Love and Work

Love and Work

Gwyneth Cravens

FAWCETT CREST • NEW YORK

A Fawcett Crest Book
Published by Ballantine Books
Copyright © 1982 by Gwyneth Cravens

Library of Congress Catalog Card Number: 81-13650

ISBN 0-449-20047-7

This edition published by arrangement with Alfred A. Knopf,
Inc.

Manufactured in the United States of America

First Ballantine Books Edition: January 1983

For Dovie and Henry

1

WHAT DO YOU DO? Angela Lee asks herself. She is preparing for today's job interview as she walks through Central Park. At parties in this city people ask, "And what do you *do?*" or "And what do *you* do?" During her seven years here, Angela has given many unenthusiastic replies—inventory clerk, temporary secretary, researcher for a writer, to name a few—and by now they have blended in her mind, like the jobs themselves, and like the interviews. Although until two weeks ago she could claim that she wrote an advice column for a love comic book, she often answers, "Oh, I don't do much of anything." This morning as she was brushing her teeth, she looked into the mirror and heard a voice in her head ask, impartially and from a great distance, "What is your fate?"

She does not think of herself as having a fate—that's for astrologers, or desperate lovers. She just wants to survive. She believes that it's best not to know how much money you have because you might have less than you thought, and she has never been able to open a box of crackers or a package of bacon along the dotted line. She would prefer to stay home, visit with friends, read, or listen to records, as she has been doing since she lost her comic-book job to the owner's son, a young man with a taste for white silk Italian shirts and gold neck chains. But her funds are about to run out and so she must find an effortless part-time way to exchange a few hours of her day for money to pay the rent and buy groceries.

There have been times when she felt more ambitious than she does today. When she was five, growing up in a trailer court in Gatch, New Mexico, her mother taught her how to embroider doilies, and Angela imagined embroidering dozens of doilies and selling them to people who came along the highway. When she was old enough to read the ads on the backs of comic books, she imagined selling Cloverine Salve door-to-door. It was not clear how much she would be paid, but one of the prizes you could earn was a Chihuahua in a teacup. In her senior year of high school, when her friends started getting engaged and she didn't even have a steady boyfriend, she stopped reading and daydreaming long enough to apply for a scholarship that would take her out of Gatch and to the state university. In college she won more scholarships, and probably would have gone to graduate school if Arthur Ray Lee had not proposed to her on their first date. She was nineteen. He was an army veteran who had gone back to school, and Angela considered him good-looking and sophisticated—he drank Scotch with soda rather than with Coca-Cola, for instance, and he wanted to move to New York City after graduation, and make a million dollars before he was thirty. In New York, the marriage did not hold up.

Today, two years after the divorce and in between enterprises of romance and employment, she feels balanced. She has finally forgotten the latest unhappy love affair, which ended badly just last month and which led her to announce to her friends, "Love does not exist. It's a matter of conditioning. I have renounced it and I advise you to do the same." So she's not ruminating about him, or about anyone else. In fact, she's not thinking about anything. For someone with a mental talking machine as powerful as hers, this silence is nearly a miracle. It is a blindingly clear January morning, the earth is frozen to iron under her boots, and a generous light wraps around the tops of the buildings beyond the bare treetops of the park and illuminates all the faces she passes. The sheen makes their features intimately familiar to her, as if she's always known everyone she sees, the children, the nursemaids, the dog-walkers, the men and women on their way to work, known them for years. The light today is like the dry mountain light of Gatch, where the shadows are always very deep and sharp. She feels fearless and clear, in harmony with her surroundings; she needs nothing, she needs no one in order to be happy and complete. Just breathing the cold fresh air, with its tang of something sweet on fire, is enough.

But the air is really not enough. She also needs a job, and she feels a slight carbonated sensation under her ribs at the thought of this new adventure. Today is going to be different, she tells herself. Something is going to happen.

As she leaves the park she is suddenly overtaken by such a rounded-out joy, mysteriously descending from nowhere, that she thinks of stories of people who were given up for dead but who recovered and for the first time realized that they were alive. She is tempted to skip the interview and go instead to the museum to see an exhibition of unicorn tapestries from the Middle Ages. Later she will recall this moment and compare it to the accounts of those airline passengers who get a funny feeling and change their flight plans, and then later learn that the plane they were supposed to take has crashed. But this morning she does not have the privilege of that hindsight, and so she heads for the interview.

"*Who do you love? Who do you love?*" Bo Diddley sings in a guttural voice. Joe Bly turns up the radio and begins sorting through the contents of his briefcase, which is on the dining table next to an empty Chianti bottle and two plates with the congealed remains of a macaroni and cheese dinner. He pushes aside papers and file folders and newspaper clippings. He cannot possibly interview anyone today. There's no time, he has too much to do. If he can find the girl's resumé, find her phone number, he can call her and say he is very sorry but he can't do it. The contents of the briefcase are all mixed up because last night he drop-kicked it across the loft and papers flew everywhere. Bitter smoke permeates the loft.

"You're burning the bacon!" Edith Berk yells from the distant bedroom, which is an unfinished, partitioned-off section in the rear. "I *said*, you are burning the bacon!"

Biting his mustache, he goes to the stove and hefts the skillet off the flame. The shrunken, vulcanized little pieces slide around in the sludgy grease. As usual, the loft is very cold. There are radiators everywhere, along the walls and under the bank of windows overlooking the street, and some of them must be nearly a hundred yers old, ornamented with cast-iron flowers and vines and coated with dozens of layers of chipping paint. The handle of the skillet is a little too hot, and Joe rests it on one of the wide windowsills near the stove. Holding the pan steady with his thigh, he pushes open a window to let out the smoke.

"Who do you love? Who do you love?"

He checks his watch, which he wears with its face on the inside of his wrist. Six minutes lost without his being the slightest bit aware. Two weeks ago, he turned thirty. He can't possibly fit everything in today. Nothing is coming together. He is losing his life with every second, it's really happening. When he scratched his head in the shower some hair fell out. The copy is late for the newsletter, and the newsletter is late going to the printer's, and this girl is coming into the office today to use up some more time in a job interview. He doesn't even want a part-time assistant. A person he doesn't know, someone he will have to train, someone he will have to work with all the time. Another responsibility. He barely has a grip on things as it is. It would be easier to keep on doing all the work himself.

Shreds of corrugated cardboard and computer punch cards blow off the lading docks and swirl in the street below. The sun is almost above the opposite row of blackened brick warehouses with their glaucous windows, and even with the window open, if he stands in the growing square of sunlight, he feels a little warmer. He has no clean shirts, no clean socks, no clean underwear.

"Arlene took me by my hand, she said 'Oowee bo, you know I understand.' Who do you love? Who do you love?"

"It just occurred to me!" Edith calls out eagerly. Her approach startles Joe. They have lived together in the loft for nine months, but her hard-soled boots striking the maple floor still make him jump. "You subconsciously burned the bacon because it's your turn to cook breakfast and you are resisting responsibility and trying to escape." She is almost shouting as she walks. She comes from a family of shouters and she thinks shouting is normal and useful, and the loft is so big that it is often necessary. She has now reached the middle of the vast, empty central space, sparsely occupied by a white sofa, a stereo, and a white flokati rug. They use this area only when they have guests or Edith's women's group comes over. She turns off the radio. "You left the window open," she says.

The closer she gets, the more Joe's shoulders tense. He wishes, as he slams down the window, that he could coil up tightly and disappear. His life is passing like a dream. Things, events, people just happen to him. After Lucy, his wife, took their newborn son and moved in with Joe's best friend, Joe swore he would never live with a woman again. He was going to become a world-wanderer, a recluse, a Zen monk, a hermit on Mount Athos. Now here is this woman marching toward him, yelling about burned bacon and open windows and his subconscious. He takes a deep breath and is about to announce that all this really must stop, that he is serious about what he said a few weeks ago, that he never intended to live with her in the first place.

"Mom sounded really bad last night." Edith's voice now becomes full and good-natured. "You know what I mean. She keeps insisting that she's fine. So why does she call me every day and say 'I just wanted to let you know that I'm feeling fine'?"

"I'm running late," Joe says.

"Don't forget to take your vitamins."

They move around each other as people move around familiar objects in the dark. Edith goes toward the kitchen. Joe goes toward the bedroom.

"On my lunch hour I'm going with Lois to a decorator warehouse that has Eames chairs," she calls after him. "And I've got class tonight, so please remember to pick up a green vegetable for dinner."

Edith, besides working six days a week as the office manager for a busy abortion clinic in Queens, is studying business administration in graduate school at night, and ever since Joe told her he wasn't sure they should be together, she has also been seeing a psychotherapist recommended by Lois, the director of the clinic. After her sessions, Edith is very cheerful and for the next few days reports to Joe on what she is discovering. Joe is being taken advantage of by the corporation, by his boss. He is overworked and that is what is affecting their relationship. If only he didn't have so many obligations, he would be happier. If only he would also see a psychotherapist. If only he didn't work all the time. If only he were more open, more responsive. Then he would be happy. If only he were happy, then she would be happy. She is anxious to help him clear up his problems. It was her idea that he hire an assistant, and she persuaded him to ask his boss about that. When Joe hires a warm body to share the work, Edith and Joe will be able to spend lots of time working on their relationship. She has discovered that mere living together is for the psychologically idle: a real relationship requires constant work. Joe is not interested in that sort of labor, especially in the late evenings and early mornings—his only free time—and in her exasperation with his inertia she has accused him of avoiding making a commitment because of his unsolved problems. Since Joe is aware that he does not know himself—one part seems to go around making deals and promises that the rest of him has to live up to in order to be honorable—he is afraid her charges may be true. One of the ways the therapist has suggested Edith help Joe work on their relationship is through sharing. Sharing what goes on at their respective jobs. Sharing household tasks. Joe brings home work most evenings and has little time to share the events of the day, but he has agreed to do the shopping, cooking, and laundry on alternate weeks. Until now, Edith has taken care of most of that.

"Should I get the ottoman that goes with the Eames chair?" she calls from the kitchen. "I think I should." She goes on talking, but he does not listen.

He stops in the middle of the loft, surrounded by the cold emptiness. He can't remember where he was going or what he wanted to do. He stares up at a soot-speckled skylight.

At this moment, a door opens, like an iris widening, like the dilation at the top of a great dome, and he is drawn upward to meet his own vast being. He is struck by a wish, a wish for a completely different life with all the disparate parts of himself pulled together, a life that is more than just getting by, a life that he must know before he dies. He can feel this in his solar plexus and in his hands and arms and in the air in front of him. By the time this wish enters the word-forge of his mind, he is no longer sure what it is, but he is certain that if a chance to fulfill it appears, he will grab it with both hands.

The Starr Whorf Corporation is located on several floors of a new building that resembles a medicine cabinet. Joe Bly's office, on the seventeenth floor, is a long, cluttered compartment with a window at the end. Books stand in piles and are wedged unevenly into shelves. The carpet is littered with stacks of newspapers and magazines, and there's a table heaped with papers and clippings. On the sunny windowsill is an empty green wine bottle. Above his desk, a bulletin board with memos, phone messages, and two photographic negatives.

Joe is hunched over his desk when Belinda, the receptionist, ushers in Angela and leaves her on the threshold. All that Angela can see is his back, which is broad. He's wearing a wrinkled, faded blue workshirt with the sleeves rolled up. Good. If he doesn't wear suits to the office, then she won't have to wear dresses or other difficult garments that require uncomfortable shoes, or stockings, not to mention drycleaning, or ironing.

When he turns to greet her, he appears surprised. Has she come too early? The surprise emanates mainly from his eyes, which are green. He has a thick mustache that curves around his mouth and encloses his chin; it gives him the appearance of a bandit or a sheriff from a frontier daguerreotype. Wyatt Earp, maybe. He's got a broad, jutting forehead and a slightly pursed mouth and a straight nose. His hair is light brown and longish; it curves over his ears and his rumpled collar. He's solidly built, maybe a little on the heavy side. Too bad. He's handsome for sure, but she prefers slender men. He has muscular arms and seems solid and rooted. As he gets to his feet and extends his hand, he knocks over his swivel chair.

Flushing, he looks from Angela to the chair and then to her outstretched hand, wondering whether to pick up the chair first or shake hands, and he thinks: My God. She stands motionless, her head tilted to one side, smiling sweetly, something way in the back of her eyes amusing her, her hair streaming and glowing reddish-gold in the bright sunlight. Her eyes, eyebrows, and hair are the same color. Her form takes the space in front of him and changes it.

"Oh—Mmm—mm—" His stutter, a mild handicap he overcame as a teenager, has returned. He is stuttering over Miss or Mrs. The resumé said she was divorced.

The office is so small and he stands so near that she feels giddy, immersed in a whirlpool of intimacy. She's still perplexed about why he is staring at her. Is there something wrong with her? She becomes aware of a low hum floating in the silence between them, some office sound.

He begins speaking rapidly in a voice slightly louder than a whisper. When he pauses in his speech, she makes low, hesitant replies and he can hear the West coming out of her throat: "Ah'm . . . Ah'll." He can feel her voice in his chest, and although he seldom remembers much from his past, he suddenly recalls a light-flooded summer between his junior and senior years in college when he lived in Montana and worked on a house-construction crew.

She knows her mouth is moving; she's talking. But she is not listening to what he says or what she says. She has the notion that they are only pretending to converse, as if they were in a movie and the director wanted a long shot without voices and so they just mouth words.

A sleeping being within each of them has jumped awake: they regard each other with amazement.

Eventually she is able to tune in on her own voice again, only to hear herself talking nonsense. "On a day like this I feel like I'm on a wonderful tightrope, the light is everywhere, every face is familiar." Can she really be running on like that? She stops. This is no way to start off a job interview. She imagines his report to the employment agency: "Please send someone sane."

Have we met before? he almost asks, but instead he picks up the fallen chair. He notices her dress, which is longish, a becoming red. "Would you . . . would you like to have lunch? It's a little early."

She grins. She has a crooked grin—it tilts up on the left side—and even, white teeth and full lips. "Sure." She pronounces it "shore."

They are already in the elevator when he remembers he's supposed to be having lunch with a lawyer from Dupont to discuss doing a corporate-law issue of the newsletter. Angela smells faintly of roses. Across the back of her coat her hair splays in thick waves, and he wants to touch it. They ride back up to the seventeenth floor and he asks Belinda to cancel the Dupont lunch.

Joe takes Angela to the nearest dim restaurant, which is paneled with dark Formica and Styrofoam beams to look like a British pub. They take a booth and order draft ale and Devonburgers.

She is only able to eat a few bites. He eats everything and still feels starved. He keeps forcing himself to stop staring at her. At her long, thin fingers, the wings of her collarbone, the mole on her cheek, her smooth forehead. He wants to make love to her, to conquer her, to plant his flag in her territory—all of that, of course. But there is something else besides his fascination. A sound is generated in a chamber of his heart. His body has been returned to him after a long absence, and he perceives everything anew. And mingled with this flood of sensations and impressions is fear. He makes a formal speech about the needs of the job.

Later the only thing she will be able to recall is that he said the Starr Whorf Corporation makes potato chips and little reflectors for highway signs and dozens of other things she never realized anyone made or owned the patents on, and that it also publishes some newsletters, mostly of a technical nature. Joe's newsletter for executives, though, is an exception. It is an exception because of the following reasons. . . .

She watches his mouth. His teeth are crooked. Why didn't his parents take him to the dentist? She watches his shoulders, which move with his words. The shirt is too small for him—it barely restrains him. She can see hairy chest between the buttons. He has a powerful source of energy somewhere between his chest and belly: she can feel his heat. After lunch he smokes a cigarette, and she can smell the tobacco in his exhalations. She thinks about kissing him.

He asks her some questions about her experience.

"Don't believe my resumé—it's not real," she says. "I mean, the facts are correct, I really did go to college and all, but it seems like it never happened to me. My plan for life has always been to do something fun, and when it stops being fun, to do something else."

He assures her that this job will be a lot of fun. What he means is that with her, it will be a lot of fun for him. As he listens to her voice and observes her random, dazzling smile, which comes and goes without much connection to what she's saying, he wishes that a word would come to him, that the sound he senses in his heart would form a word he could say to her that would be exactly right. He wants to ask her if she is feeling what he is feeling. He wants to know if she also thinks that what is occurring is extraordinary and unexpected. On the other hand, silence is better.

She says she minored in myth and she tells him a story about how elephants used to be clouds but now are forced to walk on the earth. She tells him that one column she wrote for a love comic book was entitled "Are You a Mankiller? Test Yourself!" She tells him that in dreams things shine of themselves rather than reflecting light, the way they do when you're awake. She tells him about a harrowing trip on a Mexican bus that had on its bumper the legend "Guide Me God For I Am Blind." She tells him she wants to go to Tibet, but would settle for joining a Zen monastery.

Three hours later, on a street corner, they say good-bye. The icy wind whips her long hair into their faces. He takes both her hands and squeezes them hard. Maybe this way he can telegraph the message to her. "I feel happy and confident and good for the first time in a long time," he says. "The newsletter," he quickly adds. He gives her long hands another squeeze, putting into them all the energy that he would rather use picking her up and bearing her away to the nearest horizontal surface.

"You have a motorcycle?" She thinks he might because boys in Gatch who had motorcycles all wore their watches facing inward the way he does so that they could check the time without turning over their bikes.

"Yes! I had a BMW. I just sold it last month." Later her

intuition will seem to him a marvel. Now, as they blink in the strong light and hold hands, it is perfectly in keeping with their rapport.

She shakes her head and looks genuinely sorry. "Too bad." If he still owned it, she would ask him to take her riding in the country. She would get behind him and they would ride away, toward the wide open spaces.

"I'm sorry I did sell it."

They stand there on the street corner. Finally she thanks him for the lunch and heads uptown.

She is nearly home when she realizes that he never offered her the job or even showed her the newsletter. No matter: they think alike. She is happy that they met. She *thought* something different was going to happen today.

Joe rereads Angela's resumé several times. She actually exists. The typed lines are like a code. Marital status: Divorced. What a way to sum up months, even years of pain, all those bad nights no one is spared. No private schools. Gatch, New Mexico. Gatch? And the scholarships and college honors—she must have been on her way to real achievement before her marriage.

"Found your assistant, Bly?" It is Harrison Bolt Hallowell Goodhugh—"Buff" to his friends—nearly filling Joe's doorway. He wears a baggy, wrinkled gray suit, a white shirt, and the striped tie of his fraternity. Joe's fraternity, too, except that Joe gave all his ties, along with his suits, to the cleaning lady the same day he quit his job at the university press, gave his house to his wife and former best friend, and left for Europe. "Or is the quest still on? Bly as he ought to be, traversing the world as it is?"

Goodhugh, the descendant of a President, a Supreme Court Justice, and the founder of one of the better banks in America, is the director of the newsletter division of Starr Whorf. He doesn't have to work, but he feels he owes it to his talent— he was editor of the campus literary magazine—to bring sanity and culture to the world of business and industry. He considers Joe a younger, inexperienced edition of himself, someone he can shape and improve, or at any rate that is what Goodhugh sometimes says after they have had a few Scotches together at his club.

"I—I believe I've—" Joe beings. "I interviewed, uh, a person today who seems qualified."

Goodhugh raises an eyebrow and lowers his eyelids a fraction in the manner of a weary roué. "I glimpsed you at *déjeuner*, Bly." He lounges idly against the doorframe, making it creak. "That must have been quite an interview. I went over and called your name, you know, and then I sort of tapped you on the shoulder."

"Oh, really?" Joe shakes his head. "Sorry. I didn't even notice."

"Nor did the young lady."

"We were discussing the newsletter in depth. She has a lot of good ideas." Joe adds a phrase from college days to give himself some room. "It would seem."

"It would seem," Goodhugh repeats. "Don't forget, Bly—women are just women."

Joe does not want anyone intruding on his elated mood. He picks up a pencil and turns back to the resumé, and Buff—never one to stand in the way of productivity—waves good-bye.

Joe goes to the coffee room, where he runs into Belinda Ayers, the receptionist. She is tall and slender like a piece of Ibo sculpture and she has a stately Afro and pale brown eyes. She is studying for her Master's in psychology. He gives her a brief hug. "You look very happy for a change." She is surprised. "What went wrong?"

"I have found my spiritual twin." He immediately regrets saying that.

2

JOE WALKS HOME THAT night lugging his heavy briefcase and smiling to himself. He's often wondered about people on the streets smiling to themselves. He assumed they were crazy. Now he knows it might be for another reason. Maybe they can't help it. This being who has sprung to life makes him smile. I can't help it, he imagines explaining to the band of sullen, menacing youths who control the sidewalk in front of the corner deli on his block. I'm nuts.

He unlocks the heavy metal fire door and, whistling "Who Do You Love?," enters the loft.

A strange voice throws him off balance. "Who pushed *your* button?"

Edith. Of course, it's only Edith, holding open the refrigerator door. He stops and looks around. I live here, he thinks. In this odd place, on this planet, and that person at the other end of the room is another human being, a woman named Edith, and she also lives here. How strange! What am I doing here? How did this all happen?"

"It's freezing in here, and there's no hot water either," she says.

Usually when he comes home, he drops his briefcase on one end of the dining table, fixes himself a glass of wine, or, if it has been an extraordinarily long and difficult day, a Scotch, and sits down at the table. But tonight he leaves his briefcase at the door and stands in the middle of the loft. He can remember the feeling that came over him this morning right at this spot. The door opening. He looks up at the skylight, and then slowly walks toward Edith. She is talking and opening and closing cupboards. As he looks at her, for the first time in a very long time, he wonders what has happened to her. When they met she kept her hair in a long, slick dark braid pulled tightly back from her narrow, smooth face, and with her aquiline nose and sharply focused dark eyes she reminded him of an American Indian brave. She had a leanness, a handsome, lithe way about her that made him feel at ease. Now her hair is cut close to her head and tightly curled. When did that happen? And there are lines around her mouth. From the way she is slamming doors he knows that she is struggling hard not to say anything to him, and from the way her lips press against her teeth he knows some of the things she is trying not to say. He feels very sad about her. She always expects the universe to make sense, and if it falters in that regard, as it seems to around him, she is ready to put it right.

"There's no green vegetable." She raises her eyebrows and her tone is far too amiable.

He is overcome by the magnitude of the mistake they have been making together. When they met, he was wandering around Greece and so was she. He felt safe with her. Now she wants a successful career, a real husband—not a live-in transient—and she wants two children spaced four years apart, and a fabulous apartment or a substantial town house, not a drafty factory loft in a bad neighborhood. And she wants a well-made foreign car and a place in the country. Joe does not want any of these things. He had a real wife, a son, a substantial house, a well-made foreign car. That's all over with now. He pats her on her shoulder and can feel the sharpness of the bone moving under her sweater as she once again opens the refrigerator door. He stands and stares at her. The white light of the refrigerator reflects off the angles of her face and seems to fix her rage under her skin.

The coldness of the loft, the lack of a green vegetable, and the lateness of his arrival are all due to his negligence. He did not caulk the windows as he promised, he failed to phone the landlord about the heat, he—"I'm sorry, Eed. I'll go to the store right now."

"It's probably closed." She manages a smile and shakes her head.

"I'll find one that's open."

He is glad to be outdoors again. At first he heads toward a produce market several blocks away, hurrying like the others on the street who are going home to warm, amber-lit interiors, and then he remembers Angela's smell and his step slows. Roses—a fragrance so particular and piercing that his mouth tenses and waters. He wonders what she tastes like. He almost knows. He has not seen her legs—her dress had a long skirt and she wore boots—but he knows they must be long and shapely and smooth under his palms. He almost knows everything tonight: he is about to learn something quite new and unusual, something he might have died without knowing. He feels right on the edge of the abyss of knowing everything.

As he passes a phone booth he finds his hand in his coat pocket rubbing the milled ridges of a dime. Suddenly he is afraid. What would he say to her? For the first time, Angela, I feel—. I've suddenly remembered something I'd—. And I want to—. Smiling to himself, idiotically no doubt, he walks away from the force field generated by the phone booth. He doesn't have to say anything to Angela. She knows. The streets tonight are full of beautiful women with long hair, but none of them has that floating, flowing quality of a wave outlined with gold. This image folded itself around Angela in his memory and now he is sure he felt that wave as they were meeting.

At the florist's, he gazes at the cube of lavender light within, at stacks of pots, pale green spikes emerging from trays of white pebbles, little bushes with glossy dark green leaves and clusters of pink buds. Some plants with lush, velvety leaves and big crimson bell-shaped flowers whose glowing interiors suggest a secret world intertwined with the familiar one. A world he never noticed directly before but that nevertheless always waited in the periphery of his awareness, the way he could sense shadows lengthening during the afternoon without ever looking at them. She has a throaty voice. She could have recited the multiplication tables at lunch and he would have listened with care. He enters the shop and the warm, humid, sweet air produced by growing things, and buys one of the plants with red flowers. The Greek clerk tells him it is called a gloxinia and can't stand direct light.

He walks carefully, gently cradling the tissue-wrapped living thing in his arms. The winter has been long and dull; it's been all he could do just to keep things going, between the late-night talks with Edith that come to nothing and the endless chores at work. He gets great ideas but there has been no one to help him bring them to fruition. His time is eaten away by meetings and phone calls. Now, even though it's only January, he feels that spring will be here soon. The night sky is a very deep violet, and a new moon hangs over the towers of the city. A black kid gives repeated, high karate kicks to a No Parking sign.

He memorized her phone number in a glance. Sometimes he can do that—look at something once and then never forget it. It's funny, because he can scarcely recall any of his childhood—one of his problems, Edith says. Angela's number leaped straight into brain cells that will never be used for any other information; it has an aura and a weight which pull at him each time he passes a phone booth. He realizes he is also noting which street corners have phones, marking them by moving his toes inside his boots. Across the street from the red-brick factory building where he lives, he stops at a phone booth, places the plant between his feet, and dials. No answer, but at least he's having an effect on something in her apartment, in her life. Maybe she has a lover. Of course. Several. A woman that lovely would not be available. His nose is turning to ice. The wind is searingly cold when he leaves the phone booth; it whips directly off the river and smacks him in the face. His arms ache from carrying the potted plant.

Edith bangs the oven door shut on a frozen pizza. "Midge calls it dumping," she is saying. Midge is her therapist. "These women come in and they just hysterically dump all their emotions about abortions and whatever on everybody, especially

me because I have to get their money in advance. Midge says
I'm withholding my anger and I ought to express my feelings
more. So I come home, all dumped on all day, we're up to
three hundred patients a week, and there's no green vegetable,
and you don't even care. You're not even listening.''

True, he's not. He sits at the dining table wondering if the
gloxinia will be okay in the back of the closet behind the
sleeping bags, wondering when Edith will go to bed so he can
make a phone call, and wondering what he's going to do with
his life.

Angela lies down on her couch and begins to connect the
different pieces and textures and colors of her meeting with
Joe Bly. She wants to make a single, portable image. Before
she can get very far, there is a knock at the door.

"It's just me." Sharon Abend lets herself in and comes down
the entrance hall carrying a plate heaped with meringues. "My
mother brought these and a birthday cake. I put that in the
freezer because it was so depressing. And also she gave me
something you won't believe, which is an antique wicker baby
bassinet and on the little pillow she pinned this note: 'Take the
hint, Sharoneleh!' I am really bummed out."

Sharon lives upstairs, on the top floor of the brownstone,
in an apartment that is dark despite its skylight, which is covered with soot, an iron burglar-proof grille, and a mesh cage.
Ever since Clifford Atwood suddenly moved out a year ago,
taking all his belongings, including the television, Sharon has
been depressed. She finds her place very depressing, and often
comes down to visit Angela.

Angela sits up. "I didn't know it was your birthday. Happy
birthday."

"My birthday isn't for two days." Sharon sprawls at one
end of the couch. "My mother said she was giving me stuff
early so it wouldn't interfere with my *plans*. Have a meringue.
They're not bad." She holds a meringue in her mouth, winds
a strand of her hair around her finger and tucks it behind her
ear. The strand immediately frees itself. She has a generous,
melancholy mouth, brown eyes that turn down at the outer
corners, big breasts, and a small waist. "Plans! Angela, all I
want for my birthday is a man. And he should have a brain,

too. According to my shrink, mature love for a man is impossible for me because I am in love with my father, who is a real *schmuck*."

Sharon started seeing a psychiatrist after Clifford disappeared. Angela has lost track of all the insights Sharon has told her since then—they rise and fall like seafoam—but Angela believes they are good because they make Sharon happy, if only for a day.

"You never know who you can meet and then that's it." Angela is not ready just yet to talk about Joe Bly. "Love could be just around the corner. Love could walk right in. Blam."

"I thought you thought love was a conspiracy to keep women in bondage," Sharon says. "You said that the sooner we realize we were just programmed that way, the better."

"I did?"

The downstairs doorbell rings. As Angela pushes the button in the hall to unlock the door, she imagines that it could be Joe. He could stop in. He could say that he forgot to show her the newsletter and give her a copy. She glances in an oval mirror with a dark oak frame that hangs near the door and that she bought because she had dreamed of an oval mirror in a dark, carved frame and the next day she and Sharon were driving around in the country, lost, and stopped in an antique shop, and there the mirror was. She asks herself in the mirror, Am I attractive? Would Joe Bly drop by to see me? Certainly her hair is a mess. Nevertheless, the possibility that the visitor could be Joe makes her heart jump. It could happen. He really did stare at her, and her address is on her resumé.

She opens the door slowly, her heart beating at twice its normal rate. It's Ron Nussbaum. She completely forgot about him. He is climbing the stairs with a book in his hand.

She met him a few weeks ago at a party given by Melanie Gauss, who is in a consciousness-raising group to which Angela once belonged. Melanie, although married, is about to leave her husband, and sometimes when he is out of town she gives parties and invites many single men as well as her women friends. At this particular party, she played a lot of old rock 'n' roll records and Ron invited Angela to dance. She was wearing her long red dress, and when he flung her across the room, it whipped around her ankles and threatened to trip her.

Her hair flew. She kept giggling, especially during "Young-blood" when Ron hurled himself to the floor and bit her lightly on the ankle.

Ron is tall and thin, with heavy-lidded dark brown eyes— they turn down at the corners like Sharon's—and long, soft dark hair, and a drooping mustache (there are probably men in the city who do not have drooping mustaches, but Angela does not meet them). He wears round-lensed glasses with tortoise-shell frames, and today he wears a green corduroy suit with leather elbow patches. He told Angela he was a poet, and he looks like one, like a poet who is sad but a genius, living in an attic in some cold stone city in northern Europe. He really comes from Brooklyn, and lives on the other side of the park, and he also writes criticism for *Rock Raps* magazine. "I had to drop a check off with my ex-wife," he says. "She lives a block from here. So I thought I'd see if you'd like to come out with me this evening."

Ron wanted to take her home after the party, but she refused, since she has never been able to sleep with anyone she just meets, and he has asked her out a few times since then. Finally she accepted, suggesting coffee in a neutral zone, a glassed-in sidewalk café with hanging plants in macramé baskets. He put two fingers on her hand, on the table. "I gave each of my ex-wife's breasts a name," he said. "Afterward, I changed the names. To Chlorine and Phosgene." Angela hoped a kind reply would occur to her. He wanted to know if she felt terrible and bitter about her ex. "Nope," Angela said. "When I was through with him, that was it. I can barely remember what he looks like." Ron withdrew his fingers. "It frightens me to hear you talk like that, Angela." He is a reasonably large man, and it interested her that she could upset him with a casual remark that had nothing to do with him. What if they discussed something really important?

Now, as Ron strides in, she wonders whether she could ever disconcert Joe Bly that way. The thought makes her blush as she looks up and greets Ron. He is inspired to kiss her, but she turns and the kiss lands on her forehead.

Sharon has rearranged herself: her hair is tucked behind her ears, her legs are crossed, her arm rests on the back of the couch, and her bosom is high. She lifts her fingers in greeting.

"Ron, this is Sharon," Angela says. "Nussbaum, I mean. And Sharon Abend." One summer she lay on a lawn chair in the dusty yard in front of the trailer where she and her mother lived and read through library copies of Amy Vanderbilt and Emily Post while traffic whizzed by on the highway. She learned about christening a ship and not leaving undergarments behind if her hypothetical fiancé and his family invited her as a weekend guest and not tipping their maid or chauffeur, and she memorized how introductions went but she still does them wrong, and she only remembers the right way a few seconds afterward.

"I think we've met," Sharon says. "At Hill's." Hill's is a bar where newspaper people and actors drink.

"Yes, you look somewhat familiar." Ron walks around the small living room. "Just as I thought."

Angela doesn't know if he is referring to the poster reproduction of a Tibetan mandala, or the sagging bookcases, or the once-white and now sooty walls, or the array of dusty spider plants in front of the windows. "What do you mean?"

"Lonely women always grow spider plants." He slumps down on the couch, and it creaks.

In Gatch people never made remarks like that, but Angela has gotten used to the way people behave in New York. In Gatch, you wait at the door until the person invites you inside. Then you say, "Don't mind if I do come in," as though that thought had never entered your head before. And you must always say what a nice place it is. Then the hostess offers you something to eat and drink. "Would you like something to eat?" Angela asks. "Some tea? I think I have a jar of shrimp cocktail in the icebox." She's worried about Ron's dismissal of her place. What will someone who really matters, like Joe, think of it?

"Have some meringues," Sharon says.

"Now, that's a possibility," Ron says.

"You write for *Rock Raps*, don't you?"

"Well, only for the time being." Ron has a high-pitched, well-articulated voice. "I mainly write poetry."

"I know." Sharon smiles and hands him a meringue.

"Are you the Sharon Abend who's the reporter?"

"That's me—Brenda Starr."

Angela wants to go in the bedroom and lie down and day-
dream about Joe, and while Sharon and Ron talk about friends
they have in common, Angela stands in the living-room doorway imagining Joe's first visit. He will come down the hall,
he will look around.

After a while Sharon gets up. "Well, I'm going to go upstairs
and cry a lot," she says. "In two days I will be twenty-eight,"
she explains to Ron. "I'm going banana crackers."

"Oh, please stick around," Angela says. She does not want
to be left alone with Ron. "Please."

"No, no—my phone could ring. You never know."

After she leaves, Ron hands Angela the book he has been
carrying. "Your friend has a kind of brooding prettiness," he
says.

"She's a very nice person, a lot of fun," Angela says. She
opens the book. It's poetry and it's by Ron. "Why, thank you
very much. You are the second poet I've ever known. I was
living in the Village when I met the first one." She feels awkward, and sometimes when that happens words seem to come
out of nowhere and string themselves together and issue out of
her mouth in stories that, while true, seem to her to be very
strange and she wishes she would not tell them. "He lived next
door, and one night he came over—I was married at the time—
and he told me that my feet were the most beautiful feet he
had ever seen. The next day he was running up and down the
street with a fencing sword and they took him to the hospital
and gave him shock treatments. He wrote some good poems
that he read to me. I don't think they got published."

"It's hard to get poetry published. I'm very lucky. Aren't
you going to read the inscription?"

"I was going to read it later, after you left."

"I'm not leaving. I'm going to take you out to dinner. At
an extremely nice restaurant."

"Uhhh." Angela can't think of a reason to refuse him. She
looks at the flyleaf, where he has written: "To Angela—to one
solitary from another, in the hope, strange at it may seem, that
some day we will love one another. Comrade Ron."

She puts on a long black silk skirt and borrows some high-
heeled sandals from Sharon. While they are waiting for a taxi,
the night sky behind the buildings of midtown turns exactly

the color of the pinkish-yellow lights in the windows, so that the city seems transparent. "Look at the light," Angela says.

"This light is *melon* light," Ron says, as if he owned it.

The restaurant is Russian. It's crowded, mirrored, red, and warm, and the tablecloths are pink. Ron says he is Russian, and he talks about his hero, Osip Mandelstam, and about his mother. "She secretly thinks her side of the family—Germans—is better than my father's side, the Russians, so she claims that *her* side has feet of clay. I say, 'Ma, you call that clay? It's Silly Putty!'"

Angela laughs. She likes being here with Ron. He is pleasant and entertaining. He talks through the blini and the caviar and the sour cream, and at the end, the waiter, who is dressed in what Angela takes to be a cossack outfit, brings them each a marzipan potato. She begins to worry about what will happen next.

"You're a good listener, Angela."

She nods, chewing. "Thank you very much." She's always listened to everybody about everything, from the time she was very small and the neighbor women came over to tell her mother about their operations. "Imagine—a *marzipan* potato," she says. "It looks just like a dirty old potato but it really is wonderful."

"I like you, Angela. I really do."

She gazes at the crumbs of marzipan on the plate. "That's a nice thing to say," she mumbles. Being with him is becoming puzzlingly difficult. He is definitely good-looking, and she ought to be attracted to him. If she hadn't met Joe, maybe she would feel differently.

"My wife didn't understand Mick Jagger, about how he sings 'Love in Vain,'" Ron says, reaching for her hand. "About how he sings 'with a *soooot*-case in my hand.' She didn't understand about *soooot*-case."

"It is amazing." Angela does not want to seem too agreeable at this point, because she wants to go home by herself, but she has always liked the way a former student at the London School of Economics can so convincingly sound just like Robert Johnson, the black blues singer from the thirties.

"I'm happy you think just like I do."

How can Ron make that leap without knowing her? But then she understands: she has met Joe Bly, and because of his green stare she is ready to follow him into the desert, if necessary, even wearing uncomfortable shoes. She smiles at herself.

After dinner, Ron invites her to accompany him to see a rock group perform in a club downtown. Although her feet hurt from the uncomfortable shoes she borrowed from Sharon and she just wants to go home, she does not want to be impolite and duck out of the date so early in the evening. Besides, Ron has just bought her a very nice dinner, and he is not so bad, really. He's just not Joe Bly.

The club is low-ceilinged and dark, with glitter embedded in the plaster walls, and there are a lot of transvestites around. "This is a so-called decadent rock group," Ron explains. That explains, too, the girls in the crowd with red eye shadow, green fingernails, and crewcuts. There are no tables available and so Ron takes Angela to a place where they can stand near the stage. A bare-chested man with a clothespin attached to his left nipple pinches her waist and asks, "How come you're so pretty?" She can't look at him without wincing. "That's Teen Lust," Ron says wearily. "He's very big now." On the stage, Baby Boom, who wears red tights and an Esther Williams bathing suit, prances and sings a song about his mom to a pair of gray artificial legs—the kind used to display hosiery in lingerie shops. He finishes by throwing chocolate-covered raisins to the crowd.

To get away from Teen Lust and to get a look at Ron's watch, Angela steps close to his side. He assumes she is nestling against him and puts his arm around her. She shrinks away and peers at her toes, which stick out from the hem of her skirt and signal to her for emergency aid. She thinks about Joe, about how they will become lovers. And the job. It could be interesting—Joe spoke so enthusiastically about this project, this newsletter: now it's really taking off, and who knows where it will go? She has always thought of work as something to avoid, but he made it seem like a source of excitement. He kept treating her as if she knew exactly what he had in mind. I feel good and happy and confident for the first time, he said. When she asked him about the motorcycle, the green of his eyes seemed to deepen. He held her hands, there on that sunny corner. She is wrapping herself in a many-colored, many-layered, filmy veil, and it is only the pain in her feet that summons her back to the present.

Ron is discussing the relation of musical trends fostered by people like Baby Boom and Teen Lust to the future of the self in a mass society. "These artists may somehow understand that the self must be destroyed so that the new world can be born. Very interesting." He must be rehearsing his column for *Rock Raps*. "Too bad they're so terrible."

Didn't Joe say he lived in this neighborhood? He must be nearby. She could find a phone book and look him up and just give him a call: I happened to be passing by and I needed a place to sit down and take off my shoes—do you mind? On her way to the rest room, she sees a pay telephone and a ragged directory. There are Blys, but no Joseph or J. This gives him a dimension of mystery and aloofness.

She returns to Ron and tells him that she doesn't feel well and that she has to go home. He seems alarmed. He massages her neck and offers to take her to his place and make her tea, and give her aspirin, and he has a little—

"No, no, I really have to go home. But I really do appreciate all this, I do."

"This scene—it must be too disturbing for you, too perverse. It may evoke things in your unconscious that you're not ready to deal with."

"Ah, no, no, no. It's really, uh, nice." She hopes she sounds polite. "It's just that I had this job job interview today and I guess it took a lot out of me."

By promising to see him soon, she is finally able to escape. The instant she is inside the front door of her building, she kicks off the vicious shoes, runs up the carpeted stairs to her apartment on the second floor, pulls off her clothes, throws them on the couch, opens a bottle of Coors beer, puts *Let It Bleed* on the stereo, and, forgetful of her feet, dances to one side of the album in the dark living room. She can't be bothered to turn on the light—a hanging bulb inside a Japanese paper lantern. She fills the bathtub, which she painted with blue fern-frond designs one lonesome Saturday night, and sinks into the warm deep blue that resembles a tiny forest pond if she squints through the steam, and soon she gets very sleepy.

Sometime in the night she hears a phone, and assumes it's

a dream phone, but then gets up and makes her way to the bookcase in the living room where the real phone is. But by then it's stopped ringing. She goes back to bed and to sleep. A while after that she sits up. She remembers Joe so thoroughly, the heat and bulk of his body, the hair on his chest, the pleasing tobacco smell of his breath, that it seems as if he is there with her. Some words come into her mind then, very clearly: He is exactly the one I've been wishing for. I had even forgotten I had such a wish. I didn't think someone like him could really exist. When I met him, I didn't think he was that special. Now that I think about it, though, it seems destined.

She makes up her mind, then, in a way she does not recall ever having made up her mind about anything before except her decision to get a divorce. She will do everything in her power to be with Joe Bly. It's him. He's the one.

3

JOE OPENS HIS EYES, remembers it's Saturday, and sinks into the gentle marshes of his second sleep until Edith walks the length of the loft in wooden-soled clogs and swings open the fire door with a metallic groan, a large beast disturbing the transparent cube of silence that the place ought to be when he sleeps.

"The Eames chair is being delivered today," she shouts. "So be sure not to go out until after it comes. Joe? Did you hear me?"

He sits up. The bedroom is very cold. He rubs his throat; the muscles are clenched, as if he's been arguing all night. "Yeah." The Eames chair. Lois, the owner of the clinic, has an Eames chair. Midge, the therapist, has an Eames chair. Edith has been going on her lunch hour to furniture stores looking for an Eames chair on sale. On the evenings when she and Joe are both home for dinner, she discusses the relative merits of Eames chairs and imitation Eames chairs she has encountered. He hears her on the phone talking to her friends and her mother about Eames chairs, about molded rosewood

27

plywood, about how this chair is in the Museum of Modern Art. At last she has found one—a distressed floor sample.

"I want it put across from the sofa, okay?"

"Yeah." Joe can see his breath. Shivering, he pulls on a sweater and jeans.

"I'm going to try to get off early today—I want to go see Mom. But I'll be home for dinner. Unless you want to come to Mom's and we can have dinner there."

"I have to work," Joe says.

She bangs the door shut with a cold gust.

The walls and ceiling of the bedroom are lined with foil insulation packs and the only light is a bare bulb plugged into a wall socket at knee level. Yet another thing he has to do—panel the bedroom. Tongue and groove clear pine, maybe. The rest of the loft is as finished as he'll ever get it. He built the kitchen counters and shelves. Together they sanded and polyurethaned the floor. Edith wants to move, and she tells him it's pointless for them to make too many improvements on a place they don't own.

"I love this place," Joe then will say when they have this discussion, which arises whenever he mentions finishing the bedroom. The loft is his refuge. He likes the big empty space.

The lease and the telephone are in Edith's name, however. She moved here after they split up. They had been living, since their return from Greece, with five of Joe's friends in a ramshackle former mansion, and Edith said she would just stay with Joe in his room temporarily, until she got a job. After she began working at the clinic as a bookkeeper, she started complaining about his friends. They didn't keep the bathroom or the kitchen clean; they got stoned in the middle of the night and took her food out of the refrigerator. Joe told her that he had never intended to get involved with her in the first place, that traveling together in Greece was okay, but living together was more than he wanted. He said he liked her and hoped they could be friends. She cried, moved out, found the loft, and called him up. Her father had just died and she kept enumerating all the good things she could think of. She loved her job. She had nice friends, especially Joe. "And we have so much in common," she said. "You can give me some advice about fixing this dump up. Let's experiment with friendship."

He was moved by her desperate wish to seem hearty and reasonable. When he saw the loft, he thought of an ancient cargo ship. And there was light from the windows along the street side, and from two skylights. One wall was exposed brick. The floors were bird's-eye maple. He had never seen a place like this in the city. Its possibilities drew him in. And he had come to hate sleeping alone.

As he boils water to make instant coffee, he considers getting rid of the bedroom altogether, tearing the partition down. But when does he have time for that? He really should have been a carpenter. The summer during college that he framed cheapjack houses in Missoula was the happiest he can recall. He worked from six in the morning until four in the afternoon, and then went home to a folksinger named Maryann. They lived together in her little stuccoed cinder-block house with cottonwood trees and hollyhocks in the dusty front yard. She would have a big meal ready for him, and then they would make love, and then they would walk holding hands to the coffee house where she sang about railroad trains and empty beds and the cuckoo: *"The cuckoo is a funny bird—it wobbles as it flies, and it never cries cuckoo 'till the fourth day of July."*

He suddenly remembers Angela, who is a little like Maryann, and feels a sensation in his heart like a funnel opening up, the way water opens up when it starts to go down a drain.

Maryann was all set to join him back East in the fall and live with him, and they would probably be together now if he hadn't gotten Lucy Stokes pregnant. In those days, marriage was the only honorable choice. Lucy miscarried, but they stayed together for the next four years. Joe assumed it was a permanent arrangement. It was comfortable and familiar. They had lots of friends—other couples like them. Then she got pregnant again and took up with Alec, who was Joe's best friend and his colleague at the university press as well.

Joe wishes he could hate Edith, the way he finally hated Lucy. He wishes she could enrage him. Then it would be easy for them to break up. He might even be able to persuade her to move out and let him have the loft. But Edith never enrages him. She doesn't overwhelm him or enmesh him with passion. He is secure in knowing that she cares for him more than he cares for her. She is predictable. She has made a timetable for her life: in a few months, she'll have her Master's degree in business administration and will be qualified to run a clinic. She will then move to a better clinic and run it. Then she will either start one or buy a share in one. She will invest any profits in real estate. During this time she will marry and have a family, too, before she's too old. She is going to stop smoking when she is thirty-five. She is reliable. She would never sleep with his friends, or with any other man; he's fairly sure of that. She's like the mast of a ship, tall, strong, efficient. "I want to spend the rest of my life with you," she says, and she means it. When they were motorcycling together in Greece, people assumed she was his male companion until she took her helmet and her jacket off.

He opens his briefcase on the dining table and debates smoking just one joint before he plans his day. While he's debating, he finds himself taking the plastic bag of dope—his birthday present from Edith—out of the freezer. Dope has a mind of its own, he thinks.

He puts on an old Leonard Cohen record. *"Into this furnace I ask you now to venture...."* Cohen sings about sacrifice in a tuneless complaining tone that is peculiarly moving.

Angela. Attached people radiate a closed-off, rounded-off, no-loose-ends quality. But Angela is like, like—an image of a partially woven basket rises whole in his head. All the fibers are still sticking out and the bottom of the basket—or is it the top?—is still open. The basket becomes the bare frame of an unfinished house at the end of a Western summer afternoon, when thunderheads pile up at one end of the Montana sky and the rest is a deep, dry, hot blue.

For an instant he is afraid. Angela is a danger. He surely mentioned that he was living with Edith. At lunch Angela said something about being divorced, and he said he was too, with a three-year-old son, and they grinned knowingly at each other— veterans of the wars of marriage. "I thought I'd always be married and settled," Angela said. "Me, too," Joe said. "Never again," she added. "Or at least not until General Chiang Kai-shek recaptures the Chinese mainland." And Joe had said he knew what she meant.

"Like a bird on a wire, like a drunk in a midnight choir, I have tried in my way to be free," Cohen sings.

Someone is hammering on the door. It's probably the god-damned Eames chair.

It turns out to be Gerard Clewes, in an army jacket pinned with medals although he has never served. "Congratulate me," he says, taking off his jacket. He is wearing a three-piece blue corduroy suit and sneakers. "I have just sold a poem to the august *New Republic*."

"Congratulations," Joe says. "That's quite a breakthrough."

"Actually, you should congratulate William W. Blansford, not me."

"How so?"

"That's the name I signed to the poem."

"But Bill Blansford is a famous poet." When Joe was assistant director at the university press, Blansford was one of its authors.

They go to the kitchen and Gerard gets a beer out of the refrigerator. "I of course knew perfectly well that if I did a flawless imitation of a Blansford poem and signed *my* name they would hardly have bought it. So I sort of signed his name."

"Is that legal?"

"I checked. In the United States you can use whatever name you wish." Gerard wears contact lenses and he is not comfortable with them. He usually keeps his head slightly tilted back, as if to prevent them from falling off his eyes. Joe feels responsible for Gerard. They were roommates in boarding school, where Gerard's uncle was the hockey coach, and they worked on the literary magazine there, and they were on the college newspaper together. Joe was the editor one year and Gerard was a reporter. Joe was also the editor of the literary magazine and Gerard was the associate editor. When Joe was invited to join the best and most undemocratic clubs in prep school and in college, Gerard always counted on Joe to bring him along. Usually Joe was able to persuade these clubs that Gerard had intelligence and talent and that he should not be judged by the fact that he was on scholarships or the fact that his uncle was the hockey coach. After college, when Joe was hired by the press, he persuaded the director to give Gerard a part-time job reading poetry manuscripts. Now Gerard teaches at a prep school in the city and lives in a railroad flat a few blocks away. His place is cluttered with first editions of modern poetry books, partially painted canvases—he is planning on painting his poems now—and pieces of masonite on which he glues things to remind him of future poems: a ball of hair from the brush of a Japanese woman, for instance; some cubes and rods of colored Plexiglas; an advertisement for diamonds torn from a magazine. He often invites Joe to visit, and Joe usually says he has no time, and promises that very soon he will definitely come by.

"I did it to teach Blansford a lesson. He's getting soft. This will wake him up." Gerard pulls up a chair, scraping the floor, and sits at the table. "However, enough. You said you were looking for an assistant—"

"I've found someone."

"You've actually hired him?" Gerard looks troubled.

"Practically. It's a she."

"Oh. The thing is, I've just been fired, and I thought possibly something could be worked out."

Joe thinks for a moment. No, he wants Angela. "Let me talk to Goodhugh. Maybe I can find something for you. Why were you—let go?"

"Oh, I don't know. The headmaster is a moron." Gerard doesn't want to talk about it. "I'm moving in with Elizabeth."

"Is that good?"

"As Madame LaBatt used to say when she was teaching Flaubert, when yew loff, there iss no control." Gerard always brings up prep school and it always makes Joe uncomfortable. "A propos of nothing, Alec was in town the other day."

"Oh, really?" Joe is offhand. "How is he?"

"He said he would have called you but he was just in and out. We had a quick lunch. He and Lucy are thinking of having another—of having a child."

Joe says nothing. Everyone from his former life at the university press assumes that Todd is not his son but Alec's, but both Alec and Joe know that Todd is Joe's. He looks just like Joe. Same eyes, same square forehead. Joe ought to take the train up and visit Todd soon—it's been a couple of months. Joe hates doing that, because he runs into old friends there around the campus, and he knows they think that he is a fool. A cuckold. And Alec is always putting his arm around Joe's shoulder, and Lucy makes Joe take back little jars of homemade jam—"for Edith." Alec always wants to assure Joe that he is taking good care of Todd, that now that he's the director of the press, he can afford to maintain Lucy as a housewife, which has always been her wish. Joe used to encourage her to find a profession, to do something that interested her, but she wanted to stay home. When she told him she was in love with Alec, she explained that it was Joe's fault. "You were always at work, and I was here alone, and Alec was alone, too, and didn't have a soul to help him get over his divorce."

"I don't want a job too soon—wait until my unemployment checks run out," Gerard says. "Unless there's something I could do off the books."

"I'll talk to Goodhugh," Joe says again. Goodhugh would never do something off the books. "And meanwhile, I'll be trying out this new, this new person."

"Should I know her from someplace? From college?" Gerard peels the embossed gilt label off the beer bottle.

"No, I don't think you would. Her name is Angela, Angela Lee, and she's from Gatch, New Mexico. She went to school out West someplace." Joe knows exactly where she went to school, the year she got her degree, and her major and her minor—all information from her resumé—but he does not want to seem too interested in her.

"*Gatch?* You picked her up at the bus station, presumably? She was carrying her plaid suitcase and her saddle and her lasso?"

Joe smiles. Angela had told him that she got to New York several years ago by bus and that she arrived with a plaid suitcase. "You might enjoy meeting her. She seems very— very imaginative."

"Thank God," Gerard says. "With nothing but a sea of stuffed shirts around you, it must be refreshing." Gerard often tells Joe to study aikido, or go to California and take hot sulfur baths, or to swallow a lot of mescaline—anything at all to loosen up. Joe, Gerard often says, is trapped in the mundane, the practical, the everyday, and could use a few lessons in carefree spontaneity. "I don't know how you stand the grind. I find that every day I feel more liberated," Gerard goes on. "From society, from blah-blah-blah authority, from work."

*   *   *

After Gerard leaves, Joe selects half a dozen records to play, smokes another joint, opens his briefcase on the dining table and spreads out stacks of papers. The newsletter has to be in the printer's hands by noon on Monday. If he works the rest of today, all day tomorrow, and tomorrow night, he will be able to make the revised deadline. He picks the pieces of beer label off the dining table—a table he built from Douglas fir— and rolls them into a ball and tosses it into the kitchen wastebasket. He is proud of his accurate throws. Breakthroughs in modern physics are having an impact on industry—this is what the newsletter is about this time. In fifty years, electricity will not flow through wires but through supercooled, liquid hydrogen. Goodhugh views the newsletter as a serious force, helping executives make decisions. Joe views it as a collage of information that executives can exchange while they are cruising around in corporate jets, eating corporate lunches, having corporate drinks, picking up corporate women.

I am not in that world, Joe thinks. On the other hand, what world am I in? I am always one step away from the real thing. Housing starts are up for the fiscal year that just ended.

Angela is free. Angela is in the world. It's obvious. She swims in it, breathes it, soaks it up. She has given him his body, his forgotten body. She knows the secret.

The air along the roads in Greece smelled of wild rosemary and asphalt and the sea and exhaust fumes. Traveling alone on his motorcycle, he sped through the hills and along the coasts and spoke to no one. Wrapped in the noisy vibrations of the bike and going eighty miles an hour, he was forced to concentrate fully on the road unrolling beneath him, on the balance of the bike, on the steering, and on the awesome madness of Greek drivers. He did not have to think, and that suited him very much.

For the first time, he was released from hours and days and from doing what others wanted him to do. After floating like this for a stretch, he sensed that he was about to discover something new and astonishing that could only be detected by traces it left on the accidental texture of the world. The flashing of the yellow light on the hammered waves of the Aegean, for instance. A movement of light and space that he perceived with his whole body. The way space folded around ruined slabs of altars and broken columns and rocks jutting into the sea. If he began thinking about this directly, turning it into words, it vanished.

The Eames chair is delivered in a box. He has the delivery men place the box opposite the sofa and tips them each five dollars.

The record player clicks off. Six records have played and he hasn't heard any of them. He checks his watch. The day is almost gone. He feels totally inert. But he must do the shopping. The Formica he put down on the kitchen counter is curling at one corner, revealing a dark, mossy undersurface.

Edith comes home with a black and white framed photograph of a snowdrift. She gets out her toolbox and hammers a nail into the exposed brick wall. "Lois was telling me today that I'm really good at working with people. I think she may want to promote me to assistant director—there's really no one to oversee the whole operation when she's away." She hangs up the picture.

"Good," Joe says. About the time Edith arrived, he stopped daydreaming and really got to work on the newsletter. Now his concentration is going well, and he can answer Edith without really following what she is saying, although he does wonder briefly why she has put up a photograph of a snowdrift. It's not like her.

"You know, I saved Lois at least eighty-one thousand dollars in the past year. I added it up. Before I came, she had nobody to keep close track of the books, or to get supplies at a discount, and she wasn't watching inventory. That's a big expense. People walk off with staplers, pens, rolls of tape. I put a lock on the storage cabinet and I'll bet that two-ninety-eight lock has saved hundreds of dollars."

"Good."

She moves her toolbox to the carton the Eames chair is in, cuts open the carton with a Swiss Army knife, and begins screwing the base on. Her father ran an appliance repair shop in Paterson, New Jersey, and Edith used to help him out. When the chair is assembled she drops into it, rests her feet on the ottoman, and closes her eyes. "Whew." She grips the arms, "At last."

4

"I HAVE MET MISTER absolutely right." Angela lies on her back on the floor talking on the telephone to her best friend, Helen, who now lives on a ranch in New Mexico not far from Gatch.

"Are you in love?"

"Oh, gosh." The thought makes Angela's cheeks go warm.

"The last time you called, all you could say was how stupid romantic love is, how it's all a plot to enslave women," Helen says. "I've thought about that a lot, that conversation."

It took place around Christmas, after Mark, a guitar player Angela had hoped would move in with her, had suddenly gone hitchhiking in Europe. She had especially liked Mark because he resembled Janos—he was slender, with a long, dark face and high cheekbones, and wore a faded denim jacket. Janos, Angela's way out of her marriage, was a refugee who had left Hungary with his parents. He had traveled all over the world and was temporarily staying in an apartment next door to Angela and her husband in the Village. Janos and Arthur used to stay up late drinking wine and having philosophical discussions

long after Angela went to bed. Janos was always subtly flirting
with Angela. The longer she lived in New York, the duller and
more ordinary and disappointing Arthur Lee became to Angela.
He never did what he said he was going to do—for him, talk
was enough. One plan of his was to become an ethnobotanist,
and so he enrolled in some biology courses at the New School
while working during the day for an apartment-rental agency.
A client who had once written a play said that in his opinion
Arthur had the looks and ability to become a successful actor.
Arthur had always wanted to be one, and so he quit his job
and, while Angela worked as a temporary secretary, Arthur
studied acting. In acting school he met a Columbia student who
believed the country was ripe for revolution and that the way
to help overthrow the oppressors was to talk to the workers.
Arthur cut his acting classes to do street theater in the blue-
collar sections of Elizabeth, New Jersey. He wasn't home much,
and when he was, he slept—sometimes for eighteen-hour
stretches. Janos always had seemed foreign and alluring to
Angela, and one day when she returned a copy of the Tibetan
Book of the Dead he had loaned her—he was the follower of
a Tibetan lama—they wound up in bed. Until that moment
Angela had believed that most of what she had read and heard
about sex had been made up. She was amazed to discover that
in fact great pleasure was really possible. She liked Arthur and
had assumed from their first date that they would always have
an ideal marriage, and a family. Now she could not go back
to thinking that. As the affair went on she did not know what
to do. Janos started throwing himself on the floor a hundred
and eight times a day in the ritual prostrations the lama required
of his initiates, and one evening Arthur came home and said
that he had met a longshoreman who had a great idea for making
a million dollars. They were going to become partners and go
to New Zealand and start a chain of bowling alleys. No one
there had ever heard of bowling—they stood to make a fortune.
It would finance Arthur's acting career. Angela knew she did
not want to move to New Zealand and leave Janos, and she
also knew that her future with Janos was doubtful. And she
had thoroughly lost faith in any of Arthur's schemes ever working out. He had once persuaded Helen and her husband, whom
they had met in New York, that the solution to all their problems

was for the four of them to move to New Mexico and live off the land. Tom left his law firm, used his savings to buy a ranch, and set up a business selling native grass seed to ranchers. Angela and Arthur were going to join Tom and Helen, but by then Arthur had become interested in ethnobotany. Angela wrote Helen a long letter describing her affair with Janos. She left it in an unsealed envelope next to the telephone because she didn't have any stamps. Arthur read the letter, and confessed to having had several affairs, and a few months later they separated. She had not intended to care for Janos so much, but he had become very valuable after her marriage ended: she had never imagined living alone. And yet Janos was up to sixty thousand prostrations and said he could feel the blood rushing inside his head. She never was able to think of him as a husband. He left for Dharmsala, India, and she was miserable. She nearly went West to live with Helen and Tom, but instead found herself moving uptown to an apartment in a brownstone and turning into the creature she had dreaded becoming: a single woman living alone in New York City.

Helen finds Angela's situation unthinkable. She believes that Angela ought to move out of the city, go back to Arthur or remarry, and have a couple of kids. After Angela's affairs end, she calls up Helen in tears, and Helen always says, "Come on out and we'll hang out the wash and listen to Hank Williams and go riding." And when Angela denounces marriage, men, and domesticity, Helen quietly assures her that they can still bring happiness.

"When I met him it was love at first sight," Angela now tells Helen. "I'm not afraid to say it. But I don't know if anything will come of it. I looked at him, he looked at me." At the moment Angela can't quite conjure up his face. A whole day has passed. Maybe it was only a fleeting crush. Maybe she has made him up. Talking about him will revive his fading image. "Very intense," she says. "His eyes."

"I hope it works out for you. He sounds very nice." Helen's tone is polite, as usual. She is from Fairfield, Connecticut, and grew up on a big estate with horses and servants and knows how to say correct things. "I had a dream that you and I were on a mountaintop, and we were wearing these special white robes, and there was a ceremony around a rock altar at the top.

And there were other women, too. When I woke up I felt somehow we had been initiated into a mystery." When Helen lived in New York, she and Angela used to tell each other their dreams, or at least the dreams that were magnificent and left the dreamer in a state of mind that was unusual.

Angela tries to think of a dream to tell Helen, but nothing occurs to her. "I know this is going to happen, Helen. This guy is different from the others. He is exactly perfect for me. He's solid, he's got an important job—not like Mark, or Janos. And he's serious about things."

"How can you be sure?"

"I am sure; I don't know how. He hasn't asked me out yet, but I know he will. He may not want to rush things. But something is definitely in the air. It's—like gravity. Like the tide."

"Angela, please be careful for yourself. I wish you could come out here, just for a visit. Tom is away all the time. I miss our long talks. And you have to meet our boys."

Angela has been planning to get back to New Mexico ever since she was last there, when her mother died three years ago. New York has always seemed to her like a temporary stop on the way to someplace else, and whenever she talks to Helen, Angela can feel the presence of mountains, and thin dry air, and the expanses of sagebrush-covered plain, and it all seems a part of her that she is neglecting. But now there is a howl and a cry, and Helen has to go. The three-year-old is pulling the one-year-old's hair.

Ron comes over with a dozen long-stemmed white roses. "I just wanted to see how you were feeling. I was worried about you."

"Oh, I'm fine. These are beautiful." Angela is grateful for the roses, which no man has ever given her before, because they make her into the sort of woman who receives lavish bouquets from admirers and who is therefore worthy of Joe Bly. "Would you like something to eat? I believe I have some yogurt. Something to drink?"

"No thanks. I had dinner with my ex-wife. It was terrible. She wants this creep she's seeing to move in with her, but she wants me to keep giving her alimony."

Since Angela did not want anything from Arthur except

some books, the Bob Dylan records, and an Indian pot that now sits on the mantelpiece, she doesn't understand why Ron and his ex-wife carry on.

Ron takes off his jacket, loosens his tie, unbuttons the top two buttons of his shirt, and sits down on the couch. Angela stands holding the bouquet. If she returns it to him, will he leave without hating her? If only she had another piece of furniture she could sit on so that they could conduct a formal conversation for an hour and then he would go. She finds an empty wine jug, rinses it out, and puts the roses in it and sets the jug in the middle of the living room floor and sits down next to it. "So I can smell them," she says.

"My ex is exactly like my mother," Ron says. "A banal observation but true." He talks about how his mother wants to run for Congress. His father has a big collection of antique Chinese snuff bottles. His sister lives on an oyster-dredging commune in British Columbia. His brother manages a woman nightclub singer named Brenda Bondage. Angela feels she is watching a family comedy show. She is baffled by Ron. He never has asked her where she's from, or what she likes to do, or who her friends are, or what she does for a living. Why is he pursuing her? What could he possibly have in mind?

The phone rings. It is Joe. In a whispery, low voice, he nervously apologizes for phoning at this time. "No problem!" she says cheerfully. "Not at all!"

"I just wanted to let you know that you have the job if you want it. I'm sorry I didn't give you a very complete idea of the—"

"Oh, wow! Oh, boy! That's fantastic." And why is Joe home on a Saturday night making business calls? He's either free and interested in her or hopelessly settled.

"About your salary," Joe continues. "I've spoken with Buff Goodhugh, the director of the newsletter division, and I'm afraid that starting out we can't offer you as much as I'd like." He names an amount that is more than she has ever earned. More than her mother ever earned in all the years she worked as a waitress at the Cash-In Café, tips included. Angela gives a little gasp. "Oh," she murmurs.

"Angela, I really am sorry about that amount, but within six months, I'm sure we can raise it—"

"Are you kidding? The job sounds so great—I'd pay *you!*"

Joe laughs, and she laughs, and Ron gets up from the couch. "On Monday, would you like to come in to seal the bargain? I'm looking forward very much to consummating this."

"So am I," she says. Did he say "consummating"?

"I want to get to know you, I want to know all about you. We will be collaborating very closely. I feel very, very good about having met you, about being able to work with someone intelligent and imaginative."

"Well! I feel very, very good about not having to explain everything I mean. It's great to hit it off with somebody who at least understands me." She is smiling uncontrollably and Ron is giving her odd looks. "I really enjoyed our lunch together, and having a boss like you is just—"

"I am not your boss. We will be co-equals. When can you start?"

Tonight, she almost says.

"Is a week from Monday all right?"

"Can't wait," she says.

Ron has been wandering around the apartment. And now he is fooling with the record player. Suddenly "Let It Bleed" blares out. *"We all need someone—"*

"Shhh!" Angela waves at Ron.

"I must warn you that it's going to be a lot of work, a lot of weekends, overtime, and so on," Joe says.

"I love overtime, I love working weekends. I love to work." She is babbling. She forgets it was supposed to be a part-time job. "Whatever you like."

"I want to go over everything with you, but I guess this isn't a good time to do that."

"I'll come—I'll come on Monday."

The rest of the evening, Angela smiles at Ron no matter what he talks about. She is not listening to him at all. Not any more. She keeps replaying the conversation with Joe.

"What are you going to do about me, Angela?" Ron is finally asking her a question. He has been reading her his poems. "It's four in the morning."

She remembers that she is a single woman with a lot of spider plants. Still, Joe did phone. But suppose he doesn't work out? Although she still feels no attraction for Ron, they go to bed. "It was phenomenal!" he says. For her it was not. She thought maybe he was faking his ecstasy. She feels she has lied, and so the next morning she gets up early and goes to the grocery store, and then comes back and makes biscuits, scrambled eggs with green chiles, and steak. This meal, although she would never make it just for herself, is one of her favorites.

Ron pushes the green chiles to the edge of his plate. "When I was seventeen I was in a mental hospital. I tried to kill myself, so everyone thought I was crazy. I wasn't. I had my reasons."

Angela loses her appetite.

He talks about communism. It is the last best hope of the world. The day will come when every person is a happy particle of the whole. He himself is a Marxist. Then he goes to the door, coat in hand, explaining that he must be with himself to make himself whole again, so that he can create. "The onrushing drama of your life has tired me." As he goes out the door he stops. "You really don't think you're beautiful, do you?"

She shrugs. "Why would I?" She knows she's not beautiful. The best she has hoped for since junior high is to be considered "well groomed," or "a great personality."

"I thought as much. Well, *ciao.*"

She goes back to bed and dreams about voices talking, talking, talking.

Sharon comes downstairs and Angela gives her a birthday present—a big Chinese cookie in the shape of a fish. They eat hard leftover biscuits.

"Roses!" Sharon says. "You ought to fall in love with Ron Nussbaum. Man, the day a tall, dark, handsome, brainy Jewish guy asks *me* out!"

"Ron is Jewish?" Angela has never really grasped the ethnic implications of names in the city. In Gatch there were only Anglos, Spanish-Americans, and Indians.

"A Jewish boyfriend is best," Sharon says. "A Jewish guy will get up in the night and get you a glass of water—and not from the bathroom, either. They go straight to the kitchen and they also get ice. And they'd never just walk out on you—they'd feel too guilty. I told my shrink my new motto—the

thing you fear the most never happens to you, but something
equally bad does."

"But your life just keeps getting better and better," Angela
says. She believes that even if life—her own, or anyone else's—
doesn't get better and better, it certainly ought to. "And you
have a great job. You won that reporting award, which is a
very important thing."

"Yeah, and all the guys in the city room hate me now."

"Well, anyway."

"I could get fired. Well, no, I'm in the union—but I could
get lateraled. To home furnishings or something. I could get
a brain tumor."

"But you never know—something wonderful could happen
tomorrow. Like I went to the interview for this job, and this
guy—he's really incredible. You never know. When my marriage was about over and Janos left for India to be with his
lama, I wanted to kill myself. But so many wonderful things
have happened to me since then."

"Like what?"

All Angela can think of at the moment is Joe. She pauses.
"Well, like Thai food—I'd never had that before and it's so
terrific. And, you know, you meet someone."

"You—you, Angela, actually considered suicide?"

"Maybe there was just a part of myself I didn't like and that
was what I wanted to kill."

Sharon looks intently at Angela and slowly nods. "And what
part was that?" She is getting good at the role of analyst.

But Angela is wondering what to wear when she goes to
consummate the deal with Joe. "Ah, I can't remember now.
The suicidal part, maybe."

Sharon falls back against a couch cushion. "I am twenty-
eight. I have never married. I am not even divorced. There are
no prospects on the horizon. I wish that some day in the supermarket when the Muzak is playing a handsome stranger
would sweep me up and we would dance like Fred Astaire and
Ginger Rogers." She gives a little scream, as if she had just
stepped on a splinter. "Am I just going to grow old like *this?*"

"I'm sure things will work out, Sharon."

"Let me give you some good advice. You should like Ron

and go out with him a lot. He's probably going to become somebody. People have heard of him, you know."

"He was in a mental hospital," Angela says. "Besides, I have met the man of my dreams. I have met Mr. Right. No question about it. And he is giving me a wonderful job."

"Really? You got it? Congratulations. But let me say something. You are making a big mistake falling for your boss. You know what could happen? And are you sure he's not married?"

"He said he was divorced. Thank God. I'd hate to be the other woman."

Sharon goes glum, and Angela knows she is brooding about Clifford.

As night falls, the two women watch a television interview with an elderly film director. He talks about a famous actress. He wrote a leading role for her in a movie he was making— her first—and then trained her to lower her voice and slow her speech, and to move slowly, and to insult men. When she learned to do all these things well, he introduced her to the actor who was to play opposite her. The actor and the actress immediately fell in love. "She came to me," the director says, "and that poor little thing said she didn't know what to do— he'd fallen in love with this image we'd cooked up. Actually, I was trying to create a female version of the actor, and so he really fell in love with his own image in a way. So I said to this madly-in-love girl, 'Do you really love that guy?' She said she did. So I told her, 'Darling, then you'll have to play that role for the rest of your life.' And she has!"

"What a great idea!" Angela says.

5

<hr>

"'DIFFICULTY AT THE BEGINNING,'" Katha Tibor-Nagy reads aloud from a worn yellow cloth-bound book. She sits cross-legged on the carpet opposite Angela. "'In order to find one's place in the infinity of being, one must be able both to separate and to unite.'"

Katha lives downstairs from Angela. She always has coffee, tea, milk, sugar, and eggs for Angela to borrow, and little candies in painted tins from France, and she also knows half a dozen different ways to tell fortunes. She reads Tarot cards, tea leaves, palms, the soles of the feet, and the irises of the eyes. She has three antique Chinese coins with holes in their centers to throw for the *I Ching*. Angela has been tossing these on a Kazakh carpet dense with turquoise and reddish-brown geometry. After each throw, Katha leafs through the *I Ching* for the hexagram indicated by the fall of the coins—whether they land all heads, all tails, or some permutation of these.

Angela has never thought much about her fortune, although she sometimes saves fortune-cookie slips. (One in her wallet reads: NEVER TRUST MEN IN BLUE SUITS.) But now, a few hours

before she is to meet with Joe Bly and sign a contract for a
serious job, knowledge of the future is crucial and having a
neighbor who can interpret a Chinese oracle seems a stroke of
supreme good luck. "Well, I don't so much want to find my
place in the infinity of being," Angela says. "I just want to
know what my chances are with Joe. Although I guess the other
thing would be a good idea at some point."

Katha nods. She is long-limbed and straight-backed. She
has a mass of fine, yellow kinky hair twisted into a complicated
knot at the nape of her long neck, bright blue sloe eyes, and
a slight accent. She teaches Kabuki dancing, Chinese swordsmanship, and t'ai chi at a martial-arts studio. Her apartment
has no furniture—only Chinese and Persian rugs, big cushions
covered with brightly patterned Turkish kilims, and along one
wall a huge mirror. On the other walls are pale strips of rice
paper splashed and laced with Chinese and Japanese calligraphy
which she has done herself. Sharon says that when Katha grows
old, she will become one of those regal ladies who is a mystery
to everyone: "She never married . . . she must have been a great
beauty."

"'Hesitation and hindrance,'" Katha reads.

Angela wishes that she, too, owned a little yellow book
containing the truth and the future.

"'It furthers one to remain persevering. It furthers one to
appoint helpers.'"

"It furthers Joe to appoint me? He needs me, he needs my
help. Isn't that what it means?"

"Yes and no." The tea kettle whistles, and Katha places the
open book on the carpet and gets to her feet and uncrosses her
legs with a quick, light step. "Don't be too literal," she says,
going into the kitchen. "Be Chinese. The man who translated
the *I Ching* went insane. Reconciling the East and the West in
his being was too much for him. Do you want heart tea, or
head tea, or thousand-petal tea?"

"Oh, I don't know. Heart, I guess."

The tea contains little pieces of leaves, pine needles, and
bits of fragrant bark. "I have this mystical feeling about Joe,"
Angela says. She sips her tea through her closed teeth to filter
out the vegetable matter. The cup is white, handleless, and as

smooth as a river stone. "I never felt this way before." Quickly she adds, "It's a cliché, I know."

Katha lowers her eyes. "A great love can be the beginning of something else."

"Yes?" Angela leans forward.

"If the lover becomes the essence of the person she loves . . . if the lover is entirely consumed by love, if it isn't conscious or voluntary, then you become love. Everything else disappears."

"That's Chinese?"

"No, it just happens sometimes."

Angela and Joe sit nearly knee to knee talking as the sky goes dark in the window behind them. He looks at her with such absorption that the color of his eyes grows darker, too. He is tuned to a high frequency, listening with his whole body for whatever emissions she might be giving off. His power seems to her so enormous that he must hold it in check.

She forgets herself. She forgets where they are, what they are supposed to be doing. Being together in that little darkening room floating above the city is enough. The office hierarchy, interviews with corporate vice-presidents, topics for future newsletters—these are the items they talk about. And then he suddenly describes a long trip he made after his marriage broke up.

He gave his house, an old Victorian he had restored, to his wife and to her lover, and got rid of nearly everything he owned, and took a freighter to Spain. With a little money left from an inheritance from his father, he bought a motorcycle in Bavaria and rode through Switzerland and Italy, and finally wound up in Greece. He avoided tourists sites, and when he heard English, he got back on his bike.

He does not tell Angela about the bad nights, when, as he lay in his sleeping bag, he would sometimes overhear himself silently threatening Lucy or Alec, his arms bunched up against his chest, his fists and throat tight. Or he would think of everyone back home smirking about how his wife and friend deceived him. Lucy was remarkably guileless the whole time she was sleeping with Alec, talented at making her face innocent, bland, even: the wizardry of a debutante.

He tells Angela instead about how he put himself to sleep

by listening to the noise of the sea and picturing a black breaking wave outlined with gold. "That blotted out everything," he says.

He tells her about the wild, remote regions of northern Greece. She is rapt. "There are little villages where they walk on burning coals, and there are places with festivals they say are Christian but are probably much older than that. Once I stopped in this place in Thessaly to get some bread and cheese, and there was a festival going on. These musicians were playing very strange music—it was really beautiful. It made me feel very odd, outside of myself. Lutes, a bouzouki, and some kind of pipes. Men, women, and children were in a big circle. They were wearing oak leaves in their hair. It was amazing." He stops, remembering the heat, the dust, the smell of roasting mutton, the people beckoning him to join their dance. When a man and a boy tried to pull him into the circle, he shouted "No! No!" and backed away. Their touch, casual, human, and welcoming, horrified him. There was a net thrown over everyone at birth that attached you to everyone else struggling under the net. It was terrible, and he wanted no part of it. Afterward he did not calm down for a long time. He has forgotten this until now. With Angela, his memory dilates. "Very interesting," he says.

"It sounds wonderful," Angela says. "Why did you ever leave?"

"I had this idea of going to Mount Athos. In Metéora there are a lot of eroded stone outcroppings, and in one valley, there's a monastery on top of nearly every one of them. The monks used to get up to them in a basket—someone would lower it and haul them up. I was visiting one of these—it had a ladder—and I met a German guy who was going to Mount Athos, and he told me about it. You have to get a visa from church authorities to go there. I really thought about becoming a monk. I wasn't interested in the religious part of it, but I was impressed by some of those monks. I guess they're like Zen monks. They lead very orderly, simple, peaceful lives. They meditate. Everything is taken care of—nobody has to go to the laundromat or the supermarket. And at night, the stars are incredible."

"So, did you go to Mount Athos?"

"It didn't work out." His tone is abrupt.

She has asked the wrong question. He is not exactly like her inner picture of him, which makes her stop whatever she is doing and hang there in mid-air contemplating some detail—his crooked teeth, his biceps, the way he pronounces "room" like "rum." She supposes she ought to leave. Down below on the street a siren shrieks. Then another and another. "We'll probably never know what it is," she says. "The sirens, I mean. When I first came to New York, I couldn't get over how you'd hear sirens all the time and then never read in the paper what they were for. In Gatch, everyone went outside when they heard sirens. Then there would always be a headline in the paper about it the next day."

She tells him about how she used to think sometimes that sirens sounded during school hours or in the middle of the night were warnings that Soviet bombers were coming. "I'd look around the classroom and see that the other kids were bracing themselves for a nuclear attack, too. See, everyone in Gatch knew the government-classified secret that Gatch was considered the third most important target in the Western hemisphere. We were proud as hell of that." She goes on and he leans forward, wondering where she's headed. "Outside of town, the military hollowed out this mountain and filled it with hydrogen bombs. Or that's what everybody believed."

He smiles, envisioning her as a small girl. Her eyes widen when she talks about the past. Even then she must have been very pretty. He watches the pulse in her throat.

She laughs, aware of his gaze, and smiles a little nervously, her lips flickering.

She smooths her hair away from her forehead.

He shifts in his chair and rubs his wrists on his thighs and licks his upper lip.

She glances around his office, at the clutter, the plant with beautiful red bell-shaped flowers, the two photographic negatives tacked to his bulletin board, the green wine bottle turning to a translucent silhouette on the windowsill. It has grown very dark and he has not put the light on.

He hates fluorescent light. It drains the life from faces and makes him feel intensely bored.

Difficulty at the beginning, she thinks.

He stares at her. The stare becomes so intense that she turns to the window and the twilit sky. When she finally turns back, he is still staring. They are participating in an elaborate ritual that was arranged long ago. They know their parts perfectly. The immense, overarching order of the world determined their meeting, and they are helpless. All they can do is what they are doing. When she says good-bye, she lets her fingertips rest for a second in the air just above his belt buckle.

Angela buys some new clothes, a pair of shoes, cleans her apartment, and tries to keep from calling Joe. She is filled with energy, unable to eat much, and there's no one but Joe she wants to talk to. When Ron phones she tells him she is busy doing work preparing for her new job. And she tries to figure out a way to let Joe know that he is everything she has ever wanted. Of course she can't let him know directly because he is a sideways sort of person who does one thing while believing he's doing another. To make the time go quickly, she day-dreams and dances, usually to the *Let It Bleed* album.

Finally, in mid-week, she phones Joe at the office. As soon as he answers, she discards a dozen ploys. "Just checking in. It was so great talking to you the other evening."

"It feels so good to hear your voice," he says quietly. "You sound fine." He looks up at an enigmatic postcard that arrived today, which he tacked to the bulletin board next to the negatives of Edith and of his son Todd. It's an art postcard from the Metropolitan, a romantic, wistful, delicate painting of two women in a green landscape by a green sea tending some unicorns. One woman has fair hair—she's feeding the silvery-white animals and tending a fire with a blue flame. The other woman, dark-haired, gazes at the green water and some low red hills beyond. On the back, his name and the office address are printed in block letters, and there is a strip of paper pasted across one end, a fortune from a Chinese cookie that says: TEMPTATION AWAITS YOU.

"And you're fine, too?" She wishes she could think of something to say.

"I really am fine." He is smiling, searching for a question to prolong the conversation. "Have you had an opportunity to look over the newsletters?"

"Oh, yes, yes. They're just great. I can't wait to get started."

At four or five in the morning, the phone rings and Angela first thinks it's the dream phone and then wakes herself up enough to get to it before it stops. It's Ron. "I was talking to Sharon Abend yesterday, and I've been trying like a madman to put this whole thing together, and I just want to say to you, Angela, that I know you have been hurt by men and you shouldn't withdraw from me because of your strong feelings for me. You really can trust me. Don't be afraid of those feelings. I have them, too. Could I come over? I realize that we are in love with each other is what I am trying to say to you."

"Thank you very much, but I have to go back to sleep. You're very nice and everything, but I am not conscious." As she goes back to bed, she asks the ceiling who Ron has fallen in love with. It can't be her—he doesn't even know her. Their eyes never met. Her heart never shivered in his presence. How can he talk about love?

She dreams the green of the postcard sea, the red of the hills, the waves of the hills, the ripples of the sea, a rhythmically contracting undertow.

6

BUFF GOODHUGH HAS A corner office with windows along two walls, a big oak desk, two Bank of England chairs, and a glass-fronted bookcase filled with leather-bound books with gilt lettering on their spines—the great works of the Western world—and bound volumes of *Aerosol Valve Manufacturers' Review*, *Hydroengineering News*, and *Hardware and Brass Fittings Statistics*. Angela cannot find the *Executives' Newsletter*—maybe there are not enough issues yet for a bound volume. On Goodhugh's desk is a fat black fountain pen with a gold clip, a single piece of paper—her resumé?—and a copy of Machiavelli's *The Prince* in soft red leather. "Bly is quite taken with you, Angela," Goodhugh says.

"I'm quite taken with *him*." It is Angela's first day of work at Starr Whorf. She is wearing a new blue wool dress with buttons down the front shaped like little roses. She feels bold, extravagant, and able. Once in a bar with Janos she threw darts for the first time and hit three bull's-eyes in succession. That's the way she feels today: endowed with strength and luck that actually don't belong to her but for some reason happen to be passing through. Goodhugh's blue-eyed, deeply tanned, rumpled-tie, old-boy majesty does not daunt her. Furthermore, she wants him to think she is wonderful so that he will tell Joe. "I really admire Joe, what he's doing with the newsletter and all," she adds.

Goodhugh's lower lip slides out a fraction and he passes his palm along his temple, smoothing his graying hair.

"Oh, and you, too," she adds. "I mean, you're very nice."

"Thank you, Angela. I'm pleased and delighted. I like that very much." Goodhugh is solemn.

"You are very welcome, Mr. Goodhugh."

"You may call me Buff. This is a friendly place, as I would hope and pray you'll discover to your everlasting pleasure."

She considers telling him what Katha read her out of the yellow book this morning, about the fostering and nourishing of able men, and how all that is visible must grow beyond itself, extending into the realm of the invisible, but Angela does not want to push her luck. And anyway, when she threw the coins she was thinking of Joe, not of Goodhugh. When Joe saw her arrive he bounded up the hallway toward her and took her hands, and she felt such electricity she could barely look at him. It was an echo of the oracle: "There is in man a fate that lends power to his life."

"I'm really, really glad to have you on board," Goodhugh is saying. "My whole thrust and campaign here is to get young creative adventurers and turn them loose in the corporate structure. You might say I'm sort of a maverick." Watching her, he smiles and clicks his heavy fountain pen against his fingernails.

"You must be a maverick if you're hiring me. I don't know what I'm doing here. But it sure beats writing advice columns for love comics. See, a comic book has to have one page of print so it can go through the mail as literature instead of as artwork. Did you know that? Well, I had the job writing that page—stuff about rice or banana diets, what to do on your first date, how to find true love through the stars. I used to believe in astrology until I started making it up myself." She realizes she is running on and shuts up.

Goodhugh leans back in his chair and talks for a while about the executives' newsletter. "My newsletter," he calls it. One morning, he says, he woke up with the conception of a news-letter aimed exclusively at the upper echelon of corporate ex-ecutives. Men of intelligence, taste, curiosity, discrimination. The board of directors was against it at first, but Goodhugh spent time with each of them individually and finally managed to turn them around. Then he searched for the perfect person to carry out his plan. "As it happens, I had discovered Bly years earlier, when he was still an undergraduate."

Angela, who has been thinking about how there is not much evidence of real work going on in Goodhugh's office, and wondering if she and Joe will go out to lunch together, sits up straighter and starts listening carefully when Goodhugh mentions Joe. "Oh, really?"

"Yes, I was at some alumni do and I was introduced to him. Right away I got in touch with my fraternity and I told those boys, 'Pledge Bly.' He became president of the fraternity, and he ran both the newspaper and the lit magazine—extraordinary. He would have been a Rhodes scholar if he hadn't gotten married. I must add that I believe I was modestly instrumental in getting the university press to hire him after graduation. He was extremely well wired by then. Assistant director, and everyone knew he would be appointed director in a few years. To my knowledge, that would have made him the youngest director of any university press, let's say any press of notable caliber. Unfortunately, he sort of had some domestic upheavals and troubles, and he went chasing abroad. I finally was able to reach him, after he came back, and *sans dire,* I was pleased and delighted when he agreed to do the newsletter. He was a little restless at first; he felt he didn't fit in here. 'That's the whole idea!' I told him. I said, 'It may be difficult at first, but we must try, try, try!' And now everything is splendid. I don't believe I am exaggerating or extrapolating when I venture to say that this newsletter of mine is the best thing that has ever happened to the division, in fact, to Starr Whorf."

Since Angela has only glanced at the copies Joe mailed her, she keeps quiet and nods enthusiastically. She is not interested in the percentage by which corporate profits rose in the last quarter, or in excerpts from the Senate Banking Committee's report, or in the news that housing starts have risen to a new high, seasonally adjusted, of course.

"In fact, it's the only damned newsletter in the division that is actually showing a substantial profit. Our expenses are low because we get most of our information from brokerage houses, who don't charge, and from public documents. A few months ago, I doubled the subscription price. It was a risk and a gamble—I thought we'd lose our shirts. And do you know what happened?"

"No, what happened?" Angela realizes she will have to seem interested in conversations like this if she is going to last more than two weeks here.

"The long and the short of it is that I was flooded with a thirty-four percent increase in subscriptions. The people in Delaware are seldom happy about anything—but they were happy about this."

"The people in Delaware?" Delaware is a state Angela can never find on her mental map of the country. She is still accustomed to large, square states with clear-cut borders.

"Whorf and Brunell—they own this corporation, or at least the controlling interest in it."

"Oh."

Goodhugh gets to his feet. "May I escort you to Bly's office?"

"Oh, gosh—don't bother. I can find it."

But Goodhugh puts his hand on the small of her back and propels her down the gray-carpeted corridor to Joe. "You are a fortunate and lucky man, Bly. Angela, may you prosper and flourish here. *Bonne chance!*"

"Thanks very much," Angela says. "You, too."

Angela wants everyone in the office not only to like her but to adore her, to fall in love with her, so that they will generate a conflagration of love that will inflame Joe and leave him with no choice but to seize her for his own. And so, when Joe takes her along the corridor and introduces her to Tor Bracewell, the editor of *Hydroengineering News*, Hazel McNutt, the office manager, and a series of nearly identical men in their fifties wearing dark suits, white shirts, and careful ties, Angela beams and grasps hands and tries to be earnestly gracious. By the time Joe takes her back to his office, she is giddy and tired.

"Now you can understand why I'm so re—relieved to have someone here I can talk to," Joe says in a low voice. He tells her that she will have an office of her own directly across the hall from him in what is now a storeroom as soon as it can be cleared out. "Meanwhile, I hope you don't mind sharing this—" he waves at the narrow room—"with me."

"I feel at home here." She feels high-schoolish and unnatural, but she sits down and discreetly slides her feet out of the new pumps that are chafing her heels. "I don't mind. Believe me. What is that beautiful plant?"

"Gloxinia. If you look inside the flowers it's really amazing." He is certain she will perceive what he does about them.

She promptly pokes her shoes under the chair with her toes, gets up, and peers for a long time into a flower, curving her torso over his desk. "Oh, boy," she whispers. Some old and important memory, deeply hidden, stirs. Something to do with her name being called.

Joe feels as if they are underwater together. For the first time since he arrived at Starr Whorf, for the first time on any job, for that matter, he does not want to do any work.

"Well!" Angela sits down again and takes a little notebook and a pencil out of her purse. "What do you want me to do?"

"Why don't I lay—why don't I lay out the next issue?"

"Lay it out!" She is ready to work until midnight.

"Well, usually I look through the *Congressional Record* for excerpts, and any reports from the United Nations that—that might have come out." He cannot keep his mind on what he is saying. "And then the brokerage houses issue digests of their material. . . ."

Surely the job can't be that dull. Angela sighs. This could be hard work.

". . . career outlook," Joe is saying. "The price-wage index—"

"Now there's a thought," Angela says. "Excuse me, I didn't mean to interrupt."

"No, no—go ahead."

"Well, here are these guys around, like Goodhugh, and the other people I just met—I can't remember any names. Successful businessmen and so on, middle-aged. They're really stuck here. Maybe the executives who read the newsletter would like to know about some executive who quit and started doing something completely different, like being a chimney sweep.

Or moved to Rarotonga . . . I don't know. It's probably a dumb idea. Excuse me."

"No, I think that's very interesting. I was just reading in the paper the other day about the vice-president of a ball-bearing company who quit and went to live in the Arizona desert in a tent and build a stone wall with his bare hands."

"We could be telling these executives, Look, we know you are fascinated by housing starts and frozen pork bellies, but here's something else—there's more in life!" Angela pulls her chair closer to Joe's.

Joe thinks for a moment, if what he does, touching the tip of his tongue to his upper lip and including her breasts in his vision of the newsletter idea, can be called thinking. "It would mean more work—"

"Great. I love to work. Let's do it." She feels tense and aroused.

"Midlife career changes . . ." Her enthusiasm makes Joe speak with more authority. "We'll call it that. We'll do it." He takes a pencil from behind his ear and makes a note.

"Great, great," Angela says. "Midlife career changes."

"We could find these dropouts and do some interviews."

"That would be fun."

"It would be fun."

As they talk, Angela notices that his mustache is a little longer on the left side of his mouth than on the right. When he folds his hands together and thinks in silence for a few seconds, the left thumb rests on top of the right. There are blond streaks in his hair, and she sees the beginning of a faint bald spot when the clipboard falls off his lap and he bends over to pick it up. Today he is wearing a brand-new workshirt—the fold marks are still starched into it.

"We could make that section stand out by changing the typeface," Joe says.

"We could lead off with a quote from the Frost poem—'I saw two roads within a wood, dah-dah-dah et cetera.'"

"Definitely." He grabs his inner thighs.

The spend the rest of the day talking. Lunch is forgotten. Whole garlands of notions pop into Joe's head, and as he tells them to Angela, she nods avidly and says "Great!" or sometimes makes an odd, unpredictable remark that causes a new chain of thoughts to weave through his brain.

In what seems like a few hours, they have planned the next three issues, changed the layout of the pages, and they are both hoarse. Joe stretches his arms and legs and lights a cigarette. He has been sitting in the same position for a long time. "It's dark out," he says. "It must be late."

Angela bends over and puts her shoes on. He does not want her to go. "For the first time," he says, "I am calm and content and confident. You are terrific. I love your ideas. It's so good to know you'll be here."

Angela, overcome, jumps up and grabs his hand. "Oh!" she says. "You bet."

On her way home, waiting on the crowded, chilly subway platform, amid the ozone and stale popcorn smells, she gazes into the black tunnel and prays, which she has not done since she passed the aftermath of a horrible highway accident in Mexico a few years ago. God, she says, help me get over this crush so I can manage this wonderful job.

7

"YOU'RE JUST *USING* YOUR work, the office, that god-damned briefcase full of crap—you hide behind it. You have an assistant now, so you *can't* have as much work as you did before. You're just using all that to avoid an authentic relationship." Edith is fresh from a session with Midge. She and Joe are riding downtown in a cab. She picked him up from work because she did not want to wait until he got home to express her feelings. She is working on expressing her feelings more. "Every night you get home late. Every weekend, the job. The job, the job. I'm sick of it!"

He ducks his head and shifts his haunches. A loose spring is poking up and about to burst through the cracked vinyl upholstery. She knows, he thinks. She knows about Angela even though I haven't made a move. He keeps his mouth shut. These assaults are getting more frequent, and they always stun him. Edith used to be so cheerful. He must be overlooking something very important; there is something he must not be seeing. The key piece to the puzzle. Whatever it is, it's very obvious to Edith, and even to Midge, a woman he has never met.

"You are escaping reality. That's what it adds up to."

Joe doesn't know what she means by escaping reality. If anything, reality is escaping from him. Something essential is moving farther and farther away. Meeting Angela has made him see that. But Edith could be right; reality seems to serve her purposes. She seems to know what to do with reality. Does everyone see this hopeless flaw in him? Does Angela? Goodhugh? The board of directors?

"We have a lot invested in this relationship," Edith goes on. "How can you keep retreating from this investment? How can you refuse to own the experience that we have something authentic?"

Edith never used to talk like this. He twists his mouth. He shrugs. "I—I—." He does not want to hurt her feelings. He does not want to make her feel bad.

"And that's another thing. You never express your feelings. I *know* right now that you're really angry. Midge says you are a very *angry* person. But you never express it. Never!"

"Edith—not so loud." He eyes the blur that is the cab driver's head on the other side of the smeared, scratched, bulletproof panel. Stuck to the panel above the coin box is a bright orange disk that says SCREW. "I don't feel angry, Edith, I really don't. I don't know what I feel."

"Well, *I* do! *I* know that you're really attached very deeply to me, and you really care, you *do* want to be with me. That's why we got back together—you didn't really mean to break up. Unconsciously you do want to be with me. What it adds up to is you let your anger accumulate about things in the office, and you can't express it, and so you take it out on me. You avoid. You resist sharing."

He rubs his face; his skin is hot. He will find a little place uptown, near the office. Angela came to work today wearing tight jeans, black boots, a scarlet velveteen shirt, silver beads, her hair wound up around her head. When he saw her coming toward him he quickly picked up a newspaper and pretended to read so she wouldn't think he had been waiting for her so they could have their coffee together. It is still cold, it is only February, but he carries a vision of a green and fragrant spring.

Yesterday her hand brushed his shoulder as she passed him in the narrow office, and he was aware of that touch the rest of the day. Sometimes she accidentally grazes the hair on his forearm when she reaches for a paper. She always leaves the office the instant the phone rings, out of respect for his privacy, and during her absences he misses her.

He asks the cab driver to stop, and he gets out with his briefcase and slams the door and walks the rest of the way home.

The loft is dark and cold, and there is nothing to eat. Edith is not there. He is exhausted. He drinks a coffee cup of bourbon and goes to bed.

He is asleep when Edith comes in and gently shakes his shoulder and persuades him to get up. She has cleared off the dining table and lit candles. She has been crying, and in the candlelight her face, as if weary of so much tension, has softened. In silence they eat meatball hero sandwiches she picked up at the corner deli. Her voice is tired and quiet. "Joe, I really do love you. I'm sorry."

8

"I THOUGHT THIS WAS a *part-time* job," Sharon says. "You're never home any more." She has come downstairs with a roast chicken and a cheesecake her mother dropped off.

"Well, it was going to be part-time, but the work is really interesting. And I'm getting good at it." Joe is always telling Angela how smart she is, how terrific she is at coming up with new ideas. One day before he came into work, she sharpened all his pencils. He thanked her, then said, "Never do that again. We are co-equals." A little later that day she sneaked up behind him and showered rose petals—from a bouquet Ron had sent her—over Joe's head. "Anyway, Joe is out with the flu right now, so I have to work extra."

"You are either developing a work-compulsion, or you are in a deep transference with Joe," Sharon says, biting into a drumstick. "My shrink says I was in this massive transference with Clifford. I mean, at some level I thought he was my father. So maybe Clifford couldn't take that." Sharon's friends are not allowed to mention Clifford. Only Sharon can talk about him. They used to take baths together and plan how they would become a famous media couple when he quit his job at a racing tabloid and started his own serious magazine. One day Sharon came home and thought her apartment had been burglarized. Then she discovered that only Clifford's things were missing. She called some of his friends and they told her he was all right. He never spoke to Sharon again.

"I haven't seen my father since I was three," Angela says. Her only memory is of his crooked, brown front teeth. "I don't think Joe qualifies. Oh, here's the wishbone."

"Unconsciously, I mean."

"I don't even know what my unconscious is doing," Angela says.

"Freud didn't call it the unconscious for nothing," Sharon says. "So when are you going to go out with Prince Charming?"

Angela sighs and picks meat off the wishbone. "Here's how it is. I started coming in earlier—then he started coming in earlier. We order lunch and eat sandwiches together. We work late. Before he got the flu, we were both coming in on weekends. He always says really nice things to me. He treats me like I really know what I'm doing on this job. Little does he know. And he's always touching me—on the head, or the back, or the shoulder. I'm sure he's attracted to me. There have been steamy moments. But he hasn't made a move to ask me out after work." She holds out the wishbone and wishes, as she once used to wish fervently for a pony, for Joe Bly.

"Maybe he doesn't want to date someone he has to work with." Sharon pulls on the wishbone and it cracks in Angela's favor. "Maybe he belongs to somebody."

"Well." Angela puts her half of the wishbone on a windowsill. "I have a feeling he *may* see somebody, but I think he lives alone. He never says 'we.' He says '*my* loft;' '*my* plants.' He just bought a tree for his loft."

"Why don't you just ask him what his situation is?"

"We don't talk about things like that. He never asks me about *my* situation, so I don't think I should be so nosy."

"Oh, brother."

With Joe away from the office with his flu, there is much more to do, but she is calmer and able to work better. Sometimes she forgets about him for as long as an hour and is completely absorbed in the newsletter. She comes home feeling energetic and focused and pleased with herself and all that she is doing. I could really have a career, she thinks. Where could I go from this job? But Joe—everything depends on him, on whether they will get together. She lies in bed. Ah, he's not so much, she tells herself. Another man. She has a sudden vision of all the people in her life as phantoms, continually changing and moving. Dancing particles. She thinks of the backs of men she has touched in bed in the night—not too many, really—and it seems as if her hand could pass right through each back into empty space.

One night she dreams that she has a job that involves climbing on the outside of a building high above the traffic. There is some task requiring the use of razor blades, which she carries in her mouth as she climbs. One day as she is climbing, she decides she does not want to do that any more. She climbs down and tells a man she knows. He says, "I don't understand you when you're soaring on these poetic flights." "But you like them," she asks, "the flights?" "No," he says. "Not really."

Joe lies half asleep most of the time, his hands curved over his solar plexus. His bones hurt, his skin hurts, his eyeballs are on fire. What has he done to qualify for this spectacular punishment? Maybe it's his diet. He doesn't get enough exercise. He should quit smoking, lose weight. Or maybe it's his whole way of operating. "We could use a good vacation in a warm place," Edith says. Outside, beyond his foil-pack-insulation-lined world, there is a foot of snow. "Remember how we used to smoke that hash I had and lie on the beach in Greece? On the rocks?"

"I can't leave the office when I'm so behind," he says. "I have to work."

She takes a day off to be with him during the worst part. She speaks and walks softly and brings him cups of broth. She puts a cool damp washcloth on his forehead. She pulls the covers straight and smooths the sheet. When he begins to recover, she brings the television set into the bedroom. He takes her hand. For ten days touching has only brought pain. But now her hand feels okay—cool, dry, bony, and reassuring. "Eed—thank you. Thank you for doing all this for me."

"Aaah, go on—it's nothing." She grins.

"There's no one else who would do what you've done for me in the past week." Angela is too unpredictable. She would probably go out dancing if he were on his deathbed. She said she loves to dance. Rock 'n' roll. But at the moment that Edith leans over and kisses him, her weight falling across his chest so that he has trouble breathing, he wants Angela. He has thought of her often during his moments between sleeping and waking. She could be an imaginary being.

Edith puts her arms around his neck and pulls his head against her chest. "When you're feeling better, I'd like to ask you a favor."

"What is it?" He suddenly feels very tired.

"It's no big deal—I'll tell you later."

They watch TV. A little man in a motorboat rides around inside the water tank of a toilet. The black and white picture is jumpy.

"What is the favor, Edith?"

"It's very important to me."

"You just said it was no big deal."

"Well, it's no big deal for you, but it would mean a lot, a lot to me. It would be a big plus. And it will help us both."

"Tell me." His throat is getting sore again.

"I want you to talk to Midge. Now don't get angry—see, you're already getting angry and I haven't even finished."

"I'm not getting angry." He's too sick to get angry.

"It won't take much time. It's just so we can straighten a few things out. If we're not going to be together, we might as well profit by trying to separate in a sensible way so that we don't wind up hating each other. Let's experiment with that, okay?"

"When I'm feeling better, I'll give it a lot of thought." He is startled. This is the first time Edith has brought up the idea of their splitting up. It's always been Joe in the past. Right this moment he does not want to leave this dim, warm, shiny room and go out, feverish and coughing, into the snow.

"You know something? Lois just got a twenty-one-inch color TV—says it's super."

While Joe was ill, he thought he might be permanently bed-ridden, like his mother before her death. His lassitude and weakness seemed eternal, and he forgot that he was ever vigorous and healthy and hardworking. Now it seems to him that he was never even ill.

He is eager to get back to the office, even though it's Sunday. He sits at the dining table in his bathrobe and looks down at the snowy street and drinks coffee. Edith is cleaning the refrigerator.

"You never sit in your new Eames chair, Eed."

"When do I have time?" She never talks about Eames chairs now; she's forgotten the whole quest. When she is finished with the refrigerator, it looks like the kind clinics use to hold medications. "Whew," she says, and drops into the chair next to Joe. "I have a tiny favor to ask you."

"I don't want to talk about Midge right now."

"Ah, forget that. This is really nothing. My secretary, Trudy—she's having a little get-together tonight and it would really mean so much to her if we'd come. I never ask anything of you, but this is important."

Joe hates parties and will go out of his way to avoid them, just as he crosses the street to avoid the gang of toughs who hang out by the deli. They carry ax handles and noisy radios, and they are bored and mean, looking for something to happen. But right now Joe is thinking about when he goes back to work, and how he will give Angela a hug; it will seem innocent because he was sick and away for so long. He grins and slaps his stomach—he's lost several pounds; good. "Okay," he says to Edith. "For a little while. Why don't I meet you there? I want to stop by the office and check the mail and stuff."

Edith starts to speak and then stops herself. "Sure, sweetie."

As he unlocks the door to the reception area, he hopes Angela will be there. She comes in on Sundays. But it's late, and anyway, she has a whole life he knows nothing about. Once she mentioned driving around in the country with a friend and finding an antique mirror she had dreamed about. Who was the friend?

The corridors are dark and the air is dead. His office seems dilapidated and abandoned. Certain things are missing. It takes him a minute to realize that Angela has moved out.

He steps across the corridor. The storeroom, once crammed

with old filing cabinets, stacks of dented wire in-baskets, and torn cardboard boxes containing broken paper-punches, ancient ledger books, and crumbling reams of yellow paper, is now Angela's office. He finds a lamp on the desk and turns it on. The lamp has a shade made of disks of translucent shell; it casts an amber light. The walls are freshly painted white—how did she manage that? He's been petitioning for a year to get his office painted. On the wall is a reproduction of a Persian miniature: he has to stand close to make it out. A man and woman in bed, his cheek pressed to hers, their faces rosy and serene. They lie under a scalloped blue and gold coverlet shaped like a wave and behind them, in a niche, a tall candle spurts gold flame. Next to the bed, two pairs of slippers and a bowl of red fruit. Joe has the dreamy feeling he has opened a door to a house and found another house within.

Angela's desk is impeccable. The dark blue blotter matches the blue in the picture. A scissors, a tape dispenser, and a stapler are arranged in one corner. On another corner, out of the way, is a black lacquer tray with a little blue teapot and two—two—dark blue Japanese mugs incised with flying white cranes that circle the rims. And a flowered tin box, which he opens. It contains tea leaves mixed with little pieces of fragrant bark, cloves, and flower petals. As he shuts the lid, there is an exhalation of spice. On a red filing cabinet he finds a white porcelain bowl filled with raisins and almonds. His hand is in the dish, taking, before he knows it. He pushes the sweet food into his mouth; he is suddenly starving. As he chews, standing in the sphere of warm light, he inhales deeply. Beyond the spice, there is the scent of roses and clean hair that is her particular smell. His chest fills with an expanding, searing sensation and for a second he remembers the joyous feeling of being a child on a Saturday morning with the day and its fascinations all his. But before he can remember further, the flash has vanished without casting a shadow.

He runs his hand over the top of the filing cabinet. He can feel ridges in the enamel—she must have painted it herself. He's never seen a filing cabinet that particular cinnabar red. He misses her. He has been ill; he forgot how much she nourishes him.

On the bulletin board above her desk are tacked some phone

messages—the printer, the paper supplier; of course, while he was gone she was putting out the newsletter—and some very peculiar items she has clipped from newspapers: MATTER IN SPACE TERMED LIMITED. HOW TO LOSE WEIGHT BY DAYDREAMING. LOVE QUITS POST AFTER A SHAKE-UP. FISH WAR ON SOUND HALTED BY COURT. CHANGE CREEPS INTO WORLD OF BRONX ALBANIANS. XENOPHOBIC ALBANIA IS NOT LIKELY TO CHANGE. WOMAN SAYS: I AM A WALKING TIME BOMB.

He smiles. Now he knows for sure who sent him the postcard. *Temptation awaits you.*

On her desk, on her memo pad, is a list written in her peculiar, hooked longhand. He doesn't mean to read it, but there it is, where anyone might see it.

SCORECARD

	J.	A.
1. *Scattering of rose petals over opponent*	0	1
2. *Hugs given to opponent*	5	5
3. *Songs sung to opponent*	0	3
4. *Little cheerful notes written to opp.*	3	4
5. *Food treats & cups of tea given to opp.*	0	11
6. *Solving opponent's problems*	0	3
7. *Pats on head and shoulders*	12	2
8. *Pats on abdominal area*	0	4
	20	33

He smiles with guilt and joy and the delicious sense of trespassing. The songs she sang to him. *"Hesitation stockings, hesitation shoes, even angels up in heaven got them hesitation blues . . . all your high talk will have to wait. Can I get you now or must I hesitate?"* And *"Weary blues from waitin', Lord, I been waitin' too long . . ."* and "Your Cheatin' Heart" crooned in a thin yodeling tone. Hearing a noise down the corridor, he switches off the lamp and hurries back into his office as Goodhugh appears.

"Hiya, Bly." Goodhugh claps Joe on the shoulder. "Delighted to see you. I trust you're fully recovered. I can't account for what may have transpired with the intrepid Mademoiselle Lee during your absence."

"I think everything is okay." Joe smiles from his agitated heart, thinking of Angela's scorecard, and her random scoring. "I'm glad to be back."

Goodhugh is carrying a copy of *The Will to Power*. Even though he is a businessman, and his father is an eminent bank owner, he wants his underlings, like Joe, to think of him as a Renaissance man, or, better yet, as Marcus Aurelius. Is that why Goodhugh hired Joe in the first place—because he thought he would appreciate such sensitivity? Once a portrait photographer came in to photograph Goodhugh for a business magazine, and Joe overheard Goodhugh saying, quite seriously, "Make me look as if I were a virtuoso violinist who is kind to children."

"Joe, we're hot," Goodhugh says as they walk down the hall. "I think it's time to raise the subscription price: five years for ten thousand dollars."

"Five years?" Joe has not thought about what he'll be doing in five years. He doesn't know whether to renew his own subscriptions—where will he be living in a year?

"I'm going to Whorf and Brunell and asking them for heavy backing to really put this thing over the top."

Why does this news make Joe feel terrible? They say goodbye at the men's room door and as Goodhugh goes in, he waves his book. "Read this? You should. *Bon soir!*"

It is one of those parties with big jugs of California wine and carrot sticks and thin little crackers in little wooden bowls and Simon and Garfunkel on the stereo. The first thing Joe notices when he walks in is how low the ceiling is, how little empty space is available above all the heads.

"He's here!" Edith grabs him and draws him into the din and moving mouths. It's mostly women, women from Edith's clinic, and their friends, spare women they brought along. They all seem to be wearing jeans of different colors. One woman is also wearing purple suede boots and a gray T-shirt with the legend *"Liberté, Egalité, Sororité."* What if Angela happened to be here, what if he were meeting her here? "Notice how little space there is above everyone's head," he would whisper to Angela. And she would nod knowingly. The would leave early and go home and make love.

"Oh, thank you for coming, Joe," the hostess says. She is wearing a long skirt and a regular blouse, nothing written on it. "Thanks a whole lot. This means so much to me. I told Edith already." Her name is Trudy and she has a round face and cherubic red cheeks and black curls. She is very earnest, very young. On the wall is a poster of an embracing nude couple in silhouette at a cliff edge in the sunset. "Love Makes All Things New Again," it says at the bottom.

Edith holds Joe's elbow with both hands and steers him around to introduce him to her co-workers. They are mostly in their late twenties, and they seem to him very hearty and practical and competent, like nurses. In fact, some of them are nurses. If someone started choking on a carrot stick, they would all know exactly what to do. Or if there was a fire, they would organize the fire drill and the extinguishing procedures. They don't seem at ease just standing around talking and drinking wine from plastic cups; if only someone would keel over with appendicitis, they would blossom. "Joe!" they cry with friendliness. Smiling at Edith, one woman says, "It's true—he's quite a catch." They know about him, it's clear, from the familiar way they regard him when they shake hands. They've already read his chart.

From time to time Edith sends him sharp telegrams, fierce nods, because she can detect his boredom. The others don't notice—it's too low-level an emergency. He quickly drinks a couple of cups of wine. "You forgot to bring me one," Edith says. She presses her lips together and her expression of good cheer falls away for an instant, revealing sadness and pain. What does she want from him?

"Oh, sorry." He fetches her one and then sinks back against the wall while Edith talks to a couple of women about a mix-up in a pharmaceutical order.

"Kidney pans?" he hears someone say.

He could take off his shoe and eat it. That would be interesting. He has another glass of wine. Once at a college benefit, he saw Paul Newman. Paul Newman looked very bored, and he stuck a can of beer in his tuxedo cummerbund. Joe pulls at the collar of his sweater—a gray, heavy sweater Edith knitted for him for his birthday. She made the neck too small so that when he swallows he feels he's being strangled.

"This is my sister, Lynn," Trudy is saying.

"Hi," Joe says. Lynn does not look like the other women here. She is thin and pale and wears a low-cut black dress. She puts her hand on her hip and thrusts her pelvis forward. Joe downs a big gulp of wine. She is so unlike Trudy that he supposes that one of them is adopted.

"Do you work at the clinic?" Joe is sure she doesn't, but he's suddenly too tired to say anything else.

"Of course not. I'm *Lynn Lewis!*" She explains that she is a journalist, a reporter, a feminist. She puts a long cigarette into a short cigarette holder. She has just come from a television panel discussion about wife-abuse, she says.

"Are you married?" Joe lights her cigarette.

"Of course not!" This question touches off a rage so dire that he regrets his own stupidity. While she talks about marriage and what is wrong with the institution, his gaze goes past her sloping shoulders to the poster. It is red and orange and gold, with the bodies of the embracing lovers black. It is tawdry and sentimental and it was purchased at a head shop. And it reminds Joe of love, real love, the brilliant colorless flame that Angela has sparked, that somehow without effort on his part or hers has come into being. The world is suddenly alive with possibilities; it has become a transparent whole. *Love makes all things new again.* It's true, it's true! "It's true," he says.

"And that's the way it will be until we legislate that men take an equal share of the burden."

"You are absolutely right," he tells Lynn. For all he knows, she may be. He hasn't been listening. But remembering this colorless flame, he feels gentle and warm toward everyone in the world, including the troubled woman before him who has the ability to speak continuously without breathing. She has deep blue eyes that are very lovely, and translucent skin; she's not so bad.

She stops. "But you know, I *know* who you are! A woman I work with is a friend of Angela Lee's."

Joe feels his ears heat up. "Oh, right, yes," he murmurs. "She's just started, at the, the newsletter." He scans the room for Edith. Edith is laughing with a semicircle of women; she is very popular. "So I figured the tax again," she says.

"Sharon Abend, my friend, says Angela's really concentrating on the job. It's a big break for her, and it's about time corporations like Starr Whorf started putting women in responsible positions. Or is she your girl?"

"Girl?"

"Your gofer."

"No, no, she's, she seems very good. We're co-equals. Things are going very well."

"So I hear via Sharon."

Joe says nothing. He looks keenly at Lynn. This is a trick he learned when he was a reporter on the college paper. You watch someone with an air of expectation and keep your mouth shut and your pencil raised over your notebook. A great chasm is created that way, and most people are drawn to the edge and will eventually fling themselves in—anything to fill a vacuum. It's possible that Lynn, being a reporter, will recognize this trick, but she doesn't seem very observant.

Or, for that matter, reluctant to withhold information. "Of course I understand Angela is concentrating on Ron Nussbaum, too."

"Ron Nussbaum," Joe repeats in a toneless voice, keeping his face blank. His heart lurches.

"Ronald A. Nussbaum, the poet. You know."

Joe has seen Nussbaum's poetry in magazines. Gerard Clewes probably knows him. "No, who is he?"

"Oh, *well*—you corporate types, I keep forgetting. He's won these terribly important awards. I've known him for years."

"Angela is living with him now, isn't she?" Another reporter's trick. Exaggerate and wait for a correction.

"Oh, I don't think so. He gave Angela's breasts funny names—I forget what."

Joe feels very odd. Lynn seems tiny and far away. He rubs his forehead; maybe he's not over the flu after all.

"What are you talking about?" Edith puts her arms around Joe and squeezes his chest. He quickly takes a deep breath.

"The sex life of Joe's new assistant."

"She's not my assistant. We work equally."

"Sex life? Sex life?" Edith's voice is ragged from so much talking, smoking, and drinking. "My Joe has been so overworked, you wouldn't believe it. Finally they broke down and hired a warm body to help him so we can get away once in a while." She smiles widely, artificially.

"In fact, I really have to leave now to catch up on some work." Joe's head seems ready to bump against the ceiling.

Edith's smile melts. "You promised."

"Stay and enjoy yourself, Edith. It's just that I picked up some stuff at the office and I really have to go over it before tomorrow." He wishes he could just shut up and not try to leave—it would be much simpler. Now there will be rehashing and discussion and dissection.

"Remember what Midge said."

Joe feels awful. He is making Edith suffer. He is escaping reality. He wants to live in a world like that poster over there. Midge is right.

"Midge?" Lynn asks.

"A very helpful *friend*," Edith says.

"Actually I'm getting over the flu," Joe explains to Lynn. "I'll stay thirty minutes more," he tells Edith, checking his watch. He thinks of Thoreau, an old idol. As if we could kill time without injuring eternity.

That night in bed, Edith cries and tells Joe how she felt when he said he wanted to leave the party, and how she wasn't having that great a time herself but she wanted to make Trudy happy. He thinks about Angela and this Nussbaum character. A poet—wouldn't you know! Naming her breasts. How stupid to think Angela was doing anything besides a little flirting. Obviously she would prefer a successful poet to a dud like himself. All he does is work. And hurt Edith's feelings.

He could still leave Edith. But for what? A little low-ceilinged cubicle with a bed and a chair? Like the room he rented after he left Lucy? Cold hot dogs for dinner alone? Conversations with desperate women in dim bars and at parties? Sleeping with those women, or alone, night after night until he grows old?

"I'm very sorry." He grips Edith's shoulder and she responds with a tight hug. He wants to be holding Angela. "I have to work a lot of things out."

"Did you give some thought to that favor?"

"Favor." He wants to sound as if he forgot, as if he's asking a question, but he lacks the energy to make his voice rise.

"About seeing Midge."

"All right . . . when I have time at some point."

"Thursday at three, then?"

9

ANGELA FINISHES REORDERING HER files, which are still new enough not to be out of order, and listens for the faint creaks and rustlings from across the hall that tell her Joe is still at work. Everyone else has left for the day. She waits. Today she bought a copy of the *Wall Street Journal* for the first time and she now reads that women in corporations are beginning to be taken more seriously at the managerial level. After college, when she arrived in the city with Arthur, she wanted to be a success. At what, she could not think. She then read a book about how a woman could get a great job in the business world, and eventually an executive position, if she wore one-piece outfits rather than skirts and blouses, carried mouth spray in her purse, and had a nose for new ideas. Angela, looking for a great job, made a poster that she thought would impress an advertising agency with her talents. In biology lab classes, she had been fairly adept at sketching, and so she drew a planarian, and then cut out a picture of a Volkswagen Beetle from a magazine and pasted it next to the picture of the flat-worm. Underneath she wrote some text about how neither the planarian nor the VW had changed its shape. When she went for the interview at the first advertising agency, the personnel manager declined to see Angela's ad and told her that the job mainly involved phoning airlines and making ticket reservations. Eventually Angela found work typing and doing research for an anthropologist writing a book about Ethiopia.

Joe drags his chair into her office. "I'm sorry to bother you."

"Oh, please bother me—I love it," she says. "I'll make some tea."

They sit in the warm light of her lamp—she never uses the overhead fluorescent one—and drink from the mugs with the cranes flying around the rims.

"Why don't we start some new departments in the newsletter?" She is wearing the red velveteen blouse that makes him want to stroke her. Her hair is held at the nape of her neck with a silver clasp. "I was thinking about this while you were sick. I mean, I do like it the way it is but maybe we can do some new things."

"Like what?" She must think that there is something wrong with what he's done.

"How about something like—I mean it just as an idea, just a thought—something like, oh, well, the latest breakthroughs. Maybe that's not right." She bites her lip and three horizontal lines appear in her forehead.

He lights a cigarette. He does not want to make any more changes in the newsletter. Everything happens so fast around Angela.

"Well?"

"I don't know."

She suddenly gives him the finger.

He grins. "Okay, let's hear it."

She takes a notebook out of her purse. "I wrote down some, uh, things."

This morning when he arrived at the office he gave her a fast, hard hug. It was perfectly innocent, it was okay: they are colleagues, and he had been away for ten days. He and Belinda sometimes exchanged hugs. Angela snaps open the hair clasp and her hair, released, settles across her shoulders. Her face relaxes. She sighs. "Maybe it's not such a good idea."

"No, really, tell me. We're partners."

She opens the notebook and then ignores it. "Each issue, the column could deal with some new discovery or way of doing things."

"Like unusual solutions," he says. "Dealing with a problem sideways instead of directly."

"Unusual solutions—that's great. Very good." She makes a note. "Energy," she says.

Suddenly, all at once, he feels the shape of the newsletter with this addition, a neat box. Different type, maybe with a line drawing. Inside stuff, but of general interest. "Energy alternatives. Solar power, windmills—some little company in the Southwest just sent me their prospectus."

"Wow, terrific, fantastic." She makes a note.

"This is a very good idea, Angela. And it gives us a place to put everything we don't know what to do with, everything that we think is really interesting." He stops and looks around the office and exhales. He has just remembered that she has a lover, a breast-naming poet. Well, anyway, they still make good colleagues. "What about poetry?" he asks, pleased with his slyness. "What if sometimes we just put poetry in?"

"In a newsletter for busy executives? *Po*etry?"

"Wallace Stevens was the V.-P. of an insurance company." His voice drops. "I really like Wallace Stevens." He wants her to know that there is hope for him. Nussbaum isn't the only sensitive spirit in the world.

"Okay, poetry then."

"Little known facts. Maybe reports from fields like medical engineering—those plastic heart valves. Sex research—a lot is coming up about that."

"Mmm."

Is it possible she is blushing. She is twenty-seven, divorced, and she said she had an affair with her husband's friend. And she is always flirting. With Goodhugh, with Tor Bracewell and various other office lizards. He even hears her flirting on the phone. How can she be blushing? They are simply discussing an idea, an idea that is sounding better all the time. After a while he speaks. "What was it like for you, growing up in the wide open spaces?"

"You really want to know?" No one has ever asked her that before.

"I really want to know."

As she talks he sees a broad plain covered with sagebrush and ringed with dark blue sawtoothed mountains. Dust storms that pitted her legs and face as she walked to school. Flash floods, gullywashers. Summers so hot you could fry an egg on the asphalt of the highway in front of the Cash-In Café where her mother worked for thirty-one years as a waitress until her death, in a lawn chair in front of her trailer while she and a neighbor lady were watching for shooting stars. A plague of grasshoppers that ate up all the leaves on the cottonwoods.

Suddenly an old memory of hers surfaces, the one that was touched when she looked into the gloxinia blossom. "I can remember when I first knew I was alive," she says. "I was standing next to this fence where some morning glories were in bloom, and I was looking at the inside of a flower and it was like I heard someone speaking my name, inside myself. Then I realized that my name was Angela because that was what people called me, but they couldn't mean what I felt like inside, because that didn't have a name. Then I realized everything else had an outside name but not an inside one, and I went around touching things and saying their names—fence, sidewalk, tricycle. And I used to wonder about this. How could it be that while everyone else had a name the way I did that the name only had to do with the outside part that talked to others? And if this was true, why didn't anyone ever mention it? My mother didn't even want to talk about it. I figured it must be a secret." She watches Joe, waiting for him to change the subject.

He is silent, hoping she will keep talking. Her soft voice entrances him.

She tells him about when she was eleven and she took a piece of notebook paper and wrote down how old she would be in ten years, in twenty, in thirty. She had never thought about the future until then, except just before Christmas or summer vacation, when she waited to get out of school. But when she thought about herself growing older, she felt sad about those unknown years, to be lived by a person named Angela whom she would never know, who would be larger and smarter and of course would somehow become attractive and worldly. She never doubted that she would improve as she grew. But she did wonder how to get from eleven to thirty-one. "I asked my mother, and she said, 'It just happens, darlin'—don't worry about it.' But I did worry about how to leave being eleven. How to leave Gatch. I didn't want to be like my mother. My father left her when I was real little and she waited all those years for him to come back, or for someone else to come along and take her to L.A. That's where she always wanted to go."

Angela now remembers that she used to be afraid of waking up one morning to discover that she had become an old, old woman: she would wander in confusion along the streets of Gatch, which were lined with littled faded pastel adobe houses, looking numbly beyond the town to the plain and the mountains. The region had once been at the bottom of a tropical sea, and on her way to school she used to picture warm clear waters splashing against the steep faces of the ranges and volcanoes. And what would the place be like in a million years? In a billion, when all the mountains were scoured flat by wind and rain, and the sun was a shriveled cinder in a black sky? She watched old people who had spent their lives in Gatch for some clue as to what was in store for her, but their dry, tanned-leather faces showed her nothing.

"Do you ever think of going back?" Joe asks.

"A lot. I never intended to stay in New York anyway. My ex and I used to make plans to go back and buy a ranch and live off the land with this other couple. Helen—she's my best friend—and Tom actually did it, but by then Arthur and I were divorced. Helen keeps asking when I'm coming. The Gatch area might be a nice place to settle down. The people are very friendly, and the clouds are like nothing you've seen—one cloud will be fifty thousand feet tall. Whenever things get to be too much in the city, I think about moving back there."

"I worked one summer in Montana," Joe says. "I've often thought about going back. I know what you mean about the clouds. They're three-dimensional." He puts down his mug and his cigarette. He breathes out very slowly. *And now good morrow to our waking souls, which watch not one another out of fear*, he wants to say. But he can't bring himself to do that.

There is a long silence. Neither of them moves. He stares at Angela. She stares at the Persian miniature of the rosy-cheeked couple in bed. They are so acutely aware of each other that their lips tremble on the edge of smiles that have nothing to do with smiling. She has the feeling that she has talked too much, that he can't possibly like someone with such a dusty, ordinary background.

"Oh, deadlines," she finally says. He never asks her to dinner after these late sessions. Is something wrong with her? "While you were sick, Goodhugh was complaining about the cost overruns from missed deadlines. So I was wondering— would it work to change all our deadlines to a week earlier? Maybe we could fool ourselves..." She does not finish.

He does not reply. He continues to stare at her, his eyes green and liquid.

She wants to ask him what he's thinking, but she can't get her mouth and voice to work. She is afraid to meet his gaze, but then she does, turning and facing him and looking straight into his eyes. She does not look away again.

Time stops. They hang in space.

When Angela enters her apartment, she observes herself in the hallway mirror. What was he staring at? Why? What is it? What is going on? No man has ever treated her this way. This intensity that never finds release excites and exhausts her. Maybe she should make a big move and ask him to her place. "You are crazy," she tells the mirror person, and drinks a beer, skips dinner, and goes to bed. It's a simple combination of amnesia and lust that has lured me into this circus, she thinks.

That night she dreams that she keeps encountering women in the intersections of the city who have been struck by hit-and-run drivers. She tries not to look, and a voice remarks, How bizarre. One woman kneels with her head thrown back, her throat exposed—the way she was left after being struck. Alone in the middle of the street. A girl shouts to oncoming traffic to stop, to turn back, but Angela is afraid no one can hear. However, no traffic seems to be going toward the kneeling woman. Angela walks on alone.

* * *

As Joe enters the huge lobby of Midge's building across the street from the park, he retches on his palate. Nevertheless, he made a promise to Edith. He has never broken a promise. Edith has been very kind to him, especially since his flu episode. Every morning he thinks that soon, perhaps this coming weekend, he will move out. Every evening he is relieved to have a place to sleep and eat, with no complications, and often Edith isn't even there—she's at the clinic, or visiting her mother, or shopping, or in night classes.

"Since we'll be working together, I'd like to know all I can about you," Midge says. They sit in Eames chairs in her office, which overlooks a playground. He can hear children happily screaming, and swings and seesaws creaking. The room is large and beige and plain except for several photographs of snowdrifts, all in black and white. Edith has now hung three more similar pictures on the long, empty brick wall of the loft opposite her Eames chair. Joe searches the office for a picture of a face or a human form.

Midge is wearing beige clothing—it looks to Joe like pajamas—several gold chains, a gold watch, and no rings. She smokes Gauloises. She has short, curly black hair streaked with gray.

Joe lights a cigarette. He shifts in his chair and scratches his calf, where his boot chafes. Something begins tickling inside his left ear, and he digs into it with his little finger.

"When we don't want to talk about ourselves, or talk about something specific, then we call that resistance," Midge says. "Sometimes we're afraid that people won't like us if they know the truth about us. But you should feel entirely free not to talk if that makes you comfortable. I wonder why you don't talk."

"I promised Edith I'd . . ."

"Yes? Promised?"

He shrugs.

"You are free to do as you like, but I wonder whether you and Edith have a lot invested in your relationship and whether you want to work things through."

Joe shakes his head.

"You don't agree?"

"Oh, no, sorry—my neck was just getting stiff."

She looks at her watch. "Edith will be here soon."

In the resort town that ran caiques to Mount Athos, Joe stayed at a third-class hotel while he watied for the visa from church authorities in Thessalonica that would permit him to visit the peninsula. He was having trouble with the motorcycle's ignition, and the local car repair shop was hopeless; nevertheless, he persuaded the mechanic to send away to Germany for parts. The town was filled with women. They stayed there while their men went on retreats to Mount Athos, where even female animals are forbidden. Sometimes he saw women who resembled Lucy; one woman like her even carried a baby like Todd. Edith, who did not resemble Lucy in any way, was in the hotel with two Swedish women. All three of them called "Hal-lo" and waved vigorously when he entered the hotel dining room. Did he want to go to the bar where there was dancing? Did he like skin diving? They settled themselves at his table and brought with them a bottle of ouzo.

Later, under the mythic sky and the mythic stars, by the washing of the wine-dark sea, Edith put her arm around him. The last woman to touch him had been his wife—during her pregnancy she had been so abundant and sexual in a new, odd way that Joe had felt submerged in her. Edith, who was thin and boyish, told him that she only wanted to go for a walk, just the two of them. It was chilly and late. He wanted to go to sleep. The strain of being with others, with women, of speaking English was tremendous. Under the moon of Artemis, she made urban American sounds that he had trouble sorting out into speech. She had grown up in Paterson and then her parents had moved to Queens. She was planning to get married but then it didn't work out, so after graduation she spent the summer on a kibbutz. She had some stomach trouble, probably from some mussels she had eaten the day before. She thought Greece was very clean. And really cheap. She had just bought a flokati rug for next to nothing—she'd been wanting one for ages. When she got back to the States she was going to move her belongings out of her parents' place and get an apartment in Manhattan, so she needed furnishings. She was going to get her Master's degree in business administration. Her mother worked for the phone company and wanted grandchildren before she died. Edith also said she had some super hashish.

Under the Greek sky with brilliant stars and next to the Greek sea, in a Greek town where little was familiar, Edith was familiar. She liked him, she said. She had a striking profile and alert eyes, and a voice that sounded as if she had just had a very good cup of coffee. He wanted to hold a woman again. The fact that he felt no deep desire for her made their lovemaking seem chaste and safe for him. Besides, she helped fix the motorcycle, and washed out his socks and darned them, and repacked his belongings with precision. Her intelligence and eagerness and her brisk ways were a comfort to him. After they began traveling together, if he pointed out the sheen on the sea she said it hurt her eyes and advised him to wear sunglasses. If he got drunk and confessed his wish to run naked up the road to the shrine at Delphi, she predicted a bad chest cold. None of that bothered him, once he got used to her, and anyway, their arrangement was temporary. Good friends on the road, that was all. When she suggested that they go, just for a while, to Yugoslavia, it seemed easy enough to agree. He could always visit Mount Athos later on. One morning he woke up and wondered what his son looked like now. She said she was ready to go back to the States, too. But she needed a place to stay until she found a job and got into grad school, and it was easy enough to agree to let her stay with him at his friends' place.

Joe reflects on the succession of agreements that has led him to this particular chair in this particular office and then goes blank. He can think of nothing at all until Edith enters. Then he wonders whether Angela will still be at the office when he gets back.

Edith drops into the chair next to Joe's and jerks herself out of her coat. "Whew," she says. He can feel the cold air she brought in. "I nearly didn't make it. I was held up at the clinic, but it's *super* news. Lois wants me to officially take over as assistant director. She can't give me a big raise but she's going to give me some shares and the option to buy more."

"I'm very happy for you, Edith." Midge's voice is toneless. To Joe's eye she does not look happy for anyone, including herself.

"That's great, Edith," Joe says.

Edith turns brightly from Joe to Midge and back again. She

wears her all-my-favorite-people-together-at-last expression—
the one she wears when she can get Joe to have dinner, always
boiled chicken and pot roast, with her mother.

"I wonder, Edith, if you have anything else you'd like to
talk about," Midge says.

Edith fastens her gaze on Midge and talks. She loves Joe.
They have a good thing. But there are a few problems. Joe
doesn't cooperate or share. He forgets to buy groceries. He
isn't responsive. They go to bed at different times and get up
at different times, and even though Sunday is her only day off,
he insists on going into the office. He never uses terms of
endearment. He's unrealistic about what he expects a woman
to be and he avoids honest confrontations. He bottles up his
feelings. He's always preoccupied with his job. He doesn't
listen to her, whereas she listens to him. He just leaves his
socks and underwear wherever he happens to take them off.
"We never make love—he is sexually indifferent."

"I wonder, Joe, what you are thinking, what you have to
say."

Joe can't speak. He assumes Edith has already recited her
grievances to Midge and that the two women are staging this.
But worse—he is stunned by Edith's betrayal. How can she
tell a third party all about their intimate life?

"I wonder, Joe, if there's anything that upsets you about
Edith."

He can't think of what's wrong with Edith. She does everything right. She does not leave her underwear around. It's just
that he doesn't want to be with her. Or is it something else?
He pushes his lips together and puts his hands over his mouth
and hunches forward, resting his elbows on his knees.

Afterward, he can't remember what else was discussed.
There will be more appointments, more discussions. In the cab
going back to work, he imagines spending a day and a night
making love to Angela, and then they would have breakfast
together, and he would reach across the table for her hands.
And now good morning. . . By the time he's riding up in the
elevator he's thinking that Midge isn't so bad—at least Edith
will have her to turn to when he moves out. So that she won't
be hurt the way Lucy hurt him—no, he could never do that to
anyone. But maybe Edith is right: he is an unresponsive, work-

obsessed, callous lump. Sexuality? Forget it. He's sexually indifferent. Maybe no one could love him but Edith. Maybe he's lucky to have her.

"Such a nice day to have to come back to the office," Angela calls from her desk as he passes her doorway. She is eating cheese.

He hasn't noticed what kind of day it is. "Yeah."

He is angry, Angela thinks. He's mad at me and I don't know why. Somehow his skin and hair have gotten dark; his face is heavy and lined. She'd better do something about all this. "Would you like a piece of cheese? It's gourmet."

She pronounces it "gore-may." He doesn't know whether she means to be ironic, or if she's teasing him, or if she really pronounces the word that way. She says "arn" for "iron." Or she could be making fun of him according to her private, bewildering standards. It is these standards that make him think she would consider him a jerk for abandoning Edith. He must have told her about Edith at that long lunch the day they met. Does Angela belittle him to others—to Goodhugh, to her friends? To Nussbaum? She must have strange friends. She said she loved arriving in New York and finding that it was filled with weird people—in Gatch everyone was pretty much the same. He once overheard her saying on the phone, "Sharon—homicide, not suicide."

He refuses the cheese, although he usually likes the food she gives him, the way she puts it into his mouth so that her fingertips graze his lips. He is not much of a person; it's clear from the appraisal he received this afternoon that he doesn't deserve a piece of cheese, let alone companionship from someone as good as Angela. He's just an overweight, sexless bozo without dreams or youth or plans.

She hears him thud into his swivel chair and she feels sick. Yesterday, after the long exchange of gazes, they were about to fall into each other's arms. This morning she came in ready for news: he would either ask her out, or make some declaration, or let her know he was involved with someone else. Anxious for the drama to be resolved, she arrived with her stomach in turmoil, and dark half-moons under her eyes from too little sleep, particularly after the dream about women in intersections. But Joe scarcely spoke to her. He met with Goodhugh, then went to a meeting of the board of directors, and then went out with the explanation that he had to do something he'd promised someone he'd do for a long time.

She tries to read a report on the world food shortage but her gaze keeps lifting from the page and coming to rest on a new painting Katha made for her—a Zen calligraphy, a vigorous thick-brushed inky black empty circle on a white field. In the hope that Joe will come to her and reveal himself, she will stay late. She puts on fresh lipstick and rouges her cheeks. A few times, however, he has left without telling her good night. She hates finding herself alone in the maze of suites with the heat off, the corridors dark, and without any reason to be there or to be anywhere in the world.

I will act like a normal human being, she thinks. She puts on an expensive new coat, which she bought on credit today during her lunch hour specifically to attract Joe, and a new hat, ditto. She packs her new briefcase with all the work she was not able to do today because she was waiting for Joe to deliver an answer.

She stops at his doorway. "Night!" She wishes she sounded lighthearted and spontaneous. "I'll have that list of food statistics done first thing in the morning—crack of dawn."

He avoids her eyes and nods tersely at his boots. The toes are scuffed. She is obviously going to a rendezvous. She is warm, golden—ready to be plucked and devoured. Her lips are fresh and glossy, she's wearing a blue wide-brimmed hat that makes her look like a movie star in a 1930s picture, and a coat he hasn't seen before. It is dark blue suede with splashes of white, a coat like the night sky, like an avant-garde composition he once heard in college called, in fact, "Night Sky."

Go, Angela commands herself. He doesn't even like her enough to be polite. She is probably going to be fired—that's why he was in those meetings and he never told her what went on in them the way he usually does. *Git!* she shouts in her head, as if she were shooing away a mangy dog. Herself. But new laws of physics keep her in the doorway and prevent her motion through space. "So, well, uh, see you tomorrow."

Edith will be waiting for him downstairs in a cab in five minutes. He hopes Angela will be gone by then. If Edith happens to see Angela talking to him in the lobby or out in front of the building, things will get worse than they already are. "Good-bye." His tone is so final that Angela rushes away.

Joe kicks his wastebasket. Good-bye to this woman who is on her way to meet someone, who is so full, so ready, so accomplished and at ease. And so free.

Angela enters her dark, chilly apartment and does not bother to turn on any lights. She throws her new coat and hat on the floor and looks in the refrigerator. There is a container of raspberry yogurt with a verdigris-colored tinge on the cap, and there is a bottle of Coors. She takes the beer and goes into the bedroom and sits on the edge of the bed in the dark and drinks the beer. She was in such a hurry to get to the office that she did not eat breakfast. Instead of lunch she bought the coat and hat. Her—wearing a hat—who does she think she is? She is hungry now but she can't eat. There is nothing she can do.

She puts her forearm over her eyes with such force that yellow suns flash against the back of her eyelids. It's unbelievable that she could feel so tied to someone she's never even made love with. She has poured so much of herself into Joe, into wanting Joe, into working with Joe in the belief that they were inevitably going to get together. And now. She sees she has been deluding herself. From now on she will ignore his stares and his quick, ambiguous caresses.

Eventually the beer knocks her backward on the bed and into sleep.

Toward morning she wakes up, her head and jaw aching, so hungry she wants to cry, and she thinks, continuing a debate that has gone on, submerged, through the night: But it's him. I never wanted a man the way I want him. Ever. I won't give up.

After the divorce she swore that she would never remarry and that she would never again allow herself to become dependent on a man. But when she swore that, she had not met Joe Bly. She sees HUSBAND written down his bare back and legs, the D landing on his right heel.

She hears the wheeze of the garbage trucks in the street, and from the open window comes a brief wind and a sudden smell of the river. Is this what her life has turned out to be?

Just when she always assumed it would only get better and better? When she took it for granted that the day would arrive when she would always be happy and contented? What is she settling for?

10

————•————

"THIS IS MY OLDEST friend, Gerard Clewes," Joe says to Angela.

Gerard has thick, highly arched eyebrows that give him a fixed expression of benign surprise. He wears a workshirt embroidered with clouds.

Angela jumps up from her desk and shakes Gerard's hand and grins. She wants Joe's oldest friend to have a very good impression of her. "I'm delighted," she says. She has noticed that people at Starr Whorf often say that. In Gatch if you wanted to be very formal when you were introduced, you might say "Charmed, I'm sure."

"I've heard terrific things about you from Joe," Gerard says.

"Gerard is a poet," Joe says hastily. He is pleased that he can present a poet—Angela will like him for that.

"Do you know Victor Montini by any chance?" Angela asks.

"I know his work," Gerard says.

"Well, he used to be my neighbor and he got this idea that his divine mission was to reform the Catholic church. He invented his own Mass and started going systematically to all the Catholic churches in the city and saying it. The police finally got him when he was standing on an altar in a Chinese Catholic church and they put him in the loony bin. He told me that he had a psychiatrist who said 'So—you think you're the Son of Man!' and Victor just smiled because he knew he was really just John the Baptist."

"She's charming," Gerard says to Joe, tilting his chin in a manner that makes Angela think he must be stuck up.

"Gerard is going to help us with rewrites," Joe says. "He'll come in and get material a few times a week and edit it—that way we won't be so swamped. And he'll assemble the statistical reports."

"Oh, good," Angela says. But she does not like this intrusion into their closed system. Joe never even told her about Gerard.

"Angela has come up with some wonderful ideas," Joe says. "Like getting various political commentators to write editorials."

"The first one is by the famous Derek Grinder," Angela says. "I'm having lunch with him today."

"I well remember Grinder," Gerard says. "He worked on the paper when Joe was editor and I was a humble shoeshine boy. I understand he's on his way to greatness. Well, I'm very happy to meet you. Joe needs all the cheering up he can get, and I can see that you are a little ray of sunlight for him."

Angela decides she will have to get to know Gerard very well. He is animated and thoughtful, and he understands Joe. While she tries to keep herself from getting caught up in Joe's daily moods, she is drawn into them over and over. When he is elated, he touches her and praises her; when he is down, she feels compelled to pump up his spirit. And she usually assumes that she is the cause of all his moods. Perhaps Gerard can provide an explanation. "It's great that you're going to be helping out," she says. "We ought to have lunch and get acquainted."

"I feel as if we already know each other," Gerard says. He has a soft, clear voice. Maybe he's not so stuck up after all.

Joe watches them converse, relieved that they like each other, and jealous that they do.

* * *

Joe has another session with Midge, this time without Edith present. Midge says three things he can remember: "I wonder why you seem to have trouble opening up." "I wonder if you are here to work on your relationship with Edith." And: "You seem very unhappy. I wonder if you had a troubled childhood."

He listens to the noises of the birds and the children coming from the park, and keeps his eyes on the snowdrift photographs. Why would someone want pictures of snowdrifts around? Afterward, in the taxi, he makes mental replies to her: "I have nothing to say to you." And: "You are Edith's therapist, not mine—how can I confide in you?" And: "I have a lot of work to do and I don't have time to sit around looking at pictures of snowdrifts." He would never say these things. He is always polite and noncommital, like the other members of his fraternity, like the others at the university press, like his best friend Alec when Alec moved in with Lucy. It's April and it's getting warm and he doesn't care. What he cares about is Angela's elusive behavior. She has withdrawn from him. Well, how can he compare to famous, fascinating men like Nussbaum, or Grinder?

Angela appears in his door with a clipboard and a pen, a new fountain pen, silver. She is wearing a very becoming spring dress with little orange and yellow flowers. He likes her to wear dresses so that he can look at her legs. Her hair is loose. She flips him a piece of hard raspberry candy, which he catches between his fingers in a show of fast reflexes and good coordination. "Well?"

"Well what?" She must be teasing him again.

"I'm responding to your note—'Let's talk.'"

That was from this morning, when he sat hurling paper clips into an ashtray fifteen feet away and thinking that it was time for him to discuss his situation with Angela. For all he knows, she might agree with Edith and Midge—that he is severely troubled and should not run away from his problems by moving out of the loft. However, Angela knows many surprising things, and she is a good listener. But that was this morning. This afternoon he does not want to talk.

He begins discussing Goodhugh's latest plans to expand the newsletter yet again. "We're not doing nearly enough with it—given our guaranteed audience. Goodhugh's dream is that it could compete with the *Wall Street Journal*, if we had people like Walter Lippmann writing for it."

"Walter Lippman is dead," Angela says gently.

"I know. I'm just quoting Goodhugh." He smokes his last cigarette and violently twists the pack and throws it into the wastebasket. He is feeling worse and worse. Edith wants to get married and have a baby, and she says he is the only man for her. She does not want to break up. She cries. Midge wonders whether Joe even knows Edith. Goodhugh wants him to work twenty-four hours a day. And Angela—Angela wants him to do what? Something is on her mind, but he doesn't know what. "Oh, shit." He sighs.

"What's the matter?"

A long silence. "I'm just in a bad mood." Afraid she'll think he's an emotional dud, he adds, "I feel really overworked."

"But I'm here. I'm here to help you. And now Gerard is coming in." She feels sorry for Joe. His state of mind has become more important to her than her own, than anything else. She is always trying to imagine his point of view, his likes and dislikes. If she goes to a movie she judges it according to whether Joe would like it or not. She has been seeing samurai movies with Katha, and she thinks he would like them; the movies are acquiring a special aura because of that. She feels privileged now: he has never told her before when he was upset.

"It's more than that," he says. "I think that I have to work all the time, and be responsible, and be all things to all people. Then I feel secure." He doesn't want to be precise; he doesn't want to give examples. Keep it abstract.

Angela listens intently for the real message behind his words. He is forlorn and lonesome, like a solitary tree in an arroyo, dense and twisted from wind and drought. She wants to put her mouth to his ear and tell him that his complaints are unnecessary. She is here, he is here, they must be together. It's that simple. "Why don't you consider working part-time if you feel so overworked?"

"Working part-time would be a real risk for me." He's thought of this, or rather Edith has brought it up as a solution. "On the other hand, I never get a chance to play." He gives her a quick glance.

"Oh, take the goddamn risk!" Her exasperation at the weeks

of his advances and retreats bursts out, even though she wants to be solemn and kind. "When I thought I was playing it safe and never dared to do anything. I lost everything. I was securely married and I was sure my life was going to be a certain way forever. Suddenly none of that was there. It was all washed away. I lost everything. And even when I've taken big risks and lost"—she thinks of Janos—"I still learned a lot."

Angela's irritation leads him to paraphrase Edith and Midge. "Maybe I don't know whether I would be acceptable as a person if I didn't work constantly."

"*What?*" She laughs. "Acceptable? As a *person?* You're a person no matter what you do. How you *talk!*" She rolls her eyes and drops her hands into her lap.

She is making fun of me, he thinks. Her own hidden rules again. He gets out a new cigarette pack, rips it open, and all the cigarettes fall on the floor.

Angela sees that he does not consider her response humorous. "Well, you are wonderful. Whether you work or not." She says this with such complete certainty that her voice quivers. She helps him pick up the cigarettes.

"I don't believe that," he says. "I don't believe it myself." His phone rings.

She jumps up and quickly presses his head to her breast and strokes his hair. He squeezes her arm as he answers the phone. He wants to pull her closer. "Yes, sir!" he says into the receiver.

She runs to her office and sits at her desk in a crazy daze. Why did she let herself do that? As if she were possessed. And all that blather about her philosophy of life, taking risks. Jesus!

Joe quickly ends the telephone conversation and comes into her office, bringing her pen and clipboard, the blood pounding in his temples. So Midge and Edith think he has no feelings! "Thank you, Angela. That was very nice."

She is troubled. "You're welcome," she mutters. She feels as if she might be losing control altogether. It's the end of the day now. They are alone in her office, in the lamplight. He sits down next to her.

"My first job was when I was thirteen, as a short-order cook in Cape May," he says without preliminaries. "I had a motorcycle accident the next summer, and I spent two months in the hospital. See?" He pulls his collar aside and points to a long, curved scar that runs from his collarbone to his left armpit. "The grip of the past. My mother was always sick, and then she died when I was eight. I just realized yesterday that my ex-wife was sick all the time too. I wasn't allowed near my mother much. When she died I was standing next to my father at the funeral holding his hand and I wasn't crying and I didn't know why everyone else was. Then I was sent to boarding school. My father died a few years later. I lost my virginity when I was sixteen. The headmaster also tried to seduce me. I have a sister who's sixteen years older than I am, and she was supposed to be my guardian, but she and her husband tried to sue me for my share of the estate because I was adopted and she was the real child."

Angela is afraid to speak or move for fear of stopping this outpouring of precious information.

"I was somebody's change-of-life baby, and my parents got me on the black market. I don't have any feelings about that. I guess they're repressed. Anyway, the court had my sister dropped as my guardian because of a conflict of interest, and my only living relative is an ancient great-aunt, a puritanical old maid in Massachusetts who believes that family ties must be honored and is very loyal."

Angela waits. All of this seems to be the beginning of a more elaborate revelation. But the flash flood ends as abruptly as it began. She wonders what in the world they are going to do with or to each other. "Do you have something nice in your life now?" She means: You have me.

"My loft," he says. "It's my refuge." He settles back in his chair and sighs. He touches his upper lip with the tip of his tongue. Finally he checks his watch and gets to his feet. "God, it's nearly nine."

She stands up and puts her arm around his waist in a quick clinch. "Be brave," she says.

For a second she does not move and neither does he. As she withdraws her arm, he suddenly embraces her.

Here we go.

Suddenly Angela feels she has forced things, and she pulls away, her head bent, her hair falling forward to conceal her profile, and briskly picks up papers and puts them in her briefcase. "See you tomorrow," she says.

That night she dreams of motorcycle rides and accidents and beaches and old maids the whole night and she asks herself why he resonates so powerfully with her inner life. Unreeling before her dreaming eyes is this reply:

> January 12
> accidental gunshot
> somebody's foot

"We must live by magic, we must be magicians," he says to himself, walking in the wind at midnight when he goes out for cigarettes.

"I'm really bummed out," Sharon says. "Mondo-depresso." It's Sunday night and she has just returned from spending the weekend at her parents' house in the country. "I go in their bedroom. They've got a huge mirror over the bed, on the ceiling. It could fall and kill you. And they've got one of those head-shop posters in black and chartreuse and Day-Glo orange over the headboard—it's the zodiac, except that each sign is a couple in a different sex position." She opens Angela's refrigerator. "When are you going to throw this yogurt out? It's old enough to run for President. Let's order out Chinese."

"Everyone has a sex life," Angela says. "Except me."

"And me. But Ron is telling the world he is in love with you. He keeps calling me to talk about you. Did you know he is going to inherit a lingerie factory when his mother dies?"

"I thought he was a Marxist poet."

"He can afford to be. Also, he's had lots of therapy. I think it's important to go out with guys who have had therapy."

"Ron is a perfectly decent person," Angela says, picking up the phone to call the Szechuan restaurant. "It's just that Joe—"

"I'll tell you something about Joe," Sharon says. "He—"

"When you are in love, you are in love, and all these ideas—politics, or therapy or whatever—don't amount to a hill of beans." Angela has been swimming in the possibility that Joe is lonely and needs her. She has even started painting her hallway orange. He's bound to come to her.

"You want to know something, I'll tell you something. I've been meaning to mention it. Joe is *taken.*"

Angela hangs up the phone.

"Lynn's little sister works for this abortion clinic in Queens, and one of the head honchos, or honchitas, is a woman named Edith somebody. And she *lives* with Joe Bly. I know all this because Lynn was at a party her sister gave and she met Joe. She doesn't think he's so wonderful, by the way."

Angela is having trouble breathing. Of course, it's been so obvious—how could she have kept herself from seeing it? "I have to know everything. Tell me everything."

"Well, Lynn thinks he's a bit condescending, and all that. Her little sister adores Edith. She's supposed to be fantastically organized and efficient. Everyone just loves her. She keeps being promoted, she really knows how to get things done. She supposedly saved the place from bankruptcy. Listen, she's very, very nice. Also—they had their arms around each other the whole time at the party. That was what Lynn didn't approve of. She said, 'What's a competent woman like her doing hanging onto a guy like him?' Anyway, get this—they are in something called couples therapy. Edith comes in after each session and tells Lynn's sister how it's going. Edith wants to get married and have a baby and Joe keeps getting scared about that because his marriage was a disaster so they're trying to work out a way he'll make a commitment."

"It sounds awful." It could be worse. "Maybe he just doesn't like her."

"Yeah, yeah, sure. Give me that phone—I'm starving." Sharon calls the Szechuan restaurant and orders fried dumplings, noodles with bean sauce, prawns with garlic, and chicken in spicy orange sauce. After she pushes the button down she says into the receiver, "And send a couple of men while you're at it."

Angela looks around her apartment. The formerly white walls are a sooty gray. The square of carpeting left by the previous tenant looks like matted lint. The spider plants she has forgotten to water hang in the windows like dead squid. She is an ugly person living alone and getting old and flabby in a decrepit place. Couples therapy?

"Oh, and something else I wanted to remember to tell you.

Edith told Lynn's sister that when she and Joe met, in Turkey or someplace, that it was love at first sight. So there's somebody you are better off without."

"He doesn't act taken, Sharon. I'm sure he's interested in me."

"Oh, for God's sake, Angela."

When the food arrives, Angela can't eat. "What if there really is something like absolutely true love, where you look at each other and you're never the same again?"

"In my opinion, that's adolescent." Sharon twirls some noodles on her chopsticks. "I think the best you can ever hope for in a relationship is that you don't do each other too much damage. What you're talking about is unreal. That's what my shrink says." But Angela knows Sharon must be thinking of Clifford, because she scowls the way she always does when she mentions him. "You have to make some compromises."

Angela thinks: But I will never make a compromise like that. "But what about all the love stories and epics and movies and legends about great and true and beautiful love? It must be real or people wouldn't always be interested in it."

"Well, even if you can't have him, at least you know he exists." Sharon goes upstairs and comes back down with some white chocolate hearts she bought herself on Valentine's Day and has been saving in the freezer. They eat them and watch *Casablanca* on television, each crying quietly and carefully so the other won't notice. Angela imagines Joe finding her crying in her office and consoling her.

"What did you do?" Bogart asks Bergman. "What did you think?"

11

ANGELA FALLS ASLEEP THINKING about how from now on she will be businesslike and formal at the office. Joe is taken, Joe is taken. She feels, to her surprise, relief. Now, at least, she knows why he has been behaving so confusingly. She will call up Ron and see what he's been doing lately. Also, Derek Grinder is an attractive possibility.

But in the night she gets up and wanders around the apartment. Being with Joe seems so right. It is extraordinary. Secret parts of both of them have made a pact that she cannot understand and evidently he can't either. He has to be helped. He has to be helped out of Edith's snare. *Couples therapy!* Joe must want out—that's why he stares at her, that's why he is afraid to do anything else. She hears thumping downstairs. It must be Katha, practicing aikido.

She goes downstairs and knocks on Katha's red door. Katha appears in a turquoise kimono looking effortlessly perfect. Her hair is smoothed back and tied at the nape; her forehead is framed by curly wisps of blond hair; her cheeks are naturally pink; her lashes are thick and dark. Her expression is serene.

Angela wants to cry out: Please tell me how you live so I can be that way, too! Tell me your secrets! Tell me how you live contentedly alone in a state of perfection!

They drink dragon well tea and Angela tells Katha what's been going on. Angela shapes the story to show Joe as a man rent by passion and impelled by destiny. His drama becomes singular and fascinating as Angela speaks.

"I don't see what the problem is," Katha says. "Nothing can stop you from getting together if he feels that way."

Angela is happy she has at last been able to convince someone else of the rightness, the necessity of her union with Joe. "But what about Edith?"

"Sounds like he's packing his bags from what you say. She doesn't sound very appealing or womanly. What he needs, what every man needs, is union with the feminine principle to complete himself. You don't have to *do* anything: you are already a lovely, strong woman. Just be kind to him and don't worry. But whatever you do, don't sleep with him. Not until he's free. Because once a man makes love to a woman, she no longer holds any mystery for him."

"Do you think that's still true, these days?"

"These are ancient laws within everyone. You always desire more what you can't have than what you do have." She adds, "What is not sought in the right way can't be found."

Katha massages her feet. Angela looks around and sees that she has filled two big green-glazed vases with bunches of forsythia. The room is arranged like a painting. The gracefulness and ease here make Angela calm. "You don't seem to need anything, Katha. How do you do that?"

A look crosses Katha's face that is new to Angela—a reflection of something deeply harbored and controlled. Whether it is sadness or understanding, Angela doesn't know. "I got rid of everything I could get rid of. Then I took back what I wanted. And now I like what I have. It's all illusory anyway."

"I wish I could think like that," Angela says. "But what I really wish is that I could be with Joe. I would do anything. I have never set my heart on someone this way."

Katha takes a deep breath and lets it out slowly. "When you want nothing, then you can have everything. Only then you don't want it."

Angela returns to her place invigorated. She has not known what to do before. Now she knows. She has never had a plan or a strategy before because she never cared about doing things that way. But love has knocked on her door. She is one-eyed.

Her strategy is this: she must be subtle and alluring and feminine. And she must become precisely what Edith, a woman she has never seen, is not. Angela senses energies—and will— arising from forgotten sources deep within to help her with her wish. She imagines Edith leaving Joe, and Joe, shattered, turning to Angela. She goes out with him to a bar and he gets drunk and then they go back to her place and she stretches him out on her bedroom rug and gives him a massage so tender that he starts crying. She holds him and reassures him, and in gratitude for her not taking advantage of him, he tells her he loves her. She listens to traffic noises and sinks into sleep. The bed trembles—it's a train, deep underground, disappearing into the dream tunnel.

12

MIDGE ADVISES JOE AND Edith to go on a vacation together. A way, she tells them, to authenticate the new behaviors they have learned. Some of these new behaviors resulted from a session in which Midge had Joe and Edith play with a toy train. They had to set the wheels on the tracks so the train wouldn't fall off, and take turns controlling the speed so it wouldn't derail. Joe felt like an idiot the whole time, but it was the first session he actually enjoyed. Afterward, Midge told Edith not to be so demanding and bossy and Joe to be more appreciative and cooperative. Joe began to think Midge might be sensible after all. In a private session he even mentioned his wish to move out and take up with Angela. "I wonder what would happen if you and Edith spent some time together away from the pressure of work; I wonder if then you'd know," was Midge's reply.

While Joe is in the Caribbean for ten days, Angela is sure she can sense him thinking about her, even though he kept his distance after their most recent hug. She paints the rest of her apartment and puts up new curtains and buys some plants Joe would like—gloxinias, a jasmine, and a gardenia. She persuades Sharon to find out everything she can about Edith from Lynn. She works overtime to finish the latest newsletter so that when Joe returns all he will have to do is initial it before it goes to the printer. A gift to him, so he won't feel overwhelmed by work. She buys an expensive dress with kimono-like sleeves, dark blue with red and pink Japanese-style roses. (She assumes Edith would only wear tailored clothes.) She lightens her hair a shade. (Edith, she learns, has dark brown or black hair.) She practices being cool, quiet, and self-possessed. When Ron phones her, she practices this. Derek Grinder invites her to lunch again, and she is the epitome of poise.

When Joe returns, he strides into Angela's office looking relaxed, brown, and ten pounds lighter. His hair has been cut by a resort hotel barber named Babalou. He gives her a big hug. The room seems about to spin. They could go on embracing indefinitely. "God, I'm so glad you're back!" Angela exclaims. "You look—you look beautiful."

"I feel very liberated." He is reluctant to separate himself from the perfume of her body, the roses, and the soft firm curve of her arm and neck and shoulder, the tickle of her hair against his nose. She is wearing a new dress; he can see the swell of her breasts below the blue folds. "Let's have a drink after work—are you free?"

"Sure." She hands him a peony from a bouquet on her desk. He takes it into his office and sticks it into the empty wine bottle on the windowsill.

It is spring. The air is soft, and at the end of the day a warmth remains. As they walk downtown toward a bar he likes, the sky over the World Trade Center fills with golden clouds. He tells her about the light in Greece. "You'd think it would be like the light in the Caribbean, but it's very different. It's yellow. It seems like it's very ancient light, that you could touch. It gives you a feeling of time moving very slowly. I guess that doesn't make any sense."

She turns to him, one eyebrow slightly raised. He's talking poetically. "Oh, it does," she says. They pass a hospital. "I nearly died there," she says.

"What happened?" he asks. She always says something unpredictable. What if she had actually died? This amazing being waking up after years of slumber within him would have slept on, missing this late spring afternoon.

". . . typhoid or cholera," she is saying. "But that's ridiculous. How would I have gotten cholera in New York? Maybe I was just homesick. It was the first winter away from New Mexico. It never occurred to me to buy warm clothes. I had this light trench coat I wore through college, and no gloves, no hat, no umbrella—those things still seem strange to me. I always felt hemmed in because I couldn't see the horizon. I was always wondering where I'd run to if there was a nuclear attack. The sky was always so low and dark—I kept thinking it was going to rain. And everything—the streets and buildings and sidewalks—was dirty and smeared. I used to smile at everyone I met and no one ever smiled back. I was mighty lonesome. My husband worked nights and I would listen to these all-night radio talk shows, about flying saucers and stuff. Anyway, I got sick. But I got well real fast, and afterward the doctor said he had thought I was going to die. I remember lying in the hospital, and I was very cold but I didn't care, and I realized that when you're about to die like that, you don't care enough to feel bad about it. I begged not to be buried in Queens. Whenever I see my doctor he always gives me this funny look and says, 'What in the hell did you have?'"

"Are you all through having close calls?"

"Yup."

She is so radiant, so confident, so alive that the answer comes out like a crow of joy. He is honored that she is telling him her past; he has regretted revealing so much about his own to her. They pass a little park. The crowns of the trees are a delicate, filmy green. Whenever he couldn't take Edith any more he would go snorkeling, spending hours submerged near a reef in a cove, a T-shirt protecting his burned back, drifting face down like a piece of seaweed among corals that resembled inverted roots. On the last day, Edith proposed. "Marriage as an experiment," she said. "This has been the happiest two weeks of my life." In the harsh white sunlight he could see the strain lines around her eyes and mouth. Nights, they both had a lot of rum drinks and fell asleep early, and then woke up in the night. "There's nothing to *do* here," she said.

"I'd like to know much more about you," Joe tells Angela. "All about you."

This is exactly what she has hoped for, felt, imagined, willed to happen. She turns to him and smiles, powerful and serene.

Botticelli's Venus, he thinks, and a fine sweet pain passes through his heart.

The last thing in the world Angela wants is for Joe to get to know her, especially since in the past few weeks she has set about re-creating herself. He must be made to think he is learning all he can about her when in fact he must not know anything. She takes a deep breath. "The air smells great."

"It's the sap rising." He laughs and squeezes her upper arm. The muscle he finds surprises him; he had thought her arm would be very soft.

While he was away, she worked. She sawed and hammered and scraped and painted when she wasn't working on the news-letter or having conferences with Goodhugh. With her new income, she bought a big fan palm that arches over half the living room, and a green second-hand Chinese carpet with purple wisteria blossoms. New ferns hang by the windows. The spider plants are now in Sharon's apartment, dying in the gloom. Over the bed she tacked up a red silk sari shot with gold threads that Janos once gave her with the explanation— excruciating at the time—that it was fine enough to be drawn through a wedding ring. (Angela, who threw away her ring not long after that, tried it and it was true.) When she was all through redecorating, she sat on the carpet under the fan palm listening to flamenco and admiring the graceful arch of the branches, the green of the leaves against the new white walls. Then she felt completely at ease, her own secret nameless being filling up the room. Her hands, the angle of her arms, the music, the new room. Something inside knows everything, she felt then. Knows there is no need to do anything, that there is no difference between inside and outside. She needed nothing, no one: she could flourish alone. She felt perfectly balanced. But late that night—it was the night before Joe's return—she imagined him telling her he was marrying Edith and she saw herself crying and saying, *But I'm the one who loves you!* She dialed his phone number; she would simply explain that she had a strong urge to phone. But there was no answer.

They go into a bar with old, rough cedar paneling. It's dark, with a few yellow circles of candlelight at tiny tables. He orders a retsina. She orders a kir, a drink Sharon just told her about. Neither speaks. He shifts his chair and bumps her knee and apologizes.

"About the newsletter. Goodhugh is very pleased with your work, and that's something. He never likes anything." He pauses. "I think the reason the newsletter just gets better is because you've helped tilt it toward what these corporate types secretly want—whatever they can't get from other sources. The trick is to keep on figuring out what those needs are." He checks his watch. Edith won't be home for another couple of hours. "So, uh..."

"Good." Her voice is low and throaty. She takes a sip of her drink. She wants to make it last, this mood that stretches between them and breathes like a spiderweb that can only be seen when the light is right. "There were a couple of things that came up while you were gone. Let me see." She looks up at the dark wooden rafters and scratches her head. "I can't remember. I made some notes." She feels under the table for her purse.

Her movements, her gropings, her hands and head below the little table, are so intimate and innocent at the same time that Joe is torn between enjoying the moment and worrying about what she might do next.

"Well, I guess I didn't bring my notebook." She comes back to the surface, her face flushed.

He begins talking about his vacation, telling her about snorkeling. He speaks as if he went by himself. "For some reason, the trip really made me miss Greece, a taste, the light, something I can't exactly name. Like something on the tip of my tongue." He gulps his retsina; he feels crazy. He might say anything. But it would be okay. She wouldn't mind.

"While you were gone, even before then, I felt we got out of touch with each other somehow—but only on the outside. Inside—" She touches the pale inverted triangle of skin at her breastbone. "Inside, I still feel we're close. No matter what the outside is doing." She goes on. She has broken the rules— she's actually discussing what's been going on between them, bringing it into words. She's on a roller coaster, she can't stop.

"When I first met you it was like this light flashed out from around your body. Like the light on water. Not that I saw with my eyes—I wasn't seeing anything, it was more like a perception of..." What is she saying? God.

"That's amazing!" he says. She is talking to him in the way he has daydreamed they would talk, the way he's suspected that she and her poet boyfriend talk. "In Greece I used to lie on the rocks and stare at the light on the sea, those particles of light, you know, and imagine it was a code. And in the Caribbean I found myself doing the same thing."

Everything around them disappears. There is just Angela, her oval face illuminated from below by the candle in the bowl. Her large eyes are fixed on his, the pupils wide.

He reminds himself that his reason for wanting to have a drink with her was to explain that he was working through his situation with Edith, that it might take some time, but that he nevertheless considered Angela—he looks down. He chews on his mustache. He orders another retsina from the bartender, who is whistling "Red Sails in the Sunset." "I have a confession to make," he says tentatively, watching her, watching. He feels like a little child. "I went away to think about a lot of things. And I—I thought a lot about you."

"I know." She doesn't tell him she could feel him thinking about her, long distance. Her hands, which have been resting on the table rim, are shaking. She hides them in her lap in a clenched ball. Here it comes, she tells herself. At last I will really know what is going to happen between us: he's about to say it.

"You don't fit into my notion of a formal work situation, Angela." Why does he sound so stern? "I'd—I'd rather be riding the Staten Island Ferry with you."

She swallows and nods. She is pale and intent.

"I've tried to re—, to remember when we first had lunch— I've tried and tried—did I tell you about the g-girl, the woman I met in Greece. Edith? The woman I'm living with at the moment? Did I?"

"No," she says, her surface serene. "But I gathered you were somehow involved."

There is a long silence. She waits. What else can she do? "What I have with Edith...well, it's, uh, real. It's authentic. But I miss the magic, the imagination. It's not there with her. I feel I've settled for something less than I might really want." This was not what he had planned to say. No. But then he had not known that Angela was going to talk about feeling connected with him inside. He doesn't want to make Edith look bad, and so he adds, "Edith's very humane, very efficient. She's a good administrator."

"What does she do?"

He bows his head, picks up his glass, puts it down, and rubs his fingers over his mouth while he speaks. "Mmm, uh, works in a clinic." Another silence. "She's not someone I would choose. With you, I—"

Angela is caught in an undertow that is about to spin her horizontally and sweep her out to sea. She grips the edge of the table and leans toward him.

"On the other hand, it's the best relationship I've ever had," he hears himself saying. "I trust her." He can't imagine Edith sitting in a bar with some man having a conversation like the one he's having. She's at work or she's at home, or at Midge's, or in class, and on the subway she knits socks for him.

A glaring rectangle suddenly appears behind Joe's head—someone has opened the door, and it's still light outside. Angela wants to jump up and run out. But then she won't know what Joe is working up to telling her—what the outcome of his preliminaries is to be.

He notices her gaze shift away and her engrossed mood break. He wants to bring her back. "I'm very wary of commitment though, and Edith wants to get married and have a baby. I don't—I've already been through all that."

Angela nods. "Yeah, I know what you mean. I never want to marry again."

"So Edith and I—we're just letting things go along at this point and seeing how things change." He sighs.

Angela thinks: He says that, but those aren't his words. That comes from somebody else—Edith? She makes herself smile—she has a good smile. When in doubt, smile. She toys with the candle, sliding its jar a half an inch toward him, half an inch away. A half an inch from side to side. "Is it a good relationship?"

"Uhhhhhh." He raises a hand and then drops it. "I don't

know how to categorize it." He looks at her. This is not the way he wanted things to go. He is not sure how he did want them to go, but it wasn't this way. "But, Angela—you are very special to me."

"Well, I can't pretend I don't find you very attractive," she says. She still feels sure of herself, despite his mixed news. After all, she has magic and imagination—legendary powers, powers Edith lacks. She touches his cheek. "You're so beautiful."

He tries to sort out what she just said:...can't pretend...don't find. "I'm very attracted to you, too," he says.

I've given away too much, she thinks. "I mean, there are various men I find attractive, but..."

That was it—he's been waiting for her to tell him about this poet character she's involved with. He thought then they would have in common partners that don't suit them. But various men, Jesus: he blends into a crowd of men, all "attractive," whatever she means by that. Like a men's underwear ad in a magazine.

She too feels that things are going awry. She sees that he's disconcerted and an unpleasant twist is taking over his mouth. "Maybe the sex doesn't matter, because..." She can't finish the sentence because the sex does matter. "Well, I've had various complicated affairs. Complications. Men who didn't understand me. But I feel you do."

He checks his watch. Somehow it's late.

She sickens when he does that—she knows all about watch-checking from when she was with her lover and had to get home before her husband did. And sometimes when she simply wanted to make Janos feel bad, she would pick up his wrist and study his watch.

They go out into the sunset. A rich orange has descended everywhere. "Jasmine!" he exclaims when they pass the gate of a mews. He stops. "There's a pocket of jasmine right here."

She stops and sniffs deeply. She can't smell anything. "A miracle," she says. "A smell, but no flowers."

At the northeast corner of Washington Square, he stops again, worried that she'll want to walk him to his front door. "Which way do you go?"

She points west. "Thataway—to the train." Along the way

she's pointing, along the wrought-iron spears of the park fence, purple azaleas bloom, as if they just sprang into being with the wave of her hand. "Well, see you." She turns away.

He grasps her shoulder and brings her back. He puts down his briefcase and pulls her to him—she's so small!—and kisses her. At first he is shy, thinking she'll be shocked and run away. But when she arches her back and presses against him, he slides his hands under her unbuttoned coat and around her waist. They kiss for a long time, each feeling a happy relief. Angela because now she knows how it's all going to turn out, Joe because Angela is kissing him back.

As he kisses her again and again with greater passion, she thinks, What if Edith or somebody saw us right now?

He draws away and looks around.

"I'll bet you're a good lover!" Angela is so aroused she can hardly stay on her feet.

He laughs, and then scans the park and the street. "It's all very scary."

"Well," she says, pulling away although she doesn't want to. "Go slay the dragon."

He looks puzzled, and she hopes he doesn't think she meant Edith. "Of guilt, I mean."

"I'll see you at work tomorrow."

"I *guess*." She heads toward the train station, weaving a little, smiling to herself.

Even though it's Edith's week to cook, Joe fixes dinner, his hands moving under his gaze like a pair of sorcerer's apprentices. Fried sausages, sauerkraut, bread, slices of Swiss cheese. Edith will be pleased: a new behavior on his part. He goes into the bathroom and looks in the mirror. No lipstick on his face. Angela said he was beautiful.

Edith arrives with two bags of groceries. "I really am in the mood for a good pot roast," she says, heaving the bags on the counter. "All that fish." Every night of their vacation they had chicken or fish. Joe hugs her. Her shoulders are narrow and sharp; her shoulder blades are hard. She tenses and pulls away. "I gotta use the john," she says.

Joe surrenders on the issue of which dinner they will eat.

Whistling "Ain't Misbehavin'," he flips silverware onto the dining table as if he were pitching pennies.

"Hey," she calls from the bathroom. "Everyone admired my tan today. Everyone said how great I looked."

"Good, that's very nice."

She returns to the kitchen. "You forgot the forks. You certainly seem to be in a good mood."

"Yup." He gets out forks.

"*Yup?* What way to talk is that? You're not wearing your ring." This is a silver ring that she bought at a duty-free jeweler's in the San Juan airport. It resembles, in miniature, the radiator grille of a 1953 Buick.

"I was afraid I'd lose it." He goes into the bedroom, whistling, and gets the ring from the open suitcase on the floor. He can always wear it in the evenings, with a silk smoking jacket and alligator slippers. He looks at his watch. He will see Angela in a little over fourteen hours. She kissed him back. She said she was attracted to him. She said he would be a good lover. She understands him. He told her about Edith and she still said all these things. She kissed him anyway. He crosses the dark empty central space of the loft and the shadowy humps of unused furniture. He has met the source of his joy. "Hey, Eed, you look nice."

"Well, I'm exhausted." But she grins at him. She's glad he's so cheerful. She pats his right hand, where the ring now is. "The vacation together was a good idea."

"It was good to get away, but I've got a ton of work."

"But what's with what's-her-name? Angela."

"Seems fine," he mutters. He is living in a different country now, under a different government. A force more powerful than he is has come to rule over him.

"She didn't do any work while you were gone?" Edith's voice rises in indignation. She is ready to summon Angela and straighten her out.

"Oh, she did what she was supposed to do. It's just that I have to meet with marketing, and take these corporate librarians to lunch to peddle the newsletter to them. I hate selling, I hate that part of it, and Goodhugh's always on my back about that. About expanding. Even with—with another warm b-body to help, it's going to be hard."

"Everyone's got a problem. Get me some wine." She lights a Gauloise. "I need to sit a minute before I start my pot roast. At the clinic they've all been saving up the good ones for me. Like unionizing. Lois was so glad to see my face, I tell you. You know what? I saw Midge today and she was wearing a wedding band. Florentine gold. She said we'd discuss my feelings about it next time. Did you talk to Goodhugh about the part-time idea?"

"Not yet—it didn't seem appropriate today. I don't want to get fired."

"Get outta here—he'll never fire you. You're the reason he looks so good. Anyway, I was talking to Lois today. She's going to buy that house in Connecticut. It's a summer place but she and Jim are going to winterize it. I'm going to call her real estate broker."

"What?"

"We've got to get out of here this summer. This place will be an oven. I'll take long weekends, and you'll be on part-time. We have to get out of this dump." She goes on to talk about real estate values, what she's been finding out, what a good investment a town house would be in the city, plus a country house. With her new raise, and once dividends from her shares in the clinic start coming in . . .

He relives the kiss with Angela. From now on there are going to be many obstacles. Suddenly he interrupts Edith. "I think these plans are premature. Let's let things ride for a while and see what happens."

"You're right." She claps her hand to her abdomen. "Sheesh, cramps."

For most of the night he stays up, sitting at the table with Angela's newsletter material, listening to the windows groan in the wind, and smoking. He can't concentrate or sleep. Of all the world he alone is awake.

Angela phones Helen long distance. "It's working," she says. "Joe and I are getting together."

"Oh, I'm really glad," Helen says. There is a wail in the background. "Just a minute. Jeffrey, do not put Timmy's book in the toilet! Okay, I'm back. I had a dream that you had this beautiful carpet with all kinds of maze designs, and we were dancing on it. Tell me what's new—what are you and Joe doing?"

"Well," Angela says. She realizes there is not much to tell in the way of direct action except the kiss this evening, and she feels awkward about bragging that her new self, Edith's opposite, has at last moved Joe to act. "It's very big, what we have. There is only one drawback, but it's temporary."

That night Angela dreams she is in a jet she is sure is going to crash. Her mother is the pilot. The wings dip, the engine falters and grinds. Angela puts on headphones and tunes to a silent channel to shut out the frightening noise. She is terrified, certain of the crash, of falling to her death. The plane arrives at the runway from which it had taken off. Her mother lectures her about the messiness inside the plane. Angela thinks: Ha, I could pilot this plane better than my mother!

She wakes up. It's three in the morning. She lies numb and confused, her eyes wide open in the dark, until it's light and she has to get ready for work. She imagines Joe lying awake a few miles to the south.

As she brushes her teeth, she remembers their conversation in the bar. "We will know each other for the rest of our lives," she said. Just listen to the oracle. "That's the best perspective to take," he said. She looks in the mirror at the lines under her eyes. The rest of her life! She can't wait that long. She opens the medicine cabinet to look for some cosmetic that will erase or hide the lines. On the inside of the door is written: ONE DAY AT A TIME. A sentiment she had painted there when she first moved in.

13

JOE GOES TO THE office at seven-thirty in the morning, wearing a heavy white fisherman's sweater he bought in Greece and has not put on since his return to the States.

When Angela arrives, she avoids his doorway. Later, when he comes to her office, she is very formal, as if he were someone else. She won't look at him.

"None of this crap is any good." His face is dark and troubled and he is shaking the sheaf of papers she had assembled for him as possible newsletter material. "I don't have any sense of where this issue is going."

She thought it was pretty good, until now. "Well, I—"

"And I have to take this lady, this librarian or whatever from IBM, to lunch. There's no time."

Last night Angela was sure that she was going to find out everything, learn the thing which is right, and know what to do and say. Now she is confused again.

After lunch he comes in again. "Eed is sick and I have to leave right away and take her to the doctor."

"Eed?"

"Edith." He purses his lips.

Angela turns her head so he can't see her expression.

"So I'll be back later on if anything comes up or Goodhugh wants to know."

"Okay," she says faintly. "Bye."

But Edith works in an abortion clinic. Aren't there doctors there? Or, why doesn't Edith just get herself into a taxi and go? That's what Angela would have done. With a pang she realizes that there is no one to take *her* to the doctor. She has no one who would rush from work to do that for her. She wants to cry, but instead she reads about the impending world water shortage in a United Nations document and underlines possible excerpts with a red pen.

Half an hour passes and Joe sticks his head into her office. He gives her a warm look.

"You still here?" she asks. Some emergency!

"There's something very funny that could be said about this chain of events, but I don't know what." Joe touches the back of her hand and leaves.

Another Friday, another dim, candlelit bar, this one near the office. Blues harmonica music plays. He holds her hand, picks it up, kisses the inside of her wrist, kisses her palm, reaches for her other hand, does the same, squeezes both hands. She sits smiling through his ritual. Her hair is loose and curly and red light from a shaded hanging lamp behind her chair comes through it. He can't believe she likes him, that she smiles at him. As if someone you loved had been pronounced missing and presumably dead, in Antarctica, say, but somehow managed to walk a thousand miles to shelter and safety. The backs of her hands are warm. They gaze at each other for a long time.

"I've been imagining making love to you," he says. "From the day we met."

She clears her throat. Her voice isn't working too well.

"And riding the Staten Island Ferry."

"Let's," she says. She means make love, not ride boats.

"I want to get closer to you, I want to get as intimate as possible as quickly as possible." He is drunk on the wine that only eyes may drink.

She says nothing. She is waiting for him to tell her he is leaving Edith. She will not make love with him until he has left Edith.

"Edith has never been married, never gone through a divorce—so she can't understand my reluctance. A good thing we have is the space between us—Edith and I give each other a lot of room." He shrugs and bites his mustache. "But maybe that's why I'm restive." He doesn't want to be dishonorable. If only she were a man. She has her good points.

"What are you thinking?" Angela asks.

They talk in wells.

"Well, I worry about pain coming between us," he says. "Fear. This is getting fairly intense. Very intense, I'd say."

"Well, I don't like triangles." She gives examples. How she started sleeping with her husband's friend, Janos.

"My best friend married my wife the day the divorce was final."

"Well we've found each other," Angela says. "But we have to be careful."

"We can go through life cautiously," he says. "And then never know we've lived." He looks at his watch.

She feels heartsick. He has to go because Edith is expecting him. What a cliché, she thinks. Imagine, me in a cliché.

"Maybe we should make love and get it out of the way so we can get to know each other," he says. He has to go but he can't make himself rise from the little table and leave the warm globe of candlelight, and the woman with the long soft hands across the candlelight. She bends the dark space around her. Her hair, in the reddish light, is charged. He feels something supernatural is about to happen. He looks into her eyes and he squeezes her hands, releases them, takes them, releases them. "What are we going to do?"

"What are we going to do?" she repeats. "Sometimes I think I would do anything for you."

"Oh, you're so *free*," he says.

"Yes, I am." She squares her shoulders and enjoys an instant of fierce self-admiration enriched by his admiration. Of course she is not free. She's in love. She can no more say what she really thinks than can the citizen in a totalitarian state who disagrees with the government. The followers of Lenin, Stalin, Hitler, Mao, and the rest were all probably just madly in love.

"On the one hand, when I'm with you I feel clear and fearless," Joe is saying. "On the other hand, I remember everything else in my life and I feel afraid. I've got my kid, Todd, for instance—I should see him more. And the pressure at work. And I don't know what I want to do with my life. I want to construct two sea walls so a channel can flow."

"What?" She frowns, forgetting that in her aim to be the opposite of Edith she must always be understanding. "Huh?"

"One is secrecy at work, the other is my ongoing life with Eed."

Angela pulls her hands slowly away. She can't understand what he's saying, but it sounds bad. Channel? So what can flow? But then she remembers that Edith has no magic or poetry, that she doesn't understand that side of Joe. "A sea channel," she says thoughtfully. "What did you say Edith does, anyway?"

He shrugs and kneads his lips with his fist. "Office manager." What Edith does suddenly seems shameful.

"Oh, where?" Angela sees his embarrassment and tries to keep the ravenously curious tone from her voice.

"Oh, a clinic. In Queens." He recaptures her hands. "My fear is pain between us—between you and me. But my sense is that what we have is good, and will only get better. We should proceed knowing we've already done this before and we already know what to do."

Angela drops her head so that her hair curtains her face. She is aroused, afraid, and a little dizzy. So this is how the great decisions of life are made, she thinks. She will wait this one out. She will triumph.

"I hope that the big things will take care of themselves," he says. "And all we'll have to worry about are the details."

As they step out onto the street, he puts his hand on her hair. "I loved your hair today," he says. He loved the rest of her today, too, but he doesn't want to make more of a fool of himself than he already has.

She smiles up at him, and he has to kiss her. "I can't kiss you just once," he says. He draws her into a dark doorway next to a brass Siamese connection standpipe, sets his briefcase down, and holds her and kisses her until he can't remember who he is, where he is, anything else but this moment and her mouth. She draws back for air. "Sweetheart!" she exclaims. "I guess we decided what to do," she adds.

He laughs and hugs her. He feels really free. Free to do as he likes, and why not?

She senses his levitation. "What do you want to do?"

"I want to make love to you. Tomorrow afternoon?"

She feels she could faint, but she never has, never has fainted when it would be a good thing to do, or even when it would be a bad thing to do. "Let's go to my place right now," she says. Let her body do the thinking.

He kisses her again. "This is more a good-bye kiss than a hello."

In a mutual daze, they walk to the nearest intersection. Their faces are flushed, their voices thick. He carries his briefcase awkwardly, holding it flat in front of himself, and it bangs against his thighs as he walks. He hails a cab going downtown. As he gets in, she calls, "See you at one o'clock tomorrow."

As she rides uptown in a cab through the park, which is full of blossoms in the twilight, clusters of cherry and pear trees glowing on green hillsides, she wonders what he meant about a good-bye kiss rather than a hello kiss, and what he meant about the channel and the two sea walls.

That night Angela goes with Sharon to a discount boutique in the Village. Angela has to find the right thing to wear, the perfect garment which will correspond to the new, transformed Angela, which will cause Joe to change his life for her, and which does not look as if she bought it for the occasion. They sort through stacks of sweaters.

"You know Lynn?"

"Uh-huh." Angela does not like Lynn, although she's never met her, because Lynn's sister admires Edith. "Purple, you think?" She holds up a sweater. "No, too strong." Edith would probably wear purple. Women with dark hair and dark eyes often do. She hasn't been able to tell Sharon that Joe is coming over tomorrow because Sharon will say something sensible and dispiriting.

"Anyway, Lynn is having this thing with Hoyt Golden at

work. He's her boss. I know he's a famous guy and all, but he's a creep. The latest problem is, his wife is getting better and she may be out of the loony bin soon. She's been doing something called dance therapy. When she gets out, then Hoyt can divorce her and marry Lynn, which is what Lynn wants."

"What if the divorce drives the wife crazy all over again?"

"Men can definitely drive you crazy!" It's the sales clerk. She has dark hair parted in the center and a cupid's-bow mouth painted garnet red. "It's a miracle we're not all in loony bins!"

"You said it, sister," Sharon says. "Anyway, Lynn wants to have his child no matter what. She's worried she's getting too old. She doesn't want to wait too long and then have a mongoloid or whatever. She wants to raise the child on feminist principles—nonsexist books, toys, all that stuff."

"What's dance therapy, anyway?" Angela asks absently. Something is bothering her. Something from the conversation with Joe earlier. He pursed his lips as he was talking and she got a bad taste for a moment. Then the dust cloud blows away, and she picks up a soft, low-cut, moss-green angora sweater that Joe might like and that might make her look like someone more alluring than Angela Lee will ever be.

"In dance therapy you use your body to work out your problems," the sales clerk says. "I was going to go into dance therapy myself at one time."

14

THE GIRL AND THE guy always get together in the end. The eyes meet, the hearts tremble. There may be difficulties, but in the end it works out. Angela is thinking along these lines as she prepares for the rendezvous. She had trouble sleeping, aggravated by her worry that if she didn't sleep she would appear wrung out and wrinkled, and too tense to move slowly and speak with a low voice in the new way.

On the one hand, on the other hand.

Since he said they would make love today at one she has felt taut and unreal, as if she weren't living her customary life or occupying her normal body. Unable to think. During the long night, streams of words and images funneled out of the dark into her skull. On the one hand she can see what she should do, and on the other hand what she wants to do. She used to think, when she was with Janos, that if only she weren't married, everything would be simple. Before she was married, and all her high school friends were marrying and purchasing dinette suites, she used to think that if only she were married everything would be simple. Now she is divorced. She can do as she likes. If she likes a man she can go to bed with him. Unfortunately, she doesn't feel right about that unless she really likes the man—likes him enough, say, to marry him. But of course she has vowed never to marry. Sharon goes to bed with whoever she goes out with for dinner. It doesn't seem to bother her. The same with women she knew from the consciousness-raising group. If only she felt more off-hand about Joe. On the other hand, her plan is working—he is coming to her now that she is different.

She begins a rite she has not enacted in many years.

She washes her hair, squeezes a tube of placenta-protein conditioner on it and wraps it in a hot, wet towel so heavy she can't hold her head up straight. She washes her face and spreads a spinach-colored substance made of kelp and clay over her cheeks, forehead, chin, and nose. Her eyes, set in circles of whitish skin, peer out of the mask with a hunted expression. Never mind. She runs a bath, adding rose-scented bath oil. She sinks into the blue fern tub with the mask on and cotton pads soaked in astringent covering her eyes. This is to remove any puffiness and desperation remaining from the insomniac night. She shaves her legs and under her arms. She scrubs her toes, her ankles, her knees, her elbows, and her knuckles first with a pumice stone and then with a brush. She rinses off the hardening mask and stares empty-headed at the bath water as it goes down the drain.

After her bath she rubs fragrant Mexican turtle oil on her feet, legs, hands, and arms. She puts astringent on her face and then sprays her face and neck with French mineral water. She puts on moisturizing cream. She plucks a few hairs from under her eyebrows. She pushes back her cuticles, files her nails with an emery board, and debates polishing them. No. She doesn't wear polish to work; it will look too contrived.

She unwinds the towel from her hair, combs out the tangles, and rolls the wet locks up in pink sponge rollers. It's ten o'clock.

She strips the white sheets and pillowcases from the bed and puts new tie-dyed pink ones on. *"Love is sweeping the country,"* she sings, pushing the mattress corner into the pocket of the contoured sheet. *"There's never been so much love."*

She vacuums the Chinese carpet, dusts the bookshelves and

windowsills, plucks the dead leaves from the plants, and sprays the fan palm with French mineral water. She turns the pillows around on the couch and plumps them up with swift punches. *"Passion'll soon be national!"* When her hair is dry, she removes the rollers, rubs pomade through it, and brushes it out, bending over from the waist.

She dresses in old jeans and a T-shirt and runs to the supermarket and buys a bunch of green grapes, an apple, a pear, and two purple plums and some cheese. From the liquor store, a bottle of red wine and a bottle of white wine. Retsina? Ouzo? They don't have either one. From the florist, a bunch of jonquils and daisies. It's 11:13. The various clerks are so slow. They insist on discussing the fine spring weather with her. "It's great, great," she says impatiently.

Arms full of bags, she hurries back to her apartment, and upon entering it, pretends she's Joe. What will he think of the long newly painted orange hallway leading on the one hand to the bedroom and on the other hand to the living room and kitchen? What could she leave lying around that would intrigue him? A chain saw? Some stock certificates? A love letter from Bob Dylan? A crystal ball? She has none of these things. He will have to accept her as she is. She does make sure that Ron Nussbaum's book of poems is lying near the phone on the bookshelf. *In the hope, strange as it may seem, that one day we may love one another.*

She washes the fruit, dries and polishes it with a paper towel, and arranges it in a silver bowl, a wedding present. The bowl is tarnished. She removes the fruit, polishes the bowl, and rearranges the fruit. She finds an unused vinegar cruet and puts the flowers in it. It's 12:06. Her heart pounds.

Records—the right music. He may be tense. Something quiet. *John Wesley Harding?* Too intellectual. Billie Holiday—not in the daytime. Oud music of the Armenian Middle East? Too exotic. Some Mozart quartets? He said he liked Leonard Cohen and Joe Cocker when he felt mean and low—but how could someone like Joe ever feel mean? She wants music that will compel him to stay with her. She sorts through records she hasn't looked at in years. So many scratches—will he think she's negligent, which she is, when it comes to preserving records? Ella Fitzgerald? Joan Baez? She could play some music that had depth and meaning for her but that might remind him of the worst moments of his marriage. No wonder Muzak is so popular. She stacks the Bach cello suites on the turntable and switches on the stereo so that when the doorbell rings, all she'll have to do is flip the switch and Casals's haunting resonances will flood the rooms.

She goes in the bathroom and from a cabinet under the sink pulls out a shoebox full of makeup, some of it—the mechanical eyebrow pencil and an ancient cake of black mascara—going back to high school. She sprays more French mineral water on her face, spreads moisturizer into the curves and hollows, and with her fingers dabs one shade of foundation on her cheeks and forehead and another, lighter shade around her eyes and below her nose. Too masklike. Wtih a piece of toilet paper, she wipes almost all of it off. Fingers trembling, she brushes on three shades of eyeshadow, cream, blue, and gray in striations. She draws black lines along the base of her eyelashes. Blusher. Powder. The powder is then brushed away—too floury. Eyebrows darkened a bit. Mascara. She sneezes and the mascara smears her cheeks. She removes it. More foundation under the eyes. The eyeliner has to be done over, then new mascara. It's 12:21. The wand vibrates in the shaking hands. Lip liner, lipstick, lip gloss—all in tones nearly the hue of her lips, if her lips weren't white from being nervously stretched over her clenched teeth. She sprays her face again with the French mineral water.

She beholds her creation. Does she look like she's just been hanging around the apartment yawning all morning and reading old *National Geographic*s? No. She removes the lipstick and blots away some of the eyeshadow. The idea is to seem not to be wearing any makeup at all. He will stumble upon her au naturel in her native habitat. It's 12:34.

She puts oil of tea rose behind her ears, between her breasts, in her navel, and on the backs of her knees. She goes into the bedroom and puts a little rose oil on the back of the headboard of the bed. Then she hides all her makeup, curlers, perfume, the razor, the lotions, and a box of tampons in the cabinet under the bathroom sink.

She dresses in the new green angora sweater and a pair of soft old Levis that fit like a second skin.

She puts new candles in holders and colored jars on the mantelpiece and lights the wicks briefly so they don't look new. He probably can't stay until nightfall, but who knows what will happen? It's 12:46.

She is ready now.

Hours, years have gone into her preparations. Years of training, of trial runs. All those empty summers of adolescence spent reading "Hi There Hi School!" and similar dating guides by people like Pat Boone. Hundreds, perhaps thousands of articles in *Glamour* and *Mademoiselle* and *Seventeen*. She and Carmen Garcia used to sit around in Carmen's bedroom, a cool whitewashed room in a rambling adobe house that smelled of beans bubbling and green chiles roasting, and study the laws of womanhood. You could change the shape of your face, for instance, by parting your hair differently. You could test yourself and learn whether you were the tigress type, the shy violet type, or the sporty type. In glossy magazines beautiful, clear-skinned girls posed in suits and hats and gloves under ivy-covered arches in a land with lawns and big shade trees vaguely known in Gatch as "The East." A land where it rained and people carried umbrellas and wore galoshes, and had wallpaper, and "city and country wardrobes." A green country where re-decorating, a lipbrush, and pointers in persiflage swept Mr. Right off his feet and into your waiting arms. Or was it the other way around?

Angela has read the feminists, and has discussed all the recommended topics on the National Organization for Women's lists of consciousness-raising groups. She believes in many of their ideals. But not right now. Not right now. Not at 12:51 on this Saturday in late April.

She surveys the bedroom. Everything must be perfect and alluring in case he wavers. The new orange and red striped bedspread is stretched flat. The curtains belly like orange tie-dyed sails in the spring wind, which is blowing through windows opened to air the place out. The red silk canopy over the bed shivers and flaps. Nearby, across the backyards, someone is practicing the first movement of a Mozart piano concerto.

How will they get from the living room to the bedroom? She doesn't know. Maybe he does.

* * *

Joe jumps out of bed as Edith is on her way out the door to work. "I may have to go to the office today," he says in a bored and tired way. He lights a cigarette. Usually he waits until he has his coffee. "And I think I'm supposed to have lunch with Gerard," he adds.

"I feel for you." Edith blows him a kiss and leaves and then comes back to get her knitting. "I'm going to look at some brownstones in Brooklyn Heights on my lunch hour," she says.

"I'll give you a call later in the day," he says. "In case I happen to be out or anything like that, although I'll probably be back before you are." He never gives her much information—today he overdoes it. "Maybe we'll go out for dinner," he adds.

"Super!" she says. "I won't feel like cooking." The gyne-cologist has prescribed hormones for her ovarian cysts and recommended that she have children soon, if that's what she wants, because problems may develop.

"I could be held up at the office," he says. "It could be sort of late."

"Whatever," she says. She looks pleased: he's giving their time together so much more thought than before. She probably assumes it's the result of the therapy. "And don't forget the laundry."

The moment she leaves, he showers, washes his hair, shaves, trims his mustache, dresses, and takes the laundry out to the laundromat.

While he sits in the narrow, steamy, grubby Coinomatic, which smells of sour water and detergent and is illuminated by faltering fluorescent tubes, he imagines Angela. He keeps checking the time. He will possess her in less than two hours. If it were lust, it would be simple. He'd jump her and that would be that. No, this is something more. A lot more. More than he ever thought he would encounter in this lifetime. He has to test the waters, he has to know whether Angela really feels the way he does and is ready to take the risk. Leaving Edith will not be easy. He *is* a dreamer, he does want to escape—and what has Edith ever done to hurt him? She would never go to a man's apartment and make love all afternoon. His mind clangs shut at the edge of that thought. She spends her days helping others, women who are afraid and disturbed.

He wonders what kind of man she might go out with, if she were to be drawn to someone else. Although she swears she has never been truly attracted in her entire life to anyone but Joe, she was once engaged to a medical student who broke up with her a month before the wedding. Maybe the doctors at the clinic would be stimulated by her genius for order, her neat desk, her administrative abilities. She's not bad-looking. She's kind. What if she came home and said, "Joe, I have something to tell you. We can't go on—" But that picture refuses to come alive in his brain. She promised him she would never betray him as his wife had.

"I'll never do that to you," she said. She always means what she says. She says he is in pain, that when she met him in Greece he was in retreat from reality, he was in a world of hurt. He didn't feel that way. Maybe he was in pain and didn't even know it. But if he wasn't aware of it, how could it exist for him? It existed in her mind, for him, then. He remembers Angela's full lips, her opening mouth, her tongue, her sweet taste. She is sexual in a way that Edith will never be. She understands him in a wordless way that Edith never could.

But if he leaves Edith and then Angela loses interest in him, where will he be? Alone in some dark, cold apartment with nothing in the refrigerator night after night. His thoughts churn and the washers in front of him churn.

A woman comes in pushing a stroller with two crying babies. She is dragging an overloaded laundry cart behind her. She must be about twenty-five, but she is haggard. Her blond hair is lank with oil. Her coat is a dusty black. She wears a man's plaid flannel shirt. Joe gets up and holds the door open for her. She nods distractedly at him as she passes and murmurs her thanks. The children continue to scream. Their faces are dirty and their noses are runny. The woman seems about to crack; she is barely containing herself.

What will happen to Edith if he leaves her? The doctor has advised her to have children soon, because of her condition, her ovaries. But what if she can't find another man? Decades of abortions. The image horrifies him. She will move into tough middle-age and wear suits with padded shoulders and have iron-gray hair cut short and she'll bark orders like an old WAC. No children. Just supervising abortions for others.

He folds the laundry and rushes back to the loft and puts on clean underwear, a clean workshirt, clean Levis. He smokes a joint, walking up and down the length of the huge room. The place is so goddamned cold. It's April and it's still cold. It could be an airport hangar. There's no magic here. His briefcase sits on the end of the dining table next to last night's dishes, plates with lamb chop bones surrounded by congealed fat and clumps of noodles like viscous underwater plants.

If he goes to Angela today, he will fall completely and hopelessly in love. There will be nothing for him but to cry out and bite his hand. Returning to Edith and pretending to live with her will be impossible. Weekends in the Coinomatic. The subway escalator weekdays jammed with depressed people descending under the garish lights, descending, ashen, I did not think death had undone so many . . .

He has to walk. He can't stand being in this loft. He checks his watch. He can take a cab uptown to Angela's. One o'clock. He doesn't want to arrive early. What if he ran into her date from the night before?

What is Angela's place like? He has to know. What's in her closets? Her drawers? Her purse? Her medicine cabinet?

He walks. He passes the blooming azaleas in Washington Square, and the runners who continually pant around the park like speeded-up zombies. He pauses at the corner where he kissed Angela and she kissed him back. There should be a dent in the sidewalk made by their passion, or a brass plaque dedicated by the mayor.

He has an attack of fear. He sees couples pushing baby strollers. The sun is shining. Musicians play bongos and guitars and flutes under Washington Arch. He could simply go to Angela and never return to his old life. "The terror is, all promises are kept—even happiness." In the bar, Angela quoted that line to him. Robert Penn Warren—when Joe was at the university press he once met the poet. If he hadn't run away, by now he would be director. If his wife hadn't . . . How can he make a decision? How can he be sure of Angela? She is so hidden, so elusive, she keeps him off balance.

He swallows. He will have to hail a taxi immediately if he wants to get to her place by one. But first he'll walk quickly for a few blocks to calm down. He spreads his fingers in front of him. Why are his hands shaking? He is a grown man. He has a son. He works at a high-echelon job in a big and powerful corporation. Yet his hands shake of their own accord. The joint was a mistake—instead of soothing him it has only made him more rattled. Angela will be cool and calm, her voice low and measured, and he'll be twitching like a victim of some hopeless neurological disorder.

He finds himself in a phone booth with his hand pulling a dime from his pocket. He dials, and her phone rings and rings. The booth is suffocatingly small. There is a purple sticker with a suicide prevention hotline phone number in red. Maybe she's forgotten the whole thing and gone away for the weekend with Nussbaum, who has names for her breasts. That's like her. "Did you really believe I meant it?" she would say. "For crying out West in a bucket!" A joke—her idea of a joke. If so, then—she answers in a choked voice.

"Hi, it's Joe."

"I know."

"I c-can't do it." His voice sounds high and false. "I've been walking around all morning, and I was awake all night th-thinking, and it just isn't right."

"I know," she says. "I feel the same way. This triangle business. I can't handle it."

"Right, another person's feelings are involved." When he considers Edith as "another person" she becomes insubstantial. She could be any given human being, capable of making her own way without him. Why is Angela so quick to accept his refusal? She said she really wanted to be with him, but now she sounds relieved that she won't be.

"I spent a scary night, too," she is saying.

He doesn't believe her. She is always at ease and happy.

"I can make love to you and still work with you," she goes on. "But I can't make love to you while you're, uh, attached."

So—he would have gone all the way uptown to be told no. "There's an element we have on our side," he says. Is she slipping away from him? Will she be there on Monday at work? Is this all there is to be? "Time. We have time on our side."

"I'll always know you, Joe, and I don't want to engineer a hostile situation."

Three black men in white turbans and long white gowns

pass the phone booth. "Right," Joe says. "We should make some ground rules."

"Ground rules are good," Angela says.

Joe can feel his breath bouncing off the telephone receiver. He stumbles in the little booth over his own feet and bangs his shoulder against the door panel. Why is she so goddamned agreeable? She said not long ago she didn't believe in rules. "Let's say that there will be nothing physical between us and see what happens."

"Fine," she says.

She's maddening, she's weak. "The ground rules will give us a structure." He's feeling better; this is like planning a newsletter. "We didn't have a structure before. I feel the structure will give us monkey bars to swing from. For now, that's all we can do."

"Yes, let's keep everything clear between us."

"I know we can learn to trust each other," he says.

"Right." It has never occurred to her before thay they might not be able to trust each other.

"I see you as being intense," he says. He wants to say: Let's go together to the airport right now and never look back; or: Let's never see each other again. "Please deposit another nickel or this phone call will be automatically interrupted" commands a nasal-sounding recording. He searches in vain for more change. It's better to stick with abstractions. But if he does that too much she'll think he's sterile and unspontaneous. A lunk. "And I see me as having strong, very deep feelings which might be there even if I don't show them."

Just words.

He walks slowly home. The gutters are full of old papers, broken bottles, paper cups, crumpled tissues, and dog shit. Men and women, laughing, talking, alive with happiness, pass him. That kind of life is for others. As he turns toward the loft he has to negotiate the block where packs of men in identical costumes, identical haircuts and mustaches and boots, roam and lounge, eyeing one another.

If she really cared for him as she claims to, she would demand that he come to her.

He folds the laundry while listening to Leonard Cohen turned up loud. *"Like a bird on a wire, like a drunk in a midnight choir, I have tried in my way to be free.*" What did he say to her? What did she say tó him? It has vanished in a dull vapor. He aimlessly opens and closes the kitchen cabinets. All the spices are arranged in alphabetical order, most of them never opened—Edith bought them when he moved in. And why does the sight of six boxes of Saltines neatly stacked, a two-month's supply of paper towels, and a year's supply of bath soap make him feel that his life is over?

At dinner in an awful café that Edith's boss, Lois, recommended, Joe and Edith sit amid tables of men who are mostly wearing leather bomber jackets. Joe replies in monosyllables to Edith's forceful stream of chatter about a fight in the clinic between a Puerto Rican and his wife and her brother and how she had to call the police and rush around and help the counselors calm patients who were getting hysterical by contagion. She's found a brownstone that's an absolute steal, and she is feeling much, much better—no cramps. He feels a little sick. This is what he is settling for, then, and he wonders how it will end.

"A summer house," she is saying. "I'm doing like you and hiring another assistant so this summer I can take long weekends and not feel guilty about it. Have you talked to Goodhugh yet about cutting down your hours? I've got a great plan. We've got women coming from all over the country, so we've had to start a waiting list. I told Lois to raise the rates and that I'd help her start another clinic. You know, I added up what I'm now making, benefits included, on my new calculator. It's fantastic."

"'Shock brings success,'" Katha reads. "That's from Tun changing to Chen, The Arousing. 'When a man has learned within his heart what fear and trembling mean, he is safeguarded against any terror produced by outside influences.'"

"I don't really understand that," Angela says. They are sitting on Katha's carpet, having just returned from seeing *The Tattooed Swordswoman*. Angela by now has seen enough samurai movies to have, at some level, the mistaken belief that she understands fluent Japanese.

"You will, one day," Katha says. "When the worst has happened, and still you continue to breathe."

15

JOE AND ANGELA DO all they can to avoid one another. When they do speak, they fight. "You're not taking responsibility as I'd hoped would be the case," Joe says formally.

"Well, you don't tell me what's going on so I *can* take responsibility—you try to do it all yourself!" Angels says and leaves his office. At the end of the day after one of these arguments, Belinda phones Angela from the reception desk.

"A very attractive man is headed your way, hon, and he looks anxious."

"Derek Grinder."

"You got it."

Angela checks her lipstick in her compact mirror. She has none—she's bitten it off. She reaches into her purse and extracts a lipstick from the bottom. Her hand emerges smeared with Peach Blush from a container of powdered rouge that split apart in her purse weeks ago. She tries to wipe her hand on a piece of typing paper. Derek Grinder sleeps with every woman who will let him, according to Sharon. Those who don't he never speaks to again.

Derek immediately hugs and kisses Angela although she scarcely knows him. They've had lunch twice.

Derek wears jeans, sneakers, a T-shirt with a picture of Mick Jagger on the front, and a red brocade jacket. He is small-boned and thin, appealing in a high-school yearbook way, with tidy white teeth, a tan, aviator glasses, a faint strip of blond mustache, and hair combed forward over his forehead. He must be thirty but he looks twenty-two.

Joe knows someone is with Angela. He passes her doorway, ostensibly to get coffee. It's Grinder. He is speaking intimately with Angela, cupping her elbow casually with his hand. On the return trip, Joe sees Grinder helping Angela on with her coat. He sets his coffee down so hard that it slops all over the blotter, yanks his desk drawer open, pulls out a bag of sunflower seeds, and starts cramming them into his mouth. He is trying to stop smoking.

Angela passes his doorway with Grinder. She waves gaily and smiles broadly. "Oh, Joe—I believe you and Derek know each other."

There is a kind of man who moves easily and cynically with women. Joe knew several of them in college and runs into them sometimes. They are good-looking, they can play the guitar well, they seem open-hearted and sensitive at first, and often they are from California. They look the way the deaf do, as if they've never heard a word and nothing has ever happened to them. Ideally, they should all star in television shows. Grinder is not from California, but in Joe's opinion he ought to be. Worst of all, he is gathering fame through his political columns and according to Goodhugh and other alumni, is on the "inside track" and "can write his own ticket."

"Say there, Joe," Derek says nervously.

"How's it going?" Joe replies.

There is a pause while the men appraise one another. Angela grins. She is elated—Joe is very poor at concealing his jealousy. Here is a wile she had not yet thought of. He glares surreptitiously at Angela when Derek goes over to examine the back of the door, where Joe has hung a dart board. "These are the best darts in the world," Derek says, pulling one out.

"We're delighted you're contributing to the newsletter," Joe says. "Gerard Clewes has been working on things for us too."

"Clewes, right." Derek replaces the dart.

Angela can't stand it any longer and grabs Derek's arm. "See ya," she cries.

Joe watches them go down the corridor. She is smiling, and laughing, absorbed in what Grinder is saying. She wears skirts most of the time now, she knows Joe likes that. Before the ground rules, she would wink at Joe when she caught him staring at her legs. She carries herself as if she is floating.

That night, before Edith can sit down and start talking about her day, Joe tells her that he is going to find a small apartment near the office. He doesn't want to go on with her, he doesn't want to work on their relationship, he doesn't want to get married. And he is the wrong person to be the father of Edith's children.

"What *do* you want?" Edith is mysteriously calm and in control.

"I don't know. Fewer responsibilities. Not to have to work so much. There are—new things I want to try. I don't know, really." He sounds feeble. He hates himself.

Suddenly she starts sobbing. "I pity you!" she cries. "You want to go through life without facing up to anything, without confronting anything, denying your investments."

He goes out and walks down to the tip of the island, and then through the empty streets of the financial district. A man in a ragged suit rambles along the middle of Wall Street playing a blues harmonica.

Joe walks up to the meat district and watches some men load bloody bones into a truck. Then he walks uptown to the park. He is so close to Angela's place. . . . He walks down her block and stands on the sidewalk at the bottom of the flight of slate steps that leads to the house where she lives on the second floor. The windows are dark. What if Grinder is there?

He keeps walking until the sole of his right shoe is thin enough for him to feel the cold sidewalk. As he turns the key in the loft-door lock, he feels dread. He is going to die. He is going to grow old and die, and the time will come when he is no longer here. He quickly abandons this chain of thought when it occurs to him that Edith might be awake and ready to work things through. That also makes him feel dread, but of another variety.

She is asleep, however, her form on the bed making a silhouetted horizon of hills and plateaus, and he lies down beside her.

"Joe has always dithered," Gerard says. He and Angela are having breakfast in the Village in a narrow, crowded café with steamed-up windows. A few inches away from them, at the next little table, a man and a woman are breaking up. The woman keeps reaching into her handbag, next to Angela on the banquette, for more Kleenex. Only Angela's eagerness to learn about Joe from his oldest friend interferes with her wish to eavesdrop.

"Dithered?"

"He's always been in a dither, he's always been—I'm going to have the bacon cheeseburger and a big glass of milk—"

"I always thought there was the possibility that if we lived together we might fall in love," the woman is saying. "I didn't mean to drag you down."

"Yes?" Angela leans across the table, and at the same time tries not to give herself away. "You were saying about Joe?"

"I know of no one who has not been impressed with his profound integrity. At prep school he was always the best, everyone had a kind of crush on him, I think. You know, sort of the loner, the leader of the pack, always off brooding about something."

"I've been reading *A Separate Reality*—I have to go find myself," the man says. "It's road time, for me."

"Be that as it may," the woman begins, and then breaks down, sobbing, jostling Angela as she burrows in her bag.

"I gather he's had a hard life," Angela says. "No family to speak of."

"Rather, but they had money. Probably nothing left now. When Joe was married to Lucy, I once went with him to J. Press—he had to buy some lime green pants he could wear on her father's yacht."

"Joe? Lime pants?"

"Very short hair. Years went by when I never saw him without a tie. He probably wore a tie to bed. Since Lucy left him, he's loosened up considerably, although God only knows why he persists with Edith Berk."

"You'll write, won't you?" The woman has pulled herself together and is eating a blintze. "Please?"

"I thought he was fairly settled," Angela says.

Gerard tilts his chin up even further than usual and closes his eyes. "The mystery of that couple is right up there with the mystery of the pyramids. It's frustrating to watch. She's not at all the sort you'd expect Joe to be with. She reminds me of a giraffe. At first I liked her, but she's quite cold. She's very different from Joe. They're going through a heavy scene. She's pressuring him to marry her, really a lot, and he doesn't know what to do. I guess there's something between them, but I don't know what. When I left my wife, I felt guilty because I had only affection for her, not passion. I think Joe probably likes her well enough—but they're always *experimenting* and so on. Joe said the other day that no matter what they try, things stay just the same. What a bore. And he doesn't want to get her pregnant—a sure sign he doesn't love her."

"And he already has a child," Angela says. She has an ally at last.

"Well, yes, I suppose. Joe was badly burned by his wife. I think he's afraid that any woman he loves and respects will screw him, betray him. And Edith has him in a vise—'If you leave me I'll be so, so hurt.'"

"What do you think is going to happen? Sometimes at work it's so hard."

Gerard accepts the bacon cheeseburger from the waiter and takes a bite. "Joe doesn't use a tenth of his potential because he's always dithering, dithering about the newsletter, dithering about Edith. He's never dared to live. He needs to cut through his bonds and get up and *dance!*" Gerard's last statement is offered in a voice loud enough to gain the glares of the neighboring couple. "I think you must be a lot like me," he goes on, quietly. "Basically happy."

"I didn't bring any money," the man at the next table says. "You'll have to pick up the check."

*

Esteemed Lee,
I wanted badly to take you home with me the other night

(is this presumptuous? I mean . . .) but didn't because a long-absent friend is coming to visit for a few weeks in a couple of days and I didn't want to mess up my mind, if you get my drift. This too (aforementioned visitor) shall pass.

I really had an exquisite time last night. We will eat food together again soon, I hope.

Your fan, Derek

Angela is excited by this letter, which she reads over many times before realizing she doesn't understand what Derek has in mind. Derek is very charming. Maybe she will go out with him until Joe leaves Edith. Joe is not very charming, not the sort who can blithely toss off witticisms and gossip. He dithers. Most days lately, he is tense and quiet. Whenever she tries to talk to him, he says, "There's too much work." He has the capacity to look dark or fair, and lately he looks dark. His hair is greasy, his mouth and jaw are tight, his collar is half turned under the neckband of his wrinkled shirt, and he's gained back the weight he lost. Sometimes, for no reason she can imagine, he glares at her.

Friday night she is meeting Katha for sushi and then they are going to a revival movie theater on upper Broadway to see *The Seven Samurai*. Angela packs her briefcase with some newspaper clippings and a report on the impending world forest shortage, combs her hair, checks her makeup, and then enters Joe's office. He is bent over his desk, which is covered with overlapping, untidy stacks of paper and has three ashtrays full of butts, and some half-full Styrofoam coffee cups.

He knows she's here, but he keeps working. He is filing an extension on his income tax. Last year Edith did his taxes.

"Oh, boy," Angela says, glancing over his shoulder.

He lights a cigarette from the end of the cigarette he's smoking. "Taxes," he says.

She claps her hand to her cheek. "Oh my gosh, I completely forgot. Is it too late?"

"Yes. You have to file an extension."

"How do you do that?"

As he is telling her, she wanders to the window. It's still light out. The peony she gave him has withered intact in the green wine bottle on the sill. Suddenly a giant monarch butterfly appears. "Joe! Come here! Look at this!"

Hurrying to the window, he knocks over the wastebasket. "But we're seventeen floors up—what's it doing here?" He gets a glimpse of the orange wings, the black veins and spots, and then an updraft takes the butterfly away.

"How do you do these things?" Laughter suddenly comes to him from nowhere. He lets his hand rest on the small of her back. She is wearing a rose velour shirt.

"I know someone who knows a guy who was sitting in the plaza of this little town in Peru one day," she says, "and this guy, an American, was watching an old man do these amazing things with butterflies. A butterfly would hover over the old man, the old man would make a signal and then the butterfly would land on his finger. He'd talk to the butterfly for a while and then make motions with his fingers and the butterfly would make circles in the air and then come back to his hand. Then another butterfly would come along and he would do another bunch of tricks with that one. Then he sent a butterfly to land on the gringo's hand. The gringo was scared of insects, but he just looked at the butterfly and the butterfly looked at him. Then he said, 'How do you do that?' The old man gets up and comes like a tree toward the guy and beckons him."

"And? And?" They are standing very close.

She shrugs. "My friend, Katha, who knew the guy, said that he went into the mountains with the old man and then came back to the States after a couple of years and they were having dinner in Chinatown and lightning struck a parking meter in front of the restaurant."

"We should be able to live like that. Just to be able to go when we want to follow something. We should be magicians, we should live like magicians."

Angela is inclined to remark that they need less magic and more action. But that's what Edith would probably say. Instead she tells him she is learning to read Tarot cards.

"I love fortune-tellers," he says. "Do you think you could tell my fortune?"

"Sure, when?"

"Tonight."

"Tonight? I don't have the cards with me. And if Buffalo Buff ever—"

"At your place?"

His sudden eagerness startles her. Are the ground rules still in effect? His hand is still on her back. She considers calling Katha and canceling their evening. She checks Joe's watch—too late; Katha is already on her way to the restaurant. Furthermore, the apartment is a mess, and Angela needs to wash her hair. "I can't—tonight."

He backs away and drops into the swivel chair. He lights a cigarette and picks up, at random, a letter from an assistant vice-president at Union Carbide that has gone unanswered for three weeks. "I've been a Carbider for two decades," it begins.

"I didn't know you chain-smoked," Angela says.

"It's been a bad week." He puts the letter down and tries to think of something to say to keep her with him a little longer. He saw the glance she gave his watch. But if he says one thing he will say a million things, and he isn't up to that. "Well." He rubs his thighs.

She goes back to the window to give herself something to do. The yellow lights in the buildings are beginning to come on. The sky is turning a soft pink. "It's May."

"Maybe some other time you could, uh, read my cards." He likes this idea. They aren't going to do anything indecent. She's going to "read his cards." If the police broke into her apartment and found them, and photographers, and Edith, well, Angela would just be reading his cards.

Angela is going out the door. Toward a rendezvous—with Grinder no doubt. She turns and gives him a smile.

"Tomorrow?"

"Eleven o'clock."

"And are you really going to come? Because I can't keep vacuuming the carpet each time I think you're going to come over."

"I really am going to come."

Late that night, she looks through her financial records for her income tax return, and then remembers that she filed early back in December, because she was broke and hoping for a refund.

16

SATURDAY MORNING, JOE PHONES Angela at quarter to eleven. He has a terminal hangover, having spent the evening before with Gerard at the White Horse Tavern. "A lot of things have fallen through this week," he says. "My ex-wife and her husband were supposed to bring my son and stay for a few days and that didn't work out. Edith isn't feeling too well. I can't get myself together to come and see you. It has to be an office friendship. There has to be a period of hibernation. But if our, our relationship is what I think, it will survive."

"Yes, that's true," Angela begins. She sits down on the floor, ready for a long exchange about their predicament. If only she could get to the other side of this maze; if only she could get over him. Suddenly she hears herself saying, "I can't stand this telephone shit," her voice shrill. "You'd better come right up here."

"Okay."

Fifteen minutes later he is there, out of breath. When she opens the door, she does not smile or speak.

Avoiding her eyes, he glimpses the bedroom as he follows her into the living room and gets a brief impression of reds and oranges and tunneling depths.

"Take off your shoes and make yourself at home." She goes into the kitchen.

He wanders around absorbing everything. The room is small and fresh and wholesome. She has a big palm tree and lots of plants, some in bloom. "Nice place," he says, but she doesn't hear him. She's chopping something in the kitchen.

The matchstick bamboo blinds are drawn up and warm sunshine makes squares on the Chinese carpet. On one wall are some reproductions of Persian miniatures. He tries to memorize them but it's impossible. Fountains, waterfalls, boats, animals, mountainsides, a man suspended in a grotto with serpents spitting into his ears, gazelles leaping, horsemen in battle, fruit-laden trees, archways, pavilions—the world condensed, with all its complications and rich colors and deceptive, dissolving images. A swirling purple mountainside turns out to be composed of intricate boulders and foliage, each leaf and petal exact, that in turn become crowds of faces and animals. A cloud becomes a dragon. Glutted, he turns away.

He rocks the bookcase slightly; it's out of plumb. The couch looks homemade, too—a plywood veneer box with black corduroy upholstery. As he inspects the veneer, which is beginning to peel, a cushion topples and he sees that the fabric is held around the foam rubber with safety pins. On a windowsill, next to a dried half of a wishbone, is a black lacquer box. He picks it up and turns it in his hand. It is smooth and flawless. Her boxes and bowls at the office always have good-smelling or good-tasting things inside. He opens this one. The interior is cinnabar red and contains a stiff cream-colored card covered with black calligraphy. "Angela?"

"I'll be right there," she says. She sounds annoyed. She runs water and bangs a pan.

With a thrill of expectancy he reads the card.

> *Happy Birth Day, Angela. Jung: "It is important to have a secret, a premonition of things unknown. It fills life with something impersonal, a numinosum. A man who has never experienced that has missed something important. He must sense that he lives in a world which in some respects is mysterious, that things happen and can be experienced which remain inexplicable; that not*

everything which happens can be anticipated. The unexpected and the incredible belong in this world. Only then is life whole." Love, Katha.

He quietly replaces the box, sits on the couch, and removes his boots. He is facing a shallow fireplace with a wooden mantelpiece, and on it, next to a black and red-ocher Indian pot, are candles in holders and in glass jars every color of the rainbow. The room still smells faintly of fresh paint. On the couch is a deck of cards.

She comes out of the kitchen and he looks at her directly, which he was afraid to do at first. She is wearing a short white dress, Mexican maybe, with red embroidered borders. Her hair falls in waves over her breasts. She is barefoot, and she holds a tall clear glass pitcher filled with dark red liquid and bits of orange and red fruit. "Sangria," she says.

"Now that I'm here, it's really good to see you," he says. "I'm just enjoying looking at you." He feels great delight at being alone with her. He is totally present, free of thought, as clear and fluid as spring water.

Her eyebrows slide together. She puts the pitcher carefully down on a tray on the carpet and goes back into the kitchen. He can hear her hacking something. Below, on the street, someone passes with a radio blaring a Spanish song. She returns with two wineglasses with disks of lemon on their rims and fills them with sangria. When he takes the glass from her, he sees her hand is shaking.

"What are you thinking?" he asks.

She is tasting her drink. "Whether I put enough sugar in."

She puts down her glass and abruptly leaves, then returns with a silver bowl heaped with green grapes. "I had a dream just after I met you that I rubbed green grapes on your chest," she says matter-of-factly and sits down on the couch, placing the bowl between them. "Don't worry—I'll behave. Nothing physical." She picks up the cards and hands them to him. "Shuffle and cut."

The cards are longer and heavier than normal playing cards, and their rich blues and reds remind him of medieval paintings. Each image is a dream in itself: a tower being struck by lightning, a naked woman kneeling by a pond under a star. He feels very odd. He does not feel like himself. His arms and legs seem to float, although he hasn't smoked any dope today. "You really believe these work?" He can't imagine how they would, they're silly in a way, but if she thinks they're important—well, let her read them and he'll know what she really intends.

Last night after *The Seven Samurai* Angela persuaded Katha to give her a lesson on the Tarot. Katha went over the layout and some of the central symbols and then said, "Just say the first thing you think—you're bound to be right at least some of the time. The cards are just an excuse for tapping the unconscious anyway, and the unconscious knows everything."

Angela wants to say to Joe, I don't know what I'm doing. I can't read the cards, I doubt if these things work at all. All I want is for us to love each other without any confusion or complications or misunderstandings. And she wants these words to reverberate in him with exactly the same frequency they resonate in her. But she is not able to do that, either. She therefore ignores his question.

Impressed with her silence, he shuffles the deck, cuts it three times, and hands it to her. She moves the silver bowl to the floor and smooths the black cloth between them with her pale hand. Her gesture makes a mild electricity on the back of his neck.

"There are these different stages to life," she says, dealing the cards face down in five horizontal rows. "Youth, when you devote yourself to learning what society wants from you—you learn a skill, have a family, and so on. And then about halfway through life comes the next stage, when you change direction and move away from society and its demands—that's represented by the color blue—to the inner life, spirituality, that stuff. That's represented by red."

My life is half over, Joe thinks.

"In mid-life you're at your prime," Angela goes on. She wishes she didn't sound so mechanical, so much like she was repeating data crammed at the last minute for a final exam. "At your prime, your mind and body are at their peak." She smiles at him to let him know she thinks he is in his prime. "That's when everything changes." She figures she sounds so confident because she's not saying what she really wants to say. "And if you are interested in something beyond eating and sleeping and earning money, the quest begins. The point of the Tarot is to keep you from getting stuck in the first stage of life—it's around to remind you that there is something else in life."

One by one she turns the cards over, beginning with the Magician. "The start of the journey," she says. Then comes the High Priestess, holding a book of prophecy, then the Empress who rules the world. The Lovers—Adam and Eve, hand in hand. The Hermit, Fortune—a woman pointing to the rim of the wheel of fortune while Wisdom points to its immovable center. The Hanged Man dangling by his foot. "Fear of social disgrace," Angela says, "which you have to overcome to go on." The next card is Death.

"What—?"

"Oh, don't worry. It means you must die completely to your old life, and get over your fear of death." The Devil: he glowers over the fires of hell, and a naked man and woman in chains. "Hell is getting stuck," she says. The Tower, its top knocked off by a lightning bolt. That's the way Joe feels right now. "I believe this is supposed to be purgatory, and the lightning striking is like waking up from a long dream." The Star—the woman by the pool—resembles Angela. "This is paradise, the first sign of revealed light." The Moon: "The light is growing, it's like youth. The moon moves the tides, and youth, and all of life, but it covers the sun." Next is the Sun—"The full light," she says. "The light of personal relationship." The Judgment—Joe is drawn to that one: the dead are rising from their graves at the trumpet blast. "That's the horn of light smashing through the world of phenomena." The World. He sees that it is a dancing hermaphrodite. Angela taps it with a long finger. "This is the here and now."

She looks at him. Until now she has focused on the brilliantly colored array on the field of black between them. "It means life right now as it is, not the future, not in heaven, not someplace you're rewarded with if you work hard." She takes a deep breath and turns over the final card. "This is the end of the journey."

"The Fool?" He is stepping over a cliff, his eye turned to the sky.

"He doesn't care what anyone thinks. He just wanders through the world and he knows it's a joke."

"So you start out a Magician and end up a Fool?"

"Yup, I guess so." She is sitting cross-legged now, the curve of her femur, her smooth, firm calf a few inches from his hand. Her long foot juts awkwardly toward him. Her back is straight.

She is remembering a scene from the movie last night. In the midst of the chaotic final battle, the old samurai archer draws his bow in lucid serenity.

Joe nicks the edge of the Fool card with his thumbnail. "It's funny—I thought for some reason you were going to tell me my fortune. You know—say what's going to happen to me next. Don't the cards show that?"

"I don't know. Seems like they show what could happen to anybody."

"Tell me what you really are thinking," he says.

She goes blank. She's wondering what to do and has come up against a wall.

He sees that she is strong and clear and full of deep, singular understanding. Her forehead is smooth and cool-looking; she barely fills up the space she occupies.

"Please." He really must know.

"Well, you have a conflict ahead."

"Ahead?" More conflict? A new conflict?

"And a psychological change. You either have to go with your desire and expand your—your domain I guess you could call it. Like in the fairy tales when the wandering prince comes back and claims his kingdom, his treasure, what's rightfully his. Or you could shrink back, not go on to the next stage. Allow yourself to be defeated." She is preaching; she ought to shut up. "You could become like someone you know who had energy and talent but wound up stuck in hell. Cynical, indifferent, limited."

"Goodhugh is like that now," Joe says. "He used to have a lot going for him. A lot of enthusiasm and ideas."

"Now he just manipulates and takes credit for other people's work and screws around."

"How did you know that?"

She shrugs. "Doesn't everyone?" She goes on. "Anyway, that's the choice, according to the cards. You wake up to your larger self, or you just nod off forever." God, she's talking garbage, she's just making things up. She shakes her head.

"What's the matter?"

"I just want to be with you. I don't want all this talk." She sweeps the cards to the floor. Now there is nothing between them.

She touches his toes. He is wearing gray wool hand-knit socks. Edith must have made them; he must have worn them as a talisman.

Joe feels thoroughly alive just now. Her form, her long legs, her gently stroking of his toes, the vibrant reds and blues of the cards scattered on the cool threadbare surface of the green carpet, the faint smell of roses and of new paint, the squares of light on the floor shifting as the sun moves, shadows lengthening outside his vision, the room compressed and reflected along with his and her distorted forms in the side of the silver bowl with its heap of green grapes, the floating of his arms and legs, the cries of children in the street, a piano playing a classical piece, the remote thunder of the subway train, the creaking of floorboards in the apartment above, her full mouth slightly open, her soft breathing, his own heart—he can feel it pumping, he can feel the rush of blood.

His eyes, which now fix on hers, change from blue to slate to green. She feels a sensation of falling in the center of her abdomen. She knows he is aroused.

A long time passes in which nothing happens.

"With you I always feel we're in suspended animation." His tongue is thick and unmanageable.

"Yes." It's true. That's how she feels. How is it this can happen between two people? What does it mean? Where does it lead?

She withdraws her hand from his foot. He puts his arms around her and pulls her against his chest.

As he holds her and kisses her, she thinks of Edith, and tells herself that if she doesn't withdraw now, it will be very difficult later. They have to work together. How can it be that she wants so badly to be with him, to be as close as possible—he fits so exactly the deep wish inside her body, her mind—and yet he continues in what he says is an unsatisfactory life with someone he did not choose? How is this possible? There must be some fact, some information, some practice she has overlooked. Something she doesn't yet know.

She pulls away and takes his arms from around her shoulders. This only excites him more, and he pulls her back. They are not in the office, or on a street corner, or in a bar. It's time to get this over with so that he can resume a normal life. There is nothing external to stop them from what they most want to do.

But he does stop. He reaches in his shirt pocket for his cigarettes and she sees his hands shake as he takes out a cigarette, drops the pack, drops the matches, picks them up, picks up the cigarette, and finally lights it. "I can't stop thinking," he says. "The high cost of being with you. The job . . . Edith . . . looming behind everything like a mountain range. I've just gotten back in touch with my ex-wife so that I can see my kid. I should see him more. And Edith and I may have reached a new level I want to explore."

She fetches an ashtray from the bookcase and hands it to him, and then retreats to the other end of the couch, pulls her dress primly down over her legs, and draws her knees up under her chin. New level? Explore what?

"Oh, goddamn it." He sighs. "What I mean is I don't know if I can trust you yet."

She reaches out and takes his hand. "Don't be afraid. I can tell that you like being with me. I don't know what this is that makes me want to be with you so much. It's new to me. I want to know what's going on." She is worried that she's whining. "But I guess I can figure that out on my own. The day-to-day business doesn't matter. Because I love you—"

He drops her hand. He grimaces as if she has slapped him.

She keeps talking, talking. This was not in the plan. "I've accepted that bond with you, so it frees me. I've met you at the wrong time in your life. I guess I should just keep away from you for good." She never should have said the part about love.

How can she so easily talk about loving him? She just says it. Oh, I love that shirt, oh, I love that movie, oh I love Toshiro Mifune. How can he be sure of anything she says? She's so calm! He grinds out the cigarette and looks at his watch. "For instance, I have to leave here no later than three-thirty. I don't want to have to do that."

Time? What time is it? Morning? Afternoon? She has no idea. "What time is it now?"

"Ten till three." Everything has been decided, then, and in forty minutes they will go their separate ways.

"Let's talk about the weather," she says. "Or baseball. Are the Yankees still in New York? Or did they move to California? Or was it the other team?"

Now she is making fun of him. They will talk, and not do anything, and no one will get hurt, and in forty minutes he will leave, and they will never know what they missed. He regards the litter of cards, the World dancing. The Fool. Crazy and stupid—that's what Edith would call the Tarot and all of Angela's explanations about it.

"Did you ever see this really scary science fiction movie, *Invasion from Mars* or something like that, where this little kid sees a flying saucer land in a swamp, and no one will believe him? And the aliens keep capturing the townspeople and operating on them and changing their brains so they become aliens? They look the same, but everyone has a scar on the back of the neck—and the kid goes to the sheriff for help, and the sheriff sends him away, and when he turns his back, the kid sees the sheriff has been *changed?*" Angela is talking along as fast as she used to drive over the rutted roads outside Gatch. She feels terrible, and on top of that, the story she is telling is giving her gooseflesh. "I saw it at the drive-in when I was little."

"I've seen that," Joe says. "I can never remember movies I saw when I was small, but that one sounds familiar. I couldn't sleep after I saw it."

She pours them more sangria.

"Angela, I want you to know that I've had casual affairs since I started living with Edith, but they weren't serious for me or for the other person."

"Sex isn't much of a problem for people in New York," she says. It sounds like the subject of a magazine article, and even more a lie than articles like that tend to be. Of course sex is a problem. She can't even have a cup of coffee with a man unless she really likes him. But love—that's really a problem.

She wants suddenly to surrender, to hurl herself to the floor and grab his ankles and scream Take me! She drains her glass and gets up. "Well, you better go. It's getting late for you."

"I suppose so." He puts his half-finished glass on the carpet next to his boots and goes to the window. "What plant is this?" Its leaves are a glossy deep green and it has buds just beginning to expand through their sheaths.

"Gardenia. I keep waiting for it to blossom."

"I ought to leave now." He follows her down the orange hallway to the door. He has a sensation of collapse in the depth of his guts, as if he has missed out on the essential event of his own life, as if he has misplaced an infant. He feels he's lost something, or missing something valuable. He checks his watch—he still has it. Three o'clock. He puts his hand on the doorknob. One final kiss.

She is smiling, her head tilted slightly to the right, her red-gold hair in wavy tendrils falling in a loop around the base of her neck and splaying out behind her head, her right hand between her breasts, her fingers delicately parted, her eyes slightly downcast as if she were gazing into deep water, her pelvis slightly tilted to the left, her knees together, the heel of her right foot off the floor. She is quite still in her aplomb. She seems to float. Behind her is the bedroom, the smoothly made orange and red bed, the red silken canopy enclosing it, the rosy curtains billowing. All these flowing lines, like time, urge him onward.

He is completely destroyed in the lightning of love.

"What are you thinking?" he whispers.

"You forgot your boots."

17

"MY PLAN FOR SUPPORTING myself after the divorce is to go around to all the Mexican restaurants in town and ask them for avocado pits," Melanie Gauss is saying. She and Angela are lying in the sun on deck chairs at Melanie's beach house. The waters of the bay slosh and gulls scream overhead. The air smells of coconut suntan oil. "Then I will grow the avocado pits into avocado trees and sell them, or maybe even open a store."

"Sounds good," Angela says. She's barely present. She's remembering the condensed, super-real quality of the day before with Joe, time stretched between them like a substance, thick and slow, each second breathing its own life and then surrendering its light to the next bit of time.

"Eric's a stingy bastard; he probably won't give me a cent. He'll take my charge cards. I'll have to fight tooth and nail for every little bit of child support." Melanie is from Angela's old consciousness-raising group. For the past five or six years she has been having affairs with various men—they tend to be obscure painters and young musicians waiting for the big break—

and plotting how she will leave her husband. Eric Gauss is a partner in a big law firm and has movie stars for clients. Occasionally his name is in the papers. He flies to Europe and to islands in the Caribbean to get his clients out of jams with customs officials. They have three sons in boarding schools throughout New England. Melanie exercises according to a special system for an hour every morning and rinses her face thirty times a day according to another special system. She looks much younger than she is, and her nails are long, perfect ovals. She spends a lot of time in department stores. Over the years, Angela, along with the consciousness-raising group, has encouraged Melanie to set out on her own and go through with the divorce. She has hoped that Melanie will finally leave Eric and begin an independent life the way she hopes when she watches a play that the first act will be followed by a second, in which something new occurs, and a third, in which all is resolved. But today she feels sorry for Eric. She hopes that he has a girl friend who loves him and that he will realize how Melanie uses him and leave.

But Angela is not fervent about even that: most of her energy is being funneled inward, into memory. The warm shock of their bare bodies embracing, his ecstasy and surprise, and afterward, when he turned away and put his arm over his eyes, and his whole body shook. "My guilts are like the Furies," he muttered.

She never saw a person split in two before, and she was concerned and fascinated by his rapid alternations. He hastily dressed and then rushed back to hold her, saying, "There are no words," and then knocked over the glass of sangria as he pulled on his boots, and then took her in his arms and said "I don't want to go" with such fervor and sadness that she thought he might cry. "I'm very sorry—the stain, I hope the carpet will—" and then, withdrawing abruptly from her kiss goodbye, "Just give me time!" Throughout, she felt clear-headed and sure. This detachment was very odd for her. While he made love to her, his eyes on hers until she closed them, she was that way. She wanted to absorb and memorize his passion—passion at last, thank God, out in the open—and she was afraid that if she got distracted from his throes by going through her own, she would miss something. And afterward, when he was so torn, she felt great sympathy. As he started out the door a thumping sound below made him start. "Don't worry," she said, "it's just my neighbor doing aikido."

Paul, who is Melanie's present lover and whose main occupation appears to be growing a beard, comes up from the beach. According to Melanie, he is a very talented and original folksinger with a record contract and she plans to use Eric's connections to help Paul's career. He appears to be in his early twenties. He is brown and narrow-chested, and wears faded jeans cut off at the thigh. He immediately kisses Melanie at length, and Angela, embarrassed, leaves.

The beach is littered with round stones the color of peaches and blackboards. The waves crest very slowly. She sits with her chin on her knees and holds her feet. At least they made love. At least that much has happened. After he hurried down the stairs, pulling at his mustache and looking at his watch, she stood on the landing feeling warm drops splash on her foot. Well, at least she had that much of him. "Just give me time."

She was very relieved. When Sharon came down with a carton of rum-raison ice cream, Angela couldn't eat. "Now I'm over him," she announced. "Thank the Lord."

"But, Angela," Sharon said. "Now you're the *Other Woman.*"

After a long stretch when Angela failed to eat or respond to any conversation and just stared at the wine stain on the carpet, Sharon decided to go back upstairs. "I don't think Joe has a very good effect on you. Call me when you come out of your trance."

With her finger Angela traces the inner convolutions of a conch shell laid bare by erosion—secret spirals of pink. She picks up a rock that is red and perforated like the pit of a peach or a piece of meat. The sky lowers and darkens. The memory is undergoing subtle shifts. It now seems to her that she, too, was overcome by passion, that she had experienced the pinnacle of a lifetime, that all she said, thought, and did before yesterday was mere foreplay. Even in childhood she must have sensed his presence, the way people can sometimes pick up radio broadcasts with the fillings in their teeth. From early on, an entity existed within her that could only be touched and awakened by Joe Bly. And now that this has happened, she can't return to her old state. Her body, her whole way of being in the world—these have been permanently changed.

The wind rises and blows clean through her. It starts to rain, and she hurries back to the house. Paul and Melanie are noisily taking a bath together upstairs, and so Angela sits under an awning on the deck and watches the rain.

I am really in love, she thinks, turning her hands and examining the palms. What she called "love" in the past was no longer valid. A new definition would have to be created out of sound and light and sensations and many shifting emotions. Furthermore, it was not the love she had felt for her mother, or for her husband, or for friends. This was passionate, illicit, consuming love, and nothing else mattered. If she believed in God, she would rank her love for Joe above her love for God. In fact, her love for Joe probably fills the ecological niche in her world left vacant by God. And it seems to her now that she always loved him, from the time the woman at the employment agency wrote his name on a slip of paper with the date of the interview. *Mmm, Joe Bly, what an ordinary name*, she remembers thinking. She never should have thrown that paper away.

Also, this love is not like anything Melanie, for instance, would know about. "Don't, Paul, don't—don't—don't," she is shrieking. Love as Angela now understands it is accompanied by a force that will remove all difficulties, in time. Because, she thought, pleased with this logic, the reason we are born is to love. To *love*. Through this, Joe and I became greater than our ordinary selves, if only for a moment. Their coming together was a rite, an initiation: this idea has such power that Angela, having minored in myth, makes a list of parallels. The white dress she wore, embroidered with leaves and red flowers. The clash of glances. The recognition. The abruptness. His crying out sacred names during the act (Oh Jesus, Oh God), the spilled wine, and afterward his joy and terror, with her the object and the witness of both.

The rain stops and the sky begins to clear. The sun is about to set over the bay and the surface of the water ripples gold, like a Klimt veil. Folds, runs, ribbons of gold, and then particles of gold dancing up into a fine mist over the water. Whole entities of gold mist and dark water move against one another. Here I am, Angela thinks. Alive and watching this. Amazing.

Melanie clanks and scrapes iron utensils against a wok in the kitchen. Paul appears with his guitar and a lit joint, and sits down on the edge of a deck chair. He plays and sings. He has a clear, sweet tenor that makes Angela forgive his callowness.

> *"The body dies; the body's beauty lives.*
> *So evenings die, in their green going,*
> *A wave, interminably flowing . . ."*

The sun disappears into a band of gray cloud along the horizon and then reemerges as a red, swollen egg.

"That's not the real sun." Paul offers her the joint. She shakes her head. "The real sun has already gone below the horizon. That's like, a reflection or something."

Suddenly the red egg drops into the sea.

Angela tries to intuit what Joe is doing. He must be telling Edith. He must be saying everything is different now; he has found the person with whom he is at last complete.

Joe is sitting in his bathrobe at the dining table putting together a huge picture puzzle of the Grand Coulee Dam that Edith gave him and he is also watching a sports roundup on a brand-new wide-screen television that Edith had delivered yesterday.

Edith sorts out the puzzle into border pieces, pieces of sky, of water, and of concrete with swiftness and authority, slapping each piece on the dining table in the correct category. "The fireplaces are marble—did I mention that?" She has picked out a house in Brooklyn that is very similar to Lois's house in Brooklyn, same neighborhood, and she wants Joe to go see it.

Yesterday, after he left Angela naked in her doorway, he

stumbled down the stairs and into an enormous question, his heart pounding so loud he was afraid passers-by on the street could hear it. When his mother died, he was eight and he didn't feel anything. When his father died, Joe was fifteen, and as he sat in the church listening to a minister who had never known the deceased drone on about his fine qualities, Joe asked himself if we are all cattle, born to die randomly, mindlessly: how unfair to know life if it is only going to be a temporary gift! That moment returned to him when Lucy told him she and Alec were lovers. A few seconds of free-fall between the shock and the return of the everyday world, the world whose best interests lie in burying that question. And now this question appeared again, creating in him for a time an extra presence. Why was he alive, for what purpose? He hurried back to the loft, vacuumed all two thousand square feet of it, and glued down the curling Formica on the countertop. Then he went to the seafood store and bought mussels, several pounds of them, and when he passed a produce stand heaped with oranges, eggplants, artichokes, lettuce, and cherries, he stood dumbfounded before the wet, glistening shapes. At the florist, he bought a gardenia heavy with fragrant buds.

Someday he was going to die, and there was a terrible danger that he would become permanently distracted from living his own life. The question permeated him for a time, and then began to disintegrate into several unanswerable thoughts. It was a good thing to be in love with Angela because she had opened his heart and he understood that all other experiences with women were false, mechanical, distracting him from his own real nature. Now he would have the chance to be led away from all unworthy pursuits. On the other hand, it was terrible that he had gone to her and discovered a sunken continent more amazing than Atlantis because from now on there would be conflicts and upheavals. Until now, he had just been getting by, just hanging on. Now life demanded, suddenly, that he meet it with much more of himself. As he washed and scraped the mussels—a treat for Edith; he seems to remember that in Greece she loved the mussels—he contemplated Angela. She was like no other woman. She was not easily moved, not ambitious, not one to fall for just anybody. And her effect on him is sweet. He felt kindness toward the surly clerk at the fish market, toward the burned-out speed freaks panhandling in the Square, toward the gang of toughs in front of the deli, and toward Edith and the two delivery men who arrived with the new color television set.

"Do you think it's a little too green?" Edith is asking, referring to a sportcaster's face. "By the way, I have an upset stomach—do you?"

"No." He gets up and adjusts the color knob. He does not like having to stop working on the puzzle. He has not done one since he was in the hospital after his motorcycle accident when he was a teenager. He forgot how intricate and satisfying jigsaw puzzles can be. He slept long and well last night, and today he feels refreshed and sweet, like a good child. The struggle among the different unanswerable thoughts, the confusion about which decision to make—all this has evaporated.

"Maybe it was the mussels," says Edith. A commercial comes on: happy smiling Americans with long clean limbs bicycling, roller skating, surfing, hang-gliding, and drinking soda pop while doing all these happy things. "Joe, when you're ready, I'd like to *talk*."

"Mmm."

"Okay?"

He nods. Between his thumb and forefinger he holds a piece of deep green water.

"I have had an important realization."

He puts down the piece. She must know about yesterday. He lights a cigarette. On the screen, a man does a standing broad jump. Joe wonders if it is part of the commercial or part of the show. The colors on the screen are crisper and more brilliant than anything in the loft. "Yes, Edith?"

"My insight is this—I had it Friday when I was talking to Midge: I just wanted to get married and have children because I wanted to please my mom. She always wants to know, you know, if I'm going to do it before she dies and she always says, 'If you don't marry Joe, then *I* will.' And all that's been putting tremendous psychological pressure on me. Well, the thing is, I've been thinking all along that Midge *also* thought we should get married, have children, et cetera because she just got married. So on Friday, I just asked her, I asked her, 'Midge, you secretly think it's wrong for me to keep drifting

along with Joe and not doing anything about it, don't you?'
And you know what she says? She says, she says to me, 'Of
course I don't.' Isn't that great?" As Edith talks she bends her
elbows, spreads her fingers stiffly toward Joe, and makes short,
swift, pushing gestures to emphasize her words. "Anyway, I
started thinking about how my family, and all my friends—
even Lois and Jim are getting married in June—and society—
how *everyone* has always been putting pressure on me to live
this middle-class suburban type of life. You know, be a *housewife*. But what I want to know is, what's wrong with just having
a super career? Midge thinks that what I *really* want is to take
this clinic thing and run with it. There's always going to be a
demand for abortions. Hospitals and clinics are always *crying*
for decent administrators. Midge says that if I wanted to *settle
down* and *have a family* I would be investing in a relationship
with a man who truly *wanted* that. But what I really want is
to experiment with making money and getting ahead. I want
to start that branch clinic. So the bottom line is that I *really*
didn't mean to be pressuring you about marriage after all." She
takes a deep breath, beams at him like a gawky teenager practicing friendliness, and lights a Gauloise.

Joe is thrown by her speech. He never expected to hear her
say this. But she has worked out a thorough and suitable explanation, and stated it with earnest conviction. "I don't know
what to say," Joe says.

"You're content and happy the way things are, and so am
I. You've been very happy lately, I can tell."

It's true that they made love quite vigorously last night.
Does Edith sense what he's done? Is she running twice as fast
just to keep next to him, to keep things standing still? Is she
covering up her deep disappointment in him? When they were
in the Caribbean she said to him, "When I saw you in that
hotel dining room in Greece, I said to myself, 'Edith, there is
the father of your children. I *knew*.'" How can she so quickly
shed all the hints and requests and demands and proposals she
has offered up in one way or another over the time they've
been together?

"Is something bothering you, Joe?"

"No . . . it's just—I'm just taking all this in. It's a surprise."
Maybe they can be relaxed companions after all.

"And another thing—you already really *do* have a child,
and I think we should have Todd come and stay with us as
much as possible. Especially this summer, in the country."

18

ON HER WAY TO work Monday morning, Angela becomes frightened. How can she blandly work alongside Joe as if nothing has happened? How will he treat her now? Maybe he has lost interest. She goes into a jeweler's and buys a watch set in a narrow silver cuff. At least she won't always be worrying about whether she is late. She won't have to ask people the time, or try to get glimpses of someone else's watch. There are no words, he said, and: Just give me time. All right, then.

Joe keeps checking his watch. Is Angela ever coming in? Is she ill? He is eager to see her, to exchange in a glance what would take other couples years to say to each other. "Let's have lunch, Bly." It's Goodhugh, and he is not smiling. Joe is seized by a brief sense of queasiness and panic.

When Angela does arrive, she sweeps down the corridor with her head down and her heels digging into the carpet. As she passes Joe's office she gives him an embarrassed glance and a half smile and turns into her office.

"A toasted danish and a large orange juice," she is saying into the telephone receiver when he enters. She won't look at him. She stares at the blue desk blotter. Her office smells of the fresh air she has just brought in on her clothing. "Hello," she says, her mouth turned down, as if greeting her executioner.

He thought everything was now going to be different. Edith has changed her mind about marriage; Angela has made love to him. But now Angela—if only he can catch her eyes, and ask her wordlessly if it is so. Didn't their essence collide and soar? The time they had together was so much more extraordinary than he had imagined it would be.

"I'm going to call that guy who built the car that runs on the methane from chicken shit," Angela finally says. "Does that go under breakthroughs or unusual solutions?"

"Uhh—" She still won't look at him. He wants to pick her up and turn her around and shake her so that she will remember what has happened between them. Maybe he should suggest they have lunch. But no—Goodhugh has issued an ominous invitation. Joe hears his phone ringing. "We'll talk," he mutters, backing out of her doorway.

The rest of the morning he thinks about taking the afternoon off and suggesting to her that they go to her place. On the other hand, she probably has decided he is a poor lover. And he did kick over the wineglass and stain the carpet, and rush away in a state of agitation.

"It's no good, Bly," Goodhugh says as soon as they are seated at his usual table in his club, which has dark mahogany paneling, hunting prints on the walls, a selection of used neckties in the cloakroom—Joe has to put one on in order to be allowed to penetrate further—and ancient waiters who address Goodhugh as "sir" after every utterance. *"Il ne marche pas."*

Joe feels sick. "The new format."

"It's not just the format and the design, it's everything. It's very strange and peculiar, Bly. It's not what today's upper-echelon executive wants. He wants snappy graphs and up-to-date bulletins on hard-core information that he can comprehend in a quick perusal, not bizarre maunderings about some aging company hack who decides to wear love beads and live in Malibu. What happened? You had a really tight product going. I tell you frankly and honestly, I almost stopped shipment. The people in Delaware are going to be very upset and disturbed."

"Jesus," Joe murmurs. "I just wanted to try something new."

"Well, it's new, all right. New and strange, very strange. I fully expect to be ridiculed in all the papers as soon as word gets around. What in the world caused you to do this?" Goodhugh props his chin in his hand and his elbow on the table and the crystal glasses and goblets shiver and clink.

"Has anyone else seen it? The board of directors? I gather Whorf and Brunell haven't."

"Whorf and Brunell have not seen it, nor has anyone else but me. And the poetry. You put in poetry. God, I hate Robert Frost. Whose idea was that?"

"Uh, well, Angela and I collaborated on the newsletter. She has been very good, very helpful. She's very intelligent. It is certainly not her fault if anything has gone wrong with this particular issue. It's my responsibility. Anyway, it was just an experiment." Joe has an impulse to push the table over on Goodhugh, the way it's done in the movies.

"You must understand that I still have high hopes for you, Bly. You can still be on the inside track. The newsletter is but a stepping stone for you. But you can't keep doing this sort of ahh—experimenting as you call it. This is not Woodstock, or the Weathermen of whatever—it's Starr Whorf."

"Would you be having the appetizer, sir?" asks a stooped waiter with white hair and a starched linen towel draped over his forearm.

On her lunch hour, Angela is unable to eat and instead she phones Helen. "We finally made love," she whispers. "He said it was like two sparks floating toward each other from opposite ends of the universe and finally meeting."

"He's left that woman? You said you weren't going to do anything until—"

"I know, but this is, uh, destiny, something like that. It had to happen, and it did."

"It sounds very beautiful."

"We have this terrific rapport on one level," Angela says. "And then, on another level, well, it's very scary. I feel out of control."

"That's great, though! Just a minute." Helen leaves the phone and Angela can hear dogs barking. "Tom is killing the calf today, and I had to get the dogs indoors. I get so depressed when he kills the animals, and you know, I think he enjoys it. He makes fun of me about this. But don't say anything about that if you happen to talk to him. So you think you might get married to Joe?"

"Oh, God—I would be thrilled if I got a chance to spend one night with him. But I have to get ahold of myself, because this job is also really important—it's the first job I ever really liked, that really means something to me. I don't know whether I'm coming or going, believe you me."

"My wish for you is always that you'll find the happiness I have—you know that. We both love you, Tom and I, and we really miss you."

"I feel the same about you," Angela says. "No matter what craziness I get into, I always know you're there."

When Joe returns from lunch, Angela hurries into his office, prepared to give him a surreptitious hug—enough of this strain, this distance!—but he looks so dark and so troubled, his mouth set and tight, as he slumps in his chair, that she steps aside and clenches her hands behind her back. "How was lunch? I saw you leave with Buffalo Buff."

"Uh, fine. It was o-ok-kay."

Usually he tells her what's going on with Goodhugh, what Goodhugh's latest fantasies about the newsletter are. "Any news from the stratosphere of Starr Whorf?"

He bites his mustache and shakes his head. "I've got a lot of work to do." She feels glass breaking up and down her spine. He has had her, and he hates her, and now they are forced to work together. She immediately leaves.

Back in her office she remembers him holding her and pleading. "Just give me time." She has never seen another person as moved, as affected, as Joe was only the day before yesterday. What has gone wrong? Her cubicle is too small to contain her emotions. She goes to the coffee room, forgets why she is there, returns to her desk, phones Derek Grinder and leaves a message on his answering machine, and phones Gerard.

"Things are very glum today," she says after reciting some newsletter matters to justify the call. "Evidently Joe is having problems with his private life."

"Sounds normal to me," Gerard says. "They are always sort

of on the verge of premartial divorce. Their so-called relationship is like something out of a pop psychology magazine. The only thing that will ever help Joe is for him to plunge into ecstasy, an ecstasy that will melt his shackles so that he can soar. At our fraternity when we'd have these drunken parties, everyone would be throwing bottles of rye against the wall and dancing on the mantelpiece, and Joe would just stand there off to the side in his three-piece suit holding his tankard. Afraid to live. He needs someone to light a fire under his ass."

Angela goes back into Joe's office. He is hunched over, his head bowed, his elbows on the desk blotter. "Joe!" she sings. "Joe! Stop that immediately! Get up!"

He is startled, and as he stands up, his elbow hits an ashtray and it falls to the floor. "What? What is it, Angela?"

She is smiling and snapping her fingers. "Come on, right now—let's go for a ride on the Staten Island Ferry."

He sinks down in his swivel chair. "I can't. I have so much work—" She is too strange, this woman. Frightening. Goodhugh is right. The new newsletter is a disaster, and she is the reason why.

"It can wait. Right now, let's just *go*."

"I can't," he says irritably.

Her face falls. "All right," she says, her voice cracking a little. "It's hopeless." She blinks to stop the tears and then very quickly holds her arms out like wings and flaps them. "A dance," she says brightly. "I dedicate this dance to Joe: here it is." She closes her eyes and flaps a few more times, and then stumbles back into her office ready to commit suicide. Instead, she calls Sharon.

"Have I got a problem," Sharon begins. "I ran into Clifford on the street today, right in front of the office, and he looked at me as if he'd never seen me in his life and when I said 'Clifford' he just kept staring and walking along."

"Don't cry," Angela says. "Sharon, listen—we can't let men rule our lives." She twists her new watch on her wrist; it's uncomfortably tight, and the second hand moves so quickly it makes her eyes hurt.

That afternoon goes very slowly and painfully. She hears Joe snap his briefcase shut and walk with quick steps down the corridor, and she sits feeling that her insides have been removed and buried in some remote desert. She has failed. She has failed in her aim to be poised, aloof, and low-voiced, she has failed to be the opposite of Edith, all her hard work has come to nothing.

19

ANGELA MEETS KATHA AT the martial-arts studio, where she is just finishing up a class in t'ai chi. As Angela watches the students imitating Katha, carving the air with generous arcs of their arms and low, wide steps, she feels soothed. Afterward, the students noiselessly move to the foyer, where their shoes are neatly lined up in rows.

"I had a bad day," Angela says, and then feels terrible for throwing mud on the white walls of this serene hall, which has a bare, dark polished wood floor and nothing else. "I have this fantastic job and I'm screwing up."

"I am sure you are doing things just as you should," Katha says. "Before we go to the movie, I have to clean the floor. I hope you don't mind the wait."

"No, no—let me help." The floor seems perfectly clean to Angela, but she helps Katha sweep it and mop it. When they are about halfway finished, Angela wants to take a break. Her head is choked with thoughts about Joe, the job, the endless difficulties of all of it. But Katha continues rhythmically mopping, concentrating only on the mop and the floor, and Angela finds herself doing the same. When she finishes, Katha stands motionless in the center of the room, her hands limp at her sides, her breath slow and even. Angela joins her.

As they wait in line to see a film starring Zatoichi, the Blind Swordsman ("He Don't Need No Dog!" declares a poster near the cashier's booth), Angela wants to tell Katha all her troubles, but instead she says, "You seem to know how to work. I mean, you don't work like I do, like other people do. Did you know that?"

"I try always to keep all my attention on what I'm doing, and to step quietly, and not make unnecessary noise," Katha says. "If I talk, then I can't keep all my attention on my work. Or if I am worrying or making plans or remembering something. So I gently bring my attention back to what I am doing now. Because someday, I won't be here, I won't be able to do what I do."

In the film, Zatoichi masquerades as a shabby, clumsy masseur until the wicked leader of the gang that has control of the village tries to cheat the blind swordsman at gambling. With one swipe, faster than eyes can follow, Zatoichi cuts both dice in half in mid-air, and later on, when he is thoroughly fed up with the bad guys, he kills a dozen of them and slices an ox cart in half.

Mornings, as soon as Angela wakes up, she reluctantly clamps on the wristwatch. She becomes aware of how much of the day passes without her having any sense of where it goes or what she has done. It is 9:32 and then suddenly it's noon. She does not like being manacled to time like this, but it makes her feel more responsible, more like she belongs at Starr Whorf.

Goodhugh comes into her office at 11:03 and puts his arm around her shoulder. "My dear, you are *formidable*. I just talked to Bly. I've been getting lots of calls about the newsletter—this new issue—and the *Wall Street Journal* wants to write it up. I am pleased and amazed."

"Gosh, I'm delighted," Angela says. Since she has decided to devote herself to a life of chastity and career, she is glad Goodhugh is pleased with her contributions. Let Joe treat her coolly, let him reject all her new ideas without even hearing them out. There are other newsletters. There are other divisions of Starr Whorf.

"Bly," Goodhugh calls across the corridor. "I'll see you and Angela at eleven-thirty in the conference room."

Angela has never been to a meeting of the board of directors. She keeps asking herself what she is doing at this one. If only she hadn't worn jeans today. Matters are discussed by men who look alike and whose names she can never remember. Matters of corporate interest. She observes the sweep hand of her wristwatch. So this is what happens—people trade their time, which is priceless, for money. She glances at Joe and sees that he is looking at her. He quickly drops his gaze. She watches his chest rise and fall. Okay, she will give him time.

She hears Goodhugh speaking now. He is talking about the executives' newsletter. An increase in subscription rates is highly recommended . . . renewal rate is eighty-six percent, remarkably and phenomenally high . . . the new format has attracted a great deal of favorable attention. "And in addition, Miss Angela Lee, who is with us today, will become part and parcel a member of the management team, effective June one."

"Why, I'll be," Angela says. "Thank you a whole lot, thank you very much. Thanks, really."

The men around the conference table nod their congratulations. Joe beams at her.

"Thanks again," she says.

"To my knowledge, you are the first female ever," Tor Bracewell says. He is blond, rotund, and has a rose-colored nose and fingernails as clean as a surgeon's.

"Wow," Angela says. Then she makes a mental note to stop saying wow.

She waits while the others file out so that she can walk down the corridor with Joe. She catches his elbow and he kisses her on the top of her head. "I knew it was going to be good," he says. "I told Goodhugh how much you've done for the newsletter."

She is happier to get his kiss than to be appointed to the management team, but she says, "Management team? What does that mean? What the hell kind of deal is it?"

"I think it means that on the corporate roster you'll be listed as a manager," Joe says. "And you probably get a raise. The phone company was just forced by a federal mandate to put more women into management, and so I think Starr Whorf is worried that they'll be slapped with something like that."

When they reach his office door she comes inside with him. "I have something for you." She reaches into her jeans pocket and casts three translucent golden shells, a tiny crab claw, and a piece of green sea glass on his desk. She leans close, her lips nearly touching his, and then quickly steps back.

"How nice," he says.

"I went to this friend's beach house. I've been meaning to give you these. And you know what, last night I had this dream that you were at the beach, except walking along under seven feet of green water, on the bottom of the sea, and I was walking along on the sand next to you asking you didn't you want to come out of the water, wasn't it hard to walk with the water covering your head, and you kept saying no, no, it was just fine. And I—"

Joe looks guilty and stricken as she is speaking. "Uh, hi, Buff." His face reddens.

Angela turns to find Goodhugh leaning against the door-frame looking amused. "Well, *I* dreamed that they were cutting up Moby Dick with flensing knives," he says. "And I don't see *my* analyst until four-thirty."

"Listen, Buffalo Buff, thank you for the promotion and all," Angela says. "That was a real surprise."

"Angela, I am quite certain that you will prosper and flourish here, and I want to do everything I can to bring that about. I am a lover of merit and I give preferment to the able."

"What do I have to do now that I'm on the management team?"

"Attend the weekly meetings. Did I tell you about the raise?"

"Joe mentioned that."

"And I think I can get that budget increase, Joe."

"You are a regular Mister Wonderful," Angela says.

After Goodhugh leaves, Joe murmurs, "I don't trust him. Something is up."

"Joe! How can you be that way? Now Buff is really going to bat for us."

Joe sits down and picks up a pencil. "There's so much work."

"I missed you. Let's have a drink after work."

"I can't—I have too much to do." He's pleased to see her face fall. So he still has a little power over her. Does she think he is a good lover?

"I'll work too."

Joe picks up a folder labeled "Alternative Energy Solutions."

Angela wonders what to do. A few days ago she and Joe were lying naked together; now it seems that it never happened. There is nothing in Joe's manner that betrays any recollection of their lovemaking.

Helen phones Angela from New Mexico. "When are you coming for a visit?"

"I won't have any more vacation time probably until August," Angela says. "What's new?"

"The boys have the chicken pox," Helen says. "I'm driving into town once a week and taking a belly-dancing class but don't tell Tom."

"Why not?"

"He doesn't approve of things like that. He's half Italian, remember. So when he's at home I don't go. Are you still in love?"

"Yes, but it's on hold."

"I wish I had the kind of job I could throw myself into like you're doing," Sharon says. She is lying on Angela's couch eating yogurt. "I'm super-depressed."

Angela is sitting on the carpet with piles of papers and clippings she is arranging into various folders labeled "New Ideas," "Brainstorms," "Miscellaneous," and "Garbage." "What are you depressed about?"

"Ah, I don't know. There's this new reporter. Samuel Beaufort James. One of those hotshot investigative types. He's really gorgeous—used to play football or something in college. Anyway, he asked me out."

"That sounds fantastic, Sharon."

"So, I'll go out with him. Big deal."

"But you just said he was gorgeous. Is he mean or something?"

"No, he's Southern, a real gentleman, opens doors for you and stuff. It's not that."

"Is he dumb?"

"Brilliant."

"I give up, then. What's the problem?"

"We'll go out and have a good time, and then I'll have him back to my place and ta-ta-ta-ta-ta-ta and then the next morning we'll get up, and then he'll leave."

"Yeah, right." Angela is now feeling low. "Joe—"

"And by then I'll be crazy about him, only he'll think I'm a drag because I'm depressed."

"Sounds hopeless," Angela says.

"Oh, not really," Sharon says. "He's really a terrific guy."

"Good—anyway you'll have fun."

"I doubt it." Sharon finishes the container of yogurt and sets it on the carpet and does leg lifts. "Anyway, I have to get my stomach flat by tomorrow night. You know Lynn?"

"What's the latest?"

"You saw her article on wife-beating? No? Well, she and Hoyt *broke up!* Hoyt's wife got out of the funny farm and Hoyt actually went back to her. Can you believe it?"

"Oh, no." Of course Angela doesn't know Lynn and Hoyt, but she wants all men to leave the women they are obliged to be with and go to the women they truly love. The sheer force of statistics will move Joe away from Edith.

Sharon has rented one-sixth of a house in Westhampton for every other weekend until Labor Day. "You're invited any time, Angela. There are probably going to be lots of guys around. Maybe even some who are straight."

"I don't want lots of guys."

"Yeah, I know. You want Mister Right But Emotionally Disturbed. But listen, Angela, you deserve better. He's not giving you anything. Ron Nussbaum still calls me up to talk about you, and Derek Grinder, *by the way,* was at Hill's the other day and he was asking me about you. He said, 'Angela Lee is unique. There's something of Everywoman about her.' I thought you'd like that. What does he mean?"

"I only want Joe." Angela finishes filing the papers and stacks the folders and puts them in her briefcase. "Imagine me with a real briefcase."

"And a promotion, don't forget. That probably scared the shit out of Joe."

"No, he said he was glad about it. He wants to cut down his workload and just come in a few days a week, so he's glad I'm now officially the co-director."

"And what's he doing with his spare time?"

"Uh, he wants to figure out what he really wants to do. Yeah—I know it sounds trite, but he's never really had the chance. He's always worked, except when he was in Greece for a while, and he's just always been under a lot of pressure and afraid to slow down."

"Right, but what, physically, is he actually going to be doing?"

Angela tightens her mouth and raises her eyebrows. She has told Sharon that Joe is the most intelligent, the most talented, the handsomest, the most imaginative man she has ever met, and the best lover, but she can't bring herself to say that what Joe said he wants is to learn to juggle.

Katha comes upstairs with a tray crowded with plates of stuffed grape leaves, tomatoes, and feta, and a thought for Angela.

"When you turn your back on Joe, you will gain power over your life."

"Enough power to attract Joe?"

"For once I agree with Katha," Sharon says.

The three women watch *Spellbound* on television. Ingrid Bergman's and Gregory Peck's gazes lock the moment they meet at the mental hospital. Their first kiss is accompanied by images of doors opening one after another in tunneling sequences. "It's not love," Bergman says. "I'm your doctor." Sharon applauds.

When Peck seems completely insane, a razor murderer perhaps, Chekov, the venerable, bearded psychoanalyst, tells Bergman, "We are speaking of a schizophrenic, not a valentine. . . . The mind of a woman in love is operating at the lowest level of intellect."

"Hear, hear," Sharon says.

"The mind isn't everything," Bergman replies. "What about the heart?" Angela grows very sad all of a sudden.

"Even to a woman in love," says Chekov, "this situation must seem unreasonable."

* * *

Joe makes dinner while watching *Spellbound*. Ingrid Bergman wears the same earnest, worried expression he sometimes sees in Angela's eyes. He cuts up a head of lettuce into little strips and puts it in a bowl with some mayonnaise. He puts spaghetti in a pot of boiling water and then sits down at the dining table in front of the television. Bergman senses that Peck is an imposter, that there's something deeply wrong with him. His signature doesn't match that of the person he's supposed to be.

Gerard arrives with a white stoppered jug with Chinese writing on the label. "Mao-tai," Gerard says. "It's a Chinese liquor that will take the top of your head off. All the sages drink it. Where is the charming Ms. Edith?" He makes the *s* in "Ms." buzz.

"It's a stag evening," Joe says. "She has classes tonight."

"When the mouse is away, the bees will dance."

They go to the kitchen. "I've got to find out who I am!" Peck tells Bergman.

"I've got to find out who *I* am," Gerard says. He uncorks the mao-tai and puts the bottle to his lips and tilts his head back. Then he slowly puts the bottle on the table, opens his mouth, and screams.

"Are you all right?"

Gerard nods, his eyes watering, and his face turning crimson.

"You sounded like James Brown."

"Wonderful stuff," Gerard says, coughing. "Try it."

Joe picks up the bottle and takes a pull. It's like drinking liquid nitrogen. His lungs, his spine, his heart, and his brain are instantly laced with burning neon. He coughs.

"I see you've fallen victim to color TV."

"Yeah, Edith got it. It's actually rather nice."

"All those years we memorized Latin poems—remember 'Integer Vitae'?—and we were such geniuses. Now you're a capitalist lackey glued to the tube and I'm an unemployed English teacher doing hack editing and avoiding writing. And we're starting to lose our hair. And getting fat. What happened?"

Joe drains the water from the spaghetti, which is stuck

together like rods of Venetian glass. "Anyway, I've stopped smoking."

"Have you ever considered Esalen?" Gerard asks.

After dinner, Joe makes zabaglione from a recipe in an Italian cookbook. It's the first time. It comes out perfectly—white and foamy and sweet. Angela would like it. She likes good food and eats with total concentration.

They sit at the table and Gerard rolls a joint. They smoke, and pass the bottle of mao-tai back and forth.

Gerard reminisces about school plays—he once was Brutus in *Julius Caesar*. He drinks some more mao-tai, gags, sucks in air, and breaks out in a sweat. "And do you remember *La Belle Dame Sans Merci?*"

Joe closes his eyes and nods. He is not interested in remembering the headmaster's wife. His eyes feel like a pair of hot jellyfish floating in the abyssal depths. His hair falls across his forehead. When Joe was twelve, the headmaster tried to seduce him. He took Joe into his office one night and started caressing him. Joe froze. He did not know what to do, since Branscombe and his wife had always been extremely kind to him. During school holidays when the other boys went home to their families, the Branscombes always took Joe to dinner at a nearby inn. Gerard walked into Branscombe's office that night and then walked right back out again. Joe was in terror for weeks that Gerard would tell everyone in the school, but he never did.

"How do you think things are going at the newsletter?" Joe asks. "Do you think you and Angela can manage when I start coming in part-time?"

"Of course. It's about time you were unemployed. You know, dear boy, I do believe that when we were still in prep school you were already the harried editor of the lit magazine. And then at college, you were the harried editor of the lit magazine *and* the paper, and then at the university press you were the harried assistant director. At some point, it would seem, one sort of ought to start *living*. You certainly don't want to become another Goodhugh."

"Do you think we're alike?" Joe has sometimes felt an uneasy kinship with Goodhugh, and is horrified at the possibility that he, too, could harden into a charming, platitudinous creature who is dead inside.

"You're definitely his fair-haired boy. At the moment. But if you get too good, he may turn on you."

Joe nods. He knows what Gerard means. He has seen Goodhugh's bitter edginess creep out on occasion.

"Remember what an exciting, daring rakehell Goodhugh was? And how he'd come back on alumni day with some astoundingly beautiful woman? And those legends about his gambling? Now he's such a stuffed shirt. Did you ever meet Adele Weintraub? She's a friend of Elizabeth's. Adele and Buff were a hot item for a few years and then he suddenly married, uh—"

"Cabot Aldrich—Botsy." Joe has met her. She is a long-faced blond with big teeth and a strong handshake. Sometimes he sees her picture on the society page in the act of planning a charity ball.

"Anyway, he never called Adele again, never told her he had gotten married. I don't understand that."

"I believe Botsy was pregnant—at any rate, they had a baby last year."

"There's no reason to resign yourself to someone you don't have passion for!" Gerard smacks the table. "When I met Elizabeth and left my wife, and Elizabeth left her husband, I realized that passion has its own laws, and once you know what passion is, a lot of other things no longer matter." Gerard takes another drink.

Joe takes another drink, too. He's far enough along now that the liquor no longer makes him shudder. "What do you make of Angela?" he asks, as if inquiring after some distant acquaintance.

"A bit of an odd bird, don't you think? She seems willing to work even more than you do, if that can be believed."

"She seems pretty—I don't know—fairly free about things."

"I don't know about that. I think she wants to be grounded. There's a great deal more going on with her than you'd think. She may be your star career woman, but she also has a maternal streak she is very poor at concealing."

"Really?" How is it Gerard is so familiar with Angela?

"I suppose most women do," Gerard goes on. "Angela has a nice ass—have you ever noticed?"

"Indeed I have," Joe says.

"Lucky Derek Grinder," Gerard adds.

Edith comes in, calls out a cheery hello, and then detects that both men are stoned and drunk. There are dirty dishes and pans on the dining table and on the counters and the stove. "God," she says. "I'm going to bed." Doors slam in succession, first the bathroom, then the bedroom.

"She's been working hard," Joe says.

After Gerard leaves, Joe is exhausted, and he feels terrible, but he can't fall asleep. There is so much he does not want to allow himself to think about. He presses his knuckles against his brow ridge in the dark and reviews all the loose ends he has to take care of before his part-time schedule begins.

20

ANGELA GOES WITH KATHA to see Part I and Part II of the Samurai Trilogy, starring Toshiro Mifune as Musashi Miyamoto, the greatest swordsman of medieval Japan. In samurai movies there are always many rules, and everyone knows the rules, the allegiances, the debts of honor. When the hero goes against the rules he suffers. Toshiro must learn to polish his sword and his soul. In the little smoke-filled shabby Broadway theater, with its torn dirty carpeting and keen-eyed martial-arts practitioners, blacks and Japanese, Angela thinks of Joe. She is giving him time—it's been nearly a week since they made love. A few times, working late, he has kissed her. In his office, in the elevator, in dark doorways on side streets walking her to the subway station. "Whenever I kiss you it affects me very strongly," he said. "It's very hard for me to turn away and say good-bye." It's very hard for Musashi Miyamoto to turn away from the sweet orphan girl who loves him purely and thoroughly and go away to Edo to become a great samurai. She promises to wait for him, and for years she stands by a bridge where they were to meet, running up to anyone who resembles him. But he doesn't come.

The next morning Angela enters Joe's office, her step so rapid and heavy he thinks it must be someone else.

"I have made a decision." There is a vertical line between her eyebrows he hadn't noticed before, and lines from the corners of her nostrils to the corners of her mouth. Her voice is deeper than usual. She is so serious and determined that she must be trying to keep a straight face in order to tell a new Polish joke.

He smiles at her.

"I've made a decision and it's *no*."

He gives her a long, languid gaze, remembering her arched back on the orange bed. He smiles again because he suddenly remembers, and he knows she remembers, and it's funny that she is saying no.

"No... I *think*." She picks up a Rand study on precious metals resources and throws it at the wall. "Oh, forget it!" She starts laughing, and he laughs too.

She heads for the door. She has defeated her own mission. She stops. "No," she says, turning to him. "Not now, not ever. This is the first good job I ever had, and today I wanted to pack up and leave—"

"No!" He is alarmed. His worst fear is that he will come in some morning and her desk will be cleared and she will be gone.

"But if we don't stop this, we aren't even going to be friends."

He picks up a bag of sunflower seeds and tears it open, spilling the seeds.

"I don't need all this teasing and bullshit. That's not romance." Her vehemence surprises her. "Why should I take it on? You're not easy, you know."

"All right." His stomach heaves. He wants a cigarette. Why does she do this to him? No one can upset him as quickly as she can.

"So let's figure out a way we can work together and be friends."

"Friends?" The word falls from his mouth like a crowbar hitting a sidewalk.

"Yeah." She leaves so abruptly he can feel a little puff of air from the doorway. She always leaves in the middle of their arguments and it makes him furious.

Half an hour later, while he's on the phone, she brings in a bouquet of peonies and leaves them on his desk.

Another Friday, another bar. Joe orders two draft beers and Angela goes to the rest room. Scratched on the toilet-paper holder in the stall is "I love you." Angela feels a bond with the woman who wrote those words, who probably couldn't say them to the man out at the table.

"The past few weeks things have been very good between me and Edith. It's as though the previous problems never happened. She was always insecure and possessive, but now she's been working on that and things have changed. She doesn't want to get married. She doesn't want to have a baby."

And you believe her? But Angela keeps silent.

"I feel content and happy now. We had some sessions of couples therapy and that helped. We've put a lot of work in on this relationship, and now things are beginning to shake loose." He is thinking of a recent late-night talk in which Edith told him how valuable his trust in her was, how it kept her going.

"How so?" Angela keeps her exterior as cool and as smooth as beer foam. Conversation with a business colleague. Nothing more.

"Well, I've always held back. I've never admitted my dependence on her—I've been wary of commitment. So we're going to experiment by putting our money into a joint account. Until recently I've basically been supporting her. Now she's making more. When I start working part-time I'll be taking a cut in pay, and she'll be supporting me." He smiles. It is all so adult, so reasonable. You figure out what each person wants and arrive at a balanced equation. Angela must understand the good sense of this. Her eyes are very large.

She is thinking how troubled he looks, how confused. He makes "commitment" sound like the road to dusty death. "Shoot, I could never have a joint checking account again. That was one of the best things about getting divorced—for the first time

I didn't have to ask anyone else about spending money I'd earned. I'll never give that up."

Midge would wonder whether Angela has a fear of dependency. Joe is pleased to know something about her that she doesn't know.

"I can't have a domestic life right now," Angela is saying. She is still working on being the opposite of Edith. "I need my freedom, my independence."

"When I cut down on my work hours, you and I can have more time together. With Edith, I feel secure. But with you, it's—"

"Yes?"

"Adventure." He reaches for her hand. "With you, I feel fully present—it's like electricity." He suddenly wants her more than he can safely let himself know in one moment. "I haven't allowed myself to deal with how enjoyable it was with you last Saturday. I—I've tried not to think about how g-good it was." He gazes into her eyes, and she lowers her lids.

She doesn't want to play the staring game. She doesn't want to go on with this. He is secure with Edith. Let him have her. Let them work like dogs on their difficult relationship. Anyway, she hates the word *relationship*. And all the work in the world can't make something out of nothing. She looks at him and opens her mouth. "Uh—"

He forgets everything, forgets where they are, that anything else ever existed. All he wants is to be with her without interruption inside this sealed, perfect sphere of their joined gazes. Her face is small, her chin is pointed, medieval, her hair is a golden cloud.

"I can't forget about Saturday either." The corners of her mouth turn down. She's going to cry. It astonishes him to see her shattered in an instant, completely wide open.

She makes herself get up from the table and pick up her briefcase and go past the faceless bartender standing under the rack of empty inverted wineglasses. She blinks on the sidewalk. An orange sun rests uneasily at the end of the street. People hurry past.

Just as she is getting into a cab going uptown, Joe slides in next to her.

They lie on her bed in the rose-colored twilight, and make

love, and drink wine, and make love again. As he dresses she lies still, and when he goes to the door, she follows him, her hair falling over her breasts and touching the curve of her ribs. All he can say is "Please."

After he leaves, she dozes. She dreams she is on a runway trying to guide a plane in with a radio transmitter. She has a sense of imminent catastrophe. The transmitter won't work. She tries to make it work but it won't. She is hit by a falling plane tire and then her atoms blend with it. A man in a crowd that has gathered says, "Honey, don't try to work that thing any longer—you're going to die." To the end, she keeps trying to communicate through the broken transmitter. Finally the tire melts into the runway.

21

———————•———————

"HOW DO YOU KNOW you don't love Edith?" Midge asks. She has just been comparing his relinquishing of his son with his wish to leave Edith.

Joe can't take his eyes away from Midge's wide wedding band, which is well displayed as she idly turns her Gauloise-holding hand. The sky framed by her windows is sulfur yellow. The air-conditioner hums and gurgles. He can make out the sound of bongos coming from Central Park. They are the beat of his insomnia, playing as they do all night in Washington Square when he gets up and walks. He makes a fist and taps the knuckles against his upper lip.

"I don't feel the way about Edith that I do about Angela. If I loved Edith—I mean, I must, in some way or I wouldn't have stayed with her. But why would I keep wanting Angela?"

"That's what we are trying to understand. I wonder if you are afraid of your love for Edith, afraid of getting close, afraid of knowing her and being dependent on her, and so you want to run away to this, this mythological creature, Angela."

Joe has failed to convey to Midge how Angela touches him,

aligns herself with him, becomes a magnet for him. "That doesn't feel right to me."

"We call that resistance. We can also look at this another way. I wonder whether your attraction to Angela is actually your acted-out interest in *me*."

"That really doesn't feel right. I met Angela before I met you." Acted-out interest? Isn't all of life "acting out"?

"Resistance, resistance, resistance."

A comical picture comes to Joe of himself in a beret smoking a Gauloise and speaking in a Charles Boyer accent about zee Ray-zees-tahnce. He smiles.

"So you agree with me."

Joe glances at his watch. Four more minutes. Midge's wedding band seems so final. He imagines it as a gigantic cylindrical trap. He takes a deep breath and physical pain scrapes his heart. "I want out. I don't know what to do." His throat constricts and he is suddenly close to crying.

"That's all for today," Midge says.

As soon as he passes out of her building and leaves the shade of its canopy, he forgets what he was just feeling. The air smells of hot tar and warm garbage. Angela's place is only a few blocks away. He finds a phone booth and calls her. No answer. Her absence suddenly becomes indifference. How can she not be there? It's a Saturday morning. She says she cares. How does he know he does not love Edith? Is he thoughtlessly abandoning someone dear to him? Someone who is considerate of his needs, who doesn't run screaming from his bad moods? It's just as well Angela does not answer—he promised Edith he would meet her at the loft at two because she said she has something very important to show him, and she's taking the afternoon off just for that.

The house, on a slope above a near-stagnant brook, is almost hidden by old oaks and maples and dense undergrowth. The porch roof sags under the weight of thick, twisted bittersweet vines.

"Well?" Edith pulls into the circular gravel drive, turns off the ignition, and grins. "How do you like it?"

"What's the story?" This is the second surprise of the day. The first was the new Japanese car. Edith purchased it practically at cost from her uncle, who has a dealership in New Jersey.

She grasps his hand. "Please look around, give me your honest appraisal, then I'll tell you."

The place needs reshingling, a new roof, perhaps a new porch, and the interior, which has eight rooms that open with light and air into one another and a winding staircase, must be rescued from its shabby 1950s dreariness and restored to its original 1850s clarity. He is instantly taken. His hands know just what to do here. He raps on walls, notes the jury-rigged, antique electrical wiring, opens and closes the fireplace damper, examines the beams for termite damage, checks the oil furnace in the basement, and decides that the dining-room paneling must be American chestnut—very rare. "This place is basically very sound," he says.

"I knew you'd love it! I knew it!" She gives him a hug. She has the happy vigor of an expedition leader who, after long, secretive planning—nights awake doing mental calculations, days alert to the needs of the bearers—has at last arrived at the precise destination.

"This is the place you're thinking of renting for the summer?"

"No, no. We *own* it! That's the surprise. I took out a mortgage on it. For the down payment, I used only a thousand dollars from our joint account, and the rest I took from my savings. The bank was just great about everything, very impressed by my shareholding status in the clinic—the loan officer said there was no doubt at all that I'm rising in a rapidly growing field—and you won't believe what a super-bargain this place is, especially when you think about what a fancy-schmancy area this is." She goes on to explain mortgage terms, percentages, balloon payments, and quit-claims.

"The trees are getting crowded." He gazes at the forest beyond the scruffy lawn. "The underbrush needs thinning."

"Three acres," she says, clapping her hands. "And the property next to ours is also all forested—it's part of an estate. The values here are only going to go up. So we fix the place up and then we don't like it—so what? We can sell it and make a fabulous profit. So now you don't have to mope around in the city after you go on part-time schedule—isn't that great?"

"I have to think about all this—it's very sudden."

She looks into his eyes, her own eyes dark and sharply focused, her mouth tight. "Please—please let me do this for you."

It is very difficult for Joe to get himself to Angela's place. The sight of those slate steps makes him wince every time. The invisible pianist who toils away afternoons and evenings across the backyards of the brownstones is now working on the middle movements of the piano concerto. Joe never has paid much attention to classical music, but now Mozart seems very erotic to him. He lies on his stomach on Angela's bedroom rug listening to the silvery, sweet notes as she massages him with turtle oil and then walks lightly on his back, kneading his muscles with her long, supple feet. She tells him about a movie she has just seen about a beautiful blind Yakuza swordswoman, the Crimson Bat.

Finally he forces himself to check his watch, and he rouses himself. "I'd better go now."

She puts on a new kimono, orange with blue flowers, and crouches and whirls, wielding an imaginary sword. "Hooaauuu!" she cries with ferocity.

He laughs. It is very difficult for him to leave. He could float here forever. "I'm still not together enough to do this very often."

"I know." Her expression becomes soft and sympathetic.

"It's a patchwork life. It's so strange." He thinks of Edith. How does he know he does not love her? What does Midge know that Joe does not about the way his own mind works? He overheard Edith the other day speaking on the phone in her soothing, good-cup-of-coffee voice to a friend from her women's group about how an abortion was really a very safe and simple procedure, and he was struck by her humanity and patience. And the house—what a generous gift. Exactly what suits him—not her. Grass and trees give her hay fever, and she prefers sleek, modern, finished architecture. No, the house is the result of her careful thoughtfulness. Who else would dream of going to all that trouble? She is a worthwhile person, not someone to just be discarded—Midge is right about that. Without Edith, he might just shatter into all his separate pieces.

He is grateful to Edith for holding things together, for putting up with his dour moods, for understanding his fears, his restlessness, for keeping things going, for reeling in the future with certainty and care. She wants him to see more of Todd, for instance; she wants one bedroom in the house to be fixed up just for Todd when he visits. He looks down at Angela's upturned face, her eyes closed; she is waiting for him. Angela would like the house in the forest very much. He suddenly feels sick and afraid. "This weekend," he begins, then stops.

Angela's eyes open wide and she smiles. "Yes?" She has been wanting to take him to a samurai movie; at last he'll be free to come with her.

"Oh, I was just going to mention that I'm going to the country, to Connecticut."

"Oh."

"There's a h-house. It's an incredible bargain, actually, because it needs a lot of fixing up. It used to be a farmhouse. I'm really looking forward to working on it."

Edith is obviously involved in this. There will be no invitations.

He would like to tell Angela about the graceful rooms, and the beautiful old hardwoods—the straight-grained fir flooring, the chestnut paneling, the solid red mahogany banister he found under several coats of green paint. The big fireplace with its golden-oak mantelpiece. And he would like to tell her how he's going to do the wiring himself, and the carpentry, and clear the fallen trees out of the brook, and tend the forest. She would like to hear about all these things, but he can see from her face that he has blundered into a dangerous intersection.

"I'll be pretty busy myself, weekends," she says, hoping he will assume she's seeing another man. "And you know," she goes on, wishing she would not, "I keep thinking that I had better quit Starr Whorf, quit the newsletter. All this is getting too complicated. We'd better stop seeing each other completely."

"No, *no*." Now he feels really afraid. "If anyone quits, it will be me. You stay. Stay with the newsletter. No."

He leaves in confusion. First she says she wants only to be with him, but then she implies that she sees others. Grinder always seems to be lurking around, and he sometimes hears

her giggling to him on the phone in the office. Then she tells
Joe eventually they will be together, that she has this deep
intuition about it, and now she announces that they should
never see each other again.

"They've bought a house!" Angela tells Helen. "How can we
be so close, and then he goes and does that? How can he be
leaving her if they're buying a house?"

"When are you coming out?" Helen asks. "I think you'd
better come and stay with me. The chiles I planted are flowering
now—in August you can be eating green chile enchiladas with
us. You need to get him out of your system. He's not good
for you. Although I think I dreamed about him. You were with
this man. He was dark and he looked very troubled, and he
went down to this lake, and I followed him, and comforted
him until this light broke out of his body."

Sharon appears wearing a new brown linen suit and she has
a new bowl-shaped haircut with stylish platinum streaks. "Let's
go out and celebrate at a Mexican restaurant," she says. "I got
the raise!" For the past few months, Sharon has been trying to
get a raise but she has been so pessimistic that Angela thought
that the subject had joined Clifford on the forbidden-topics list.
But now Sharon is beaming.

Over guacamole, Sharon talks about Sam, the investigative
reporter. "I actually think he's interested. We've gone out *five*
times."

"Single?"

"Separated."

"Good." Angela tells Sharon about Joe and Edith and the
house.

"You want to know my advice? Just lie low. When he gets
away from that job, and she'll be the breadwinner, what happens to his famous virility? He'll seek you out, believe me.
Especially if you can make him feel guilty."

"I wonder how they can be buying a house when Joe is
cutting down on his job."

"She now owns a piece of the clinic. I hear from Lynn that
Trudy says Edith has generally taken over the place and the
director doesn't even come in very much."

"How can he like her and like me at the same time?"

"Maybe he only likes one of you. Oh, Angela, don't look so down. You have a wonderful exciting career going, you're attractive, single, smart. New York is a wonderful place to be."

Joe cleans out the house and sets up a woodworking shop in the basement. There is so much to do here, and he can see just what to do and how to do it. The wiring, for instance. He did some of the electrical work on the house he and Lucy had, and he's always wanted to know more about that. He reads how-to books on the subject. The insulation—that's easy. The re-shingling—it will be easier to hire someone, a team, to do that. He and Edith talk about the house all the time now, sometimes lying awake late at night in the city. She takes such pleasure in seeing how much he enjoys her gift—and he likes seeing that side of her. Between setting up the branch clinic and studying for her final exams, Edith does not have much time to come up. Joe doesn't mind being alone here. Lately he's found he's no longer afraid to fall asleep alone.

As he works, his mind often drifts to Angela, and he asks himself, with some indignation, why he can't live simultaneously in two worlds. What's wrong with that? Amphibians live happily in water and in air. The problem is, really, the office. Angela and Gerard, whatever it is between them. Well, let them have the goddamned newsletter; it's out of his hands now anyway, it's gone out of control. At the last meeting the three of them held, she suggested they give each subscriber a singing telegram to celebrate the anniversary of the newsletter, and she half-seriously offered to do the singing herself. Let them make it as crazy and subversive as they like. And Good-hugh can go to hell.

He squeezes a plastic bottle of white glue and dribbles it along the back of the peeling wainscoting in the foyer, stepping carefully over the ruby-glass chandelier which Edith bought at an antiques auction and which rests on a piece of foam rubber on the floor. Edith wants to put the chandelier up in the dining room right away, but Joe wants to run wiring through the gas pipes that end in a jet over the dining table, and that will take time. If Angela was really burning to be with him, she would

tell him so. She would tell him to leave Edith instead of pretending Edith does not exist.

He runs out of glue before the job is finished. The village
is only a fifteen-minute walk away if he cuts through the woods
adjoining the property. Striding through the dark green humid
shade, he whistles "Who Do You Love?" At the hardware store
he remembers that he also needs a couple of household fire
extinguishers, a smoke alarm, a pair of wirecutters, a whet-
stone, a bow saw so that he can go to work on the fallen trees,
a maul for splitting firewood, and a ten-pound bag of charcoal
for the barbecue. "That's some load you got," Dan says. He
is a big man with a black spade beard, a ponytail, and Oshkosh
overalls who works behind the counter. "Your car out front?"

"No—Edith is in the city until tomorrow evening," Joe says.
"I came up on the train." He and Dan have gotten to be friends
because Joe comes to the hardware store so often. It turns out
that they went to the same college, and although Dan is three
years younger than Joe, and a dropout, he knew about Joe
because of the college paper. Now Dan has a small farm outside
town with two Jersey cows and a dozen chickens, and he talks
in a rural sort of way.

"I could run this shit by your place after I get off work,"
Dan says.

"No, no thanks—it's okay. I need some of this stuff right
now. I can carry it. It's not too far."

"Tell you what. Borrow my motorcycle. It's right out back.
I've got my truck in town today, so I won't be needing the
bike. You can bring it back tomorrow."

"You're sure?"

"Hell, yes, you son-of-a-bitch! Take it!"

It's an old, battered Harley-Davidson, and Joe doesn't like
Harleys, but he straps the bags to the carrier rack, climbs on,
and kicks the starter down with his boot heel. The motorcycle
shudders awake between his legs and roars like a bull, and as
Joe makes a circle in the dusty, weedy yard, he feels the old
joy, forgotten since Greece, return. He takes the long way
home, and on a straight road that divides two fields he opens
up until the bike reaches its top speed—only about sixty. Never
mind. At that speed the still summer air becomes a cool, brisk

wind, sweet and exhilarating, and the low hills drop from beneath the wheels as if he were flying.

The next morning he wakes up ready to return the Harley. As he makes coffee, he decides to buy a new BMW motorcycle and keep it here in the country; he didn't know that's what he's missed so much. What if Edith doesn't like it? She never liked the old one, and kept after him until it was easier to sell it than to hear her talk about how expensive it was to garage and how dangerous it was. In case she objects, he has a solution. He will buy the neighboring forest tract—according to Dan, it's for sale. He could then build a little cabin with a lean-to on the side and store firewood and the BMW there. He could go there whenever he wanted solitude. Get some kerosene lamps, make a table, a chair, a bed.

His breath catches and he imagines, oblivious to the fact that he is brushing his teeth, living in the cabin instead of with Edith. He has never had his own place. It will be all his, he will make everything. Angela might come to him then. He will build the bed with four cedar posts, which he will carve. When he tells her about it, she will sit up in bed, straighten her back, tilt her head to one side, and gaze down into invisible depths the way she usually does when they leave words behind, when his essence and hers touch like two rivers braiding together. He spits and bares his teeth at the mirror and is taken aback by how bad they look, brown and twisted. One of these days he ought to do something—probably his Starr Whorf medical insurance would cover getting them fixed. Then he would re-semble Derek Grinder, at least in the mouth.

Holding all these resonant possibilities in his mind as if they were hollow, shiny spheres, he goes outside to the circular drive where the motorcycle sits in the dappled early-morning shade. It is a sunny Saturday morning, and he has the day all to himself until Edith arrives around seven. Saturdays from his childhood arise, and he remembers waking up and realizing that there was no school—this was before his mother died, before he was sent to boarding school—and he would run outside with a toy balsawood glider onto a broad lawn that sloped down to a marshy inlet and rush through the wet grass in his pajamas until the maid called him in to eat breakfast and to tell his mother good morning. He doesn't know if this happened only once or many times. It's coalesced into a solid single memory now, a door blown open, revealing a surprise of air and light and levitation.

He gets on the motorcycle, guns it, makes a tight curve around the driveway, and accelerates as he heads down the hill. The Harley immediately goes into a skid on the loose gravel—how could he forget aobut the dangers of loose gravel?—and he finds himself moving in slow motion through the air. This has already happened, he thinks. For a few seconds he sees himself as if looking down from a great distance: one knee bent, the other leg stuck straight out, his back parallel to the ground as he begins to descend, the bike continuing by itself in an arc down the hill and off the road into the bushes. How wonderful, this flying! he thinks. I could do it forever!

He comes to with his chin on a stone, his mouth full of blood and his ears ringing. When he gets to his feet he has a weightless, drunken sensation and has lost touch with his arms and legs. His hands are scraped and bleeding. How interesting, he thinks.

He lies on the porch on a dusty overstuffed sofa with maddening cabbage roses that Edith wants hauled to the dump and watches sunlight slide along a splintering wooden column and then vanish as crows screech. By the time Edith arrives, the world is red, bleeding into black at the edges.

Edith drives him back to the city and accompanies him to the oral surgeon and waits in the reception room for three hours. He notices, when he comes back to consciousness, that she is letting her hair get longer and that her expression is one of deep, tender absorption. She walks him, his mouth packed with bloody gauze, out to her car, supporting him with both arms so that he does not stagger and fall. "What would have happened to you if I hadn't come along?" she asks. She intends toughness but in fact she seems very fragile and in love. He is touched. For the next month, while the orthodontist wires, caps, and pulls teeth, he will have to take codeine for the pain.

Angela flies to the plant in Akron to learn exactly how the newsletter gets printed. Back in New York, she talks to representatives of paper companies and discovers a cheaper source for the same quality of stock. She tells Goodhugh about this and from then on Starr Whorf prints all its newsletters on the bargain paper. She takes copies of the newsletter to graphics studios to get consultations on better design. She rewrites Gerard's copy and checks his statistical reports, which he sometimes fabricates. She takes captains of industry to lunch and interviews them. She learns to order omelettes so that she can eat with her left hand while taking notes with her right.

The president of a can company asks her to fly with him in his private jet to his private island in the Caribbean. She refuses but she does start buying shoes and purses that match, and wearing hose even on hot days. Goodhugh takes her to lunch and offers her a job as the assistant director of a division of Starr Whorf in San Francisco—something in the sugar business. She refuses.

Ron Nussbaum sends her a postcard with a photograph of Port Said that says on the back, "You have missed a great opportunity." Derek Grinder calls her and says that soon he is going to be asking her out. "When?" she asks. How can she refuse a non-invitation? "In not more than six weeks, possibly less."

She comes home nights from the air-conditioned office to her hot apartment, dances to one side of *Let It Bleed*, drinks a beer, takes a shower, and lies in bed awake until three or four in the morning. In the backyard, cats yowl and mate. Sometimes the Puerto Ricans down at the end of the block have a party with live salsa bands and booming Fender basses. Songs about *amor* and *muerte* and *fuego* throb through the night. As she is about to fall asleep one night, someone nearby accidentally turns the wrong knob on the stereo and Janis Joplin screams *"It just caiiiiin't beeeee! Oh no!"*

When Joe occasionally comes to her place and they make love she experiences no pleasure. It's all in the preparation and the recollection. In his arms, she pretends ecstasy, which is genuine enough beforehand and later. Why she is numb at the moment, she does not know. She forgets that part. The mechanism that drew her to him has become submerged, and now it's faulty from having to operate for so long in the wrong element. She daydreams, though, of absolute union with him, their atoms intermingled, an impossible blending of souls that is produced from the heat and light of their coming together. She gasps in the solitude of her office at this prospect.

Angela interviews a young British astronomer who remarks, in a kind way, "I sense that you, like New York, are always teetering on the brink of disaster."

"Why are you always scaring yourself?" she asks Joe.

He is pulling on his jeans and looking frightened. The scrapes on his face and arms have nearly healed.

"You love to scare yourself, don't you?"

"I've always rehearsed disasters, even when I was little, so I wouldn't be surprised," he says. With his tongue he checks the temporary caps that conceal his broken front teeth.

"Deep down I don't think you're scared at all."

He pulls his shirt on and buttons it crooked. He exhales and relief comes to him. He smiles. "I believe you're right. With this accident, I wasn't afraid. I had a sense of déjà-vu."

"I never think what's going to happen next," she says, twisting her hair up and pinning it. Her breasts shake as she moves and talks. "Once I was going across the Brooklyn Bridge in a cab at night, and listening to that hum those cables or whatever make and looking out at the lights, the city and all, and I got a sense of my whole life, like a little piece of music you catch in the middle when you're turning the radio dial."

At work she shows him what she's been doing in his absence. The new estimates she's worked up for the next fiscal year. The corners she's cut. The innovations. She's looking into computers—if they had a terminal, they could type the material into a word-processor and skip having to deal with the printer. It would be cheaper in the long run, and a damned sight quicker. She shows him the sketches of new designs. "Good, good," he says, but he doesn't seem very enthusiastic. Not ever as enthusiastic as she wants him to be. He doesn't say, for instance, that as a reward he wants her to live with him and be his love. He does say, however, that his son is in town for the week, and that he doesn't know what to do with him.

22

JOE SITS ON A hump of black schist shaped like the back of a giant turtle. Last night it rained, and this afternoon the park is clean. The leaves glisten, the meadow has a sheen, and the blank blue sky fits quite precisely over the tops of the skyscrapers. His son plays at the base of the rock, singing to himself and picking handfuls of grass and throwing them as hard as he can at the rock.

"How are you doing, Todd?"

"Not fine." The boy looks so much like his mother. The pale hair, the plump arms, and even the ability to seem emotionless.

"Come here."

"Don't want to."

"Todd." Joe sits a minute longer and then goes down to the grass and squats beside Todd, who refuses to look at him. "What is it?"

"I want to go home. I want my mommy and daddy." He screws up his mouth to keep from crying.

"*I'm* your daddy." For the past few days Todd has called

him daddy without any questions or confusion. Lucy has always been careful to let Todd know that Alec is only his stepfather.

"You're my fake dad," Todd says. "I want Alec."

Joe clamps his mouth shut and then quickly opens it: the new wires dig into his gums with every abrupt movement. His jaws ache. He takes a codeine tablet. He should never have tried to see Todd. Edith tries to be friendly, but the strain is obvious. Yesterday she made plans for Todd—lunch in a nice restaurant, a movie, then a trip to the zoo. But Todd would only eat his fingernails at lunch; after fifteen minutes in the movie he wanted to leave; and he fell asleep in the car on the way to the zoo and was in a bad temper afterward. The more Edith nervously tried to make him happy, the worse matters grew. This morning, Todd refused the fried egg Edith made him, then the granola he asked for instead, and then the toast Joe made him. Then he threw a plastic bucket full of toy wind-up robots on the table and broke a plate that was part of a set Edith had ordered from England.

Joe places his hand on the damp, silky crown of his son's head. For a second he recalls what it was like to be small and not know what was going on: his mother was slowly dying (although he could not have known that at the time) in an upstairs room with red curtains; his father was usually away at the knitting mill he owned and when home, he seldom spoke. The succession of housekeepers. Why did his parents want to adopt him in the first place? Then, his mother's death, and boarding school, the shock and bewilderment of suddenly finding himself on a train alone going to a place far from home, a place he had never seen, with a pair of magnetic Shmoos the housekeeper gave him. He can still feel in his fingers the mysterious, tiny force of their magnetism. "Listen, Todd. I am your real dad. Even though you live with your mother and Alec, I am your real dad."

"I want to go home."

"We can't. My, uh, friend is coming with a picnic lunch. Won't that be fun?"

"No."

So there is to be no repairing of the damage. Joe sighs. He has no place in life like others do. Since Todd's birth he has been holding onto the idea that it mattered that he must stay alive, must keep working, because Todd needed him. Todd, after all, is his only blood relation.

"Hey, who's this?" How long has Angela been standing there? Her hair is bound into two long, thick shiny braids like a Valkyrie, her face half-hidden by big sunglasses. She is wearing faded jeans, an embroidered green undershirt, and sandals. She sets down two well-packed shopping bags and ignores Joe altogether. "My name is Todd," she says. "What's yours?"

"*My* name is Todd, I'm the Todd." The boy is indignant. His nose is running and Joe searches his pockets for a Kleenex.

"Oh, then I must be the Angela." She immediately falls down and sprawls beside him. "Help!" she screams, and starts rolling down the grassy slope. Todd lookes at her and at Joe and then runs down the slope after her. "Are you a animal gal?" he asks.

She grabs his ankles and pulls him down beside her. He screams and sits up. She sits up and does nothing.

"Todd—" Joe begins.

Angela holds up a hand to warn him off. Todd keeps screaming. Finally he stops. "Okay, now it's *my* turn to scream." Angela screams in a near-perfect imitation of Todd. "Now it's your turn."

Todd screams, and Angela screams, and Joe looks around to see if the police are coming. But there's no one in sight.

Now they are talking. "Do you have shoes on your feet?" Angela asks.

"Yeah," Todd replies with scorn.

"Do you have legs connected to your feet? Are they connected to your body? Is your backbone connected to your head-bone?"

"Yes, yes, yes," Todd says. He is now quite calm. He watches Angela to see what will happen next.

"Lunch." Angela spreads an old cotton bedspread on the grass and sets out fried chicken. "It's still warm—after I fried it up I wrapped it in newspaper. And there's homemade biscuits, and lemonade, and potato salad."

"He didn't eat breakfast," Joe says. "This is terrific."

"Maybe we shouldn't let him have lunch then."

But Todd is holding a paper plate out. "Please?"

Joe watches her serve Todd. She knows exactly how much food to give him, and she knows to fill the paper cup only a third full of lemonade. "Both hands," she says, giving it to him. Joe never imagined this side to her.

"He's just like you," Angela says. "He looks exactly like you. The green eyes, everything. Todd, you look just like this guy here. You know him?"

"Yeah."

"What do you call him?"

"He's my dad."

"Really? I thought maybe you were brothers."

"Nope, he's my dad."

"You're sure?"

"He's my *dad!*" Todd roars with annoyance.

"Okay—if you say so."

Angela doubles up her fists and menaces Joe. "Are you this boy's dad?"

"Yes! Yes!" Joe says, laughing. "Well, that's enough excitement." He's sometimes afraid Angela will go too far.

"The forehead, the voice—he's like you," she says. "Were you stubborn too? What am I saying? Yes, you are."

"I don't remember. I can only remember a couple of things from my childhood. How about *that?*" He says it with defiance, expecting her to say, Boy, that's really sick and repressed.

But she's holding Todd and flirting with him. "Once upon a time there were three noodles and they lived in a house in the woods. There was a mama noodle and a daddy noodle, and a little . . ."

Joe is relieved. The day is going to go all right. She likes Todd. She is a natural mother. She has never said anything about wanting children—too busy protesting how much she values her freedom. He wants to ask her how she feels about having children, but that's too dangerous a question. But don't most women deep down really want kids? Lucy always did.

They walk through the park, past the Great Lawn, where softball games are beginning in the hot sun of late afternoon. Men and women in brightly colored team T-shirts and baseball caps kick up puffs of dust and shout to one another. "I wonder why Starr Whorf doesn't have a team," Joe says. "The newsletter division could probably qualify for one of the advertising or publishing softball leagues."

"Ah, I hate baseball. Do you like it?"

"I don't care one way or another." Todd is stumbling with exhaustion. Joe picks him up and carries him, and by the time they reach a bench and sit down, he is asleep, his face sticky and blackened, his cheeks red under the dirt.

"Thank you for all this, Angela. You seem—really good at this."

"I used to do it for a living."

"Really?"

"Sure. When I was a kid I started babysitting, and then I put myself through college doing it. Mother's helper. I also worked in the libarary, and cleaned houses, and did secretarial."

"Oh—I didn't know that."

"I try to be a woman of mystery, that's why."

They sit watching the dozen or so interlocking softball games. The players tend to look very earnest. "How do they keep track of which game they're in?" Angela asks.

"Maybe some of the players are simultaneously in two or more games."

She puts her hand on his shoulder. Todd snores softly. "Jeepers, this is really nice, Joe."

"I know what you mean. Not so charged." Today she has become an entirely different person. Distinctly unethereal. Someone who has worked hard all her life. "What did you *do* where you grew up?"

"Gatch?" She shrugs. "Not much. There was no park. No museums. A little library—I read every book. A lot of dust and tumbleweeds and frijoles. I didn't hear classical music until I was in high school. It sounded like water to me—forests and lakes and streams."

"It must seem very different, very strange to be living here, then."

"Yup. I always feel out of place."

Behind the buildings to the west, the sky is turning gold. It will be time to go soon. He wishes that he and Angela and Todd were going home, to a house that was his, that belonged to him. They would cook lamb chops and artichokes, and give Todd a bath, and read to him, and put him to bed in his little room overlooking the garden, and then go to their own bedroom and make love, and sleep soundly next to each other all night. He sits up straight with a jerk and Todd wakes up for a second, drunkenly laughs, a bubble coming from his lips, and then falls back asleep. Joe bobs his head stiffly from side to side. The codeine is wearing off.

"Does your neck bother you?"

"I had to have some more gum surgery two days ago, and then the doctor put these wires in my mouth, and my jaw and neck have been aching ever since."

"I noticed that you didn't eat any chicken. You mean you've got *braces?*" She pulls down his lower lip to see. "Wow."

He is embarrassed. "Well, the dentist said as long as I had to get caps on the front teeth, and I thought because I never, I mean when I was a kid, I didn't—anyway, I still have the corporation insurance, and it covered the accident too, and it seemed like a good time—"

"You are my favorite teenage guy." She goes behind the bench and puts her hands softly on his shoulders and gently massages the cords of muscles from his collarbone to the back of his skull. Her fingers are sure and supple, continuously moving and pressing, but not too hard. He watches the golden light flooding the park, and listens to the blended shouts and noises of all the games, and smells the dust and the sweet leaves of the plane trees and feels his breathing child asprawl on his knees. If you do not decide, says a voice in his heart, someone else will decide for you.

She finishes by tracing the contours of his ears, her touch so faint tht he might be dreaming it. He feels at ease and sleepy. She comes around the bench and sits next to him, placing Todd's feet on her lap. "Thank you," Joe says. "You're a very kind person."

"I enjoyed it."

"Not as much as I did. You've taken very good care of me, and Todd. You've been very good to me. Thank you." He hears himself sounding stilted. He grasps her naked foot and ankle and softly kisses her. "That's all I can do," he says. "Consider yourself vigorously kissed."

She smiles. Her hair is in frizzy tendrils around her face, having pulled out of her braids. There is a lemonade stain on her shirt between her breasts. The reflected light from the sunset makes her dusty skin luminous.

The sky overhead is an enormous cube of warm gold now, and the rocks jutting through the lawns are like parts of another world thrusting itself into this one.

She goes home, exhausted, and makes coffee. She will have to stay up most of the night to catch up on the work she did not do today. Joe has told her that he is going to take a leave of absence, so the full burden of the newsletter is now going to become hers. He has no idea what he's going to do. Besides working on the house, maybe he'll wander around the city like he's always wished he had time to do, or even take juggling lessons.

The pianist can play nearly all of the Mozart concerto through without stopping. All night the cats screech outside her window. Toward dawn, she falls into bed and cries.

23

"IT PROBABLY WON'T WORK out," Sharon says. She and Angela sit on Sharon's dark brown sofa and eat cottage cheese and cantaloupe. The bassinet from Sharon's mother now holds the surviving spider plants. Lately, when Angela is depressed and has the time, she comes up to see Sharon. Sharon, however, is seldom home these days; she is often at Sam's apartment. "I don't understand why he's so nice to me. He keeps telling me I'm really a little ole delicate Southern belle and he says he's going to get me a hoop skirt. I mean he's so nice—twenty-four hours a day he's nice."

Angela refrains from pointing out that Southern men are always nice and that their niceness may not reflect what they are actually thinking. She wants Sharon to be happy, and Sam is so alien to Sharon that there is hope. "'Get it while you can,'" Angela sings. "'A little love and affection.'" She is scarcely able these days to talk about any subject besides Joe. His complexities, his situation with Edith, his accident, his baffling alternations in emotion are endlessly absorbing to her. She has just described in great detail her afternoon in the park

with Joe and Todd. Now, like the other memories, it has become perfect, complete, burnished.

Sam arrives with his guitar. He is even bigger than Joe,
barrel-chested. Muscles bulge under his yellow T-shirt. He has
thinning red hair and a full mustache. He kisses Sharon and
gives Angela a hug. "How you doin'?"

Angela tells him. He has already heard about Joe, his complexities, his situation with Edith, his accident, his baffling
alternations in emotion.

"You hang in there, honey," Sam says, tuning his guitar,
"and he'll have to come to you." He sings "Rocky Raccoon"
in a fine, clear voice.

Angela phones Helen. "The kids have summer colds and I've
been up nights with them," Helen says.

"How's the belly-dancing?"

"Great. I'm also taking yoga at the dance studio from a
wonderful man. He's Armenian. We do breathing exercises
and concentrate on a candle flame. But if you happen to talk
to Tom for some reason, don't say anything."

"I won't."

"It's beautiful here. Every afternoon the thunderheads come
down the canyons and we have fifteen minutes of rain. Things
just cool right off." Helen is beginning to sound like a native.
"And there's a big new shopping mall going up outside of
town. When you visit I'll take you to see it. How's everything,
Angela?"

Angela, lost for a moment in the vision of the thunderheads,
has an attack of homesickness. She tells Helen about Joe, about
his complexities, his situation with Edith, his accident, his
baffling alternations in emotion.

"Sounds like you really are involved," Helen says.

Angela buys a gold band, antique, set with a square-cut garnet.
She wears it on her ring finger, which lately has felt more and
more vacant. After her divorce, she was glad not to have the
irritation of a ring, and she was glad to sleep spread out in the
middle of the bed. Now she has taken to sleeping on one side.
A few weeks later in a jeweler's window in the Village she

sees another gold band, red-gold, thick, old-fashioned, and she buys that.

The first time Joe saw her in the office with her rings, he was afraid. A ring meant something serious. He didn't think they meant marriage or engagement exactly, but he assumed that men always gave women rings, that a woman wouldn't buy a ring for herself. Now she wears three or four of them, and when he squeezes her hand he feels more metal than skin; he finds them a silly affectation.

"I feel strange and depressed," he says, sitting at his desk one sulfurous, steamy, dead-air morning.

She wriggles her fingers and the rings click. "Take up thy bed and walk!" she cries. "I always feel like a faith healer around you." She tells him a fact she has just learned—that chickens are imprinted from the moment they hatch with a fear reaction to a silhouette of a sparrow hawk. Then she shows him a report on subscriptions: they are up by 11 ½ percent.

Angela has four recurring fantasies as she rides the densely packed, fetid subway to and from the office.

One: She is walking in the park and meets a Tibetan who is a master of ancient, secret wisdom. He asks her to become his disciple and teaches her all he knows, and after that she is no longer vulnerable. She is radiant, she is immortal, she doesn't care what anybody does or thinks, and she no longer needs men.

Two: She is walking in the park and a flying saucer lands. "Where is Angela?" the aliens ask. They lead her up the ramp to the flying saucer. It turns out that she was just visiting earth on a tourist visa and forgot about it and got trapped in this body that is never the right weight, can't wear shades of purple, and gets headaches and heartaches. The friendly aliens—her own people—cure her and free her, and she is no longer vulnerable. She is radiant, immortal, and doesn't need Joe.

Three: She is walking in the park and finds a coupon entitling her to spend two weeks at the finest health and beauty spa in the world. She is welcomed by kind attendants who feed her delicious things, massage her, and remove flab, wrinkles, folds, and the creases that divorce and disappointment have left on her face and body, all to the sound of the Schubert Trout

Quintet, and they also fix her hair and her makeup and redecorate her apartment, and provide her with a flawlessly coordinated wardrobe. After that, she needs nothing.

Four: She and Joe marry and live on a farm with forests and lakes and rivers and deserts and canyons and an ocean, and her hair grows very long, and she winds it up on the top of her head and wears graceful calico skirts, and grinds wheat by hand for the bread she bakes every morning for their children, and they drink herb tea at night by the big stone fireplace and make love and listen to Country Joe and the Fish and Bach and read Wallace Stevens poems aloud to each other in pools of light cast by candles, and they always love each other passionately and deeply no matter what.

The day before Joe's leave of absence begins, Angela gives him an old book she found in a magicians' store near Times Square—*Simple Steps to the Ancient Art of Juggling.* She also gives him a copy of the *I Ching* and three antique bronze coins from a shop in Chinatown. "You're going to be free now," she declares. "These things will help you take your fate in your own hands."

What is she really saying? What does she really want him to do? He takes her gifts, remembers to smile, and puts them in a shopping bag with other things he has taken from his desk and bulletin board, like the unicorn postcard. *Temptation awaits you.* "This is very nice of you." He feels he is at the edge of a cliff in the night—why is he taking this leave of absence? Is he giving into himself, into some dangerous impulse—like the one that led to getting his front teeth broken? Poverty, ruin, a flophouse—it could happen.

"I don't know why I'm doing this. I don't want you to leave." She stands before him, slender, wavering, smiling nervously. "I hope you come back real soon—it's not the same with you gone. It's not fun. I don't get any great ideas without you around. I hope this is not like what happened to this woman I heard about. Her husband built a tower at the end of their backyard as a place to paint pictures, but really he would just take girls back there to screw. One day she asked him to take out the garbage and for the first time ever he did it without complaining, only he never came back."

"I don't get it," Joe says. He is barely able to listen to her. She is telling him how unreliable he is.

"Oh, never mind." She grabs his hands. "See you in the fall."

Later when he goes into her office to give her a kiss and remind her that from time to time he will be coming in—into the city, into the office—she is gone. He waits for a few minutes and then, lugging his briefcase and the heavy shopping bag, walks home, feeling afraid.

Gerard arrives at the office three hours late. "I can't get used to working in the morning," he says to Angela. "All that false cheer that goes on here until about noon makes me sick. How can everyone lie? We all want to kill one another—that's the truth."

"Do you have the housing-starts graph and the I.R.S. report?"

"No. Please! Please don't hit me! I couldn't take it. Go ahead—fire me. Fire the only genius on the premises. I hope you're not going to become an obsessive-compulsive like Joe. As soon as I have my breakfast, I'll do the housing starts. I can't wait." He pats her on the back. "Angela—you are indubitably wonderful."

That night Angela leaves the office at about nine. Her stomach is queasy from a dozen cups of coffee, her eyes burn, and she feels extremely alert. When she gets home, she drinks three beers but she still can't relax. It's too hot to dance to *Let It Bleed*. She lies in the dark under the canopy. Why is it that no matter how hard she works she is always able at the same time to worry about Joe? She is not focused. She does not work the way Katha does, with singular attention. She is one issue late already, thanks to Goodhugh's decision—she learned about it when she read a one-paragraph interview with him in the *Wall Street Journal*—to produce the newsletter every two weeks rather than monthly. It's a good thing she doesn't have a regular boyfriend—when would she have the time?

Confusion, boredom with the confusion, boredom with this endlessly undefined condition, boredom with talking and thinking solely about Joe—how can all this spiral out of one pure, weightless instant of joy? She is no longer herself; she can't even remember what she was like before Joe. She can't remember at the end of the day what she's done. Her eye is always turned inward, reliving moments with Joe, planning new ones. She wishes for a resolution, any resolution. But by any resolution she really means the resolution that will be what she wants more than she has ever wanted anything in her life: Joe. Unconditionally.

A few miles to the south, Joe sits watching Johnny Carson and putting together a picture puzzle of a Cézanne still life. Very challenging. Edith just gave it to him—she sent away to the Tate Gallery for it. When he does two things at once like this, his mind stops and he feels at peace. Sometimes, in the night, he thinks: Which woman shall it be? Or neither? Maybe they both will go, canceling each other out in a tidily solved equation. As different as they seem from each other, Edith and Angela merge in his mind: She wants me to love her; she wants more of me; she expects too much of me; she looks hurt when I say I'm not sure.

Joe and Angela are just two organisms out of billions. Not even their subatomic particles are solid. From a microscopic viewpoint, they are simply giant moist sponges with wind blowing through them. When she cries each night, her tears are to release chemicals of stress from her body. When his state alters in her presence and light bouncing off objects becomes clearer and sounds become crisper, it is because of a narcotic formed in his endocrine glands. Both Joe and Angela possess billions of brain cells carrying memory traces of every kind. Why then, amid the Latin verbs, the instant of sunlight on a blade of grass, the twitch of a curtain with a sudden gust, the din of cicadas at noon, the smell of a plank of newly sawed Douglas fir, the phone number of a long-forgotten friend—why then, given this vast collection of possible memories, sensations, and thoughts, do they devote so much inner energy to each other?

Angela wakes up in the hot night, the sheet twisted and clinging to her damp feet. She can't stop the onrushing roar of her own mind. She can neither sleep nor make herself wake up. She rises and puts on her kimono and goes downstairs and knocks on Katha's door.

Katha opens the door right away. She is wearing an unwrinkled white cotton shift and Angela is struck by how thin she is. Has Katha always been like this? Her shoulders are bony; her collarbone forms a high ridge. She regards Angela with a delicate empathy.

Angela suddenly grabs Katha's elbows and the touch of cool skin brings her out of her nightmare.

"If that's how it is, if it's making you feel crazy, then go to him." Katha squeezes oranges and makes two glasses of juice.

"I can't go to him—Edith is there, and on the weekends they're at this place in the country."

"As soon as Edith leaves for work—go to him. Why hold back?"

Angela sits on the red and blue lozenges of the Kazakh carpet and sips the juice. "I feel better now. Thank you."

Katha sits down opposite Angela. "What are your plans for the rest of the summer? Are you going away?"

"I somehow thought that by now Joe and I would be together, and we'd go someplace. I just—"

"Angela." Katha pats her hand. "I was just wondering because I have some friends in the country with a lovely garden and they're going to Europe and they need someone to stay there and keep an eye on things while they're away. I was going to do it, but now I won't be able to."

"Why is that?"

"Oh, some matters are keeping me here in the city. Nothing important. I told my friends I would try to find someone."

"I can't think straight right now. But it sounds nice. Katha—do you mind this? I mean, do you mind the way I just came down here in the middle of the night and started bawling?"

"No." Katha's gaze is level and at ease. "I don't mind anything."

"Boy, I do," Angela says. "I mind everything."

Katha has Angela throw the Chinese coins and opens her yellow book. "'Contemplation of my life decides the choice between advance and retreat,'" she reads. "'This self-contemplation means the overcoming of naïve egotism in the person who sees everything solely from his own standpoint. He begins to reflect and in this way acquires objectivity. However, self-knowledge does not mean preoccupation with one's own thoughts; rather, it means concern about the effects one creates.'"

"I can never remember this wisdom when I need it," Angela says.

"It doesn't matter. Things are just as they are if you understand. Things are just as they are if you don't understand."

The sky, reflected in Katha's mirror wall, is turning white. Angela goes back upstairs and falls face down on the bed like a tired child. A breeze from the river, smelling of the sea, cools the room. There is the faraway scream of gulls. She sleeps for a couple of hours, the point of her cheekbone driven hard into the bunched-up pillow, and then takes the jammed subway downtown, drinks coffee in a coffee shop until ten, and phones Joe. "I want to *talk*."

His loft is immense and mostly empty. A lot of plants, some chrome and leather furniture, and a spotless white fleecy carpet. Some black and white photographs of sand dunes along a brick wall. A long plain dining table with half a dozen dark brown jars of vitamins in the center and a big television at one end, and several thousand jigsaw puzzle pieces. No imagination here, Angela thinks.

Joe is wearing paint-spattered white cut-offs and an unbuttoned shirt. His legs are brown, the hair on them is curly and light.

She keeps looking around, past him, feeling horrible. It's true then, he really lives someplace, here, and he does not live by himself.

"Can I make you a cup of tea?"

"Yeah."

He sees that her face is taut and pale, and there are smudges under her eyes, and her hair is damp. Strands of it cling to her neck. A smell of sweat mingles with the smell of roses. Will her roses remain after she leaves and be detected by Edith? Angela seems about to cry, or as if she has been crying. She always gets so emotional about everything: it's his fault. He sees that she is looking around with a peculiar avidity and an odd expression—disapproval?—crosses her face. She bites her lip. "May I use the bathroom?"

He points it out to her, and on the way she gets a glimpse of the bedroom: foil insulation packs, a mattress on the floor.

The bathroom smells of disinfectant. There are no cosmetics or perfumes visible. There are two toothbrushes, one light blue, one dark blue. There is a bottle of dandruff shampoo. His? Hers? She imagines Joe and Edith in the shower stall, hidden behind the milky, starry glass, shampooing together. On the toilet tank is a box of tampons—the only sign so far that a woman lives here. She longs to open the medicine cabinet but she's afraid it will make a distinctive noise.

They sit on the sofa, which is very long and which is upholstered in a cream-colored nubby fabric that scratches the backs of her legs. Everything in the room looks new. She sits at one end and sips from an oversized mug and he sits at the opposite end and smokes. As soon as she leaves he will stop smoking for good.

"I'm confused," she says, finally. "It isn't worth it to me for us to keep on seeing each other and making love if it endangers our—our relationship."

"What we have, I feel, is a friendship that will always go on," he says. "But then there is also this powerful attraction, this electricity. I don't know what that's all about. Now that I'm on leave of absence, we can be together more."

"Do you care for me?"

"Very much. Do you care for me?"

"Very much."

They rearrange old labels.

"What are you going to do?" she asks.

He shakes his head. "I've been separating subjective truth about Edith from objective truth."

Angela doesn't understand this. But she presses on. "You said you were afraid with Edith that you were settling for less than you really wanted."

"That might just be my subjective evaluation. For instance, she hasn't gotten involved with my kid the way I would like, but now I think that's because I've been so nervous about that— sending out signals that kept her away." Edith recently reported this theory of Midge's to him. "Now I'm monitoring this."

Angela feels she is slipping down the face of a glass mountain. "This is all so abstract to me. What are you saying?"

"I haven't yet fully committed myself to Edith. The areas in the relationship I felt were lacking are probably ones that I haven't invested enough in to get anything back." He speaks as if temporarily inhabited by an extraterrestrial from the Planet Psychotherapy. She wonders if this is how he and Edith talk. This is not the Joe she knows.

"I don't want any barriers between you and me." Joe feels he is being as honest as he can. For some reason, he is also very afraid, and he hopes she doesn't pick up on that—although she seems to miss very little. "With you, I enjoy the here-and-now. Later, when I'm with Edith, in some completely different situation, it all seems unreal. And I always get the feeling that you believe that in some other time, in some other place, we will get together." He has forgotten for the moment his own wish that Edith would somehow dissolve, would turn out never to have existed, and he and Angela would go away together to a forest, to the Alaskan wilderness, and build a cabin.

Angela does not point out to him that all he has said to her over the months they've been seeing each other is that he needs time, that it's taking time to get out of this thing with Edith.

And Joe does not remind Angela that she once said she wouldn't respect him if he just dumped Edith without considering the consequences.

Angela decides that now it must be over. The waiting is finished. She will not lie in his arms again. Too painful.

He puts his ashtray and cigarettes on the floor and leans back and stares at her. Her sadness has dissolved the artificiality that has been building up in her face over the past few months. She looks more the way she did when they met. Natural. She is beautiful. Why does the curve of her knee, emerging from her skirt, why does the line of her thigh excite him so? Why should this be? And why does the wave of her hair follow the curve of her shoulder so beautifully?

And then he ceases to think altogether, and the air between them disappears when she returns his gaze, her eyes clear and slightly widened, her mouth parting.

His green irises call her into a green world, a green shade. She breathes with him. She can sense his pulse. She is aware of every pore. Finally she makes herself stand up. He gets up and embraces her.

They lie on the flokati rug. He is excited, frightened, and

as if in a dream, unable to move. She takes off his clothing and her sandals. "Don't stop there," he murmurs.

As he arches his back and groans, she sees his head twist and his lips draw away from his teeth in an odd grimace. She has never seen this before. He immediately gets up and dresses. He does not look at her.

She wants to gather up her clothes and run out the door without looking back. But she dresses and sits beside him. Didn't they agree, not an hour earlier, to prevent barriers from rising between them? Now he won't look at her or speak.

"You look worried," she says.

"I'm fine, I'm fine. Is there something wrong with you?"

"I'm afraid this will drive us apart."

"We have to not let it." He gets to his feet. "Well, bye."

She is out on the hot street. Garbage in black bags is piled high on the sidewalk. There is a smell of rotting garbage and dog shit. The sky is thick and yellow, and hangs over the rooftops. A bearded, shirtless man with a painting under each arm walks by, a red rag tied around his head. She walks to the corner. Across the street in front of a deli is a gang of boys with transistor radios and baseball bats. Which way shall she go? What will she do? She looks down and sees two children, a boy and a girl, about three years old and stark naked. "Where is your mother?" a woman is asking them.

The loft remains filled with Angela's presence. Joe vacuums the rug and then, raking his fingers through its long wool in search of her golden, radioactive hairs, he feels wrapped in something smooth and silken and living. It was good of her to come to him—what a risk it must have been for her. She has an elusive delicacy, and she seems to understand his fear. She has a streak of sweetness, an essential goodness.

When Edith comes home with a list she's had Trudy type up of things he is supposed to pick up to take to the country, he can barely speak or move. "Are you all right?"

"I, uh—"

"And get the *big* cans of solvent—that mantelpiece must have a hundred years of paint on it." She gives him a keen look. "And come right here—you look like you need a great big warm hug."

24

"AH THANK YOU'RE GETTIN' screwed," Sam says. "Either you've got him and he doesn't know it, or he's a *creep*." He picks up his guitar and plays and sings. *"My creole belle, I love you well—my darlin' baby, mah creole belle!"* He stops and tunes the guitar.

Angela has been telling him her troubles with Joe while Sharon is in the kitchen cooking dinner. Sharon can't stand to hear about Joe any more.

"It's so painful," Angela says, about to cry.

"But have you seen this movie, *Papillon?* If you thank *you* got a lot of problems, you ought to see *Papillon*—it's about these two guys who try to escape from Devil's Island." He resumes singing. *"When the stars do shine, Ah'll make you mine, mah darlin' bay-bee, mah creole belle!"*

Angela goes into the kitchen. Sharon is making roast prime ribs of beef, Yorkshire pudding, and a Julia Child potato-and-cheese casserole. She is sweating and pale; her freckles stand out. "I love him," she whispers to Angela. "I absolutely love him."

"That's great, Sharon." Angela's response is automatic. For some time now she has had only a little attention left over to give to people other than Joe. And she makes everyone else's behavior connect, willy-nilly, with his. "At least Sam's *available.*"

"Yeah, except. Except he happens to be married. I mean, he's separated, but he says he's still not over his wife. She's from Alabama and she goes to church regularly and wears a hat and gloves."

"Let me see if I understand this," Sam says after dinner. He seems to find Angela's situation as intriguing as a C.I.A. covert operation. "Joe's girl friend is giving up marriage and having children to work full-time and have a career so she can support him while he takes off from work to spend more time with you."

"It's an experiment," Angela says. "He says Edith is insecure and possessive."

Derek Grinder calls Angela at the office. "You're great," he says. His voice is hoarse.

"You're great." Angela is amazed that anyone could think she was anything. A man who knows she exists.

"I just woke up from a long, complicated dream. I was flying. And you know what Freud says about *that.*"

Joe never dreams. Angela in fact feels obliged to do all his dreaming for him. She is still very tired from the latest confusing episode, at his loft. Why do their encounters take on this Battle-of-the-Titans quality? Derek is shorter, thinner. Evidently available. "I've been reading through the copies of the newsletters you sent. They really are improving. Do you mind if I quote from one of them in my column? About how old the universe is?"

"Feel free."

"You're terrific—every time I talk to you I get a great idea."

"You do? Like what?"

"I never tell—my ideas could be stolen."

He starts talking about politics. Angela thinks about Joe, and then about what to order sent up for lunch. She has nothing to say about the President, about the imminent collapse of the political system, etc., etc. These matters, as far she is able to tell, have nothing to do with her life. A BLT would be good.

"And I was sitting next to this actor at Hill's," Derek is now saying. "He says, 'Derek you really should stop smoking. The potassium nitrate in the cigarette paper reduces your aura.' And I said, 'How can I worry about the size of something I can't even *see?*' "

Angela laughs. It feels odd in her throat, laughter.

"My shrink tells me I should find someone like me. You're like me, Angela. Funny and serious."

"Thank you." She wonders if this is a compliment.

He talks and talks. He must be starving.

"I hope you don't mind my saying I find you very pretty. I'd like to get together with you soon."

"Gosh, thanks, well—"

"At some point."

"At some point," she says.

"And not in the too remote future, either."

Alec comes to the city to a convention of publishers from university presses, and asks Joe if he can stay at the loft. The day he is to arrive, Edith comes home from work wearing a new purple and white flower-print dress and soft-soled, purple espadrilles. Her hair is in a new style, gently waved around her face. She carries a white box containing chocolate torte from a new French bakery that has just opened nearby.

When Alec arrives, he hugs Joe and kisses Edith on the mouth. Joe blanks out. He and Alec used to be so close; when they worked together at the press they could talk about practically anything for hours. About poetry, politics, women, carpentry, the avant-garde. They had lunch together nearly every day, and Alec and his wife were always over for dinner, or Lucy and Joe were at Alec's. Joe recalls a lot of spaghetti and Chianti. Design Research furniture. Vivaldi on the stereo. And he recalls looking around at the faces of his two friends and his wife in the yellow candlelight and thinking, We will always be together like this. Joe knows, logically, that there is no longer any reason to hate Alec. Edith has pointed that out. Lucy now butters Alec's English muffins instead of Joe's, that's all. And Lucy has become dowdy, skinning her hair back in a severe ponytail and wearing T-shirts and long shapeless skirts and clogs—not exactly Helen of Troy.

Alec is in a restless fever. He has always paced and fidgeted and talked fast, but this evening he seems like a caricature of himself. He has skinny arms and black-rimmed eyeglasses and curly black hair, and he has grown long sideburns, which make his face narrow and wolflike. He gives Joe an enlarged photograph he took of Todd in the bathtub. Todd looks solemn and guarded, and he holds his elbows close to his sides, his knees drawn up. Todd has announced that he does not want to visit Joe and Edith again.

Edith and Alec get along very well, and Joe is relieved that she is willing to do all the talking. She tells Alec about the house and shows him the Eames chair and her expanding collection of photographs of snowdrifts. "I know you like Scotch," she says, and fixes him a Scotch and water.

"May I say that you look very lovely, Edith?" Alec glances at Joe. Joe pulls on his mustache.

Edith tells Alec about her career plans. She'll get her Master's in August. Lois, who is trying to relax and get pregnant, has moved to her country place in Connecticut and so Edith is now acting director. The Brooklyn branch is not even open yet and it already has a waiting list. Edith is trying to convince Lois to set up some branches in other cities, too.

They go to an Italian restaurant, Alec's choice. "The press is going rather well this year," Alec begins. Four middle-aged musicians stroll in wearing the garb of medieval students—tights, pantaloons, crimson velvet jackets strewn with ribbons and medals—and they sing and play mandolins and guitars so loudly that conversation is impossible.

"Isn't this wonderful!" Edith shouts.

Alec, shredding a matchbook, gives her a dreamy, sidelong look and smiles at Joe and says something. Joe, not comprehending, shrugs and nods and takes a big drink of Chianti.

After the musicians leave, Alec starts talking about Lucy. She wants to have another baby to keep Todd from getting spoiled. "Frankly, I just think she wants to keep on being a housewife and a new baby would give her a perfect excuse," Alec says. "I've urged her to get a job, maybe a part-time nursery-teacher job or something along those lines, but she says Todd needs her all the time. But she might write a children's book—she's been thinking about doing that. We had Bill Blansford over for dinner—we're doing an exquisite edition of his new poems—and she was asking him all about what kind of typewriter to buy."

Joe begins to have trouble following Alec's words; it's as if he's listening to a tape being played backwards, or as if he has suddenly been parachuted into a nightclub in Albania. Angela would appreciate that observation. He watches Edith saying something to Alec, and he can't understand her, either. Has something happened to his brain? He's been smoking more dope lately—could it be that? Smiling and nodding, he pretends to participate in the conversation.

Back at the loft, Edith serves the chocolate torte. "I know you love chocolate, Alec." She seems much nicer to Alec than she ever is to Joe; Alec always looks like he's starving. When they work on a jigsaw puzzle of Monet's lily pads, Joe puts his hand on Edith's thigh under the table.

"You know, I would dearly love to photograph the two of you in the nude," Alec says, getting up and pacing. He unplugs the refrigerator, blows the dust off the plug, and sticks it back in the wall socket.

"Oh, let's!" Edith exclaims. "It would be super—we could get enlargements and frame them."

"Well," Joe says. The last nude woman he saw in the loft was Angela. "I don't really—"

Edith makes up a bed for Alec on the sofa and goes into the bedroom after kissing both men good night. "Got any cognac?" Alec asks.

Joe finds an inch of brandy in the bottom of a bottle under the sink. Alec insists on dividing it equally in two tumblers. "Joe, it's so great to see you, to talk with you. I've missed that."

"Me, too."

"Sometimes when something happens at the press, or when something happens between me and Lucy, I think: What would Joe have to say about this? When I was going through that divorce, man, you were a *brick*." Alec cups his hands, presses them to his upper lip, and looks at Joe intently.

"I don't have anyone I can speak with like that now either,"

Joe says, "I see Gerard, he's doing some work for the newsletter at the moment, but—ah, I don't know." Gerard has never behaved as Joe's equal; he always insists on being the subordinate and at the same time he keeps suggesting that Joe doesn't know how to live fully and needs some ecstasy lessons. "He's gotten away from writing poetry lately."

"Too bad—Gerard has always been a very sweet person, and one hell of a poet." Alec speaks without any interest whatsoever in what he is saying. He finishes his brandy. "Joe, something is going on that I have to tell you about."

Joe does not want to know what Alec is going to say; he wants to go to bed and go to sleep.

"I am in love. I don't know if you've ever—" Alec hesitates and glances toward the bedroom end of the loft—"really completely absolutely fallen for some woman. This has never happened to me before. It's all I can think about."

Joe stares at Alec. Is Alec saying he was never in love with Lucy? It's too much to think about coherently.

"She's Jamaican. She's a student who's been working part-time for me. Ah, God." Alec takes off his glasses and rubs his eyes with his knuckles.

What if Alec leaves Lucy? How will she survive? Her parents are rich, but how will she survive emotionally? What will happen to Todd? "Maybe it's just a passing thing. These things happen."

"No, old friend. This is *amor*. I absolutely don't know what I'm going to do."

"Does Lucy know?"

"Good God, no! But sooner or later, I'm going to have to tell her."

Angela phones in sick the two days that Joe comes into the office. The rest of the week she asks Belinda to hold her calls and take messages. Joe calls four times. Angela does not return the calls, and when she is at home, she lets the phone ring.

Gerard has moved into a loft and he is giving a big party. Angela knows that Joe will probably be there with Edith, and she debates with Sharon about whether or not she should go. But of course she must go, she is compelled to go, and she buys a dress for the occasion, a light blue jersey dress that clings to her breasts, hips, and calves. "Don't torture yourself," Sharon says. "You must follow your heart," Katha says.

Gerard's loft was once a leather-goods factory, and it still has piles of leather scraps in the corners. It is gloomy and dusty, lit by fluorescent lights. She had no idea Gerard had so many friends. A long table with bottles of liquor. The Rolling Stones on a big tape deck. As she stands in the corner nearest the freight elevator, a short, plump, blond man in a red ascot comes up to her. "Did you know that there are many different kinds of anchovies?"

"Shoot, I sure didn't."

"It's not a well-known fact, but—"

Gerard comes leaping toward her in great pirouettes. His face is flushed. "You must dance with me, Angela—Ron Nussbaum tells me you are a terrific dancer."

"He's here?"

"Oh, somewhere."

It's "Honky Tonk Woman." Angela is relieved that she can dance; otherwise she might start screaming, or implode. She is afraid she will see Joe and Edith.

"I met a div-or-cee from New York City, had to put up some kind of a fight!" Angela sings along. She jumps and whirls and flails her arms. Gerard is so stoned he can barely stay on his feet. Her hair lashes back and forth, and she is possessed by a manic fury. *"She blew my nose and then she blew my mind!"* she screams along with Mick Jagger. Suddenly she gets a sense of how comical she and Gerard must look, how crazed and desperate, but when she looks quickly around the room, she finds that everyone else is dancing that way, too. She closes her eyes and keeps moving.

"May I cut in? May I cut in?" It is Derek Grinder.

"Please do!" Gerard gasps. "I can't take any more." He bows and reels away.

Derek takes Angela in his arms.

"Let's dance, then," Angela says.

Derek is wearing a black T-shirt with the legend "Quanta and Reality for Breakfast" and jeans. He looks about sixteen. "I never dance," he says.

"Oh, you have to. I really want to dance and dance tonight." She hopes she doesn't sound too frantic. Suddenly she sees

Joe's back. His elbow is being clutched by a tall, dark woman with a big nose. Edith must be Greek or Italian. She is wearing a purple pantsuit and espadrilles. Angela is ripped by nausea.

"Only for you, then," Derek says. He waltzes with her while everyone else is dancing to Chuck Berry.

"Nadine—honey, is that you?" Chuck Berry sings.

Angela wishes she were not here. Is that Ron Nussbaum? Is he going toward Joe and Edith? Derek starts kissing Angela's shoulder.

"I have to go," he says. "I just promised Gerard I'd drop by. I hate parties, and I have plantar warts on the soles of my feet."

They have waltzed up behind Joe and Edith. Edith's arm is now across Joe's back; Angela can see the weave in the purple linen. "We're having a *super* time restoring the place!" she is telling someone. Her voice is loud and nasal. She is quite handsome—a little taller than Joe; Joe seems to have shrunk; his head is pulled into his collar.

Janis Joplin starts to sing "Ball and Chain." "I'll see you out," Angela says. *"Oh, noooooooo!"* she screams along with the record.

"Angela, Angela!" She stops. She is afraid to turn around and see who is calling her. Finally she does turn, and it's Ron with a pretty, dark-haired woman wearing long rhinestone earrings. "I'd like you to meet my *fiancée*, Gibbons Loring," Ron says. "She told me she'd forgive me if you and I had one dance."

"This is my *husband*, Derek Grinder," Angela says, "and we're just leaving."

They ride downstairs in the freight elevator. Derek has his bicycle chained to a Stop sign.

"Can I ride it a minute?" she asks. She has not ridden a bike since Gatch. She gets on and wobbles, and makes a little circle on the sidewalk, then another. She begins laughing. The laughter wells up from under her ribs and makes a sweet taste in her mouth. Derek grabs the handlebars and stops the bike and begins kissing her. He kisses her for a long time.

"I'll be right back." She goes upstairs and finds her shoes and purse where she hid them behind the propped-open fire

door. She keeps her eyes on her feet so that she won't see Joe
and Edith.

Derek pedals through the empty streets with Angela seated
sidesaddle on the crossbar. There's a cool night wind; they
could be sailing. His knees brush softly and rhythmically against
her.

He lives in a warehouse, on a floor above the offices of a
floor-tile business. It is divided up into a maze of little musty
rooms. In one, there is nothing but a dark wooden hat rack
which has a mirror and is carved with scrolls and acorns. A
black and white cat meows. Derek takes Angela through the
bathroom—the bathtub contains a shattered blue coffee mug—
to a hallway lined with books, and into a room with nothing
but four black velvet pillows and a stereo. He puts Rod Stewart
on the record player, "Mandolin Wind," excuses himself to
feed his cat, returns, and removes her dress. "You're really
beautiful," he says. "I didn't realize."

He has a long, compact body, muscular—probably from so
much bike-riding. "You taste like nectar," he says. "You smell
like grapes as they're just fermenting." She is impressed with
his metaphors. As they make love he seems to her tender and
happy and above all, calm. He is light; she misses Joe's weight,
but she is relieved to be with someone else. Later, he brushes
his cat. "My cat is starved for attention."

Angela feels sorry for Derek. He lives in this strange place
and he must be very lonely.

He takes her into yet another room, which has a four-poster
bed with a patchwork quilt. He lies down and makes a space
to his left. All night he sleeps with his arm stretched out,
holding her.

She wakes up not knowing where she is. Derek looks different without his glasses on. Like a ten-year-old with some
down on his upper lip. She remembers the party, and Joe there.
Why is it she should care so much for Joe and they have never
spent a night together, while it seems so simple to do with this
man she barely knows? She considers removing the fragments
of the cup from the bathtub and taking a shower, but then gets
an eerie feeling about that. Derek wakes up, makes love to
her, and takes her into a room with a hotplate, a refrigerator,
a sink, an old Philco radio, a bed, and a desk with a typewriter.

He makes her a cup of instant coffee with warm tap water and they each eat a peach, and then he holds her hand and walks her to the subway past trucks loaded with bolts of cloth and rags and ribbons. Angela feels lucky. She could get to care for this man.

"You intimidate me," Derek says. "You're so dramatic."

"Me?"

They kiss. "You are beautiful," he says. She is grateful; Joe has never said a word about her looks. She doesn't believe Derek, but she likes being told she's beautiful.

"I hope I see you soon." She was not going to refer to the future; it just slipped out. She begins descending the subway steps. A dank hot exhalation strikes her face. She smiles back at Derek.

"Now my mind is all messed up," Derek says.

Joe phones Angela at her apartment. It's a Saturday morning—why doesn't she answer? Why hasn't she returned his calls this week? What has he done now? The day spreads out in front of him like a vacant lot littered with car parts.

When he hears a knock on the fire door he hopes it's her, but it's only the window washer. He is hairless except for one greasy gray strand that clings to the back of his head, and he has two teeth, one twisted. He wears ancient gray twill and boots without bootlaces. He carries a bucket, a roll of newspapers, and a nearly empty plastic bottle of ammonia.

"All I ask is hot water," he says. As he rubs the sheets of newspaper soaked in hot water and ammonia against the windowpanes, producing an atonal series of squeaks and throaty rubbing sounds, he replies in kind, talking in squeaks and rubs.

He speaks window, Joe thinks: I could end up like him. What did the window washer think when he realized, at some point many years ago, that his life was half over? Did he ever wonder why he was alive? Did he ever have a more ambitious calling? Was there ever a woman? Women? What sacrifices has he made? Joe feels suddenly self-conscious, as if the man might read Joe's thoughts as he polishes away the dirt and soot from the glass.

Joe dials Angela's number again. No answer. It was not fair of her to leave the party with Grinder. She was taking

advantage of the situation. He hates to think about her roaming
freely but he can't stop himself. If he had Angela all to himself,
he would really know her. He would know himself. Why he
is here and what he is supposed to do. With her, he feels on
the verge of a big discovery. With Edith he feels walled-off;
a shallow breather. But Angela—there's no future with her:
she believes in fortune-telling and massage. She doesn't even
remember to pay her income tax. She says Joe is extraordinary,
a terrific lover, capable of great things. Edith does not think
those things. Edith thinks that if he doesn't change his socks
every day, his feet stink. And Edith is right.

"I did these windas in 1941 when this was the Cohn Fastener
Factory," the window washer says when Joe pays him. "Oughta
get new glass, that old glass is oxidized up." But the windows
are so clean they have disappeared.

Joe hopes that when he's that old he at least will know how
to do one thing well. This would be a good remark to make
to Angela. He thinks of the half-moon curve of her belly and
dials her number. No answer. He has always been good at
poker; sooner or later she's bound to tip her hand, to give
herself away. All he has to do is watch her for a clue. But
sometimes she just disappears inside herself, like a cat swallowing its tail. Once they were sitting in a bar so dark that no
one would be able to recognize them, and she did that. After
he asked her what she was thinking, she waited a while and
then said: "That everything is a gift. I could never have lived,
never been awake, but here I am." And then she lifted up her
chin and straightened her back, and took off: "The candlelight
here is a gift, and the people at the other tables, and that blues
guitar playing, and you—being with you is a gift." She can be
very farfetched and romantic at times, but she is so earnest,
her words are so heartfelt, that what she is saying must mean
a lot to her, and it stirs him. Stuff like: "Here I am, a point of
consciousness, perceiving the miraculous secret." For him, she
is the secret, a hieroglyph. If he could read it, he would know
the world. But she won't return his calls.

Edith phones. "Did the window washer come yet?"

"Yes."

"Did he do a good job?"

"Yes."

"Is everything okay?"

"Sure."

"You sound—introverted."

He has nothing to say to this.

"Don't forget to pick up the jigsaw blades, and maybe you should put gas in the car so we can leave as soon as I get home from work."

"Okay."

"Love ya, sweetie!" She is artificially perky—someone must have come into her office.

When he had to work all the time, he imagined how exhilarating it would be to have enough time to wander around the city. Now, going out is a chore. Even so, he is glad to have something to do: jigsaw blades and gas. With the right blade and a router bit he should be able to duplicate the gingerbread porch trim that's rotting away under the bittersweet vines.

He goes outside. It's like stepping into a brick kiln. The air is thick and smoldering, the sky, like porous stone. Diesel fumes given off by the idling tractor trailers at the lading docks catch in his throat. It is even too hot for the gang at the corner. A woman sticks her head out of the door of the deli. She wears pink curlers. "Lee-roy!" she shouts.

He passes a crowd of teenaged girls. They are wearing short skirts and halter tops and they eat ice-cream cones. Tongues, breasts, exposed navels, bare legs flash past Joe. His hands want to reach out to them. In the square, men and women, arms around one another, thighs pressed together, lie on the parched grass or loll on benches next to transistor radios all tuned to the same throbbing song, viscous with lust: *"Ah, ah, uhhhh, give me every inch of your love!"* Women sit on the rim of the fountain, their skirts pushed up around their thighs, their breasts about to spill out of their low-cut tops, and swish their feet in the water. He has never gotten enough of Angela. He wants to eat a cheeseburger, but the wires hurt his mouth. He wants to make love to Angela, but she has disappeared, taking with her the secret part of himself that she brought to life.

As he walks on, he smells smoke and discovers that the street has been blocked off by police cars and several fire trucks.

A big crowd has gathered. An old factory building is burning. Not one that he had ever particularly noticed. About six stories high, with flames visible in every upper window, and black smoke erupting through the roof, which has collapsed. He can feel the heat, heat upon the heat of the day. A policeman is leaning against a barricade drinking a Coke. "What happened?" Joe asks him. "Was anyone hurt?"

"Naah. A couple people were living there illegally, and they got right out. It started about four this morning and it's probably going to burn for a couple of days."

"A couple of days?"

"Sure—I've seen it before. These buildings have old wood, it's well-seasoned, it burns real hot, you know, enough to melt metal. Once one of those floors gets going, that's the ball game. It might as well be a lumberyard. Anyway, the owner had the sprinkler system turned off so there wasn't a chance."

"You think it was arson?"

"Maybe." The cop shrugs. "Coulda been the electric, something of that nature. These old factories, they got old machinery, old wiring, and the owners don't want to do anything about it because they're trying to sell and get out. They lose everything in the fire and make out like bandits—arson or no."

Joe watches for a while until the heat makes him uncomfortable and then he walks on. The wiring and the sprinkler system in his loft are sound—he checked them when he was renovating. Nothing to worry about. What would it feel like to lose everything—who would you be, then? Would you even exist?

He goes into a hardware store. Before Angela walked into his office, life was peaceful and intelligible. He and Edith were good companions, weren't they? In those days? He inhales the oily, metallic, air-conditioned air and fingers jigsaw blades. I am going through a very bad time, he says to himself. How am I ever going to get free?

"The way to get over an unattainable man, Angela, is to make a demand on him," Buff Goodhugh says.

He has taken her to lunch—"Sorry, I'd take you to my club but they don't allow women"—at a midtown restaurant near Sixth Avenue with carved walnut paneling and brass chandeliers and a German maître d' who says, "Good day, Mr. Good-hugh."

Angela is not sure whether Goodhugh knows about her and Joe. (Belinda, of course, makes knowing remarks each time she brings Angela her telephone messages.) "Thanks for the tip, Buffalo Buff."

"Make a demand on him and he evaporates."

She eats a clam. "Where did you learn that?"

"My analyst. Oh, I used to get around a bit. But security—I've realized—is far more important than romance and passion. Single people are the wrack and ruin of American society. People should get married and stop causing trouble, you know."

As if all single people could simply marry in an instant and cure society. Angela smiles at the thought of roving gangs of troubled unmarried people wreaking havoc. Belinda has told her that Goodhugh has a beautiful new mistress. Ruth Fein-stein—the vice-president of a company that makes false eye-lashes and fingernails. "You are absolutely right, Buff." Even if she argued with him, he wouldn't hear her.

"Take Bly," Goodhugh continues. He evidently has a plan: this lunch is not a social occasion. "He can't make up his mind about anything. It would seem that he would settle down and accept his fate as a responsible adult. He's over thirty, he has children, girls I believe. But one week he wants to quit his job. The next week he wants to start a new newsletter."

Angela has not heard anything about that project.

"The week after that he wants to come in only on Wednes-days. Then he takes a leave of absence. Now, as you know, I myself think the world of him, and he's managed splendidly and made Starr Whorf a few dollars—so I'm willing to see him through any new project he might design, and aid and assist him in finding himself. But first some major change will have to be undertaken in the structure of Starr Whorf. *Entre nous,* the entire board of directors has got to go. They're run-ning us into the ground, and at the rate they're going, we'll all be on the streets in two years. There's not much air left in the tank at the moment."

Angela wonders how Goodhugh can do anything about the board of directors. He is under them.

"It is better to be feared than to be loved, you know."

Angela doesn't know how this follows from what he just said. She nods, however.

"As of course you know, if you play your cards right, you have a magnificent and excellent future here. Just what exactly have you been doing on the executives' newsletter?"

"Well." She takes a long drink from her glass of white wine. She doesn't want to say she is now running the whole thing, because that will slight Joe, and Joe has said he doesn't trust Goodhugh. She doesn't want to give him any ammunition. On the other hand, she doesn't want to seem to be doing less than she's paid to do, particularly since her most recent raise. "Some of everything—design, layout, writing, rewriting, editing, interviewing, talking to the people in marketing and the printer."

"Do you think you could spend a minute going over a report I'm working up for presentation? You have taste and good sense, and you could be a help to me."

"Why, I'd be proud to."

As they leave the restaurant, he puts his hand on her shoulder. "It's when you get over passion that you can really appreciate someone and feel secure." His tone is gentle and his face has softened. She realizes that he has suffered, just as she is suffering. He, too, is looking for reasons, mottoes, assurances.

"Well, I think security is a fantasy," she says. "Everything can change in a minute. The bomb can fall. The dam can bust." She knows, though, that his idea of security includes a wife, a baby, a mistress, and an inherited disposable income of around two thousand dollars a day. "But maybe I'm just crazy." She grimaces and waves, her rings clicking. Goodhugh must be aware of her hopeless situation. She must radiate defeat and loss. As they cross Fifth Avenue, Goodhugh says, "It's always a relief to me to return to the East Side."

Back at the office, she stumbles over Gerard, who is lying on the carpet with his hands folded across his chest and his eyes closed. He resembles a carved sarcophagus.

"What did Goodhugh have to say?" He gets up.

She shakes her head. She thinks of Goodhugh's uncharacteristic sympathy and tears come to her eyes. Has he heard of her terminal illness, passion? As with a terminal illness, there seems to be nothing she or anyone else can do. Even Katha's suggestion to go to Joe didn't work. All treatments have failed. She blows her nose.

Gerard puts his arm around her. "Don't let the old bastard get to you—he'll never fire you."

"It's not Goodhugh. He's fine. It's really nothing. There's so much damned *work*."

When Angela gets home she phones Derek Grinder and reaches his telephone answering machine. "Committee to Re-Elect," Derek's voice says. "This is Angela Lee speaking to you in person," she says for her tape-recorded message.

A few minutes later, Derek phones.

"I just called to say hi," Angela says.

"I just called to say hi," Derek says.

"How are you?"

"I'm fine. How are you?"

"I'm fine. How are you?"

"I'm fine. How are you?"

"Uh, it's a nice day." Angela is completely thrown.

"Yes, it's a nice day."

There is a long silence. She has made a bad mistake. "What have you been up to, lately?"

"I'm working on a long but actually brief essay for the *Times*."

"I'm glad you're alive and well." She regrets having mailed him a sponge with a decal of a bosomy diving girl and the legend "Greetings from Sag Harbor." Those whom the gods wish to destroy, they first introduce to Derek Grinder.

Sharon is at Sam's. Katha is out. Angela lies on her bed drinking a beer and listening to the phone ring. Rain is coming. The sky goes iron and the air turns cool and the ailanthus boughs outside her window start to flail in the rising wind. The pianist goes over and over a passage from the Mozart concerto. A jet roars overhead. Angela takes a piece of paper and her silver pen and makes a list of compliments men have paid to her. "Buff: sense and good taste. Derek: beautiful, like peach, grapes, etc. Joe: ?" She feels worthless. But she has gotten through another day without calling Joe.

25

JOE GOES THROUGH THE woods spraying each dead tree with an orange *X* so that even after the leaves are down in the fall he will be able to go on cutting firewood. Then he works through the heat of the day in a clearing. Ignoring the gnats, he pulls fallen trees out of the brook and cuts up the ones that aren't waterlogged with a bow saw—he's afraid of chainsaws. Some of the logs could be notched and used to build a cabin. He will leave those for the last, and then decide.

He is relieved to be alone. Edith has not been able to get away from her job as often as she thought she would. When she arrives on Friday nights she is tense from the drive but she feels she can't sit down until she's cleaned the kitchen. During the weekend she struggles with her hay fever, stays inside studying, or drives around to antiques dealers and prices furniture. When she was able to get a few days off, Todd was visiting, and Edith decided to go back to the city early. It was a good thing, too: no matter what Edith tries, she and Todd don't get along. But she says she's working on this.

One morning he walks into the village to inquire at the real estate office about the tract of land adjoining Edith's. Between the real estate office and the sandal shop is a store called the Compleat Juggler. When he looks in the window, an odd, prickling, oscillating sensation rises in his chest. He has leafed through the juggling book Angela gave him, but he never bought the balls. Maybe someone at the store gives lessons. A few minutes of practice every morning, and by the time his leave of absence is over . . .

But there is a sign on the glass door: "On Vac. Be Back Soon." Dust has collected in the display window. A spider has constructed a web between a jester's cap and a magic wand from which colored scarves spill. Pressing his face close to the glass, he can see three different kinds of Tarot decks fanned out inside a circle made of red, green, and blue balls. There are white saucers containing incense cones and amber crystals of frankincense; there are paper doves, bottles of invisible ink, and magic boxes. In the back he can see shelves with books, soaps, and little figurines; a popcorn machine; an orange-and-black flowered kimono pinned to the wall like a butterfly; posters from Japanese samurai movies; and an antique brass cash register. The floor is painted in alternating diamonds of black and white. This is Angela's kind of place, all right.

Yes, the land is for sale, eventually, the broker tells Joe. Right now it's tied up in an estate settlement.

Joe buys a crowbar at the hardware store and walks back through the forest. He has lost Angela. There is so much within him that could destroy him, the way it destroyed what he had with Angela.

He pries up the splintering, rainbeaten floorboards of the porch with the crowbar. First he was just going to replace the trim, and to do that, he had to get a longhandled clippers to cut away the heavy tangle of bittersweet slumping over the porch roof. When the vines were cut away, sunlight hit the floorboards and he saw what bad shape they were in. There is so much to do around this place. There's no way he will be able to winterize it before cold weather hits. And he's got to cut firewood. And the wiring—when will he get to that? Edith is anxious to install the chandelier.

As he works, he looks through the window into the house. The cathedral ceiling of the main room of the house is like the inside of a boat's hull: curved ribs of reddish-brown cedar, beautifully fitted joists and beams held by pegs. He has stripped the mantelpiece of its paint and oiled it, and now the rich, old, close-grained oak glows softly. It will be very cozy when it's cold enough for him to build a fire—the yellow light flickering in the reddish room.

A delivery truck arrives with a refrigerator Edith bought: it has an ice-maker and an ice-water dispenser. And then Edith drives up with a cherrywood dining table roped to the roof of the car. He helps her lug it into the dining room. Her cheeks are red and her eyes are lustrous. "Whew!" she says. "Won't the table look perfect under the chandelier when we get it installed! Oh, look what you've done to the porch, wonderful, super! We have to have Lois and Jim over soon."

For dinner she makes taramosalata, spinach and feta strudel, and serves baklava she brought from the city. Afterward, he dozes over a jigsaw puzzle of an abstract impressionist painting, Jackson Pollock, until the phone rings.

Edith answers, and he hears her sympathy voice. "I'm sure everything will be perfectly all right," she says in her rich, soothing, confident tone. "There is absolutely no reason to worry. He will be back."

Joe is sweaty and grimy, and he gets up to take a shower and go to bed, but Edith grabs him as he passes and covers the phone receiver. "It's Lucy!" she whispers.

Joe does not want to speak to Lucy, but Lucy insists, and so does Edith, pushing the phone into his face. Alec is living in a motel with some Jamaican girl and he refuses to come to his senses and come home, and Todd is very anxious, and Lucy doesn't know what to do. "It's his *responsibility*. He's my *husband*. He's *supposed* to be here. Joe, you've got to make him come back. Here's the number of the motel. Just phone him and tell him, remind him of his responsibilities. He has obligations and he has to live up to them."

Joe phones Alec. "Lucy is very upset, and Edith is worried about her and wanted me to call. Is everything okay?"

"I'm in heaven," Alec says. "You think Lucy will manage all right? What did she say? Tell me exactly what she said."

Joe is very tired. Why has he been chosen to referee? He

goes through Lucy's list of complaints. "She feels you're not being responsible, that you've forgotten your obligations."

"Did she ever mention love? Did she ever say, 'I love Alec and I want him to come back'? Anything of that nature?"

"No..."

"See what I mean?"

"Well, maybe it's necessary," Joe says lamely. "Maybe sometimes it's necessary to make certain sacrifices."

That night Joe and Edith have a long discussion about Alec and Lucy. "Alec has always been childish and thoughtless," Joe says.

"He probably doesn't know how much he's hurting poor Lucy," Edith says.

And so they talk late into the cool summer night, companionable and relieved to be working on a relationship other than their own.

26

<hr style="width:40%">

"I'M GOING TO TAKE the Cure," Angela tells Sharon. "I worked extra and I'm one whole newsletter ahead, so Good-hugh is willing to give me some time off. I'm going to house-sit for Katha's friends."

"Good luck." Sharon is depressed. She lies on Angela's couch eating slices of smoked mozzarella. "I guess I'll be in Westhampton with Sam."

"Things are not going well?"

"Oh, yeah. Sam says he wants to spend his vacation with me."

"That's really great." Angela remembers with a twinge her hope that she and Joe would spend August together.

"I won't be seeing my shrink for a month. What if this August I really do go crazy?" Sharon scowls and twists a strand of hair behind her ear. "My shrink says I'm just using Sam to avoid my real feelings for *him*."

"Isn't it possible that you care for Sam, and Sam cares for you? Isn't it possible that in the old way of things, Tarzan and

Jane and all of that, that you want to be together? Man and woman? Why does this shrink have to meddle?"

"I have these patterns about men, that's why. Sam has all these hang-ups about his wife. But I'm beginning to wonder—every time I go into that brown office and lie down on that awful brown leather couch, I just hope he's going to stay awake—my shrink, I mean. He keeps asking me don't I realize how deeply attracted to him I am."

"Are you?"

"Angela. He's five feet tall, he's very fat, he's about fifty. No, I am not attracted to him. And he has terrible taste. I pay him all this money and every time I go in he's got some new *tchotchke*, like a spiny blowfish in a Lucite box."

Angela is staying in a big old fieldstone house—it used to be an inn—with a barn, fields curving down to a wide stream with a covered bridge, and a pine woods. In the cool, dim parlor over the fireplace, there is a portrait of the family who live there. She did not meet them, but she feels as if she knows them. The father is tall, blond, bearded, handsome, and manly. The mother has a cloud of red hair, regular, chiseled features, a pale oval face, and a warm smile. They are posed behind a Victorian loveseat. On the loveseat are their two little girls. They are blond and pretty, and they wear dotted-swiss fluff dresses, white ankle socks, and black mary janes. They all gaze into the camera with flawless serenity: We are the Ideals, of course we are serene. Mrs. Ideal has left many notes, written in a round, left-handed script with plenty of exclamation points. "Pick the zucchini when it's *small!*" "TV turned on at the wall switch—*not* at TV!" "Blanch broccoli, seal in plastic bags, then into freezer!" "*Please* help yourself to everything!"

The first few days she does almost nothing. She sleeps a great deal, and wanders around the property, and cools her feet in the shallow, pebbly stream. At night in an overstuffed chair next to the fireplace by the yellow light of a hand-painted globe lamp, she reads Wallace Stevens.

> This is, therefore, the intensest rendezvous.
> It is in that thought that we collect ourselves,
> Out of all the indifferences, into one thing . . .

> *Out of this same light, out of the central mind,*
> *We make a dwelling in the evening air,*
> *In which being there together is enough.*

She puts the book down and looks through the Ideals' record collection, which is huge. Lots of Mozart. The complete piano concertos. She puts one on the stereo, and writes Joe a letter. "I can't forget what it was like to lie in your arms. I am in a beautiful place and love you and miss you. I hope you will come." And so on. She draws an extravagantly labeled map on the back and writes her phone number at the top of the page.

The thing that is to happen between us has not yet happened, she tells herself.

The garden is overflowing with its harvest. Eggplants bend over with the weight of their glossy purple fruit. Tomatoes spill onto the ground. Green beans as long as her hands make the vines sag. She picks vegetables and makes them into salads and Chinese stir-fry and freezes them as Mrs. Ideal has directed. She reaches deep into the dark loam for the roots of weeds. She turns over the compost with a pitchfork and each day adds kitchen garbage.

In the evenings she spreads the vegetables she has picked for dinner out on a table on the screen porch and contemplates them. In the clear green twilight, they glow like jewels. She sits listening to the insect din, which grows more frantic with each night as the summer diminishes. She smells the dew collecting and watches the soft light leave the fields, the pine grove, and finally the sky. She listens to her own breathing and contemplates her hands, lying still in her lap like two babies.

She idly picks up books—*The Big Sleep, War and Peace*—and finds herself reading them backwards chapter by chapter. Next to the bed, she discovers the complete works of a call girl who views sex with anyone as just that. Sex. The prostitute doesn't seem to know about the terrible disease of love and its dread, wearing-down force. Angela envies her.

She closes her eyes in the cool night, with a dog barking a long way away, and imagines what it is like to be dead. The end of the body. And what if Joe were dead, too?

—*Is it true? That we never got together? It seemed so real.*

—*No. We never did get together. I don't understand. All I wanted was to be with you.*

—*That's all I wanted, too.*

But now they have, in death, lost everything: time, their bodies. Sensation, emotion, hearts, brains.

On the other hand, maybe they won't be able to distinguish after death which experiences they dreamed about and which ones they lived.

In the mornings, she bicycles through the fragrant pine woods, the copper needles that pad the ground muffling all sounds, and bathes in the stream naked.

The second week, she drifts less. I am taking the Cure, she thinks. Each day I am away from Joe I recover a little more of myself, and someday I will be whole. Whole in a new way. She scythes the hay growing up around the barn. She hauls wheelbarrow loads of decayed leaves from the locust trees around the house to the garden. "Mulch if you like!" Mrs. Ideal wrote. "Keep the weeds down!"

Laura, the daughter of a neighbor, comes to mow the lawn. She is sturdy, brown, big-boned, square-jawed, and has dark hair in a long ponytail. She seems much older and wearier than a sixteen-year-old ought to. Angela invites her to stay for dinner and learns that the girl's mother is dead and that she has to take care of her younger brothers and sisters. Laura tells Angela the local gossip. "The woman in that big modern house with all the glass just sits in her bathtub and drinks all day," Laura says. "I sometimes help out with the housekeeping. She has two kids. Her husband left her for a seventeen-year-old model named Winky."

Angela still has an exceptional fondness for stories about men who leave everything to start a new life.

"He and Winky moved to New Hope and started a batik factory. He used to be on Wall Street."

"Good," Angela says. "I mean, at least he's doing what he wants."

"And the Scotts, who live in that big place off Dark Hollow?" Laura continues. "Mr. Scott used to be an important lawyer in Philadelphia and he and Mrs. Scott were always fighting, then one day he packed up all his things and threw them in his car but it broke down at the end of their drive so now he just lives in his car and earns money babysitting."

"Not good," Angela says.

The way Angela thinks about Joe is changing, maybe from the solitude, the strenuous labor of each day, and the quiet evenings on the porch when she sits and allows her mind simply to reflect everything around her. He has begun to depart from the totality of her thinking. He is not always with her. She knows now that he is not going to phone, or answer her letter. He isn't in the garden, in the dirt, the compost, or the hay. Or in the other room working while she sits on the porch. He really is another person, and he really is somewhere else. An ex-imaginary playmate. When she takes deep naps during the heat of the day, she awakens refreshed, a sweetness in her throat. In the mirror she sees that she has become lithe and tanned and clear-eyed.

One night she has a long uncomfortable dream in which she is in a movie theater watching close-up films of herself. She sees how so many of her characteristics, mannerisms, and thoughts are imitations of others she has known over the years. Straining to be what she is not—like a dancing dog in a tutu. She feels a horror at this thick overlay of falseness. Where is she? Where is the real person underneath all that? When she awakens she thinks, I must change, I must find my genuine self.

Her last evening here, she sits on the porch eating a soup she has just made from zucchini, basil, chicken broth, and cream. She can taste everything. With each bite she remembers the sun in the garden, the warm green zucchinis, the basil, pungent and sweet, moving in the breeze. I am well, she thinks. I am happy.

She hears the crunch of car wheels on gravel in the drive and assumes it is Laura. When she hears the scuff of sandals on the flagstone walk she calls out, "Come in and set a spell!" in her biggest drawl.

When she sees that the person coming in the screen porch is Joe, she is afraid she has conjured him up, imagined him, that it is his double, summoned by her belief that she is cured.

He looks washed out under the yellow porch light, and thinner. He needs a shave.

She wishes it were not him, arriving to destroy the perfection of this summer night. Anyone but him. But she greets him heartily. "Hello! Hi!" she cries enthusiastically. She hugs him, and he grips her upper arms. "Hey—I sure didn't expect this."

"I've been driving for four hours." His voice is barely audible. "I left Edith."

"Oh, no!" Her cry is involuntary. "I mean, I don't believe it."

"She knows. She knows everything." Joe does not look at her.

"What happened?" Angela feels slapped by guilt. Did Sharon tell Lynn, did Lynn tell Trudy, did Trudy tell Edith? Was it something Angela did? She puts her arm around his waist and seats him at the table. She has a sudden recollection of when she was small and seated large dolls and teddy bears at a little table-and-chair set.

He left her, and he has come to me, she thinks, explaining it to herself almost aloud so that she will be able to comprehend it. She feels she is telling herself a story: And then, and then . . .

He removes a folded piece of paper from the pocket of his workshirt and hands it to her.

"Would you like something to eat? A drink?"

"A drink."

She takes the paper and goes into the kitchen and snaps on the light. She blinks in the brightness. It is the letter she wrote him—x's scrawled across the bottom of the page, the whimsical map on the back saying "Here there be Tygers." She shudders. A teenage letter. All she can find in the way of alcohol is a bottle of crème de menthe she brings out with a glass of ice cubes. "She saw it."

"Yeah."

"She opens your mail?" She wishes she didn't sound so nasty.

"No, I was staying at the house and I left it on top of the refrigerator. She came up early from the city and it fell when she opened the door."

Angela feels very sorry for Edith. She must be suffering. She can taste Edith's tears in the back of her throat, where the breath strikes when she opens her mouth to speak. She wants to apologize, and to say how badly she feels about everything.

She puts her hand on his shoulder. It feels unelectric, slack. They still have not looked directly at each other.

"How about some zucchini soup?"

He shakes his head.

He says very little the rest of the evening. "Nice place." "Good restoration job." And: "Look at how thick those beams are." His voice is spiritless. She puts him to bed as if he were an overexhausted child and lies down next to him. He lies flat on his back, his arms at his sides, trembling.

She can't sleep. This is the first night they have ever spent together. He is clearly in no mood to make love. She does not want him to be here. Not like this, anyway. Toward morning she falls asleep thinking, I am alone, as I have been nearly every night for years. She is frightened awake by a tearing, hoarse animal noise.

It's Joe, crying.

27

ANGELA LIES ON THE floor of her living room next to the window fan. She has placed the telephone near her hand. It is Labor Day, and there is a heat wave. The street has been closed off to traffic and a volleyball game is in progress. Men shout. Dogs bark. Radios play salsa music. The relentless pianist practices. He can play the concerto almost all the way through without stopping; he's up to the beginning bars of the final movement. Sharon is in Westhampton with Sam. Katha is away on some mysterious errand.

Angela waits for Joe to call. She barely slept during the night, and got up at five, and now the waiting has taken on a density, a life of its own. He was going to go back to the house in Connecticut to get the rest of his things, then he was going to move his belongings from the loft into storage, and then he was going to get in touch with Angela.

"*Por ti seré, mi amor, mi vida!*" a radio blares.

She has been afraid to use the phone for fear of tying up the line, but finally she calls long-distance information and gets the phone number of the house—in Edith's name, of course.

From time to time during the day she dials the number, then hangs up before it rings. She dials the loft. No answer. Toward the end of the afternoon, she tries the house again. Edith answers. Angela hangs up.

Joe sits on his side while Edith gives him a sponge bath. Propped up on his elbow, he goes in and out of sleep. He is aware of her touch, brisk and certain. The water is lukewarm. They are in a little country hospital.

When Joe arrived at the house in his rented car, Edith was standing at the top of the porch steps. She was wearing shorts, her knees knobby and blackened, her hands on her hips. The new porch flooring was stacked on skids in the driveway.

The whole trip up Joe had felt nauseated and faint. He stared at her knees and wondered if she had been cleaning out the cellar.

"You are just going to run away from your responsibilities your entire life," Edith said. "You don't give a damn about your obligations to others, do you? Look at this porch—how am *I* going to rebuild it?"

Joe shook his head. "I'll get my stuff. I don't feel too well."

"It's because you are repressing. You are repressing your hatred, your anger, and you're repressing your feelings for me by running away, escaping, going to—" But she can't say Angela's name without her voice breaking. "You don't care how much you're hurting me."

"I'll just sit on the step a minute." He was sweating, his abdomen clenched in a spasm of pain.

In the ambulance, she held a cool, wet washcloth on his forehead and urged the driver to speed it up. After the operation, after Joe woke up, Edith told him that the surgeon was surprised that someone could have been walking around like that with a ruptured appendix.

In the night, when the sedatives wear off, he opens his eyes, realizes where he is and what has happened, and sees Edith sitting in a chair next to his bed, her head askew in sleep. "Eed?"

She is instantly awake, her hand on his arm.

* * *

Joe is supposed to come into the office and meet with Goodhugh today, Angela's first day back at work. She keeps waiting for him to pass by her doorway. She has so much work to do that she does not get up from her desk until the end of the afternoon. Belinda stops by to tell her how good she is looking and to ask about her vacation. Tor Bracewell puts his head in the door and welcomes her back. Gerard phones to tell her he won't be able to make it in today.

"Have you heard from Joe?" she asks.

"I haven't. I assume Edith has him doing occupational therapy in the country."

Goodhugh comes in and, as usual, puts one foot on Angela's desk and rests his elbow on his knee. He is wearing loafers but no socks. *"Comment ça va?"*

"Elle verse de l'eau chaude sur les feuilles de thé," Angela says. It's the only French she has retained from school.

"Bly called a while ago. He won't be in for another few weeks."

"Oh, really?" Angela is unnaturally blasé. She can hear her phoniness, and feel her face hardening.

"He was at his country place and he got a ruptured appendix, evidently."

"Oh. Gosh." He is sick, maybe alone. He didn't turn to her when she could really have helped him. "Where? Did he say where?"

"Calm down, dear girl. I don't know *where* he is, but it would seem that he is in competent hands, in a hospital."

Has she blundered into a soap opera? With Joe, nearly every day brings a new crisis overlapping with an older, unresolved one. Even so—she will go to him. He needs her. She has not waited all this time for nothing, has she?

"Are you going to need some help with the newsletter? I suppose you were counting on Bly's return—"

She smiles. She is good at smiling. "Nope—I can manage."

The physician who runs the hospital considers Edith his medical colleague. Before and after visiting hours she stops by his office to chat, and reports to Joe on their talks. The doctor says that if she ever wants to open an abortion clinic he would be happy to have her associated with his hospital. "He says this town needs more medical personnel of my caliber," she says. "We could move up here—after the house is fixed up. Wouldn't that be great? You could just quit your job, or commute."

She doesn't like the way the nurse's aide makes the bed, so she remakes it. She reads to him aloud from news magazines. She brings him a little fuzzy wind-up dog that shakes its head and chimes "How Much Is That Doggy in the Window?" She watches him with a soft, sweet expression that is new to him. It seems to Joe that he has always lain in this bed, in this hospital room with the fan turning overhead and the insects outside pinging against the window screens, always breathed this scrubbed-wood and alcohol odor. He and Edith do not talk about his going to Angela, although after Edith returned the car he rented, she said jauntily, "I have a new insight I have to remember to tell Midge: every relationship has its pluses and minuses."

One morning a new patient is brought into the ward and put in the bed next to Joe's. His name is Tim and his leg is shattered. When he comes out of the anesthetic he tells Joe that he was riding on the back of a friend's motorcycle when the friend ran a red light. A car hit them. His friend was not hurt at all, and the bike just needs a rear wheel.

Joe is glad to have someone to talk to. Edith has been coming mornings and evenings, but she has to go back to work. And he doesn't feel like reading. And he certainly doesn't feel like thinking. When he recalls Angela, a memory of intense abdominal pain intrudes, along with the colorless cold taste in the back of his throat of anesthetic, and he is reminded of the itching around the sutures.

"I've been in two motorcycle accidents," Joe says. "But I still like motorcycles."

"Me too," Tim says. He has a faint, whiskery brown beard and hair in a ponytail. "What kind you got?"

"I used to have a BMW."

They talk about motorcycles, and the Catholic church, which Tim says is the largest landowner in the world, and a reclusive millionaire Tim once worked for, planting trees on his property. "This guy had a real phobia about bird shit. He believed that if food was brought to his table uncovered, bird shit would fall into it. His servants hated him, so they were always putting bird shit in his food." Now Tim makes pottery and has a small shop in the village. "And I'm really into meditation. In fact, some friends of mine are coming tonight to do this healing meditation. I hope you don't mind."

"No, no. What's involved?"

"Well, an ordinary meditation would be just sitting still and observing yourself, your thoughts—you just let them roll on by. But a healing meditation, you direct your inner energy at what needs to be healed."

That evening when Edith arrives, Joe tells her that in a few minutes the meditators are going to come. "Sheesh," Edith says. "What next?"

"So I guess we have to be quiet."

"No, it's okay, really," Tim says.

"Well, I've got to drive to the city tomorrow. I think I'll go home and pack. Is there anything you'd like me to bring?"

"No—but you don't have to go now."

"I couldn't stand not being able to talk." Edith kisses him and brushes her nose against his, and gives his cheek a pinch. Then she straightens the top sheet of his bed, and tidies up the magazines, the ashtray, and the water glass on the bedside table.

"Thank you," Joe calls after her as she goes out the door. He does not want her to go. "I really appreciate everything."

"Naah, don't mention it," Edith says. "I'll try to get Friday off and come up Thursday night."

"You're a lucky son-of-a-bitch," Tim says. "I wish I had a chick like that. My old lady just ran off with a hammer dulcimer player. I couldn't fucking believe she would do that." He let his fist fall on his mattress. "Her name was Wakanda."

Something is making Joe feel good. What is it? It's a faint memory, he can just catch its tail. Edith. He was very pleased at how jealous she was of Angela. He hates to admit being pleased about that, but it's true. He closes his eyes and dreams about a cup, a blue cup with white cranes flying around the rim, and when he opens his eyes, he feels he is missing out on something. "And the terror is . . . and the terror is . . ." How did that line go? Loss, pain, nausea. And what was it he was going to do?

28

ANGELA PHONES ALL THE hospitals in the area where she thinks Joe is. When she finally locates the right hospital, a woman tells her that he is asleep. Angela leaves a message for Joe. Then she calls back and cancels it: Edith might see it.

She phones Derek Grinder. She would prefer not to, but he is the only available man on the horizon. He did say she was beautiful and peachlike.

"It's Angela Lee, the walking legend," Derek says.

"More like a running account." She says she has to do an errand right near his office. "Maybe you have time for a drink or something?"

"I'm not unbusy, but feel free to drop by or not."

Derek's office is small, with an armchair, a television, bookcases, and several thousand books and magazines in stacks everywhere. Shirts, trousers, jeans, neckties, and a fringed leather jacket hang from a hat rack. On his desk is a Xerox of his face and a letter written in purple ink on scalloped blue paper which he quickly covers up with a newspaper. He has gotten a haircut and now his hair juts over his forehead in little spikes. He resembles a frightened bird. "I'm depressed," he says. "Just look at this." He picks up a paper plate that has a sandwich on it covered with blue mold.

She thinks: He is capable of harming me. "What's wrong?"

He bites his lip and presses his fingers to his upper lip. His eyes, worried and remote, glitter behind his aviator glasses. "My problems are not inconsiderable."

"It's okay," she says. Maybe they can just be pals. "I've got problems too."

"I'm too self-centered to want to hear them."

"Okay. Maybe I'll see you around." She goes to the door. Is this the same Derek Grinder who bicycled her to his place and held her all night?

"Please don't leave. I know my cigarette breath is vile. But you are a morally fine person, aren't you? You are the most moral person I know."

"Moral?" She doesn't understand. He doesn't know her very well, they have never discussed morality, and she doesn't even know exactly, really, firmly, what the word means. It's like *heuristic* or *ontological*. On occasion she has looked these words up, but then she always forgets.

"Let's go have a hamburger."

"All right—are you sure?"

"Maybe a corned beef sandwich would possibly be better, don't you think? Or do you?"

They go to a sandwich shop where the Muzak plays "Tea for Two" and the sugar packs on each table have pictures of the presidents on them. "Here's Nixon for you," Angela says.

"People offer me drugs as a test," Derek says. "And when I refuse, they think I'm uptight. I grew up in a very superstitious household—eighteenth-century rationality prevailed. I'm half Jewish and half Christian Scientist."

He is so troubled and complicated that Angela welcomes him as a distraction from Joe. She listens. She asks questions. He tells her about a long difficult love affair and how that overlapped with another long difficult love affair, and how he proposed to both women and then changed his mind. He takes her on the back of his bicycle through the park to her apartment. It is a leafy, end-of-summer night. She sings blues songs as they ride. *"I'm tired, tired of your wicked low-down dirty ways, the Good Book say you been dirty all your days."*

"Your apartment is so clean," he says as they enter it. "The dirt in mine is spooking me. It never did before. When we were bicycling up the West Side it seemed to me like a crouching monster was after me—all those intellectuals, reformers, apartments with high ceilings, people in carcoats."

Angela didn't see anyone in carcoats; the weather is still warm. "Yeah, I know what you mean. Would you like something to eat or drink?"

She is happy to lie in someone's arms, and Derek is a keen lover. Feverish, almost. As she is falling asleep, he says, "Let's have a fight, okay?"

"Why? I'm not mad at you."

"No, you are. I can tell. Let's have a fight and get it out in the open."

"Okay—you go first."

"Well, I don't like you going out with that Samuel James. I know he's supposedly the world's greatest investigative reporter, but I've met him and he's a hustler."

"I don't go out with Sam—Sharon, upstairs, goes out with Sam."

"You're just saying that."

"Do you want me to call up Sharon and ask her to come down? She'll tell you."

"Of course—she'll say whatever you want. She's your friend."

"Could we finish this fight in the morning?"

"I actually like Sam—he's a fine person, don't you think? Or do you?"

In the night she thinks about Joe, and wonders how she can reach him without tangling with Edith. "Italian watches down the hearstverse," Derek says in his sleep.

In the morning, she puts a Bach violin sonata on the stereo and he takes a bath in her fern-patterned tub. "This is like a dream!" he says. She makes hot biscuits and scrambled eggs for him. "I feel worthless," he says.

"Oh, no, you're not worthless. You are a well-known political columnist, your star is rising, you are a good lover, you—"

But he is up and going out the door. "I have to go away now," he says.

One morning in September, Angela hears Joe making his way down the corridor, greeting people. Everyone is glad to see him. She overhears Belinda offering to bring him coffee and Tor Bracewell telling him a Polish joke.

Finally he arrives in her office. He is well-tanned and the lines around his eyes and mouth have been smoothed out. He has lost some weight: there are no gaps between the buttons of his new shirt, a starched and ironed Brooks Brothers. "I've just come by to see Goodhugh about some things," he says.

Angela looks harried and faded. Did she always have that crease between her eyebrows, even when she smiled? Her smile is taut, and if uncontrolled it might suddenly veer into another expression. The phone rings. It's the proofreader—she has hired someone to do that because Gerard lets too many errors go by. "Yes, it should say 'molybdenum' at the top of page four, column one," she says in a fast voice. "Yes, 'frozen sow hyphen belly futures' is correct." He watches her put the tip of her forefinger between her teeth and bite it while she is listening. "Yeah, rush it over by messenger," she says, hanging up.

"Hi," he says.

She stands up and hugs him. "Joe—what happened? I waited to hear from you. I would have gone to the hospital. I wanted to—"

"It's fine, it's really fine."

"You look good."

"Thanks. I've been meditating. There's this meditation group up there, and they do these healing meditations. I don't know if it helped, but I feel much better."

"Great." She frowns and checks her watch—the messenger had better get here fast. "Here's the latest newsletter, if you're interested."

The layout is all changed around. More open spaces. A new typeface. Not things he would have done: he liked it to have a hectic, jumpy appearance; now it's slick.

"What do you think?" Her eyes are wide and pleading. Her upper lip trembles.

"It's fine, it's great, it's really coming together."

"Maybe we can talk soon." Her voice drops. "I want to see you." A switch from the professional colleague to the woman in doubt.

"I can't—I'm just in town for the day."

"Let's talk alternative energy, Bly." Goodhugh appears in the doorway. "How are you?"

"Never better," Joe says.

"We'll have lunch at my club."

Angela feels excluded. It is true, then—Joe is going to start work on a new project. And he must be back with Edith. He seems to have forgotten everything that ever happened between Angela and himself. When Goodhugh leaves, she slides her hand between the buttons of Joe's shirt and rubs the hair on his belly. "What do you think of Derek Grinder?" She has tried every wile—why not repeat the jealousy wile?

He closes his eyes for a minute. "Derek seems like a nice man. Uh, very gentle." Joe keeps his voice nonchalant. "Why?"

"Oh, I've got a big crush on him." She withdraws her hand. "When will you be back in town?"

"In about a month. Goodhugh is letting me extend my leave. I might do some traveling. I'm thinking a lot about what I really want to do next, about what I want out of life."

You are an idiot, she thinks.

"Poor Derek, he says he feels worthless." Angela would like to discuss Joe with Sharon, but Sharon says she has reached her limit. She has never met Joe, but she hates him.

"Maybe he *is* worthless," Sharon says.

They are driving in Sharon's car on the back roads of the Catskills, and they are lost.

"With him you always get the rind, Angela, never the pulp. Maybe there is no pulp."

"Well, I like him. He's—interesting. And what else do I have going for me right now?" Joe is spending a month thinking things over. Maybe, maybe! Just give me time, he said in the spring.

"You know Derek has a reputation for going out with anything female. How often do you see him?"

"A couple of times a week. The rest of the time he's busy working on his column, or some essay. I don't think he sees anyone else. He's very lonely, I think, and depressed. He's got some problems, but he's working on them." Angela really wants to like Derek, to be his girl friend, the woman he takes to Hill's, to parties where there are exciting people, actors, politicians, writers. Until Joe leaves Edith, Angela and Derek could live together in his strange loft, maybe rent a house in the country together. Go to Italy together. He may be troubled, but at least he is not living with Edith Berk. "Do you ever hear anything from Trudy or Lynn about Edith?"

"Not much—just that she bought that house and they're having a great time fixing it up," Sharon says. "The shrink told Edith to find therapeutic things for Joe to do. Look at that beautiful hillside! I wish I was with Sam in Scotland."

Derek phones Angela. "I lie, and then people respond to my lies, and they are unknowingly lying then and I hate them for lying."

"How do you mean that?"

"For instance, you are tying up the phone right now and I am expecting a call from someone. And I don't want her feelings to be hurt by getting a busy signal."

"Wait a minute—" He phoned her, and now he tells her she is tying up his phone? "I don't get this."

"The implications are *obvious*, aren't they?"

"Oh, fuck you!" Angela screams, and slams down the phone.

She buys new clothes. She has decided to stop wearing jeans and boots to the office. Instead, she will now wear skirts and blazers and silk blouses and shoes with heels. Each piece of clothing is evaluated according to how Joe might react to it when he returns to the office. It is surprising to her that she can work so hard, so continuously, with such concentration when Joe and Derek enmesh her thoughts so often and demand of her imaginary conversations in which she straightens them out, sets them on the right track, and they love her for it.

29

JOE STAYS IN THE country and works on the house. He finishes the porch and paints the new trim a deep blue, a lovely color Edith picked out. He reglazes the storm windows and paints their frames blue, too. He stacks the firewood he has cut on the porch. He works on the wiring, although not too often because it is so tedious. Edith comes up on the weekends to scrape the floors. She is the full director of the Queens and Brooklyn clinics and she and Lois are opening a Philadelphia branch. Edith seldom troubles Joe about anything these days. This new quality bothers and intrigues him: first she bought this house, and the new car to get to the house, and in the fall she wants to make a down payment on a house in the city with money she made investing in a real estate deal in Paterson with an uncle. She doesn't seem to need him for anything. She has not mentioned Angela since the day his appendix ruptured. Their joint checking account has a lot of money in it—mostly hers, since his leave of absence began and since she has acquired more shares from Lois. He is glad when she comes up from the city. Except for seeing Tim or Dan when he walks to the village, he talks to no one.

She has not mentioned marriage or having a baby in a long time—even though Lois and Jim got married, and Lois is trying to get pregnant before she is too old to have a baby. And it was Edith who finally persuaded Alec to return to Lucy for Todd's sake.

The Friday evening before Joe's leave of absence ends, he is building a fire in the fireplace, when the phone rings. Edith answers and goes into her sympathy voice. "I'm *sure* everything will be all right." It's a long conversation with so much gynecological terminology that he assumes she is speaking to a patient. He watches the flames spurt and thinks out the kitchen wiring. That part will be so tricky that he ought to hire an electrician.

Edith hangs up and sits on the floor next to the fireplace and is very quiet.

"What is it?" Joe asks.

"Mom."

"Yes?"

"She has to have a hysterectomy. She didn't want me to worry, so she's been keeping it a secret. She has to go into the hospital on Monday."

"Is it serious, do you think?" Joe remembers something about his mother having to have one at some point, but then his mother was always ill.

"She's worried that it's malignant."

Joe puts his arms around Edith. She begins sobbing. "Eed— is there anything I can do?"

"Oh, I couldn't ask you to do anything—it's all right." She takes his arms away from her shoulders, gets up, goes upstairs, and closes the bedroom door behind her.

Saturday morning Angela is awakened by the sickly sweet smell of the paint on the radiator heating up. A wind is blowing. She sits up and swings her feet to the red carpet next to the bed. She senses a big change. Maybe the government has collapsed during the night. Maybe aliens have landed.

She goes downstairs and has tea with Katha, whose skin is

pearllike and translucent, making her eyes an intense, burning blue. She is thinner than ever. "Are you on a diet, Katha?"

Katha smiles, the corners of her long eyes turning up. "I don't eat meat."

"How are the t'ai chi classes going?"

"I won't be teaching this fall. I thought I would take some time off. I may go to a Zen meditation center upstate for a few weeks, too."

"Katha, I woke up feeling something has happened, something was different. Would you do the *I Ching* for me?"

"Maybe it's you who changed, overnight. Have you ever had this feeling before?"

"The day before I got the call about my mother's death."

Katha does not consult the *I Ching* for Angela; instead, she gives her the yellow book and three coins.

"You've had this a long time—these coins are old. I couldn't take it."

"Please—I know it will be upstairs if I need it for anything. Consider it a loan for as long as you like."

Angela goes into the office and works the rest of the day rewriting Goodhugh's report. His training in writing, he has explained with pride, comes from his mother having read *Moby Dick* aloud to him when he was five. Goodhugh's sentences tend to be written in reverse order, as if directly translated from, say, German, and often the content is so cryptic that she finally has to phone Goodhugh at his summer house in East Hampton to ask what he means.

"I mean that all the officers in the corporation have to be fired. The whole board of directors has got to go, lock, stock, and barrel, and that's what I am presenting, *entre nous*, to Whorf and Brunell. Find some way to put that—I can't come right out and say it."

Angela comes into the office late Monday morning. Her hair has been cut, and it hangs, loose and wavy and somewhat fashionable, to her shoulders. She wears a navy blazer, a white silk blouse, and a gray skirt. She has just come from a cool, dimly lit salon with beige décor where women in pink smocks cut and style hair and put clay and seaweed and almond paste on the faces of other women who want to be loved and no one

speaks above a whisper. Angela keeps swallowing and clenching her hands. Today Joe comes back. Her heart rattles.

In the corridor she runs into Goodhugh. "My dear." He puts
his arm around her shoulders. "I met with Whorf and Brunell
this morning and they sat down and read the report. They were
very impressed with my clarity and precision—traits I have
assiduously cultivated, thank God. And you, Angela—you
helped. What you did for me was brilliant, deft, and kind."
He walks her to her office. Why is he being so expansive?
"And if I may be so bold, I would add that you look very
sortable today, dear girl."

She goes directly into her office. She can sense Joe in his.
Belinda pokes her head in the door. "Are you okay, hon?"

"Sure—why wouldn't I be?"

"Just checking."

She departs, and Angela wonders why she was being so
solicitous.

Angela sits and breathes and looks at her hands until Joe
finally comes in. He removes some papers from a chair and
sits down. He glances at the little bowl—no treats today. Both
mugs are dirty, and one has a chip in the rim. Papers and books
and magazines are piled on the desk, the floor, and the filing
cabinet. The Persian miniature hangs crooked. Angela sees him
looking around. She says nothing.

"How are you?" he asks.

"I'm terrific. And you?" She maintains a rigid correctness
and keeps her lips tense. "Did you have a nice leave of absence?"

He shakes his head no. "It was fine, it was eventful."

"Did you travel?"

"Not too much. I was mostly in the country."

"But you got a puzzle ring," she says.

"A puzzle ring? This?" He lifts his hand. On his right little
finger is a ring made of twists of thick silver wire.

"You know, the kind that fall apart into separate pieces.
Isn't that what it is?"

He sees she is serious. "It doesn't do that, but, yes, it's a
puzzle ring."

His face becomes sad and slack. She surmises that he has

had a bad time of it lately. His pain is like little needles in her chest. "Why don't we have lunch?"

"I'm tied up today."

"A drink, after work?"

"I have some, uh, obligations." He and Edith are going to the hospital to visit her mother and cheer her up with the news.

"How about breakfast tomorrow?"

"Okay." Then he blurts it out: "I got married Saturday. I'm sorry I didn't tell you but we did it very suddenly."

"I kind of thought something like that had happened. Well—congratulations."

He looks miserable. He tried to call Angela Saturday morning while Edith was in the shower. To get her to help him stop what was going to happen. But she was not at home. She was with Grinder or God knows who else. Now it is too late, and she is smiling knowingly. "Well, it was a surprise to *me*." The giddiness with which it all was done now seems dreamlike to him. Edith was completely prepared. She knew all there was to know about getting married in the village: where the Justice of the Peace lived, which silversmith had the matching rings. Her friend the physician at the hospital even backdated their blood tests so they wouldn't have to wait three days. Saturday morning, Edith said, "If we don't get married today we never will." Saturday afternoon Lois and Jim arrived to be witnesses and Joe and Edith became husband and wife.

"I feel so—grown up," Joe says. His voice is dull. His eyes seek hers.

Angela sits very still. Her hands remain folded and motionless in her lap. She barely breathes. "You planning to have kids?"

He is startled by her question. "No. Well, I don't think." Edith hasn't mentioned that.

"I hope you'll be a good husband and not screw around."

He smiles at her, showing his new, orderly white teeth, touches her hair, and leaves.

Going home after work, Angela is surprised that people are hurrying along the sidewalks and standing in the street waving for taxis and crowding through the subway turnstiles. As if nothing has happened. She wants the world to end, right now.

In fact, nothing does end. Children scream in the playground in the park across from the subway station as she emerges from underground. The newspaper stand is still on the corner. Dogs are walked. Gravity still works. The sun, inflamed and distorted in the September haze, sinks at the end of her street. It will probably rise in the morning. None of this, none of this should be allowed to continue.

She is aware of every step she takes as she walks to her building. She lies asprawl in her bathtub until the water grows cold. The phone rings and she doesn't answer it. She can feel the merciless passage of time in her bones, in the walls, in the disappearing light of day. The world is empty of everything. Love knocked. When she was complety destroyed in the lightning of love, both old and new things disappeared. And now nothing is left.

Even the edges of the buildings in the clear light of the next morning are engraved with her loss. Love itself has come to her, made her one-eyed, and what she wants, or he wants, or what their friends, or Edith wants—none of this is important.

An odd feature of her memory is that when she recalls the worst stretches of her past, what she remembers is not pain but some other quality, something liquid and fleeting and luminous. The fall that she and her husband finally exhausted their marriage, and Janos left her, she wandered for hours in the park, and what she remembers is the light. It was a clear dry autumn with night frosts that made the trees through the park glow crimson and gold. Today, as she walks through the park to meet Joe, she sees great sheets of light. On the reservoir, in bands across the sky, through the leaves, gold light behind red leaves, red light behind golden buildings, blue and plum shadows. The entire tremendous city is backlit. The day she told her husband to leave, what she remembers is not his face, or the way he left, or what he took, but a bad rainstorm, and two pigeons taking shelter under the pediment of a brownstone across the street.

Her friends tell her that her childhood sounds very bleak, but what she remembers are the great washes of light over the mountains and the mesa, and the sweetness of the sudden moist air just at sunset when the desert plants and the cottonwood surrendered their nectar. In the kitchen over the spice rack,

Katha has a stiff white board that she calligraphed. It says: "Wind, breeze, nectar; moreover, this body ends in ashes: O sacrifice, remember! Whatever is done, remember!"

Angela and Joe have both daydreamed about having breakfast together after a night of ecstasy, but it has never happened that way. The night he spent with her was terrible, and in the morning neither of them could eat. This morning they meet at a Schrafft's. He has not slept much and neither has she.

They look at menus and talk about work. Now that the newsletter is going well, Goodhugh wants him to start another one, something entirely different. Maybe it will be about alternative energy sources. "It's the same old same old—Goodhugh was opposed to my proposal for the executives' newsletter until it began to work. Now he wants me to think up new ways to make money."

"You mean the executives' newsletter was your idea?"

"Yes. I researched the concept, and went around to a lot of corporations and talked to the corporate librarians about getting information, and to executives to get a grasp of what they wanted to see in a newsletter. Goodhugh was against it—finally I took it to the board of directors and they okayed it."

"Do you know," Angela says, "that the first day I was on the job he told me how he had started it?"

"Well, that's not true." Joe doesn't mind; he knows what Goodhugh is like. He is pleased with how well the conversation with Angela is going. They will still be able to work together. "Now this new project, whatever it turns out to be, I want you to collaborate with me. I value your inspiration, your ideas."

She starts to cry. "Why did you do it?"

He absently flicks at the new ring with his thumbnail; it's a little small for his smallest finger. "Get married?" He has never seen Angela cry. He never thought of her as the kind who cries. Furthermore, she is sobbing like a child. He reaches across the table and covers her hand, which is holding a spoon.

"I don't know why I did it." The sound of his own voice, speaking the truth, stops his thoughts and feelings for a few seconds. Then he feels he should apologize, and come up with some explanations that will make Angela understand why it was necessary. "Edith's mother—she wanted it, she's wanted it for a long time. And my kid was getting confused—Lucy decided he shouldn't visit me as long as I wasn't in a stable situation. And, uh, I guess by getting married I'm admitting my dependence on another person." The last remark comes from Midge, via Edith, and he can tell by the way Angela glares at him as she blows her nose and abruptly stops sobbing that she knows it's not Joe speaking.

These are reasons to marry? Angela thinks this, but says nothing.

"It's an experiment," he says. He hates himself.

"I guess I'll have the fried eggs and hash browns," Angela tells the waitress.

She stares out the window for a while at people going to work. The women wear fresh lipstick, the men are in neatly pressed trousers, crisp shirts. Their expressions seem to be of happy anticipation: What will happen to me today? What fine surprises are in store for me? Angela feels no anticipation. Her eggs grow cold.

Joe watches her troubled face. Doesn't she realize it's her fault that he's married to someone else? If only she had been a little more organized, a little more predictable, a little less flighty; if only she hadn't been so critical of domesticity.

She holds her breath and wills herself to be calm. Her vision blackens, there is a roaring in her ears, and she is suddenly aware of her whole being at once, her life spiraling outward from a cluster of molecules, gathering force and color, her whole life widening and speeding up and colliding with other lives. Things have always just happened to her. She exists in whirling fragments held together by momentum and pushed this way and that, oblivious. Meeting Joe changed her. She is no longer her old self. She can never go back to the way she was. Who is she? She exhales, the restaurant reappears, and Joe with it. She gazes into his eyes and says, "You were my great passion, my real love."

He returns her gaze. Now that he is safely behind bars where he can do no further harm. "And I felt exactly the same way about you."

In the middle of the night, she telephones Helen and cries.

"It's all right, it's all right," Helen says. "You can come here, you can be with us. Tom and I love you. It's been so sunny and warm you can't believe it. You come out here, and we'll make chiles rellenos and go for drives up in the mountains and look at the aspens—they're all yellow now. And we'll hang out the clothes. We'll listen to Hank Williams. How soon can you be on a plane?"

"I'll quit. I'll quit my job and come out, maybe tomorrow."

But in the morning she has to present a summary to the board of directors about the newsletter's revenues for the past three months. They are up, and Joe feels she should get the credit for that because he was away most of that period. Afterward, Goodhugh tells her she is priceless and invaluable. "I can't be certain about Bly," he says in a low voice. "But I know you'll keep carrying the ball."

30

ANGELA ENROLLS IN AN exercise class, cleans her apartment with frenzied thoroughness, and asks Goodhugh for a transfer to some other newsletter or, preferably, to another division in another state. He tells her to be patient. "Enormous things impend, *ma chérie*."

She and Joe avoid each other as much as possible, communicating through terse memos. One day they have to discuss the newsletter budget. "Maybe I can talk to Goodhugh about these cuts and work out a compromise," Joe says.

"I *hate* compromises!" Angela shouts, and leaves his office.

Another day, they discuss future topics. "What about adventure?" Joe asks.

"Adventure," Gerard says. "What running dogs of capitalism do for thrills? Most of humanity wouldn't know an adventure if it punched them in the eye."

"Well, what do people do for adventure these days?" Joe picks up a pencil and puts the eraser end between his teeth. He hasn't had a cigarette in ten days.

"They watch color TV and do jigsaw puzzles," Angela says in an edgy voice, and leaves.

Joe is beginning to remember all the lovely moments with Angela, and he can't forget what she said to him in Schrafft's. And so it is a daily shock to him to discover what she is like now: harsh, wan, complaining. When he decreased the margin size of the newsletter, she was furious. You were my great passion, she told him. He remembers bending over her in bed, and the delicious, frightening feeling of climbing up the stairs to her apartment, watching her long legs above him going up the stairs in the dim light. He remembers the way she swept the Tarot cards to the floor, and how she looked down, self-contained and perfect, standing on one foot in the hallway when he was going to leave and then didn't. How he took her in his arms, and then they went into the bedroom and lay under the red canopy. He remembers how her face looked the first time he entered her.

Edith spends a lot of time at her mother's, and sometimes sleeps over there. Her mother is able to get up and walk, and the tumor was not malignant after all, but she needs Edith's company. Edith phones him from the clinic to tell him she has found the perfect house in Brooklyn, in Park Slope. It's a steal. Hardwood floors, three fireplaces, bay windows, wrought-iron balconies, a tiny garden. When he tells her that he loves the loft and does not want to move, she says, "My grandfather sewed *schmattes* for forty years in a sweatshop in one of those sickening lofts."

One Saturday morning Angela goes downstairs to Katha's. Katha is throwing things from an old leather steamer trunk into a black plastic garbage bag. Angela sees old letters and photographs. The letters are written in a European hand, slanting inky black characters on stiff, yellowed paper. The photos are European-looking, too: misty sepia-toned unsmiling faces. A little blond, curly-haired girl on the knee of a man in a tweed suit and an ascot. At the bottom is written, in faded blue ink, "Gstaad, 1954."

"Who are these people, Katha?"

"Some relations." Katha moves slowly, deliberately, shoving handfuls of old airmail envelopes into the bag. Her wrists are knobby and Angela can see the blue veins in the backs of her hands. The dusty pink silk lining of the trunk gives off an ancient powdery perfume, Chanel No. 5 perhaps. "How have you been feeling these days?"

"Awful. Crazy. Confused." Angela would expand on these conditions, but she is bored with them. "I really can't believe what's happened with Joe. I was so certain it would all work out, that we would get together."

Katha twists the top of the bag tightly and knots it. "There is only one certainty."

One evening before a deadline, Gerard comes by Angela's place with an interview with a corporate vice-president of Litton Industries that he has written and that Angela will probably have to stay up late rewriting. She offers him a glass of wine.

"What's going on at the office?" Gerard asks.

"You mean—with Joe?"

"Right. He wavers—one day he's going to get me a key job on this new newsletter he's planning, and he's going to speak to Goodhugh about getting me a raise, and then the next day he's a robot. Of course most of humanity is mechanical and dead—but I always thought Joe had potential. Now he seems to be turning to mush."

"I've noticed that myself," Angela says.

"For instance, this getting married. It's bizarre. He doesn't even *like* Edith. They barely get along."

"He doesn't like his new bride?" She can't keep the bitterness down when she says "bride." It comes out like a snarl. And she always thought of it as a pretty word, like "veil."

"They're both very cold and remote toward each other. She's sort of an awkward kid with a lot of ambition, and he's this lump, this rock. Very peculiar."

She takes a sharp breath. She wants to know everything, even though it makes her feel terrible. She would prefer to hear that Joe is totally swept up by his marriage, dazzled by his love for Edith. Then Angela would know it was over, that she had no hope. "Does Joe ever talk about his situation?"

"Oh, formerly. Before the marriage, he was saying that they kept trying one thing after another, experimenting, but no matter whey they did, ostensibly nothing worked. And also that she was pressuring him constantly about marriage and children—neither of which he wanted. I don't know what made him do it."

Angela excuses herself and goes into the bathroom and holds tightly with both hands to the edge of the sink and cries. Her whole body shakes with her crying: it comes from the deepest part of herself. She is like a field mouse being shaken by a hawk. She tries to choke back her sobs.

"Angela? Angela? Are you all right? Say there—"

"I love him," she groans, her voice hoarse and nasal.

Gerard ushers her back to the living room and sits her down on the couch and holds her hand. "I had no idea," he says. "You mentioned being involved with some Prince Charming, but I assumed you were referring to Derek Grinder."

"No, no, no. It's Joe. I've always been in love with Joe. We were lovers. Derek was nothing."

"I'm taken aback," Gerard says.

She tells Gerard the whole story. As she tells it, she finds herself shaping it in a way that does not admit that Joe might have good reasons for choosing Edith over her. She does not allow for ambiguity, for the possibility that he may live simultaneously in two coherent worlds. "He really cared for me, I know he did. It was the most intense experience for both of us. And then he did this insane thing, just when I thought he was leaving her to come to me."

"I'm more baffled than ever by his marriage—but you know, he did leave her and come to you."

"For one night, sure, but he was in shock. And he was just going back to get his stuff. Then he got sick and that seemed to stop everything."

"Would you like to hear a poem I wrote one time when a woman I loved left me?"

Angela does not want to hear any poetry, but Gerard has been listening to her for a couple of hours. "Sure."

> *"There is only one dream.*
> *There is only one taxi.*
> *There is only one fear.*
> *There is only one story."*

"What am I going to do, Gerard? I'm going crazy. And I have to keep working with him."

"Tell him everything. Tell him you love him. He may have understood that all along, unconsciously maybe, intuitively, and maybe it scared him. But that doesn't matter so much, does it? He's in a miserable situation now. Tell him everything."

"It's too late. The door is closed."

"Only in Establishment terms. Go ahead, tell him. He may have blocked out his feelings for you, or what you feel for him. We old-school WASPs have very thick exoskeletons you know. You've been very cautious. There's a time when caution just gets in the way. It occurs to me that Joe went along with Edith's scheme because he thought you didn't care about him. You often talk about Grinder, and everyone knows how you feel about domesticity. You keep saying you never want to remarry or even live with a man again. That you want to be an independent adventuress."

"Well, I wanted to seem like the opposite of Edith."

"I can assure you that you would never have to *do* anything to accomplish that. I can't think of anyone more different from Edith than you are." Gerard closes his eyes and shakes his head. Then he sighs and gets up. "And maybe I can be of some help. I'll talk to Joe—"

"Oh, no—this is our secret, if he ever thought I had told anyone, he'd feel betrayed. I'm sure. Please—"

"Oh, I won't be crude. I'll just find out what's going on inside his thick skull. You're a dear woman, and he deserves someone like you."

After he leaves, Angela dials Joe's number. Edith answers.

"I was just calling Joe about some material," she says brightly. "An interview we have to get to the printer's by nine tomorrow morning."

"Joe isn't free," Edith says good-naturedly. "I'll give him the message."

"Okay, thank you very much."

"Is this Angela?"

"Yes."

"Hi!" Her tone is very friendly. If they had met under different circumstances, Angels would probably like her. "I'm

Edith—Edith Berk!" Is part of the experiment that Edith will not change her name to Bly?

Angela falls asleep feeling relief and hope. At last she has told the secret to someone who knows both of them. Gerard is knowing and wise; surely, when he says they ought to overthrow caution and rush into each other's arms, he is only being objective. She goes over what she is going to tell Joe.

In the morning she wakes up with her head clear. She doesn't have to tell Joe anything. He knows how she felt, how she still feels, and yet he decided to marry Edith. Hi, *I'm* Edith—Edith Berk!

It's over.

She phones Derek and apologizes for shouting at him and hanging up on him.

"Please forgive me for saying this, Angela, but you really are cute when you're mad. I found that very attractive when you told me off. I was turned on. Let's work on this."

At the office, Angela is lighthearted. She laughs and hands Joe a bronze-colored chrysanthemum. What was bothering her? Probably trouble with Grinder. She's moody anyway. But now she's flirting with him the old way. She squeezes his arm slowly and gently, and he reaches out for her. She raps his hand with a pencil and leaves. Now he is off balance again—just when he thought he knew where they stood with each other.

Joe has very little time these days. Closing down the country house for the winter, getting the house in Park Slope in shape to move into, and coming up with a proposal for a new newsletter for Goodhugh keep him busy nights and weekends. He's glad of that—he'd rather not have time to think. This summer he had too much time, and it only led to pain.

Gerard telephones Angela. "I had dinner with Joe last night. He says he's been reduced to being a housewife. Edith doesn't have time to do the cooking or cleaning or shopping. I think things are bad between them, very bad. My impression is that within a year he'll leave. All that talk, the therapy, the experimenting will only exacerbate the inner pain that he now thinks 'working things out' with Edith will assuage. Meanwhile, waiting a year is a lot of pain for you. But he will certainly leave."

"A year? Did he mention me?"

"Oh, no, never—he's only ever brought you up in a sort of vague, businesslike way."

"I don't think I can stand waiting any longer. I've already been waiting the better part of a year. The caring is there for him, that hasn't gone away, but—"

"You must ask yourself what it means that you're interested in someone who still has these sealed-in-concrete ideas about marriage. At any rate, I think he's going to leave her, or engineer a breakup that will have that result, maybe directly."

"Well, I know you can get Joe to do anything you want him to do through guilt. I couldn't do that, but *she* can. What if she gets pregnant?"

"She does operate that way," Gerard says. "That doesn't bother some people. But you have to pity her—she doesn't know what passion is, she doesn't know what those laws are. She has to settle for working things out, talking things out. And then, she's not home very much—she's a go-getter, she doesn't mind working her tail off, and she's very effective when it comes to planning things and carrying them out. I have to give her credit—she's fairly invincible, and she's got her claws in quite deep."

"What is Joe's mental state, as far as you can tell?"

"Well, I asked him directly what he thought about marriage, about being married, and he said, 'Well, we're working some difficulties out.' He's like someone who's had all his blood removed."

Angela lies on Sharon's chocolate-colored sofa drinking a milk-shake through a straw. "I am so depressed," she says. She has eleven months and twenty-nine more days to wait for Joe.

"Why do you say that?" Sharon is indignant. "You have everything going for you—a fantastic, glamorous job, your boss adores you, you don't have a weight problem. Derek always mentions you when I run into him. And Ron Nussbaum, believe it or not, still calls me up and asks me what went wrong between you two." Sharon does ten side-bends.

"Derek is not Joe. Ron is not Joe. I do my job, but all I think about is Joe. I wish I could have a brain operation that would make me forget I ever met him. Actually, more than my brain would have to be operated on."

"Let me tell you something very funny. I was telling my shrink how devastated I'd be if Sam ever left me—how Sam really helped me get over Clifford and how he makes me feel wonderful about myself. You know what my shrink said? He said that probably within a three-block radius I could find a man I could happily spend the rest of my life with."

Angela starts to cry. There is only one man in this city as far as she is concerned. All the rest are shadows.

Derek telephones in high spirits. Three different magazines and one newspaper are publishing and quoting his lucid comments on the downfall of American democracy and the constitutional system and the Central Intelligence Agency's role in all of this. He is going to be interviewed on TV. "And I've been thinking about you, Angela. What you need is a ten-speed bicycle. That would get rid of your hostile energies, wouldn't it? Or don't you think it would?"

Angela imagines flying through the streets on a bicycle as light as air, her hair streaming behind her, her thighs becoming tight and firm. No more descents into subways before and after work. "You're right. What kind should I get?" She imagines wheeling her bike down the office corridor, looking radiant. *Actually, Joe, since I began biking I am a new woman.*

"I will take you to the best bike store in town and help you pick one out on Friday. Why don't I meet you at your place at six?"

"Terrific. And we can have dinner there afterward."

"I think that would absolutely be the greatest thing in the world." She can hear his smile over the phone. She forgot that he has a great smile, lots of square white teeth.

"You're effervescent today," Joe says. Angela stands in the center of his office demonstrating the shortest dance in the world. "I didn't see it," he says.

"That's because it's so short."

Gerard comes in. "Angela, you look stunning. That dress— I see you traveling through India on the train in it." Gerard puts his arm around her. She and Gerard smile at Joe.

Joe does not care for this increased solidarity. Are they

lovers? "Let's discuss this next newsletter. I have a lot of work to do, and I have to leave early because the movers are coming."

In formal tones, Joe conducts a meeting about whether political material should continue to be included in the newsletter. "Derek says that executives and corporations are political idiots," Angela says. "That's what's wrong with the country."

"Then it seems logical that we ought to make some feeble effort to raise their consciousnesses," Gerard says. "Assuming they possess consciousnesses to raise."

"Derek also says that it's the corporate hierarchy of power that really runs the country but that its political strategies are heavy-handed."

"Frankly," Joe says, feeling ganged-up on, "I've lost interest in current events. I quit reading the newspapers last summer."

"Derek would classify you as a moral idiot, I guess," Angela says.

"And you are a moral genius, I suppose?"

Angela flashes him her smile. "It's true—he thinks I'm morally wonderful." She starts laughing. "I can't keep a straight face."

Joe glares at her legs. He flushes. He does not know what to do when she needles him like this. She is so offhand, so unpredictable. "I don't know what you're talking about," he says.

Angela leaves work early, goes to a store on Fourteenth Street that sells Mexican chiles, and then home to prepare enchiladas. Derek said he was fond of Mexican food. By six-fifteen she has prepared the enchiladas and put them in the refrigerator and bathed and put on makeup and clothes suitable for wearing to a bike store. At seven o'clock, she phones Derek's office. He is not in. She phones his home, and a taped message replies. "This is Derek Grinder, unindicted co-conspirator." The message goes on at length. "This is Angela Lee and I just called to say I am not a crook and it would be wrong." Later what she left on the tape seems stupid and she wants to phone and erase it somehow. Instead, at nine when she phones again, she says, "Derek, where are you? I thought you were coming to my place at six."

Sharon comes downstairs. "I had this new insight today." She looks in the refrigerator. "What's this *food* doing in here?"

"What's your insight?"

"My insight is that insights don't help. At some point you just have to start living. By the way, did you see Lynn Lewis's big piece on sisterhood, sex, and jealousy?"

"No, I don't get those magazines."

Sharon explains that the article is not in a feminist publication but in a real magazine. "Who's coming for din-din?"

"Derek, in theory."

"You know what my shrink said about Derek?"

"No, and why would your shrink be talking about Derek?"

"I was using Derek as an example. How he's thirty-two but looks sixteen and runs around in jeans and T-shirts. The Peter Pan complex. My shrink says guys like Derek are afraid they're homosexual and have to sleep with a lot of women to prove they're not, and also to prove they are young and carefree. Of course they're just unable to have an adult relationship like a mature man. And the women are driven to throw heavy objects."

"Derek sleeps with a lot of women?" Angela is thinking about the smashed coffee mug in his bathtub. It was there two or three months ago, and it was there last week. He has bathed at her place only a few times, but he is never dirty.

"Oh, *you* know that!" Sharon says irritably. "Everyone knows that."

"It's funny," Angela says, fiddling with her freshly washed hair. "I thought that he was a lonely guy who needed someone to listen to his problems. And I thought he might be so enchanted with me that he wouldn't want to go out with other women."

"You'd better read Lynn's latest article, then."

Angela heats up the enchiladas and she and Sharon sit down to dinner. "Hey—let's get Katha up here, too," Angela says.

"It's Friday night," Sharon says.

"So?"

"She never answers the door on Friday nights. Didn't you know?"

"Is she orthodox Jewish or something?"

"Naahh. She's not Jewish at all. She always has a visitor on Fridays. A man. Very *distingué*. But he never stays the night. Sometimes when I come home late, he's coming out of her apartment. He looks like David Niven, except I'm not absolutely sure because he always keeps his head down."

"I'm staggered," Angela says. "Katha never mentioned—"

"Oh, don't say anything, ever. It's a big secret."

They watch *Planet of the Prehistoric Women*.

Sharon brings down the magazine with Lynn's article, and before Angela goes to sleep, she lies in bed drinking a beer and leafing through the magazine. The piece begins, "Why would a sane, calm, intelligent, reasonable feminist such as myself smash a coffee mug in my most recent lover's bathtub?"

In the night Angela hears someone crying and wakes up to discover her own face and pillow wet with tears. She used to cry when she was thirteen; after her wedding, she thought she was grown up and would no longer need to cry except if someone died. Then she cried so much during her divorce, even though it was what she wanted, that she thought she was losing weight through tear-loss. But here she is, crying again. Surely this will end soon.

31

JOE IS STANDING IN the center of the loft holding a push broom. Why is it that the place always seemed so clean but now, with the furniture gone, there are balls and skeins of dust everywhere? Sealed cardboard boxes, furniture, and the Eames chair, shrouded in sheets, stand by the door. The huge, silent room is filled with light. The bank of windows is like the bridge of a ship. Once again he is struck by the possibilities of the place. He never got around to using it, to living here the way it had summoned him to live when he first saw it, to match the exuberance of space and air.

Now he is moving to a dark, enclosed place with many small rooms, a place he did not choose. Why am I moving, then? he asks himself. Because I am Edith's husband and it's where she wants to live; she has never liked this place. Marriage is a cooperative venture. As Midge points out, Edith has made sacrifices for him—given up having a baby, for instance—and so it's only fair that he reciprocate. And because the house is closer to both clinics, she will be able to be home more, and avoid long subway rides, and since she works more hours a week than he does, it's only fair that they live in a place convenient for her. It all makes sense. Sacrifices must be made.

Something careens through his brain faster than a neutrino passing through the earth. A compressed thought concerning the arbitrariness of decisions. A person buys a house because it's close to his job. He can't then move from the house because it's close to his job, and he can't leave his job because it's close to his house. And yet there is an entire world to live in, and there are millions of jobs. Why then does he live as if he has no choice? This thought is like the column of dust motes in the sunlight by the windows, and it flashes away when the phone rings.

"Joe?" The voice quivers and then drops into a sob.

"Angela? Are you all right?"

"I'm fine, thank you. No, I'm not. It just hit me that you really are married. I really did love you. I still do. I feel just plain awful. I was trying to use Derek to get over you and it didn't work. Something important between you and me has been lost."

She goes on like this, crying out old phrases from dozens of 3:00 a.m. interior dialogues. Hopeless. Paradoxically, she wishes with force that her words, cried out in this way—honest at last; no holds barred!—will salvage everything, will call to Joe as no other words have succeeded in calling to him. He will awaken from his narrow dream and come to her.

"I had no idea," Joe whispers. "You didn't say this before. I didn't know all this was going on. I thought you were okay." He gazes across the flat sea of polyurethaned maple. He has made a very big mistake. "I'm glad you're telling me all this. It's important, very important to me." He thinks about people who commit suicide because they believe nobody loves them, then are warmly eulogized. "Because—Angela, listen a minute—because I still have very powerful feelings for you. I don't know where to put them. I try to hold them at arm's length."

"I have the same problem, Joe. What can we do?"

"I don't know. I just wasn't aware that you—"

He takes a cab to Angela's and they sit on her couch and hold each other. She is in a disheveled T-shirt and jeans with holes in the knees, her hair is damp, her eyes are red and very large. She seems helpless. She is completely open, all those doors with odd locks flung open, those hidden boxes containing calligraphed messages—they are all open to him just now. He could ask her anything and learn the truth today. "It's good, anyway, that we know something about each other we didn't know before," he says. He is too sad to ask her any questions.

They both think about how things might have been different. If only.

This is the woman I am supposed to be with, Joe thinks. Love can exist without having to work at it. Like light, like air. I never believed that.

She is waiting for him to say that he will now leave Edith for good.

He thinks about the sealed cartons full of his belongings, his books and records and clothing, mingled with Edith's. "I'm trying something new now, this marriage. I've made a commitment. I can't just abandon it."

"No, you're not that kind of person." She is drained. She looks soft and real and exactly like who she truly is.

He can't say that he still is unable to think of his marriage as permanent. Permanence vanished with his first marriage. After the first death there is no other. He does not want to seem dishonorable by confessing his intuition that eventually he will not be with Edith. Angela can't ask him to leave Edith, and he can't ask Angela to be loyal to him until he does. He weighs these conditions as if hefting sash weights. What can he say? "Time. We have time."

"Time takes everything away," Angela says.

32

"MY ANALYST TOLD ME something significant," Good-hugh says one day in December. He has gotten in the habit of stopping by Angela's office after he returns from his analyst. "About men and women. The way a woman can get a man and keep him is to find out what kind of woman he secretly wants to kill. When a man is in bed with a woman, he is killing her. If you find out the kind of woman he secretly wants to kill, and become her, he will be obsessed with you. *C'est facile!*" So the whole office must know about her and Joe— or maybe he's referring cryptically to his own mistress, who shows up in a sealskin coat and waits for him by the elevators outside the reception area every evening.

Derek comes to the office just as Angela is going out to lunch. He walks alongside her down the street as she heads for a coffee shop. "I didn't show up at your place that night because some kids knocked me off my bicycle. They smashed my glasses and tore my jacket. They almost got the bike." At lunch he says he wants to talk things through. Yes, Lynn Lewis did smash that cup in his bathtub, but that was a long time ago, and now they are just fairly good but not close friends. He gets her to laugh by doing an imitation of a stoned airhead who is an ardent supporter of Vegetable Liberation. That night he takes her to a horror movie and to dinner at McDonald's. Maybe, Angela thinks, we are going to be a couple after all.

He telephones her every day, and they start spending weekends together.

"I'm sorry I'm such a boring failure," he says one Sunday night at his place while they are watching a football game. He has been trying to explain football to her for several weeks now. "I'm sorry to always be belaboring you with my problems."

"Oh, no—I don't mind at all. They are really, uh, interesting. I really do like you."

"And I really do hate people who like me. Sorry to be so blunt, but that's the truth. I was famous in college for my Christlike sweetness, but that's all a lie."

"Let's talk about this, Derek." Angela, hoping that eventually things will get straightened out so they can make love, manages to stay awake listening, and reassuring him until dawn, when she dozes off. He wakes her up. "You've just proved to me that you don't want to examine the relationship," he says.

Angela seldom sees Joe. He okays the newsletter before it goes to the printer, but most of the time he is in an office next to the company library on the eighteenth floor researching a proposal for the newsletter on alternative energy resources. Goodhugh calls it, depending on his mood, "Bly's hippie crackpot scheme," and "the best and most significant work this division will ever produce."

One day shortly before Christmas, it is snowing, and Joe, unable to think about energy resources, comes by her office to ask her to ride with him on the Staten Island Ferry. When he sees her, looking tired and very, very pretty—her hair has grown long and wild again and she wears a brown suit with a copper-colored silk blouse—he realizes that such a voyage would not be taken by old pals, which is what he thinks they could become to each other. Instead he invites her to lunch at a new Greek restaurant near the office.

It has whitewashed, rough-plastered walls, blue tiles, and

earthenware jugs on the tables. He helps her off with her coat, the night-sky coat, flecked now with melting snowflakes, and they sit opposite each other at a little unsteady table with a rough-hewn top. She removes her blue hat, which is now softened and battered and wet.

"I always meant to tell you how much I like your coat and that hat," he says.

"Thank you," she says primly.

As they read the menus, he sighs. "I miss Greece. I've got to go back."

"Oh, you should. Go!"

They put down their menus. "What's new?" he says.

She bursts into tears. For the next half hour she is unable to speak. A couple of times she moves her mouth. "Ah'm, ah—I."

"I wish I could do something." What a bad idea this was!

"I have to go through this alone," she finally says. "I thought I could handle being with you, but I can't."

He orders for both of them—egg-lemon chicken soup and a variety of appetizers.

He starts telling Angela about his new project. Crucial data about energy resources from all over the world will be supplied to subscribers—not only to executives and corporations, but also to think tanks and universities. "It's cross-pollination. We take free information provided by, say, some geodesic dome company out in the Southwest, and give it to aquaculture people in Massachusetts. So the newsletter is an exchange, a network, a clearinghouse."

"That's terrific, Joe." She thinks for a moment and tastes her soup. "That is so good. But you know—why not use a computer? I've been checking out using a computer on the executives' newsletter for a long time now, and talking to guys in the business, and I really think that's where we've got to be headed. See, each subscriber buys, or rents, a terminal. Just like you have a telephone? And you provide a daily service— a screen, or a teletype print-out. You need some crackerjack researchers, though." Her eyes brighten, and she is fueled by a hope that once again she and Joe might collaborate. They were always so good at that. Better than either of them working alone.

He is thinking this, too. He has not only missed her as a lover but also as a colleague, a source of ideas and enthusiasm and sparks. She has regained her self-assurance. He begins to gaze at her in the old way, but when he sees her eyes fill with tears again, he looks away. "I'm very excited about this, about what you just said," he tells the taramosalata. "Let's have lunch, or breakfast, every week, and keep this discussion alive."

As they step outside into the falling snow, the sun breaks through. "What an oxymoronic day," Angela says.

He turns to her and she looks up at him. He slowly lifts her hair, trapped under her coat, and spreads it across her back, and he kisses her.

Although she still believes that a kiss could change everything, this particular kiss does not move a particle of dust. Each morning she thinks: Another morning. At night she thinks: Another night. She still has trouble sleeping. One cold night she gets up and finds the yellow *I Ching* Katha gave her and leafs through it. *Waiting* (Nourishment). *The Lake. The Marrying Maiden.... No blame.... It furthers one.... A fox crossing a frozen river....* She jumps up, pulls a blanket around her shoulders, and goes downstairs and knocks on Katha's door.

Katha is awake, of course. Does she ever sleep? But her face, once smooth, is puffy. The skin under her eyes is swollen. Her hair, partly concealed by a scarf, has become so thin that Angela can see her scalp. She wears a quilted red brocade Mandarin robe with a black frayed silk collar. Angela grabs Katha's arms, and can feel the bones through the padded silk. "Katha! What is wrong with you? Are you sick? What has been happening?"

Katha smiles, and it's like a fire in a collapsing house. Whatever inner, smooth, coiled-up force she carried before, it is now on the outside, almost visible.

"All this time, I could see, I knew—but I didn't think of you, I didn't ask." Angela feels ice cold, and her chest is about to cave in.

"Angela, come in, sit down. I'll put the kettle on."

The apartment is very neat, as always, but there are fewer objects. On the floor is the Kazakh rug, alone on the bare, polished wood. The big mirror is gone. Lined up against one wall are three old steamer trunks. And there is a faint, pungent odor that makes Angela think of the creosote bushes that grow on the mesa outside Gatch.

"I'm dying," Katha says matter-of-factly, as if she were saying, "It's snowing."

Angela swallows and stares at her. "There must be something we can do. Some medicine." She wants to scream *No*.

"I am taking medicine—look at this silly swollen face."

They talk for a long time, drinking two pots of tea. Katha explains the clinical details. The surges toward health and now this long, deepening relapse. Angela has the odd hope that if they can just keep awake talking about it, the cancer will shrink away. "You've got to fight it," she says.

"I have, for two years longer than the doctors said I could make it. But lately I understand something new. I'll show you." She goes into her bedroom, moving slowly but still gliding the way she always has, her back straight, her head level. She returns with a picture she has cut out of a magazine. Three cheetahs are devouring a gazelle who is still living, its head and neck arched eloquently over its predators.

"Katha, this is terrible."

"No. It is the truth. It's the way life is, life lives on life, and when I look at this, I think: Yes."

"You have always been so kind to me, and listened to me blubber, and now you're comforting me again. About—you."

"No, I don't think of it that way."

"Katha, I'm sorry if I sound nosy, I don't mean to have bad manners, but—"

"Yes?" Katha is in the kitchen, throwing yet another handful of green tea in the celadon-blue pot.

"Do you mind that you didn't marry or have children?"

"I was married. I had a child."

"What happened?"

"My husband, my daughter—she was eight—were shot and killed."

"Oh, God, Katha." Angela wants to ask how, when, and where, but stops herself.

"Their lives were complete, for them, at that moment. Not for me—but for them."

The degree of Katha's suffering makes Angela feel that she

has lived in a self-indulgent way, absorbed in her own daily dramas, with no sympathy left over for anyone else.

"I have no complaints," Katha says. "Life has been generous to me. I am thankful for the gift of life, of consciousness."

"Tell me what I can do for you, Katha."

"I will have to think."

They drink their tea in the cups as smooth and white as river stones. "I do have a request—it's a very big favor."

"I'll do it."

"You've got to promise me."

"I promise." Angela is crying.

"What's the date? The twentieth? This week, over the holidays, I want you to go away somewhere you've been wanting to go."

"And—?"

"That's all. For me, can you do that?"

"Katha—I couldn't." What Angela has in mind is nursing Katha.

"You just promised."

"I think I should stay here, in case you need anything."

"I am very well taken care of, I assure you."

"Let's talk about marriage," Derek says one night. They are lying in the room that has nothing in it but cushions and a stereo. "I wonder if that wouldn't help me."

She looks at him and has no feelings. She has been very despondent about Katha. She has a plane ticket to fly to New Mexico to spend a week with Helen and Tom on their ranch. Marriage? She has poured so much hatred toward Joe's marriage that the word itself is tainted. "I'm pretty wary," she says. "I've been through all that. But sometimes I think it would be good for me to be a little more settled. Live together or something."

"It really is interesting, isn't it, the whole idea? Or don't you think so? Or do you? I found it very provocative when I met you and learned you were divorced—I knew that meant you weren't looking for a husband. Most of the women I know have never been married." He pulls at his lip and looks worried.

They don't make love at all that weekend. When she calls him on Monday evening, he says he can't talk. "I've got all this writing, and I'm so depressed. I'll call you tomorrow, I promise. I'll see you for lunch tomorrow."

He does not call or appear the next day, or the next. Toward the end of the week she calls him. He says he can't see her—he's too depressed. "Why don't I come down to your place and cheer you up? I'm going away in a few days, you know." In the past she has often been able to get him out of his dark moods; he has told her she always says and does the right thing, and makes him feel great, and he finds her trustworthy. That his first impression of her was that she was eager, involved, full of emotion—and of course she was, for Joe.

"How long are we going to go on beating the dead horse of this so-called relationship?" Derek asks.

"What? What do you mean?"

"Haven't you had enough of this so-called relationship?"

"Derek, come over right now—let's talk about this." Being with Derek is hard work, but it's better than nothing.

"I can't come over right now because I have a friend here and I don't want to hurt her feelings."

"You little creep!" Angela shouts and bangs down the phone.

"You will have to be absolutely on fire with genius to bring it off," Gerard tells Joe as they eat Devonburgers at the restaurant where Joe took Angela for the first time a year ago. "Otherwise it's going to be just another newsletter. Put yourself on the *qui vive*."

"I certainly welcome any suggestions you have." They sat in a booth in the corner, and she told him how she wanted to go to Tibet, and that objects in dreams are self-luminous.

"I hope you'll gallop with it, and keep it spontaneous and fun. These ecology tomes are so dull, so constricted, so good and gray. How about something with pizzazz?"

Joe sighs. He can barely get through the day, let alone consider pizzazz. Some days he is really interested in energy resources; other days he stays at home and broods. He suggested to Edith that they go to Greece for two weeks, but she doesn't have the time. Nothing is guiding him now. He changes the subject. "How's the executives' newsletter going?"

"About the same. Angela is away for a week, and—"

"Really? Where?"

"She's visiting a friend in New Mexico. She's been threatening lately to move back there and live on a ranch."

"I don't see her doing that," Joe says carefully.

"No, of course not. But she's been very—ah, very low lately. Something big is bothering her, I think." Gerard looks at Joe and Joe looks at his watch.

"She's difficult to understand, it would seem," Joe says. "She's now official director of the newsletter, with a good raise, Goodhugh likes her. But she gets so—emotional."

Gerard nods and shrugs at the same time. "I think she wants more than the job. She wants to appear as a free spirit, but I think she yearns for someone to settle her down and give her children."

"Maybe so." Joe shifts in the booth and finishes his beer. "You've mentioned that—I don't know." Is Gerard in love with her? "How's Elizabeth?"

"She's doing very well—she just got a job as an assistant buyer for a fur company. We seem to keep getting along fairly well." He pauses. "In a way, we're the mirror of each other, and in another way, complete opposites, like love and hate, or work and play. She's the realist, I'm the fantasist. We have to make love frequently or the oppositeness, the rage of it, builds up. Do you find that in your—in your situation?"

Joe grinds his teeth and looks over his shoulder for the waiter. "Check, please." He and Edith seldom make love: she's either out of town at one of the clincs, or she's tired, or he's tired. "Edith is very interested in power these days," he says. "Money and power. I have to respect her business sense—she's always right. The clinics are getting a very good reputation for being well-run. But there are difficulties. We're working on them."

Gerard starts to say something and then stops himself. "Someone once asked Freud what he thought a normal person should be able to do well." he then says. "And all Freud said was *'lieben und arbeiten'*—to love and to work. Usually I don't care for Freud, but that impressed me. Now that the love side of my life seems to be getting clearer, I want to get serious about my work."

"I'm glad to hear that, Gerard." But Joe is a little sad—he has always counted on Gerard to be the frivolous one.

33

HELEN IS STILL VERY exotic-looking. She has high cheek-bones, slanting gray eyes, and thick black straight hair, and today in the airport, she wears a long black velveteen dress and a heavy Navajo squash-blossom fertility necklace. But she has new lines around her mouth and eyes and her skin has become leathery and dark. She seems worn down. In New York, no one ever thought she was from Fairfield, Connecticut; people always imagined she was from Kazakhstan, or Crete, or Abyssinia. When Angela embraces her, Helen stiffens slightly and pulls back.

They walk through the airport, and when they get out to the parking lot, Angela blinks in the harsh sunlight. "How do you like my new pickup truck?" Helen speaks in a monotone which is new to Angela.

"It's great—a Navajo Cadillac," Angela says. An old Gatch joke. Helen is silent. "I flew right over that mountain where they store the bombs. You know, Arthur would never believe me about that."

On her previous flight to New Mexico, she and her husband

flew over the mountain that had been the source of so many
rumors during her childhood. It was then that she saw that on
the side hidden from Gatch there was a railroad switchback
that led to two enormous trapezoidal metallic doors. That entire
face of the mountain had been neatly smoothed, so that it
resembled the Great Pyramid. Arthur refused to look out the
window at this wonder, saying, "If the government stored bombs
there, *you* certainly wouldn't know about it."

"Do you think the mountain could give off any radiation
that would hurt my kids?" Helen asks.

"They might turn out like me. I grew up next to that mountain." For a moment Angela has found an explanation for why
she is the way she is, why she always feels like an alien—it's
the radiation, of course! But then that must mean that Carmen
Garcia, her best friend at Gatch High, and the Indians who
always sat in the back of the classroom and never took off their
jackets, and the hoods in the parking lot, and the cheerleaders
have all become mutants, too. So much for being unique. "I
don't think there's anything radioactive in those bombs, anyway," Angela says. "It's after they explode that you get the
radiation."

Angela wants to tell Helen all the bad things that have been
going on, but Helen is so remote and quiet that Angela finds
herself chattering about whatever she sees out the window—a
new shopping mall, billboards, sixteen fast-food franchises one
after another along the freeway. At last they are out on the
open highway with nothing in view but a barren brown stretch
interrupted by occasional mesas and volcanoes. "Say, let's
drive through Gatch on the way to the ranch—it's not much
of a detour."

"Okay," Helen says. "I have an Indian girl babysitting.
She's pretty nice, but the kids cry whenever I leave so I don't
leave much. How do we get to Gatch?"

"This sure is funny. Gatch used to be on the only main
highway in the entire state. Everyone knew where it was.
Everyone driving through stopped there for gas and a bowl of
chili verde at the Cash-In Café."

"Now everybody just stays on the new Interstate," Helen
says. Her hands grip the steering wheel very tightly; the veins
and cords of muscles stand out under the tanned skin.

They turn off onto a winding road that goes through some low sagebrush-covered hills and eventually arrive at a huge, brown plain dotted with tumbleweeds and ringed by sawtoothed blue mountains. Angela has been asking about Helen's kids—they've just gotten over the flu—and so she is surprised when tears come to her eyes before she has registered the fact that they have reached the landscape where she first came into consciousness. She remembers peering into the morning glory flower and realizing that part of her had a name and part of her was nameless.

"Well, where is it?" Helen asks.

"It's in the middle, about halfway toward the mountains, on the old highway. We'll see it any minute now."

Helen turns off the paved road, which cuts across the edge of the plain, onto a dirt road that leads toward the center.

"Boy, these roads," Angela says. "We used to drive out here and neck and drink beer and listen to the radio—to Tiny Morie and the Night Rockers with Al Hurricane Sanchez. Later on, Al changed his name to Al Hurricane Nelson." Angela sees the bomb-storage mountain but keeps quiet about it. There is still a twelve-foot-high chainlink fence between the road and the mountain.

They drive on for several miles and still don't see any signs of a town. The wind blows tumbleweeds past the windshield every now and then. Finally a few low houses appear.

"I can't believe you lived here," Helen says.

"Neither can I."

Russian thistles dried to the color of bone stick out of cracks in the abandoned highway. The main street, the section of highway that runs through the town, still has a few stores standing, but their windows are smashed. The Cash-In Café, where her mother worked, is gone altogether, and yellow, dried weeds stand in the vacant lot that was once the trailer court where Angela can remember a birthday party she went to wearing a yellow dress, and a little man inside a very big, hollow tree beckoned her to enter, and she did, and within she saw a spiral staircase going upward and downward. She has grown up believing there was a huge old tree in that place, but now she knows that could not have been so. But the birthday party remains clear in her memory, and so does the little man and the tree. The school, which resembled a pueblo-style bomb shelter, has been bulldozed. Undigested pieces of concrete protrude from the sand.

They drive down some of the side streets. A few rusting cars, and car parts, litter some of the yards. All the front doors are missing, and most of the windows. On the ground, pieces of broken glass flash in the strong light. No grass, no trees—but there never was much green here. "Wait," Angela says. "There were some cottonwoods at the end of this street, by the arroyo. Big cottonwoods. What happened to them?"

They get out of the car and look at the red gash of the arroyo. A few greasewood shrubs. No trees. Could they have been washed away in a flash flood? Is this the wrong place? Perhaps Gatch never really existed. Angela wonders if she will wake up and find she is living a completely different, detailed, absorbing life elsewhere. Gatch as she knew it is only some chemical traces and electrical charges in a tiny area of her brain, in a couple of cells, and she has forty-five billion brain cells. A whole town, shrunken to a few molecules. She picks up a piece of rusty corrugated tin—probably somebody's roof.

"Watch out—you could get tetanus," Helen says.

Angela lets it go, and the wind whips it away, across the arroyo, with a rumbling sound.

"There's a sign over there," Helen says. They walk over and read it, and learn that they are trespassing on federal property, on the Gatch Bombing Range.

They get back in the truck, Helen steps hard on the accelerator, and they speed back to the highway.

"How's Tom doing?" Angela asks.

Helen blinks, winces, and stares at the road. "I had an affair with my yoga instructor, the Armenian." Her face is carved, her mouth a straight line. "Tom found out. He's left."

"Oh, no!" Angela cries. She remembers the last time she saw Helen and Tom, sitting in a restaurant in New York with their shoulders touching, their faces quite peaceful. Things were already going badly between Angela and Arthur, but Helen and Tom were perfect: Helen was pregnant and Tom was out of his mind with joy. Angela now recalls a recent dream in which Helen gave her her own baby to care for. Angela held it and nursed it.

"I thought I could keep up the compromise but it didn't work."

"Compromise? I always thought you and Tom were madly in love."

"No. I wasn't, anyway. Oh, I don't know. Maybe Tom was. At some point. I thought I'd reconciled myself to the situation."

"You never mentioned any of this to me!"

"Well, it was just something between me and Tom, and I didn't want to talk about it. And then after he left, I didn't want to bother you because I knew you were having a rough time in New York."

Angela thinks of Helen alone on two hundred and twenty acres, mostly bare brown hills, with two small children. "And how about the yoga instructor?"

"Oh—him." She shakes her head.

Helen has had two years of college at a finishing school which boarded her horse. She does not know how to type. She worked at the phone company to put Tom through law school and since then he has never allowed her to have a job. "What are you going to do, Helen?"

"Catch another man who can support me, I guess." Her voice is flat.

"What can I do for you?"

"Nothing. It's okay."

When they pull up at the ranch house, the Indian girl comes out carrying the two little boys. They cry when they see Angela and run to their mother. Helen turns to Angela and pats her cheek. "I'm so happy you're here."

At sunset Angela stands on a thin crust of snow between the hen house and the ranch house. Two warm fresh eggs rest in her jacket pocket, and she curls her hand gently around them. Far away, among the leafless cottonwoods along the irrigation ditch, dogs are barking. Underfoot, the snow crackles as it turns to ice as fast as the sun goes down. To the west, behind the mountains, the sky is gold. I have been in exile, she thinks, and hot tears again come into her eyes. The city seems farther away than Pluto, and just as bizarre and uninhabitable. Where can she go? What is she supposed to do with her life? Who is she supposed to be? In the back of her mind she always maintained the thought that if nothing else worked out, she could return to Gatch and sleep in her little fold-out bed in the rear of the trailer, listening to the sounds of her mother's sleeping breath coming from the front. No mother, no trailer, no Gatch. The air is sweet with cedar smoke.

She walks toward the house. Through the French doors she can see a fire burning in the big curved adobe fireplace. The boys are playing in front of the fire screen. Over the fireplace Helen has tacked up a sampler she embroidered when she was a girl in Fairfield: "You are welcome as the flowers in May." Angela imagines that she and Joe are married, that this is her home, those are her children.

After Helen feeds the children and puts them to bed, she turns on the television, and she and Angela do yoga along with a man in black on the screen. "Afterward I don't feel depressed, I feel really good," Helen says. While they imitate the postures the little boys come out and wander around in the room waving their bottles. Angela wonders, doing a shoulder stand, if a four-year-old should still have a bottle, or still be in diapers, but says nothing. Helen puts them to bed several more times while Angela fixes dinner. "If I don't sit with them until they fall asleep, they never do," Helen says.

After dinner, Helen and Angela sit on a Navajo rug in front of the fire and drink Kahlua.

"Someday, when the boys are older, we could go on a trip together," Helen says. "To India, or Bali, or Ceylon."

"That would be nice," Angela says. "We could go to Ladakh." Katha went there once, a long time ago.

"I often have a dream that we're climbing a sacred mountain. This morning I woke up wishing and wishing for something, I don't know what."

The fire pops, and a coyote yips. Helen jumps up and opens the French doors and shouts, "Go, scat, shoo!" A cold wind sweeps through the house, and she closes the doors. "I don't want that damned coyote getting in the hen house. They dig under the fence." The dogs start barking, and the coyote yips again and then it's quiet.

Angela looks at the fire through the translucent reddish-brown liquid in her glass. She is drunk. The altitude: she has risen six thousand feet since she got up this morning. She thinks about Katha and their good-bye hug: Katha has become like an ibis, regal and linear. "I'm remembering all the good things that have happened in my life," she said. "And that are still happening."

The children cough during the night, and they wake up before sunrise, and they hang on to Helen most of the day. She can't converse without interrupting herself to fix a bottle, change a diaper, take a toy out of one sticky hand and return it to the aggrieved party. They have round smooth faces and large blue eyes and sweet voices when they're content. They cry and run after Helen if she leaves the room. She serves them without showing any annoyance, and rocks them to sleep each night.

At the airport, when Angela says good-bye, Helen starts to cry, and Angela cries, too. It was easier for them to be friends at a distance.

Angela is glad to get back to the city, and to see so many people. She is happy to see the variegated crowd lined up to get produce weighed by the Koreans at the vegetable stall on the corner. In the dingy corner supermarket, which smells of rotten bananas and has sawdust-littered aisles cluttered with stacks of cartons, canned goods, bags of dog food, and lines of people waiting with their shopping carts, a man in a blood-stained white jacket hurls packages of hamburger into a meat bin and sings. *"Ayyy, mujer ingrata, mujer ingrata!* For you I kill myself, ungrateful woman!"

Angela knocks on Katha's door but there is no answer. Feeling queasy, she knocks on Sharon's door.

"It's good to see you," Sharon says. "I was worried that you wouldn't come back."

"Of course I'm back," Angela says. "I'm a native now."

"Oh, Angela!" Sharon suddenly looks very dismal. "Here, sit down, let me give you something to eat."

"It's okay—I just went to the store. What is it?"

"Katha—she's gone."

She gives Angela the rolled-up Kazakh rug Katha left her. "I went to the memorial service at the t'ai chi studio. There was a beautiful Japanese flower arrangement—plum branches. Some people stood up and said what they liked about her. It turned out no one knew she was in a lot of pain for the last six months. But she left everything in order. And that mystery guy—he was shattered. He sat in the front row, and then as soon as the service was over, he ran out. He's probably an ambassador or something, probably has a wife and kids. Afterward everyone was invited to a banquet in Chinatown— Katha had planned the whole thing. With bottles of Scotch on every table. It was her treat."

Angela goes down to her apartment, unrolls the rug, and sits on it. She asks herself what she has left to lose.

34

WHEN ANGELA RETURNS TO the office, she considers going upstairs to see Joe. As a test. She feels that now she will be indifferent to him. Goodhugh, Belinda, Bracewell, and miscellaneous others greet her warmly. "We missed your sunny face," Belinda says.

"*My* face—sunny?"

Goodhugh has now attained a position created by Whorf and Brunell especially for him at his suggestion: corporate director. And he has hired a man named Mark F. Sennett to manage the newsletter division. So far, Sennett has had Goodhugh's old office recarpeted and fired seven people. When Angela asks Goodhugh what is going on, he says, *"Ma chérie,* once upon a time there was an Italian duke who knew how to lay the foundation for his power. He started taking over Italy, bit by bit. When he took the Romagna, he found it had been governed by weak, ineffectual rulers and it was in disarray and disorder. So he appointed a man named de Orco to teach the subjects obedience. De Orco was cruel and thorough, and he had carte blanche. By the time he had whipped the province into shape, all the subjects hated and despised him. So the duke decided he ought to show that if any cruelty had taken place, it was because of de Orco—the duke, naturally, didn't want everyone hating *him*. So the duke had de Orco cut in half and placed in the public square. To quote our dear friend Machiavelli, 'The ferocity of this spectacle caused the people satisfaction and amazement.'"

"God, that's awful," Angela says. "Are you going to change, now that you're a big cheese?"

"It's what we call hardball, dear girl. Hardball. But you can rest assured that you are the ornament and shield of the newsletter division. And Sennett is quite taken with you."

Joe's project is not going well. He has no one he can talk to about it. Gerard would be helpful, but lately he has been working hard on a book of poetry in order to qualify for a grant and is never free. Angela—Angela avoids him. Across the hall there's a bookkeeper, a woman with floating green eyes, maroon hair cut like a boy's, and a lascivious smile. Sometimes he tosses paper clips into her ashtray from his office. One day he spreads out his folders and feels totally helpless. Adriana pops in. Maybe she has some ideas. He tells her he can't cope.

"Let's go to my place and get stoned and fuck," Adriana says.

She is married to a psychotherapist, and she has said that they have an open marriage. She tells Joe not to be nervous— her husband is away at a three-day mind and body conference. Adriana does not frighten or enmesh Joe. As soon as she has an orgasm, she falls asleep. Why can't his dealings with other women be this simple, this innocent? "Poor Joe," she often says, sighing. She tells him that he and Edith should have children. She gives him a book of color photographs of developing human embryos and invites him and Edith to have dinner with her and her husband, but Edith has to make frequent trips to New Haven, where she is setting up another clinic, and can't make it.

One icy Saturday afternoon, Joe walks uptown to the white brick building where Adriana lives. As he is about to knock on Adriana's door, Buff Goodhugh walks out. Joe freezes with his fist in the air near Goodhugh's tie, the tie of their fraternity.

"Say, Bly," Goodhugh says.

"Buff," Joe says.

"I'm in something of a hurry." Goodhugh, buttoning his opcoat, makes for the elevator.

After that, Joe does not go to Adriana's any more, or toss paper airplanes into her office, although she still sometimes sits on his desk and strokes his hair, or puts her arms around his neck and murmurs, "Poor, poor Joe!"

The winter is slow to end, and the days pass in an empty haze. He sits in his chilly, bare office—he has never gotten around to fixing it up—and stares out the window at the people moving, as if on dozens of TV screens, in the fluorescent-lit offices across the street. One window still displays a red and gold Merry Christmas banner facing outward. In another window, random letters are taped up: *aiiouiaa*.

He is a year older. For his birthday Edith gave him an ounce of Thai hashish and a framed blow-up of the two of them sitting naked, their bodies artistically arranged, on the flokati rug. She has hung the picture in the entrance hall of their house in Brooklyn.

The preliminary proposal for the energy-alternatives newsletter has been given to Goodhugh and Goodhugh has not yet responded. Meanwhile, Joe tries to put together a sample newsletter. He is being paid three times his old salary to convert a ream of paper into a million-dollar concept. "Today's challenge . . ." he types. "The Starr Whorf Newsletter Group would like to invite . . ." he types. What has happened? He used to be a bright young man.

A few days before graduation from prep school—he was valedictorian—he received acceptances from Harvard, Yale, and Princeton. He took it for granted that doors would always fly open for him as he approached. Now he knows this is not true. "The depleted energy resources must . . ." he types. He wonders if Goodhugh has cleverly managed to shunt him away from a chance to rise in the corporation. Is this his destiny— to found and edit newsletters while Goodhugh takes all the credit? "Time is running out," he types, and stops.

He leaves early, takes the subway home to Brooklyn, comes into an unlit, cold house, feeds Edith's new Abyssinian cat, eats four cold hot dogs standing over the sink, smokes some

hashish in a little brass pipe Edith gave him, and lies in be
watching television until he falls asleep dreaming of infinit
rows of penguins dancing in chorus lines.

One day he has lunch at the Harvard Club with an assistan
director of public relations from an oil company. He is a few
years younger than Joe, and he has long sideburns. He wear
a pink striped shirt, an Italian suit, an elegant gold watch, an
polished loafers with little gold chains, and he has a tan, eve
though it's February. In an animated, concerned way, with
crease appearing and disappearing rhythmically between hi
eyebrows, the man speaks about long-range planning. The fu
ture. In five years. Down the road, in ten years. By the yea
2000. There are some major problems, sure, who said ther
weren't? But on the other hand . . .

Joe blanks out. He stares at a popover on his plate, an
then at the dark wood paneling, the red carpet, and all the men
young, middle-aged, old, sitting at tables eating and conversin
as if they had a reason to live, as if life had a purpose. "I be
your pardon?" he says to the public relations executive.

"I was just saying, perhaps you can give me some input o
this."

Joe drifts away again.

". . . some feedback," the man is saying.

Joe stands up and puts his napkin on the table. "You'll hav
to excuse me. I'm very sorry."

"What is your frank and honest opinion?" Goodhugh asks An
gela. On his desk, in a black leather binder, is Joe's sketch o
the energy-alternatives newsletter. "Do you think we shoul
put money into this?"

"Nope. It might work as a modest little newsletter, but
don't understand this push to make it into something so in-
flated." She has read through the material several times an
she can't understand much of it. She can't understand wha
has happened to the grace and wit and vigor that she used t
find so inspiring about Joe's work. And she doesn't see how
Joe could effectively run an operation with more than tw
people because he insists on doing all the work himself an
yet this proposal calls for a staff of ten. But she doesn't say
that. "I think it would be smart to stop this project before i

gets out of hand." Maybe Joe would come back and work with her on the newsletter, and it would be the way it was. She has sometimes wished that Joe would carry out his offer to invite her to help him set up his new project, but of course that is impossible for both of them. "It stinks."

"You sound vehement, Angela. It doesn't become you."

"Well, you asked what I really think, and that's what I think. Joe is destined to do great things—I've always felt that. But this rinky-dink newsletter is not one of them."

"Sennett thinks Joe's concept is very big. We're investing a million."

Sennett has a small, stiff red mustache and red curly hair, and, according to Belinda, his suits come from Dunhill's. He summons Angela to his office by telephone and shows her his new framed Finnish abstract tapestry, which is to hang above a new rosewood table.

"How do you like it, baby?"

"It looks like a tropical skin disease, Mr. Sennett," Angela says, clasping her hands at her waist.

"Are you making a little jokie?"

"Just a very little jokie." Angela notes that he is wearing a heavy gold class ring.

He asks her to sit down and tells her about his dynamite idea. "Executive advertising, doll. With order forms. You know, there are executive digital alarm clocks, executive briefcases with a special pocket for a squash racquet, all these terrifically elegant, *power* items. So—do you see?"

"No, not exactly."

"Advertising—in the newsletter. Mail-order. It's so obvious I don't understand why nobody has thought of it before."

"When Joe Bly started the newsletter, the plan was not to have advertising, but to make money with a high subscription fee," Angela says. "The idea is that executives are too busy to read ads and just want short takes on hard information. They don't want to pay a fortune for a subscription and then wind up looking at the kind of ads you see in airline magazines."

"I can pick up this phone and in ten minutes I can sell advertising space that will bring in, oh, ten thousand dollars."

"Have you talked to Buff about this?"

"No need to—I'm the one in charge. He's a busy man—we can't be nickel and diming him."

"I'll ask him if you don't want to," Angela says. "I get along very well with Buff."

"That won't be necessary," Sennett says, and Angela realizes she has gone too far. But she wouldn't mind being fired. She is bored with the newsletter.

"There's another matter I want to discuss with you," Sennett continues. "Your assistant. He's out."

"I know he's a little odd, but he's a good person," Angela says. "Look, I'll talk to him—"

"Corners have to be cut. He just happens to be one of those corners. If you read your own newsletter you'd know about the economic downturn."

"I don't see how there are going to be enough hours in the day for me to do it all myself. I work nights and weekends as it is."

"No problem. If you run pages of ads for executive items, those are pages you don't have to fill with anything else."

"I think you better talk to Buff. And to Joe—this is Joe's newsletter, really, and I hate to think decisions are being made that don't include him."

"Bly is inoperable in this matter." He gives her a slow, appraising look. "Attached to him though you may be."

"Oh, cut it out," Angela says, going to the door.

"How about a drink with me after work?"

"No, thanks—I don't have the time."

"Tomorrow."

"I probably won't have any free time for about ten years, Mr. Sennett."

She returns to her office and sits at her desk clenching her shaking hands and panting. She could quit, right now, she could walk out. But all her things are here—her teapot, her pictures. And who would do the newsletter? It would not be fair to Joe—she promised him she would keep it going. And she promised Goodhugh. Still trembling, she takes the elevator up one floor to see Goodhugh. On the way down the corridor, passing Joe's office, she hears female laughter and slows her step.

Adriana Thompson is sitting on Joe's desk flipping paper

clips at him. She wears a skirt slit to the thigh. Angela has heard men in the elevator and the coffee room discussing Adriana as openly as they do the Yankees. All Angela knows about her is that she is a bookkeeper and that it takes her about six months to do the work necessary on Angela's expense-account vouchers so that Angela can get reimbursed.

Goodhugh keeps Angela waiting on a couch in his secretary's office for about half an hour. Finally he asks her to come in. "Sennett is a twit and I hate him," she says.

"Angela—how unlike you," Goodhugh says. *"Calmez-vous."*

"Don't say that to me!" she shouts. "Everything around here is getting crazy and you just sit up here and toss out French phrases to impress everyone. How can you let him fire Gerard? Is it that everyone is betting on Joe's energy newsletter? Is that it? Is that why mine is being cut back to the bone? And what is this bullshit about advertising?"

"Angela, Angela, please." Goodhugh's face is red and his eyes are hard.

"A pack of twits from fancy schools," Angela goes on. "You just—you don't—" She gasps. She suddenly hears her own voice. She feels her mouth moving, and senses her furious facial expression. She must seem berserk. Why is she doing this? "Oh, God," she murmurs. "I'm sorry. You've always helped me. Oh, please, please. Let me apologize."

"Dear girl," Goodhugh says coolly.

"I really didn't mean any of that. I'd do anything to keep my job. I love it, really." She hears herself babbling on, begging, contradicting herself. No matter what she says, it only gets worse. She wants to keep talking until everything can be brought back to the way it was before she had her outburst, but Goodhugh dismisses her.

"Please, just forget what I've said," she says, still pleading as she leaves. "I want you to understand—"

"Consider it forgotten," Goodhugh says, interrupting her, his expression dour.

35

ANGELA COMES HOME AND throws her coat on the floor and looks in the refrigerator. Empty. She is too tired and too full of rage to go to the store. She goes upstairs to borrow a beer from Sharon. She wants to announce how unjust everything is, and to prove that Goodhugh, Sennett, and Joe are ogres out to destroy her.

"It's been an awful day, Sharon," she begins.

"Yeah," Sharon says. She is very dreamy and slow and distracted. "A strange day. Sam just left."

Angela looks in Sharon's refrigerator. No beer.

"I think I'm going to get this place painted—white. And get rid of all this brown crap."

"Sharon?"

Sharon is walking around her dim living room hugging herself and smiling. "I broke up with him," she says. "I asked him to leave. I said we'd always be good friends, and I intend to make sure of that, because I really love him—but." She puts her hand on the plant-filled bassinet. "This really would look better with a baby in it, don't you think?"

"Sharon—"

"I never broke up with someone before. It's a great feeling. I told him he wasn't finished with his wife yet, that he had to get that settled. I'm handling this—I'm not collapsing. God, how mature I'm getting!"

Angela, annoyed, goes back to her apartment and paces around. A dozen plans go through her brain. She will resign. She will tell Goodhugh to go to hell, she will kick Sennett as hard as she can. . . . Suddenly her apartment seems claustrophobic and littered. She wants to go out and walk, but a woman alone does not go for a walk in this neighborhood at night. She does what her mother used to do in the middle of the night. She scours the stove, and then goes on to clean the rest of the kitchen. Then she starts in the living room, rolling up the Kazakh rug. Katha is dead.

Katha is dead, and suddenly Angela really knows it, and misses her acutely. She can see Katha turn and lower her eyes and smile, but she can't remember exactly how she sounded, how her faint accent went. She thought she had gotten used to Katha's death right away—that's what Katha probably would have liked. But she continues to undergo a transformation in Angela's mind into a former person, someone who no longer exists and can no longer be of help. That plain fact is like a cold bar of steel which Angela feels forced to assimilate into her chest.

Clearing away the piles of books and magazines that have accumulated on top of the bookcases—she hasn't really cleaned the place since Joe got married—she comes across the book of poems Ron Nussbaum inscribed to her. Why couldn't he have been Joe? Ron was so generous, and Joe has never given her anything.

She takes down the mandala poster and rolls it up—it has faded, and anyway she never looks at it any more. Its chief purpose was to remind her of Janos, and she does not want to think of him ever again. Another creep. She starts clearing the mantelpiece of its several generations of candles, many of them in translucent colored jars. She is working very fast now. Her eyes are burning and it must be late, but it doesn't matter. She grabs up the jars one by one and throws them in a garbage bag—who needs candlelight when lovers are out of the question? The last jar is cracked, and the wax has oozed out and glued the bottom of the jar to the mantelpiece. She gives the jar a swift jerk and it comes apart and a jagged piece of glass slices deeply into her little finger.

She inhales sharply and grabs her finger below the cut. The room suddenly balloons and she watches herself think and move. Her thoughts form orderly rows: I have hurt myself, cut a vein. I knew the jar was cracked and was going to break and I pulled on it anyway. I'm hurt and I'm alone. As though moving by remote control, she goes into the bathroom and rinses her finger. For the first time, she realizes quite thoroughly that her flesh is temporary, that it can be torn.

She feels very faint. She wraps the finger up in paper towels and lies down in bed. Her flesh can be torn—it's not plastic. What in her draws her recklessly toward jagged glass? Toward the pain with Joe? What in her made her say those things to Goodhugh? What will happen to her if she keeps this up? She feels a horror about herself. Who is she? What is leading her along? She remembers her dream of the previous summer, of being in a theater watching close-up films of herself and feeling humiliated by the show of artificial behavior that seemed to come from outside her true self. Now, recalling her outburst at Goodhugh, she feels more horror and shame. Does she even exist?

You are the one watching the movie, a voice says in her head. And she remembers something Katha used to quote: "Two birds sit in a tree, fast friends. One eats the sweet fruit. The other watches." But this does not comfort her.

"I've finished the book and applied for the grant." Gerard is looking very spruce. He's gotten a haircut and lost some weight. "I'm really enjoying working hard. I'm going to try to do a lot of readings and finish another book by the end of the year."

"You seem different," Angela says. They are having breakfast in a little café in the Village. Gerard orders a bacon cheeseburger.

"I can't really account for it—I just started getting serious. I think it's similar to what happens to junkies—as they get into their thirties, they spontaneously give heroin up."

"And what did you give up?" Angela wants to know what

others have done to get themselves unstuck. She has tried Zen meditation, staring at her bedroom wall every morning for twenty minutes, and she goes to Katha's old studio for t'ai chi lessons. She has been reading about the right hemisphere of the brain and the wonders it holds. She imagines it as an ocean liner floating just below the curvature of the earth. There's a band playing, and on a calm night she can hear the notes blowing across the water. And on this ship there must be people dancing, and in the saloon, rare and lovely paintings. If only she could make radio contact! Anything to change her from the way she is, doing the same old destructive things day after day.

"I don't know," Gerard says, meditatively chewing. "I think seeing the trap Joe has gotten himself in scared me—seeing how he has always had all this potential and now he just sits around, stoned most of the time. It was good that I got fired, too. And I read something somewhere about if you want to stop being a thief then you have to stop stealing. I suppose that's obvious, but it wasn't to me. I think I've given up just trying to get by. Of course I'm very lucky to have Elizabeth."

"Have you talked to Joe lately?" She still thinks of him a great deal, and when she happens to see him in the elevator, her heart still speeds up. But he always looks so melancholy and withdrawn that she keeps her distance.

"I don't see him too often because I'm keeping to a strict work schedule. He told me the last time we talked that he was very bored, and just gets stoned and looks at his plants. I guess they're bankrolling the newsletter—"

"A million dollars. Goodhugh has encouraged Sennett to put Joe on the line for that."

"I'll be very surprised if Joe is able to bring it off in his present condition. I hope he does—if it becomes a success then he might wake up and come into his own, as it were."

"What about Edith? Are they going to stick it out?"

Gerard tilts his head back and looks more surprised than usual. "It still matters to you?"

"You gave their marriage a year—the year will be up in about four months."

"Angela, even if their marriage goes, you don't want him the way he is now. *You'd* turn into another Edith—you'd have to get him to do whatever you wanted him to do. *You'd* have to lead him around by the nose. I suppose there's some wile you might be able to use to spark him—if you think it's worth it."

But she has run out of wiles. If there is any wile she hasn't used, she would like to know what it is. She has used the jealousy wile, the therapeutic wile, the passive wile, the aggressive wile, the raw sex wile, the honesty wile, the wiles of anger, of indifference, of superiority, of inferiority, of neglect, and of nobility. She figures that she has single-handedly caused a national wile shortage. Now she is bankrupt, burned out in the fires of love.

She is ashes, and there is peace for her in that. It makes everything easier. The fire has passed through her town and destroyed everything. She assumes there is nothing left to burn.

At night before she goes to sleep she stands in front of the oval mirror in the hallway and says to herself, "You do not exist! You do not exist! You do not exist!"

Angela has to force herself to go into the office most days. She has set herself a rule: she must be at her desk by ten. She remembers with sadness the days when she couldn't wait to get to work. Now the newsletter is a burden. She misses Gerard's company, and she realizes that she has never been very interested in solid, hard-hitting info for executives. It was Joe's enthusiasm that infused her. And now the job has become tedious, with no let-up from deadlines, the ringing phone, or the avalanches of reports and statistical tables and documents and surveys. Worse still, Sennett keeps making sexual innuendos, and Goodhugh barely speaks to her.

She daydreams about a new job as she eats breakfast at her desk and idly peruses the classified section. Gal/Guy Fri . . . audio-visual . . . word-processor . . . steamfitter . . . yoga & lunch. She could move to California and start over, dye her hair black, change her name, buy a Triumph convertible . . .

She gets a call from the British astronomer who once said she was teetering on the brink of disaster. He is now living in New York directing documentaries for television. He takes her to lunch and offers her a job putting together a script about women in corporations, women managers in particular.

"Who would give two cents to see a program like that?"

"I think it's a terribly important issue," he says. "I have generous funding."

"I couldn't quit my job just for this one-shot deal."

"Do it in your spare time, then."

"My *what?*"

36

ONE DAY IT'S SPRING, all of a sudden, and she hears an odd noise outside. She leans out of her apartment window and sees a man in a saffron robe with a shaved head walking along beating a skin drum. That night she goes to a party Melanie Gauss is giving. Wearing a clingy, flowery ankle-length dress, Angela circulates and flirts and spills May wine down her front, and winds up standing in the corner most of the evening talking with a tall man with black curly hair, heavy eyebrows, sharp blue eyes, and an animated face. He speaks very rapidly in a low voice and he is extremely polite. They discover they have a mutual interest—plutonium. For the newsletter she has assembled some statistics about how much plutonium, the most dangerous and toxic substance in the world, is lost each year by the atomic energy industry. He has just read the same book on this subject she is reading. A woman stands with her arms crossed over her chest about six feet away, scowling and watching them. Angela turns to include her in their conversation, but she walks away.

Angela feels happy and at ease with this man, whose name

is Nick Reymond and who is one of the few men present who is not one of Melanie's protégés. He has just started his own company with a couple of other people creating educational computer games for children. He makes her laugh. Whenever she moves closer to him in an attempt to flirt, he backs away the exact distance.

"Well, I'm going home now," she finally says. "It's late."

"I've really enjoyed talking with you," he says, and she can't tell whether he's just being polite or he means it. "I hope we meet again."

"Me, too."

As she is leaving the party, she sees the scowling woman go up to Nick and grasp his arm. Oh, well, Angela thinks.

She falls into a taxi and asks the driver to go through the park. The leaves are just coming out and the night air is sweet with sap. She leans her head back. What is a New Mexico girl doing washed up on this crazy island, this condensed, intricate city, far from the mountains and piñon trees and dust, and whatever for? The West is huge and simple: the line of the horizon, the big blue jumble of mountains at the edge of the plain, the vast night, transparent, black, starry, a whole landscape as big and as empty as Mars.

Before she gets into bed, she goes to the bedroom window to close the curtains and sees a naked man with a pleasing body standing in a second-floor window in a house across the backyards. She remembers the male body—it has been so long— and silently thanks him.

Joe drives up to Connecticut and unlocks the house. The air inside is stale and mildewed and the house smells of old ashes left in the fireplace. There is so much more work that needs to be done. The wiring, for instance—so far he's only done the basement and one bedroom. It will take maybe two or three more years to finish the place, to restore it properly. He drives into the village. He finds Tim in the pottery store.

"Hey, man," Tim says.

They talk for a while, and then Tim asks Joe to come to his house that evening. "We're having this meditation, because there's this lady who's got leukemia and we've been trying to help her."

Joe does not see a way to refuse.

Tim lives on the shore of a lake in a boat house. He has put in a bathroom, a kitchen, and a wood-burning cast-iron stove, and he's still working on the insulation. The main room is lined with shiny foil insulation packs. Several people are seated on the floor on an old hooked rug.

"This is Mary," Tim says.

A frail red-haired woman who resembles a little under-nourished boy smiles with desperate friendliness at Joe, and when she does, the tendons in her neck stand out.

More and more people at Starr Whorf are getting fired, and Joe wishes he were next. He knows exactly what the alternative-energy newsletter should look like, feel like, read like, but it still lacks a spark, a soul, and he has to drag himself to the office to work on it.

One spring morning Joe gets off the subway several stops before the office and walks past his old loft and into Washington Square. All the azaleas are blooming. He stands at the corner where he kissed Angela. What happened? Why didn't they get together? It seemed so certain that they would.

He goes to a phone booth and calls her at work. He has phoned her a few times, and stopped by her office, but she always seems to be too busy to talk. She won't look at him. He has wanted to speak with her about the new newsletter. With her, he is always able to come up with new ideas. He looks back on their collaborations as virtuoso duets. "I'd like to discuss my project with you," he says. "How about having lunch?"

"I'm leaving today at the end of the morning," she says.

"Is everything okay?"

"Yeah." She sounds tired and ill-tempered. "I was in the office until midnight last night, and the messenger just came to take the stuff to the printer. Anyway, I decided to start the weekend early."

"I have to go up to your part of town," he says. "Can I see you?"

37

JOE SITS ON A bench on the sidewalk under a plane tree across the street from Angela's subway stop. He watches white clouds pile up over the towers of midtown.

As she emerges from underground, Angela can feel him watching her. She glimpses him on the bench, but pretends not to see him, to be absorbed in the diminishing perspective of the avenue. He hurries across the street to her.

"Let's walk in the park." She leads him away from her apartment. She wears a short skirt and the sunglasses with big lenses, and so he focuses on her mouth and her legs.

"I threw the *I Ching* coins you gave me," he says. "Last night. It came out Eighteen."

"Which one is that?"

He can't see her eyes, so he can't tell if she's humoring him. "Decay—Work on What Has Been Spoiled."

"And?"

"I can't remember what it said." He catches her hand as they walk. She still smells like roses. "How is it with you—these days?"

"Oh, I'm helping with this TV documentary about women in corporations. I'm thinking of quitting my job. And I'm thinking about going in with some other people and buying a brownstone—you know, maybe about six people living together. It's cheaper than renting. But I'm also thinking about moving to California. Maybe I'll go this summer to a Zen meditation center out there for a while."

"I meditate sometimes." He tells her about the dying woman. "It really made an impression on me, trying to concentrate on this woman who was suffering." He wants to tell Angela how he has started remembering his mother, bits of her—her broken-off, faded straw-colored hair spread on the pillow, her long, thin hand reaching out to take his when he sat by her bed, her kind eyes. Angela would understand about that.

"I know what you mean. My friend, Katha, died this winter. I'm still not used to it."

They walk along the bridle path. The cherries are blooming, and the viburnum. "And you—how are things with you, Joe?"

He sighs and kicks up puffs of gray dust as he walks. "I'm—unhappy. I feel claustrophobic." He adds quickly, "About the job."

"But you never come into the office—Belinda says you've been working at home."

"Yes, but the pressure is still there, the feeling that I'm not free. I'm restless. I want to travel. To Asia, maybe, Malaysia."

Under a cast-iron bridge she stops and looks up at him. "Are you unhappier than you were a year ago, or happier?"

He slumps in reply, his face becoming so dark and sad that a pang goes through her heart.

"It's hard . . . working for Starr Whorf, for Goodhugh and those people he's bringing in." As he speaks, he twists his wedding ring on his little finger and kneads the skin around it with his thumb. He is in pain, she sees, and for a moment she believes once again that she can free him from it.

"Well, I'm doing okay at the job," she says. "But I don't want to live alone any more. I want to live with someone, but I know now that there's no security without passion. So I figure that the best situation would be to live with several good friends and not put domestic weight on relationships that belong elsewhere. If you tie up with someone for security, then you don't have it, because you're always restlessly looking for passion."

"Yeah," he says.

She's preaching, and they both know it. She shuts up.

They walk along for several minutes in silence. She is very alert. She just watches him and imagines a white radiance moving along his back in an arc, and a black weight resting in his brain. She supposes he must still be sleeping with Adriana.

"Separations can be good," he says.

"What are you talking about?" Gerard has told Angela that Edith is away most of the time setting up a chain of clinics. Joe must be thinking about that.

"To sort out things," he says. Even though he and Angela have been apart, something living continues to move back and forth between them. Nothing has been lost, has it?

"In a marriage, you mean?" Angela is saying. She wants to preach at him some more, to get him to admit that he made a mistake in choosing Edith. "I guess separations could make or break a marriage. There's always the chance that you find yourself dreading the reunion."

Edith will be back Sunday night. It is Friday afternoon. Sometimes he's glad to see her, to have some company. They usually don't have much to talk about, and she has to spend some of her time away from work visiting her mother. Sometimes he has dreaded seeing Edith, but he's always glad not to have to sleep alone. He says nothing, but he nods.

"How's life in Brooklyn, city of magic?"

"I think we're going to sell the brownstone and move back to Manhattan. It's a hassle, being all the way out there. You can't get taxis."

"Joe, is there anything you like, or that you do, that makes you happy?"

He is silent.

They are walking around the reservoir now. A flock of sea gulls drifts in the center. Pear trees shed their petals on the path. She regards him as a doctor might regard a terminally ill patient. She has always thought there was something she could do that would make him change his life, but at last she is seeing that he has always chosen to go along with Edith's decisions. They'll probably have a baby one of these days.

"I've discovered I can't rescue anybody," she says.

She must mean Derek Grinder, Joe thinks.

"So where in Manhattan are you thinking of moving to?" she asks. "Are you going to get a brownstone? Another loft? You plan to get something near the office?"

"Oh, who knows?" Edith talks all the time now about buying an apartment on Park Avenue or Fifth Avenue. She is trying to convince Lois to open a clinic in Manhattan. Edith tells Joe she thinks he would be a lot happier if they lived near his office in a good building with a doorman.

"What is it, Joe?" Angela is getting weary of this difficult conversation. Months of thought and emotion are being squeezed into bloodless abstract phrases.

"Oh, Edith and I—"

"Yes?"

"We aren't communicating."

"Oh, why?" She keeps her voice neutral.

"Just a phase, I suppose, part of a cycle."

"Well, that's okay—you're immortal." Angela wishes she could take back the sharpness of that. Have he and Edith ever "communicated"? Have they ever had a week free from "working on their relationship"? But she bites her lip.

"It's going to rain," Joe says. "It's been unusually hot today." He puts his arm around her and leads her to an open lawn with a single perfectly formed oak in the center. Its leaves are full and glossy. They sit down under it, and then she slides herself down and stretches out her legs and rests her head on a protruding gray root.

She closes her eyes and imagines being a maiden in a fairy tale who appears to die in the forest. The leaves fall, then the snow covers her. She seems dead. Then she begins to sink into the earth, among the roots, to go deeper and deeper as winter deepens. Finally all motion freezes. Then the days begin to lengthen and grow warm and it is time for her to push upward. She doesn't want to. She wants to remain under the earth, frozen forever. No, something says. You have to finish this. She pushes back up through the earth, the green maiden of spring, and opens her eyes.

Joe has been watching her lips make delicate movements as she lies there motionless, her long hands folded on her chest. What is she thinking? He still wants to know, after all this time, what she is really thinking, what it is like to be inside her mind gazing outward. He bends over her.

She looks beyond him to the branches overhead framing the endless emptiness. The dark leaves, the clouds, the park, the man next to her, all her feelings about him—just phenomena floating in a great void. For an instant immense doors swing open and she glimpses the everyday world streaming out of the emptiness, being created at every moment, flourishing, dying away, and shriveling back into emptiness. She turns to Joe and removes her sunglasses.

They watch each other. Together they're like a very fragile vessel being filled beyond its capacity.

"It's still there, isn't it?" Joe says.

She nods. She is thinking of a samurai movie in which a teacher of swordsmanship tells the hero, Expect nothing, be ready for everything.

Big drops start to fall, and there is a sudden smell of dust, and thunder, and Joe and Angela run hand in hand to her apartment.

They sit in their damp clothes on the red rug in her bedroom by the window and watch the lightning flashes in the black sky and the ailanthus branches leap in the wind, revealing their silver undersides. She brings out glasses and a tall, cool green bottle of wine. Her voice is quiet and crisp in the comfortable room, and the rug is soft. He feels he is on a floating island. Her pulse is quiet, her breath slow and even. The phone starts to ring and she unplugs it. He peels the foil from the wine bottle and makes a little metal ball of it between his fingers. The wine is sweet in the back of his mouth, like spring water.

They begin kissing. She hears a clink in a wineglass and assumes he is discarding his wedding ring. They are both completely taken with desire. They give up.

There is a new ease and lightness between them. Expect nothing, be ready for everything. She can almost feel what it is like to be in his skin, and he does not know where his body ends and hers begins.

Afterward, they reluctantly pull apart, their skin hot and

wet, their hair damp and sticking to their cheeks. She lifts her hair from his face. He gets the wineglasses and the bottle, and she sees the ball of foil in his glass. Her own glass is still full, and she empties it over his head. "To cool you off," she says, laughing.

But the wine burns his eyes, and she has to run to get a wet washcloth for him. He waits until she is lying down and pours wine from her throat to her legs.

He spends the night with her and he fixes her zabaglione for breakfast. He has imagined doing this many times. He repairs the leg of her bed, which collapsed when they made love in the night, with matchsticks, a screwdriver, and a hammer. "This won't last," he says. "I'm very sorry about it."

"I'm glad you broke my bed. It's wonderful."

They bathe, and she washes his hair. He leans back against her in the blue tub. "You are ethereal and gorgeous," he says. "If you ever have a daughter, she will be ethereal and gorgeous."

"Well, I'll be. I never thought you'd say such a thing. Thank you very much."

"I assumed you knew I thought that. You are a little conceited about your looks, I think."

If he knew how hard she worked to keep herself from veering into deep homeliness. But she says nothing, and looks wise when he tilts his head back to see what she is thinking.

"Have you ever slept with Goodhugh?" he asks.

"No, I don't find him too appealing in that way."

"What about Gerard?"

"Gerard! Of course not. Anyway—he and Elizabeth. They're so connected, so close." She won't admit that of all the men on the planet, she only finds Joe attractive.

"I'm troubled by the implication in that," he says. He suddenly remembers Edith. He had completely hidden her behind the joy and silliness of the last day or so.

"Ah—don't worry about it," Angela says. But he trembles and seems ready to sob. She holds him tightly. Then she leaps out of the bathtub crying "Hey!" and leaves the bathroom. She returns with a big bunch of green grapes which she rubs against his chest. He laughs, remembering the dream she told him a long time ago. He takes the remaining grapes from her and squeezes them over her shoulders and her hair.

He stays on, and they enjoy each other, and they don't speak about anything serious. She cups her hands with her thumbs to her lips and whistles "Greensleeves" through them, and teaches him how it's done. They seem to be outside of time, outside of considerations about, for instance, whether he will stay for good, whether he will finally leave Edith, whether Angela will welcome him, and be as good to him, as loving, as she is now, on this floating island. Wasn't she talking about plans to live with someone?

They fall across the bed, across the rug, across the couch like children, rolling and wrestling, and making love all the ways they have imagined for so long.

Joe is always polite. "May I open another bottle of wine? May I leave my clothes off a little while longer?"

"Are you kidding? I love to watch your body." She is naked, holding a red watering can and watering her plants. She is growing a lemon tree from seed, and the gardenias are opening.

"But I'm so fat." He takes the roll of flesh around his waist in both hands and shakes it.

"I've never thought of you that way. You are solid, big. I like that."

"I didn't used to have this extra weight," Joe says. She must be just trying to make him feel better. "I started gaining after— well, in the past few years."

"You are sort of built like Toshiro Mifune," she says. "The young Toshiro. You have that low center of gravity, and you walk like him, too."

"I'm flattered."

Sooner or later, they will have to leave her apartment. They are not royal lovers who will be brought food in golden vessels. The sparrows in the backyard will not fly down with morsels in their beaks for the two of them. Although both of these events seem possible to Angela. It is as if a golden circle has been drawn around them.

But they must step out of it, and she is worrying about whether, when Edith is due back, Joe will leave. If she asks him to stay, to stay for good, it might be pressuring him, it might smash the delicate mood between them. He has been unhappy for so long because of Edith's pressuring. Joe is worrying about whether to go back to his place to get his belongings and leave a note for Edith, and about why Angela has made no move to invite him to stay.

At any rate, they go that evening, walking with their arms around each other, their legs pressed together, to a movie theater on Broadway where *Samurai Rebellion* is playing.

38

ANGELA HAS SEEN TWENTY-THREE samurai movies already this spring—the theater has been running a festival—and she has seen *Samurai Rebellion*. After she saw it, she decided that it was a movie Joe should see, but she had no idea how she ever would be able to make that happen. Now it is happening of itself, like everything else this weekend. Like their waking up at the same time in the middle of the night and reaching for each other.

They take their seats in the musty, narrow theater, and then Joe gets up. "Do you want a Coke?" She shakes her head.

He finds a pay phone next to the popcorn machine and dials the number of the apartment of Edith's assistant director in New Haven, where Edith stays. "Oh, Edith is out for the evening," a man tells Joe. Is this the assistant's boyfriend? Edith has never been too clear about her arrangements there, or maybe she was and Joe didn't pay attention. "I'm not sure if she'll be back tonight." The carpet, a grease-blackened red, is strewn with popcorn. Two men nearby discuss Toshiro's sword techniques. "He definitely has *ki*, he's definitely authentic," says one. He is tall, with a pointed black beard and a shaven head. "Just watch his feet."

Joe returns to his seat. It is easy to find because Angela's reddish-blond corona of hair glows in the dark. She is wearing a light dress that buttons down the front, and he can see the luminous triangle of skin between her breasts and the curve of her knee like a half moon. He puts his hand on her knee. She puts her hand on his hand, and feels it trembling.

There is a trailer for a coming film that shows a Ninja protecting two women from an onslaught of arrows by spreading his arms. The arrows magically curve around him. In another scene, the Ninja leaps backwards onto a parapet fifty feet overhead.

"That's a i-ll-*oo*sion," someone behind Joe says.

Toshiro plays an obedient veteran samurai who has endured a long marriage to a harridan. Their son has married the cast-off concubine of the son of a powerful neighboring lord. She has an infant son from this former liaison whom the family loves, especially Toshiro. But the lord dies, his son comes to power and demands that the baby, as the only heir, be returned to his castle. Toshiro pleads with his own lord not to let this happen, but he is weak, and also considers Toshiro a has-been, ready to retire. Toshiro's wife ridicules him, too, and urges him to acquiesce. But Toshiro announces that the woman and child will stay with him and that he will no longer serve his lord. He orders his nagging wife to leave, gets out his swords, and tells the maid to lay out mats in the courtyard. "Why?" she asks. Until now, the pace has been very slow.

"So we don't slip in the blood," Toshiro replies. The audience sighs and cheers.

From that point on, Toshiro becomes very powerful and determined. He kills all the lord's samurai when they try to force him to surrender the baby by killing Toshiro's son and daughter-in-law. Then, sword in hand, Toshiro picks up the baby and swears they will seek justice in Edo. More cheers from the audience. Toshiro, his face ravaged, his clothing bloody, the baby in his arms, sets out for Edo, only to be stopped by more samurai. Soon after he has hidden the baby in a safe place, he is cut down by gunfire.

Joe and Angela go to a deli and buy groceries, and go back to Angela's. Neither can eat much.

"What did you think of the movie, how Toshiro finally tells his boss and his wife to go to hell?"

"It was interesting," Joe says. "The consequences were very bloody. Those films are an acquired taste, it would seem."

He feels exhausted. Where is he? What is he doing? He stares at the glowing orange and turquoise geometrical shapes of the Persian carpet and then he picks up Angela and carries her into the bedroom and lays her on the bed. She is so small, so light! He lies down next to her and gazes at her with such intensity that she closes her eyes.

"What are you thinking?" He must know, he must know now.

"I'm not, I'm feeling."

He makes love to her very slowly and then is suddenly overcome by sleep. She sees that he is even dreaming; his eyeballs move under the lids. She carefully moves to slide under the covers without awakening him. But he opens his eyes, sits up, and leaves for the bathroom.

When he returns, he starts picking up his clothing.

"You leaving?"

"I have to feed the cat." The cat is one Edith bought for herself after doing a lot of research on cats and shopping around for a couple of months. It is a red Abyssinian and Edith is never around to take care of it.

"Cats have nine lives," Angela says irritably. "Come here."

But he continues to dress. She starts to cry. "I'm so tired of all this. I've tried everything. My feeling for you goes very deep. I've tried to put it into words, I've tried to analyze it, I've tried to forget, to hate it. Nothing has worked. People give me advice, and they're right, but it doesn't seem to matter. I don't know what it is. I don't understand why we can't be together."

He is about to tell her that the past few days have been the happiest he can remember when there is a knock on the door. He grabs his shoes and backs toward the bed, away from the door.

"Just a minute," Angela calls out. She waves at him, intending for it to be a calming gesture, but it only makes him back away further and collapse into himself. She puts on a kimono and pulls the bedroom door shut as she opens the apartment door a crack.

"It's Sharon. This is a heavy one."

"Sharon—I can't—"

Sharon is pale and the rims of her eyes are red. "I've got to talk to you."

"Uh, I'm in the middle of something," Angela whispers. But she can see that Sharon is in pain. "What is it?"

"My shrink asked me on Friday if I would go to bed with him and I was so bummed out about that I had to talk to somebody, but I couldn't exactly talk to *him* about it, could I? And you didn't answer when I knocked and you didn't answer your phone. I didn't want you to know about this, I feel so guilty—"

"Yes?" Angela looks over her shoulder, half afraid that Joe will leave through the window on a rope of bedsheets.

"Well, Ron Nussbaum is always calling me up and asking about you. And he happened to call up, so I told him what was bothering me, and he invited me to come to his place and talk about it. Anyway, I spent the weekend with him!"

"And?"

"It was wonderful, but I feel so guilty—I mean, I always thought you and Ron—"

"Sharon, I'm very glad, believe me. You and Ron are perfect for each other. But I can't talk now—Joe is here."

Joe hears whispering through the door. It's got to be one of her lovers. Why should he be punished for these days of happiness?

When Angela comes back she sighs and sits on the bed. "That was Sharon, my friend from upstairs. She was very upset about something."

"Well, I've got to leave—you can talk to her."

She catches his elbows and looks up at him. "I've taken a lot of big risks for you," she says.

"Yes—you have." He has not thought of this before; he only thought he was taking risks.

"Since I met you there's no other man I've cared about. I've been through a lot." She is whining now; she prays she will be able to stop, but no—she goes on. "I have suffered."

He knows this is so. He knows she must sleep by herself most nights. Her apartment has a solitary atmosphere; no hand but hers turns back the sheets or squeezes the toothpaste tube. She has waited and waited for him, despite all his warnings that she must not. Now she sits, broken and teary and red-faced, under the ridiculous red silk canopy that flutters with the explosions of her words. He hates himself for his cruelty and blindness. Shall he tell her? Shall he tell her how happy she has made him, how she has filled out his life in unexpected corners, in surprises of beauty? Shall he tell her how he loves her, how she has begun a new life in him? But that would only make her cry more. And he certainly does not understand why he is being randomly shredded by some vast, mindless animal. He holds her. "I really trust you, Angela. I don't know why you scare me so much."

39

EDITH COMES HOME FROM New Haven late the next night with six books on infant and child care and natural childbirth. "We'll have to move," she says happily. "I'm having a baby!" She goes to the phone and calls her mother, and her friends. "And I was so worried that my cysts would be a problem, or I would be too old," he hears her saying. "Thank God for amniocentesis. Yeah, Joe is super-thrilled."

Sometimes Joe and Angela meet in the elevator. When the first issue of the alternative-energy newsletter is published, a bouquet of twenty-four long-stemmed red roses is delivered to his desk. He has to go to the florist's to get a description of the person who sent them. He waits for her to confess, but she never does. Sometimes she says barbed things to him, like "I've given you up for dead."

He hires a pretty assistant just out of college. In bed she tells Joe all the problems she is having with her lover, who has become a follower of the Reverend Sun Myung Moon.

Nick Reymond calls up Angela. "Trans World Airlines," she says when she answers her phone. She doesn't care what impression she makes any more. She has been a recluse all summer. Sharon has moved in with Ron Nussbaum and sublet her place to two men who have decorated it entirely in black. "I've found that you may never get what you truly want," Sharon said when she was packing. "But something equally good can happen to you." Angela never sees Sharon now—what they had in common must have been pain over men. "Would you like to have lunch?" Nick asks. "We can whisper sweet nothings about software into each other's ears."

She accepts. She continues to have business lunches, but she refuses dates. It's just simpler. At lunch with Nick she laughs the whole time. She is surprised that he would remember her. "I have a very good memory," he says. His eyes are very blue. He refers to an opening in his company and then invites her to dinner. She has been thinking for a long time about leaving Starr Whorf—almost everyone she knows has been fired, and she's probably next, even though the newsletter, now that it carries ads, is making a high profit. She's been given another television script to work on, and she has thought of looking for more work in TV.

Nick keeps taking her to lunch, and to dinner, and then to Yankee games and to a pub where they throw darts. He never tells her what he thinks of her or even whether he likes her. He is solicitous but not intrusive. Angela finds out from Melanie that he is no longer with the woman who scowled, and then she accepts his invitation to fly to Boston for a weekend. He never does offer her a job with his company. In fact, now that the company he started has become very profitable, he's selling it so that he can devote his time to a new business involving a scheme to create a fleet of sail-powered ocean-going freighters. He loves samurai movies—he has even seen a Toshiro movie she hasn't—and he gives her a wooden saki box autographed by Toshiro. One evening he comes to her apartment for dinner and never goes home. Sometimes she says, "Are you *still* here?" He buys good coffee beans and a coffee grinder and brews excellent coffee. He teaches her to sail on Long Island Sound. He takes her to French restaurants. She gains ten pounds, and she laughs all the time. She never realized until now that it was possible to enjoy being with someone calmly, day and night.

One day Goodhugh asks Angela to come to his office. He has been cold to her ever since she shouted at him nearly a year ago, and she assumes it's her turn to be fired. Instead, he is friendly and confiding. He tells her that Starr Whorf is in big trouble. There have been setbacks in several divisions. "And Bly got us to invest a million dollars in that goddamned energy newsletter, and it's bombing. A staff of ten and he still tries to do everything by himself. His people don't know what's going on. They keep complaining to Sennett. Do you think you could help him?"

"No," she says. "I don't think I could. Thanks for thinking of me, though." The last time she saw Joe, she was walking down a corridor. He made a point of walking along next to her. Neither of them spoke. "I just bought some land, a forest tract," he finally said. "Well, even Hitler had his good points," she replied. "He was a vegetarian." She went to the elevator, and as she stepped in, leaving him, he said, "I know you hate me."

Nick takes her to St. Croix for two weeks and teaches her to play backgammon and to snorkel. One afternoon she falls asleep on the beach and dreams that she goes into a movie theater where Joe is watching the screen. He is aloof and silent. Finally he turns to her. "I have given you every chance at work for some time. Do you like me or not? I would give anything to know." He begs her. But he lacks the erotic power of Joe as she knew him. She lets him kiss her and feels nothing. "And I even have to plead with you for a little kiss," he complains.

"You know, at some point soon I would like us to start living together," Nick says on the plane back to the States.

"That would be a pretty big step for me," Angela says.

"Well, we actually are living together."

"You're right."

"So we should look for a nice big place."

"This seems too good to be true," Angela says. "I can't believe this can be happening to me."

When Angela returns to work, she sees Goodhugh in the corridor. "Hey, Buffalo Buff, how you doing?" she calls. He ignores her. She stops by Tor Bracewell's office and sees that it is empty, the desk bare, the pictures down. She goes to

Belinda, who is typing her Master's thesis and has pages spread across the desk and on the carpet in front of the switchboard. "What's going on?" Angela asks. "This place is like Siberia."

Belinda fixes her large light brown eyes on Angela. "The newsletter division is in big trouble. And Joe especially. I think you know."

"I don't, I don't." Nevertheless, Angela feels guilty. She is somehow responsible. In her effort to stop caring for Joe, she has hated him, she has said things about him that were low and mean and unnecessary, she has refused to help him with his job, and as far as she knows, he has only praised her to others. She once dreamed of revenge, but she has been so happy with Nick, and Joe has looked so miserable for so long, that even her mildest fantasies of retribution have vanished. Nevertheless, Belinda has observed everything over the years, Joe's and Angela's arrivals and departures and unreturned phone calls and silences in the lobby and quick hugs in the coffee room. "Is Joe going to get the ax?"

Belinda nods. "Whorf and Brunell hate the energy newsletter. Poor Joe, as if things weren't already difficult enough for him. He reminds me of that song from *Tommy*—'*Touch me, feel me, see me, hear me, heal me,*' or however it goes."

"Where's Tor Bracewell?"

"Oh, him. He was fired about three months ago, but Sennett let him keep coming in until he could find a new job because Tor was with the company for so long. Eleven years, I think."

Angela goes into Goodhugh's office. "What's going on here? Can't you help Joe? He's done so much for you, for the division."

Goodhugh picks up a sheaf of papers and leafs through them.

"I really want to know, Buff. Is something wrong?"

He starts making phone calls, and she leaves.

She goes back to her office and sinks into her chair. A mysterious epidemic has broken out. Nick fetches her for lunch, and as they are waiting for the elevator, Joe passes them. He is pale and unshaven, and he looks ill.

"Hi, Joe." Angela wants to reassure him. But he ducks his head and hurries past.

The rest of the day passes in a vacuum. Mark Sennett calls her into his office and while an old man shines his shoes tells her that someone has been hired to help her with the newsletter. "You might have let me interview him before you hired him," Angela says. "I'm the one who has to work with him."

"That's not the strategy I employ around here," Sennett says.

The man Sennett has hired, at twice Angela's salary, to work on the newsletter is a recent business school graduate from San Diego, and this is his first job. He resembles Sennett, and is short, with a class ring, a little mustache, and hot-combed hair. On his first day, he has an enormous oak desk brought into Joe's old office and positioned so that when Angela comes in to meet him and sits across from him, she has to blink from the glare coming straight in at her through the window.

"We are going to reorganize," he tells Angela.

"Reorganize what?"

"The newsletter. I've already gone over my list of concepts with Mr. Sennett and Mr. Goodhugh, and I'll tell you what I have in mind. But first—" He opens his desk drawer and gets out a long, narrow box. "Here—these are pencils with my name on them and they need sharpening."

"I'll sharpen your fucking head," Angela says. She leaves the same day and never comes back.

40

ONE SUMMER DAY, THREE years later, Joe and Gerard meet for lunch at a sushi bar in midtown. They don't get together very often now that Gerard is a poet-in-residence at a college in New Jersey. After they discuss what they are going to order, they have trouble conversing until they hit on the topic of Starr Whorf.

"I hear it's going under," Joe says. "Goodhugh and his family bought it, you know—or at least the controlling interest in it, and now it's on the verge of bankruptcy."

"It was too bad they canceled the executives' newsletter," Gerard says. "It was always so good. Have you ever thought that Goodhugh might have engineered that whole energy newsletter catastrophe?"

"Yes—partly to get rid of me, but mainly to discredit the board of directors by showing that they backed weird stuff that lost money. Then Whorf and Brunell put him on top."

"Maybe you were the sacrificial lamb in that one," Gerard says. "Burned on the altar. Anyway, that was Angela Lee's theory."

"Angela—do you ever see her?"

"Rarely. She's always traveling—have you seen any of her documentaries on TV? Her last one was about Ladakh—some country next to Tibet."

"I don't have much time for television." He usually doesn't get home until nearly nine o'clock. Angela—God!

"Working hard?"

"Very." He describes his job as vice-president of a management consulting firm. "It's going pretty well, but what I would really like to do is start my own little press. You know, like it was back at the university press. Beautiful stock, cloth binding, well done. I don't know when I'll get the time for that, though. So, you do sometimes see Angela? How is she?"

"She seems very well. She's either living with or married to a very interesting entrepreneur—I met him once. Very active, very intelligent. I think Angela has calmed down a lot."

"She always was—fairly emotional."

"Yes, she was. You know, she really—" Gerard stops himself. "And Edith—how is she?"

"The same. Very busy. She bought out her partner, and now she's got clinics in Boston, New Haven, Queens, Manhattan, Brooklyn, and Philadelphia, and she's just opening one in Washington, D.C., so she's down there most of the time."

After lunch, out on the street, Gerard asks about the house.

"These things take time," Joe says. "It's mostly restored, but between the job and my kid there's still a lot that's unfinished. You and Elizabeth will have to come up some time."

"Great," Gerard says.

They shake hands, and Joe walks away, realizing with sadness that he and Gerard probably won't want to meet again.

That night, Joe has a dream that he remembers all the next day. He is speeding with Angela along an open, straight highway in Montana. There is no traffic, nothing in their way. The sky is huge and blue, and her presence beside him fills him with acute longing. The radio is on loud—Bo Diddley, the Rolling Stones, Chuck Berry—all the best rock. They are very happy, the two of them, and he knows they're going to make love. Then a police siren screams and he has to stop under an overpass that has appeared and someone is ordering his arrest.

41

IT IS A PERFECT golden day in early fall a year or two later. The air is clear and dry. The playing fields in Central Park are dusty and trampled. The sky is full of big, three-dimensional clouds that remind Angela of the sky over Gatch. Except that Gatch no longer exists—she always has to remind herself that Gatch, and Katha, and other parts of the world she once knew are nothing now. The towers that rim the park reflect gold and blue, and their silvery windows catch clouds in motion.

Hundreds of people are playing softball. They wear various team T-shirts and run through one another's games. Angela, who is illegally on the team of the company Belinda works for as an industrial psychologist because Belinda is the captain, does not wear a team T-shirt. She wears an old jersey that says "Where the Hell Is the Cosmos Mystery Area????" and baggy jeans and sandals.

The other team arrives in new-looking navy-blue shirts with white lettering that says "Renwick" and they all wear matching baseball caps and push shopping carts full of beer cartons, bags of potato chips, and bats, bases, and gloves.

"Now remember," Belinda says, huddling with her team, which is composed of women, and boys from the mailroom, "our goal this season is to lose, and we are probably gonna make that goal by the end of the season. So far we've only won one game. So—remember, strike out when possible, and if you happen to swing, don't hit the ball very hard."

Angela plays second base. The Renwick team makes one run after another. They have many men, and many women who have come along to cheer. They cheer the most when a man comes up to bat who is tall, thin, and smooth-faced, with horn-rimmed glasses and a short haircut that makes him look very boyish. "Joe! Joe! Go, Joe!" the women cry with special fervor. Angela regards the clouds, the towers of the Dakota, the treetops. Suddenly the man hits a home run and passes her, tapping the base with the toe of his blue running shoe. She notices that he is much older than she thought: she gets a glimpse of tightened, lined skin stretched over his cheekbones—the face of a somewhat wizened, balding boy.

At last Belinda's team is up at bat. When it's Angela's turn, Nick, who has arrived, shouts encouragement from the sidelines: "Confuse them with minor premises! Undercut their ontology!" She sets down her beer and steps up to the plate. The pitcher is a pretty young woman who keeps looking helplessly over her shoulder to the man playing first base and lobbing balls with her forearm that miss the plate by about ten feet. Suddenly Angela feels like really hitting the ball, and she knows she's going to do that. She forgets Belinda's admonition to lose. When a pitch finally comes her way, she swings hard and nicks a foul. "That's a piece of it, Angela!" Nick calls. Then she hits a line drive and, laughing as she runs, makes it almost to second base before she is tagged out.

Later, when her team heads for the field, the thin man who hit the home run and who plays first base looks into her eyes as they pass near the pitcher's mound. "Hello," he says. He seems familiar.

She nods politely and shouts to Belinda, "Where's my glove?"

It *is* Angela, Joe thinks. She has gained weight, and chopped off her hair, which is much darker. She is stolid and muscular and tan. She chats and laughs and clowns with her teammates. He wants to speak to her, to say anything, something. She never asked anything of him, he thinks. That was the thing about her that was different. He rehearses a few possible greetings—"You don't know who I am, do you?"—with an amused grin. Or: "Angela! It's Joe, Joe Bly." After the game he walks directly toward her. "Hi," he says again. She nods politely again, their eyes meet briefly, and she walks on in the opposite direction. Mysterious as ever. Did she recognize him and decide to ignore him? Or does he look so different from when she last saw him that she no longer knows him?

She realizes, as she crosses the baseball diamond, that it's Joe Bly. How odd that she feels no more than if he were a stranger, how odd that at first she didn't even recognize him. She turns and sees him walking quickly across the playing field. He has to hurry to Grand Central to catch the 7:43, and she drifts away with her teammates.

"Well!" Belinda says to Angela. "Did you get a chance to talk to Joe?"

"Isn't it incredible that that was Joe Bly? Shoot, I barely recognized him." She thinks of the women encouraging him, helping him, calling his name, his name only. She is astonished that the man in that body was the same man who was connected with all those concentrated, fervent feelings, thoughts, and dreams that had captured her for so long and made her body, her life their own. And she almost failed to recognize him— how could that be? She suddenly feels outside herself, a little dazed. "Did you talk to him? How is he?"

"Well, he told me that he runs ten miles every day and he's become a vegetarian. He's set up a small press near his place in Connecticut. When it gets going he wants to quit Renwick."

"Gosh." Angela is still having trouble putting together her memory of Joe Bly with the present Joe. And where did all that intensity go? What a disaster it would have been if they'd gotten together!

"By the way," Belinda continues. "Did I ever mention to you that the day he interviewed you for the job he came back and told me, 'I have met my spiritual twin'?"

42

IT'S A YEAR AFTER the baseball game, the next fall. As Joe drives up the hill and sees the fire, his first thought is about how beautiful its shape is, a rippling fan of solid orange light that casts a red fog against the low night sky.

"Oh my God," Edith says. She is holding a big flat cardboard box containing a pizza. Rebecca, their daughter, leans over the seat whistling through her cupped hands. Joe recently taught her how to do this, and now she goes around sounding at all hours like a mourning dove. Roped to the roof of the car is a bentwood rocking chair.

"I hear sirens," Joe says. He is aware of how carefully he is driving, as if that might help. "One of the neighbors must have called." It's a good idea to remain calm so that the child does not get scared. He pulls off the white gravel circular drive—made pink by the flames—onto the lawn so that he won't block the fire trucks.

"The whole thing," Edith says.

"Mom, Dad, the house is burning!"

They sit in the car, which smells of warm cheese, tomato sauce, and smoke, and do not move.

"At least we were all away," Joe says.

"Look! The frame is burning, the whole thing," Edith says. "I don't believe this. Is this really happening?"

"Dad? Could I ask you something?" His daughter only has questions. "Will we build a new house? Just like the old one? Where does the house *go* when it's burned? Where does a fire go when you put it out? Does it just go somewhere else? Or does it turn into something we can't see? Could I have some pizza? Dad, when people get old, do they just get small and disappear? Where do they go? Dad?"

"In a minute, sweetheart."

"What are we going to do? What are we going to do?" Edith has never asked him that question before.

The house was made almost entirely of wood, old, well-seasoned wood. That's why it glows so as it burns. He thinks of the years he spent restoring the place: stripping the banister and the mantelpiece, finding a blacksmith who could copy the original wrought-iron door pulls and latches, painting the inner curlicues of the frieze molding in the dining room. Just this morning he finished the last of the wiring and installed Edith's antique ruby-glass chandelier over the dining table. They left it on when they went for pizza just so they could admire its splendor when they pulled into the drive. Edith wanted to see how it would look to visitors.

"Dad, do old people just turn into little babies? Dad?" Rebecca resumes blowing through her fingers, the melancholy cooing blending with the dying screams of the sirens as the fire trucks come to a halt in the drive and men in black slickers leap out. "Dad? Why was I born?"

"We'll rebuild, we'll rebuild, we'll get through this, won't we?" Edith keeps asking. Her voice is hoarse, her eyes are red. She sits on the edge of the motel bed, making a list for the insurance company. "Cuisinart. Espresso-maker." At the foot of her bed, on a cot, their daughter sleeps with two fingers jammed into her mouth. "We'll get another place, and restore it exactly the same way. What about that? Sheesh, and I have to fly to Washington tomorrow."

Joe lies on his bed, his legs crossed, his hands cupped behind his head, and looks at the glittery plaster ceiling. The room and its flimsy, worn furnishings make him think of a movie set. The filming will eventually end and he will resume his real life. There is a faint, acrid smell—smoke has clung to their clothing.

"Thank God my furs were still in storage. Betamax. The Eames chair."

Joe suddenly feels like air, like light. As if he could be anywhere, and take on any form. He glances over at Edith. Over the years, without his noticing it, she has become womanly, rounded out, coherent. Her black hair, streaked with early gray, is glossy and stylishly shaped around her face. Her eyes are carefully made up, outlined to make her look sloe-eyed. Her profile is striking, and even in distress, her mouth is full and interesting.

The next day, running through the forest on his property, he remembers Angela. Not the one with the cropped hair and the tough batting stance who whacked the line drive. No, he remembers his private beloved, with the flowing hair and the light step and the sweet taste who sometimes uttered spontaneous poetry in a Western drawl. She smelled of roses. After they no longer saw each other, he would sometimes follow a woman on the street if she smelled of roses. Then a rose perfume like hers became popular, and lots of women, including some he made love to, smelled like Angela. Like Ali Baba chalking an *X* on every door in town to foil his pursuers. She always talked about the light. Do you see this, she would say, how the light is different in this part of the room from that part, up near the ceiling?

He stops near the stream and squats and tilts his head back and gazes into the crown of an oak turning golden, and to the clear sky beyond, clear as water. All the power of his feelings for Angela suddenly returns to him, not as memory but as a present sensation, a rush in the blood. The person he loved as Angela no longer exists for him, and so he is left with love itself, this life within his life—a life he had given up on altogether. He remains looking upward for some time—he is not sure how long, because time no longer matters. Not for a lover. He knows he has done nothing to deserve this—it has just come to him out of the blue. And similarly, a chain of recollections quite outside those he is usually able, with some effort, to find when he thinks of his childhood, comes to him now. His mother holding him up to look at seals splashing in a zoo pool. The smell of an apple. The taste of fall air. The particular blue used in the pictures of his first reader. The feeling under his palms of an old blanket he liked. Over all the years he felt pain, and loss, and isolation, his life continued to give him sensations and air, and new things to learn, and love, and work. All these things came to him while he was preoccupied, and most of the time he didn't notice. Those impressions, so much richer and deeper than the everyday life he has kept his attention on, were there all along and they continue.

His heart warms and opens and he is flooded with such a sense of being alive, of being nothing at all, that he could fly. He is thankful that he is alive and aware of being alive. The light caught in the branches is a sweet substance, descending, that he soaks in. He walks on through the forest, his boots crunching the leaves, and sees everything—every leaf, every twig, each one different, intricate, part of the whole. The world is familiar and glowing and deep, and it has a ringing sound. He senses his body moving through the long coiled passage that is his life. Where does the fire go when it goes out? He and Angela were never even properly a couple, scarcely lovers—but what love burned between them. She has vanished, and now he rests completely in love: his heart is so electric that he worries for an instant about a seizure. All the pain and loss, the dull days and years, have been miraculously swept away by a light that issues from every thing and every direction.

He walks through the village feeling that he knows intimately everyone he passes: their faces are touched with light and readily reveal the essence that shapes their features. An old woman stoops to fasten a leash to the collar of her dachshund; two boys lounge against the door of a pickup truck talking. He knows these strangers as directly as a dream knows its dreamer. He stops at the little office over the hardware store where he has set up his press. The cabinetry he built has the dull red-gold patina of newly finished pine. The air smells of ink and paper. A stack of newly bound books sits on the windowsill next to a gloxinia. Whoever works here, he thinks as if he had entered the room for the first time, is a happy man.

He returns to the burned-out house, which is now a foundation, a chimney, and a skeleton of collapsed, charred bones. Pools of water filmed with soot stand in the driveway. The air is heavy with the smell of wet charred wood. Edith is waiting in the car with Rebecca. The bentwood rocker, the last piece of furniture Edith needed to complete the parlor, remains roped to the roof.

"I'm not going with you," he says as he walks toward the car. "I'm going to buy a tent at the sporting-goods store."

"I've got a plane to catch," Edith says. "Come on."

"I'm going to build a house. It's going to be my house, built the way I want, on the land I bought. If you like, you can stay with me in the tent while I build it."

"You're out of your mind. What about your job?"

"I'll quit—the press will be making enough money soon. I'll have to get the house built before winter. Would you like that?" he says to his daughter. Is she really his daughter? He'll never be sure. She has black hair and dark eyes, and she regards him with humor and delight. "Won't that be fun?"

"Where will we go to the bathroom?" the little girl asks.

"In the woods, like the bears do."

"Yeah, and what about when it snows?" Edith asks.

"I'll get a good tent, the kind they use in Antarctica."

"Dad, when the snow melts, where does the white go?"

Edith starts the engine. "I have to leave now."

He turns to the ruin. The black spikes of a few remaining uprights cast shadows across the soot-streaked lawn. He thinks of the beautiful chestnut paneling he loved, the oak and mahogany fixtures—cheap and commonplace when the house was built, rare now. When he was traveling alone in Greece and visited ancient altars where sacrifices were burned, he puzzled over why a man would surrender what he loved best—the most beautiful woman, the finest bull. He was sure it had to be something you loved or the sacrifice would not work, you would not be freed. He feels awe for the slow, patient operation of the hidden part of his being in perfecting this sacrifice, the long hours he lay on his back in the dank crawl-space under the dining room floor hefting a drill and wire cutters, the years, in fact, that it took him to rewire every room. The hidden world was alive and working all along without his knowing it, the hidden world in which shadows lengthen day after day, and objects in dreams shine of themselves.

"Joe," Edith says quietly.

He turns to her. She looks small and afraid. He wants to tell her that it is wonderful to lose everything, but he doesn't want to frighten her. She is beautiful, and so is their child, and it seems to him that they must have just been created an instant ago. Remembering that he is in love, and feeling a surge of joy and astonishment, he opens the car door. "Move over," he says. "I'm driving."

43

THROUGHOUT THE SUMMER, ANGELA cultivates her garden behind the house she and Nick bought in the country. It is her first garden, and she works with attention and care. She shovels, hoes, and rakes. She sows and weeds. She clears away rocks and logs and twigs, and carts wheelbarrow loads of manure and humus. She pinches off yellow leaves and ties up meandering vines and stakes tomatoes. She brushes caterpillars and slugs off leaves and releases praying mantises. She picks eggplants and chiles and roses. Nick sometimes asks her if she ought to work so strenuously so late in her pregnancy. But she feels very well, and enjoys stretching and bending and lifting as she never has before. Most nights she sleeps deeply and wanders with ease in the universe of her body, her hand resting on her moving, growing abdomen, her work continuing on a subtler level in a series of engrossing dreams.

She dreams that she is sitting on the Kazakh carpet, watching Katha do t'ai chi. As Katha molds the air with slow graceful arcs, Angela says, "I didn't realize you were still alive—or, wait, am I just watching a film of you?" "Now you are beginning to understand," Katha says in her delicately accented voice. "I am dead, but I continue to exist as a pattern in your mind, and from that you can benefit." This is the first dream. On subsequent nights, she meets people from her past toward whom she still bears grudges. Sometimes she asks them why they hurt her, and they reply with various explanations that are satisfactory not only in the dreams but also when she awakens.

She dreams of Janos running a vegetable stall with his young wife by Lake Titicaca. His shack is small but neat, and he makes room for Angela and her daughter to sleep there when they visit. Angela helps Janos and his wife sell fruit at a festival. She is glad he has finally found someone he can love and something he likes to do, even if only in her dreams.

She dreams of Derek. He is living in the basement of a brownstone on a pleasant street. There are big windows so that she can see into the basement. He is married to a dozen or so women, Lynn Lewis among them. Some are still in their wedding gowns. He appears well-fed. His little mustache is gone. He shakes her hand through the window and tells her that he is a speechwriter for the President of the United States. "I found he needed me," he says.

She meets Goodhugh walking along the east side of Fifth Avenue and offers him a handful of M&M candies, dropping them into his outstretched palms. "Let's be friends," she says. He takes her elbow and they walk along chatting and greeting strangers.

After each of these dreams, Angela feels that a weight has been dissolved, even though she was unaware she was carrying any burden. She is not a person who has ever easily surrendered a grudge. Even when she has wanted to forgive others, she has not really been able to. Now it is being done for her, through the magic of dreams.

One morning she wakes up at dawn. A cardinal is singing. She has been dreaming about Joe Bly, but she can't remember anything more than that. She remembers what he was like, his solidity, his heat, his embraces, all those endless, hypnotic green gazes. I really loved him, she thinks—not the thin stranger at the ball game, who would never interest me, but the old Joe. What a fool I was for him! How crazy! And he must have really loved me, sometimes.

She knows, then, that what they formed together had a complete shape, a fullness, a symmetry at the limits of deep feeling. It was enough. She hopes that at last he is happy—as happy as she is now.

About the Author

Gwyneth Cravens is the author of two previous novels. Her work has appeared in *The New Yorker*, *The New York Times Magazine*, *Harper's*, and other magazines. She lives in New York City and is currently working on a new novel.